AMERICA'S CHILDREN

America's Children

JAMES THACKARA

CHATTO & WINDUS

THE HOGARTH PRESS
LONDON

Published in 1984 by
Chatto & Windus · The Hogarth Press
40 William IV Street
London WC2N 4DF

British Library Cataloguing in Publication Data
Thackara, James
I. Title
813'.54[F]   PS3574.H/

ISBN 0–7011–2780–5
ISBN 0–7011–2781–3 Pbk

AUTHOR'S NOTE
This book is a chronicle novel. As in classicism,
the narrative is a poetic invention, while the
details of events are widely known. Sources for
these are in the excellent works of Jungk, Stern,
York, Chevalier, Davis, Nelson, Sherwin, Ried
and the records of the US Atomic Energy Commission.

Grateful acknowledgement is made to Faber & Faber Ltd. and to Alfred A. Knopf,
Inc., for permission to reprint an extract from the poem, 'Esthétique du Mal', from
the *Collected Poems* of Wallace Stevens.

Typeset by Inforum Ltd, Portsmouth

Printed in Great Britain by
Redwood Burn Ltd
Trowbridge, Wiltshire

THE DESERT

THE DESERT

In a time when men were born free, and Cyclon was the word for a sudden whirlwind, two brothers had a horse ranch in the foothills of the Sangre de Cristos.

From the Rocky Mountains, the great divide, the Rio Grande runs straight south, like marrow through the bone-harsh country of the pueblo Indians, before it bends to make the long border with Mexico and empty itself in the Gulf. It is a fossil-red desert scarcely less virgin or cruel than when the explorer de Vaca first saw it, elevated by his ordeal as a slave of the Indians to a shaman among them. Or when Coronado toiled over this petrified sea in his dream of the mythical Seven Cities, and first saw the earth-shaped fortress mesa of Acoma. It was always a place where people came to start again, a land where people could imagine they had left a great deal behind. A wasteland which navigators remembered and forgot again, while nothing changed for the Indians of the pueblos: of the double mud-and-straw pueblo of Taos under a sacred mountain, with its roof ladders and protruding beams; of Walpi perched in the desert wind on a one-way crag; of Zuni on the Colorado, and lofty Acoma, and the cave-cities of Mesa Verde.

For these were the Mycenae and Athens, the Jerusalem and the Bethlehem of North America, but more timeless in having no written history. Before de Vaca there was only a great mystery. Everything there was to be told of people must be remembered and spoken by a single man. So the words were very slow and heavy, and the legends as well loved as the land. At every turn the limits of life could be felt, so the people were simple and imaginative, and hard. Then de Vaca came and there was a new legend . . . of the great mystery consuming these invaders, who were forever starting again and leaving a great deal behind. Then that which the explorers had left behind also came to the Rio Grande. The modern age began.

Around the cathedral of Bishop Lamy, Santa Fé grew up. Manuelito marked a treaty with the General Sherman, and the last pueblo Indians were penned on reservations. The trader family of Wetherills guided New York scientists to the cave ruins of Mesa

3

Verde, and soon the great bow, the magic feathers and mummies that remained were in musuem cabinets. The Rockies, the Great River, the unmarked pueblo land and its mysteries were possessed. Then far away there was an unequalled war, and an English story-teller came to Taos. There he laboured at a curious task, no less than to plough under the Christian crop of his soul, and reseed it with the gods of Mexican Indians. A cycle had come around.

In 1929, five years after this Englishman moved on, another sick *civilizado* came to the Rio Grande to begin again. This Easterner's pride was devastated by a European girl, his mind by the New Physics of the German universities, and his body by an alpine consumption. He returned to the little pine ranch of his student days, *Pero Caliente* under the Sangre de Cristos, and settled down to regain his health. And making love to the lonely desert, gradually it was given back.

Like all the others, Robert Oppenheimer imagined he had left a lot behind. While horses carried him on overnight pack trips from the Pecos into the prehistoric silence, past the tearoom on the Rio Grande of an unknown poetess named Edith Warner, then up Los Alamos Mesa's precipitous dirt trails marked only by puma tracks, gentle waves of a rattlesnake or driftwood of antelope bones, what Robert Oppenheimer imagined he had left behind in Europe continued to sicken and change. It changed so rapidly, within a matter of years, that the deep past and the deep future could scarcely be distinguished. In Germany, scenes were taking place which seemed to have nothing to do with the slouched, flop-hatted rider on a paint pony creeping up the silent Mesa trail over a deep canyon of juniper and cottonwood, with a rainbow arcing down.

Finally the rider reached the plateau alone, and dismounted on the stone shelf to breathe into his weak lungs the dry, scented air. He staggered slightly in his black pants and boots, and the eyes in the delicate face glittered unhealthily. Standing minute on the body of the land, he looked out to the distant blue haze.

Far on his left, the smoky snow peaks of the Sangre de Cristos drifted beside a solid-white cumulus over Taos. The afternoon sun was yellow on the cloud. From left to right the stratified gorge of the Rio Grande snaked south to the rust and grey plain of the Albuquerque desert. Here and there in the distances rose topless

4

stone mountains, shapes significant and inexplicable as petrified ships, images of prehistoric migration, or eroded fossil warnings from less kind worlds.

The horse nosed the tiny figure on the ledge. The man started, and took a step forward. Feeling so diminished and alone with himself, Robert tried to imagine ever having felt the drug of great minds. Was that image really him, the embarrassing student of German days, orating in a Göttingen amphitheatre to his own professors? At the question, Robert experienced an emotion like jealousy. Yes, it would be good if he could have *them* all here with him, he thought. The romance of Europe was coming back. The sick American stood bareheaded, conjuring under the innocent desert sky.

Truly, they had been like master-singers at some gothic cathedral of learning. Sluggishly, Robert remembered the excitement of intellectual upheavals among Europe's star- and atom-gazing minds. A high society of Truth untouched by common affairs, as the high-energy nucleus seemed impervious to the electron bombardments of the physicists. What would they think of him here, in this desert of stone and limitless sky? Robert thought, wiping his temples. Hilbert or James Franck, or his old teacher Max Born? What would the gentle Dane Bohr think, or the Russian Gamov, always fleeing his homeland across mountain borders, or Wolfgang Pauli, and Dirac taking mystic flights through the atom, speechless before the blackboard? Or Houtermans with his idea of suns as a fusing of nuclei? Or the Russian Kapitza, with Chadwick in England discovering the strange, weak neutron . . . and delirious Heisenberg (their subtle charming faces went by), Heisenberg, who had fallen over a kerb one day, and when offered a hand had shouted, 'Do not touch me . . . I am solving it!' Yes, and sanctifying this old, worn landscape of the senses on which common folk lived, strung between the unknowably vast and the microscopic, between the force of suns and the devastating power locked in atoms, was the high priest of Physics at the Kaiser Wilhelm Institute in Berlin-Dahlem, Albert Einstein. Had an American moved as an equal among these masters? Would they recognize him *here*, on this ignorant earth of kivas and pueblos?

Through the canyon haze, the peaks of the Sangres had come

into the sun. Robert felt the solitude of his lonely canyon rim. How vulnerable tuberculosis made him. Thinking of his colleagues in this unbroken silence left a feverish feeling. At his back the horse, knowing only the one Nature, hung its head patiently and looked for grass. The consumptive squinted out hungrily into the wavering distances, and it was a hunger for life.

Soon the man put on his slouch hat and pulled up into the saddle. The horse began the steep canyon trail in slow, sinking jerks. There was only the hiss of gravel and heavy-rasping pant. The vast silence waited, far out. The prophet and his lonely place were separated. Tomorrow night he would be a ride by railway to the west, on San Francisco Bay.

Across Los Alamos Mesa eleven springs went by, like dust. Nothing changed.

Over the scorched canyons of the Rio Grande it was another morning. In the cool rock shadows the dew was still down, and the seven sets of hooves raised no red film as Doctor Oppenheimer guided the Europeans up the steep turns and ledges. They made a file, the Austrian, the German-Jew and his wife, the Italian, Robert's boss Lawrence of the Berkeley laboratory, and his brother Frank at the rear. As they climbed near Robert's place, the voices trailed far below in the canyon shade. The figure in the tight black Mexican breeches and knee boots kicked his horse recklessly up the steep twists, swinging out on unprotected ledges. Finally he emerged on the stone panorama into the hot wind, and jumped down.

Robert stood again on the lovely body of the land. He had not talked cyclotrons or neutron bombardment with Isidor or Hans, Emilio or Ernest or Frank. But physics was between them like a drug. And as Robert grabbed for his slouch hat and turned slowly on the ledge, drinking in the shimmering country, what he saw was cosmic detritus, atmosphere, and solar heat gradients, Light, rays, elements, forces and particle lives. An architecture of force-fields, where he had once loved an epic canvas of pueblos and conquistadores. Not winds, light, colours and rocks, but numbers and signs streaming and snaking through the morning light . . . painting formulae, systems, spectra and magnetic fields, and all particles governed by laws he held in his mind.

Like a doctor with his mistress's body, Robert thought. Only this body, the land, was infinity. It was what the last eleven years had done to physics. And they had taught Robert Oppenheimer another revolution, the one spreading from Russia. He would be joined with that when he married Kitty next week, lusty little Kitty who had lived with scientific Marxists, and the heroes of Spain.

You have to have it all, don't you . . . Robert laughed softly. And behind him the horse, hearing the silence of the Mesa unnecessarily broken, laid back its ears.

This morning Robert needed to be close to this place, he needed its beauty to isolate him. He paced to the verge of the drop. The others would not be here for ten minutes.

But science was just down the trail. And what of the other refugees from the old scholar-elite of Germany, Robert Oppenheimer thought, and history filled his head. Yes, the sacred circle of enlightenment had finally burst in '33, when they jeered Einstein off the podium at the Kaiser Wilhelm. Now they were scattered like seeds . . . Einstein to Princeton with Gamov, and Houtermans in Russia where Peter Kapitza was said to be Stalin's captive. Robert's old teacher Max Born was in Edinburgh with a student called Fuchs . . . while Bohr was teaching Teller, Weiskopf and Von Weiszäker in a Dutch castle. Even here in the Sangres, Robert could feel their physical peril. But the supreme adventure of the mind had kept on – with Frisch and Peierls at Cambridge under Chadwick; even in Nazi Berlin, Hahn and Strassman somehow were keeping up their contest with Joliot-Curie in Paris . . . to reach the unimaginable energy, *violence*, everyone guessed was in a single atom. Yet it was in Mussolini's Rome that this same Emilio Segre – now below on Robert's horse – had bombarded heavy metals with neutrons and produced 'transuranics', elements made by man. That was mankind's second physical peril, Robert thought, without controlling his exhilaration. Leo Szilard had gone alone among their physics elite preaching some 'veil of mysteries' be drawn over the terrible powers hidden in nature. But just last year Joliot-Curie had made public the first details of the 'dangerous neutron', and Lise Meitner had for the first time spoken aloud the words 'nuclear fission'. Every-

7

one in high-energy physics had heard how Szilard went then to Long Island, to their high priest. Everyone knew Einstein had signed a letter to the American President, Delano Roosevelt. A prophesy of some great mystery that was to come.

So Robert's concentration flew out, standing on the canyon rim under the deep sky, looking south from Los Alamos. He scarcely saw the heat haze forming on the far desert. For they were all, all at the rim of a new age. Only in the last months, an American in Robert's own lab, MacMillan, had finally isolated those Segre-Fermi-Joliot transuranic elements. And they were Element 93, Neptunium, and Element 94: *Plutonium*.

'Nineteen forty, anno domini!' Robert said into the wind.

And thinking of the revolutionary dawn to which the last eleven years had brought them all, he did not feel the unchanging Mesa's eleven bitter winters, or its eleven parched summers. Not as the farmers and goatherds of the canyons, who knew nothing else. As he stood again on the promontory high over the red valley of the Rio Grande, the man felt very sure his sickness was left behind.

Standing with the slouch hat and bridle held in his hands, an infinitesimal figure against the blue-hazed distances of the desert, Robert Oppenheimer narrowed his eyes to see. And gone now was the bloodless skin, the tight sharp features and large glittering eyes. The man's skin was brown and clear and the tall, spindly body filled out. The eyes, eyes American girls had called beautiful, looked out with a restless irony. Forgotten was that hungry, plaintive gratitude for life. Instead, standing braced on the rock as the hot gale snapped his scarf and tore at his shirt until it roared like a flag, the man felt an exultation, a sense of greatness and of his own freedom too wilful to be humbled even by this waste. The emotion was so intense that a wave of embarrassment instantly followed, and the man shifted his boots. Yes, I must bring Kitty to this place, he thought, and she will make love to me here.

The spell of the moment was broken. He gathered the reins and swung on to the horse's back.

PART ONE

Chapter 1

Four eggs crackled on the wood stove. In the log kitchen at *Pero Caliente* there was a smell of breakfast. Frank Oppenheimer leaned back by the open door with his flute. Over the stack of books he could see the grass slopes, the perimeter of spruces and the corral. As his eyes followed the figure among the horses, he was glad the others had left, even that Jackie had stayed home. Frank blew in the mouthpiece. In the early morning just the tone sounded good.

'Hey, Rob!'

Down in the corral his brother waved and swung the saddle on to the fence rail. Frank sat down and began playing the *allegro vivace*. Presently Robert stood moodily in the door, powdered with dust. 'You should be doing that full time,' he said.

'Thanks. But would you explain something to me?'

'I didn't mean giving up physics.' Robert looked at the frying pan appraisingly.

'There are five horses down there,' Frank went on, 'and you have to ride the unbroken one. It makes me mad.'

'But think what the saddle must mean to him.'

'Why not quantize it and see?' Frank said.

'We'll have no quantizing down here.' Robert slipped the eggs on two tin plates and walked his shuffling uneven walk out into the sun. Frank padded after him over the pine needles with the coffee tin. Feeling his brother brooding so early in the morning, Frank experienced a little wave of anxiety. He preferred Robbie telling him how to run his life.

The snow on the Sangres looked very close over the forest hills. The air was spiced with pine. Over the meadows the dawn shadows were warming.

'Speaking of quantizing, Frank,' Robert went on without picking up his fork. 'Have you ever asked yourself what our chums from the labs think seeing us play around with horses?'

Robert looked across the plates at his younger brother, eyebrows knit. He was thinking of his intense emotion yesterday on the Mesa. Robert needed Frank to guess it. Looking up at him between bites, Frank thought it was marriage and he was moved.

'Robbie? How do you feel about it?' Frank said quietly.

'Ah, that.' Embarrassed at their misunderstanding, Robert began his eggs. 'Well, a lot better than Levin about to marry *his* Kitty. Did it occur to you,' Robert said. 'A Pittsburgh political romantic and biologist, born in Germany? What could be closer to our family?'

'And a vamp too.' Frank was silent, wondering about princesses, then about all the books they used to read together here. '*Anna Karenina*, now there was a book! Still it's been good this time. I don't want to go back West.'

'Or New York?' Robert shrugged. 'Frank, tell me. How did you ever listen to that garbage about how wonderful your brother was?'

'To New York, the coast, anywhere!' Frank waved it away.

'I guess we feel the same about New York,' said Robert. 'You know, Papa's chauffeurs and cooks, Mama's goodness.'

'You outgrew it.' Frank shook his woolly head. 'I guess there's a lot more to this country. I'll tell you what it was for me, Robbie. You never went to that rally in Madison Square Garden, for the Brigade.'

The two skinny brothers faced each other, leaning on the picnic table above the clearing.

'*No pasaran!*' Robert spoke the Republican oath, rolling the r's and hardening the a's. 'You knew friends of Kitty's arranged that rally?'

'She's pretty far from it now.'

'The farther the better.' Robert's eyes veiled. 'If I start thinking about what's going on back in France, I'll boil over.'

'Kitty won't let you stick to that.'

'Am I so easily influenced?'

'It's a family trait.'

Robert put down his fork. The shadow from the tree-tops had left his face.

'When I think of pogroms, Frank,' Robert said so quietly that even in the morning hush Frank barely heard it, 'it makes me think of bombs!'

'*No pasaran*, eh?' Frank shook his head. 'Anyway, bombs won't solve any more than rallies do.'

Robert pushed his plate on the table and looked up. 'It all seems

12

pretty unreal from out here.'

Frank changed the subject. 'You didn't tell me how Edith was yesterday.'

'The poetess and her Indian chief.' Robert smiled. 'Obscure but splendid.'

'What's her obscurity got to do with it?' Frank said.

'It's what I meant about horses.'

'You were a terrific host!' Frank objected.

'I'm tired of being the host.' Robert took out his pipe. 'Segre and Bethe can be the hosts . . . I'll do their work.'

'Robbie, you'll have your moment,' Frank said gently.

'I'm thirty-six, Frank.'

The brothers sat a while in the silence. 'Do you know who was at this table yesterday?'

Frank shrugged. 'Who?'

'Destiny, fate knocking at the door,' Robert said.

'What a door. You know where their work could lead.'

'Galileo, Frank? The truth is the truth.'

'A vacation's a vacation. Robbie, you always loved it here.'

His handsome brother looked across with a crooked smile. 'I'm sorry Frank. I'm spoiling it for you.'

'For yourself,' Frank grinned. 'You'll need your strength.'

'She makes things work for me, Frank. Jean never did,' Robert squinted up at the sun. 'You know I feel the same about here,' he went on. 'Only there's never been a moment like now. Not in all history.'

'Famous last words. I'll settle for this.'

'I want to settle for it too. Only my mind keeps slipping off.' Robert frowned nervously. 'I want to love what we've got, but it scares me. What if there's nothing else? Never anything else?'

'But that's the *beauty* of it!' Frank burst out.

'That's it, Frank!' Robert laughed happily. He slapped the table. 'You've solved it . . . that's the solution.'

While they talked, a wintry film had spread on the sky. Across the river the rich gold dawn had dulled on the slopes, the red flesh of the desert darkened.

Robert stood up, still filling the pipe. 'You're right, the labs are not so wonderful,' he said. 'Most of the crew are quite ignorant.

13

Imagine grown men who blush like bobbysoxers at words like poetry, or love. Thank heaven for a few friends like Haakon Chevalier. Or students like Serber, Lomanitz, Neddermeyer.'

'They think you're some genius,' Frank said.

'Listen, Frank . . .'

Robert was in a new mood. Walking up the knoll, he turned and squinted over Frank's head, down the slopes into the Albuquerque desert. 'Without Bach or Buddha, Frank, mesons and quanta and isotopes are no more than mechanics.' Robert was excited. 'I don't need hero worship. Just to feel I'm running more than a garage full of jealous grease-monkeys and electricians. And you're right.' He waved his pipe around the horizon. 'Beside *this*, those cities were a floating over the surface. I was coming here all along.'

Alone at the table, Frank picked at his breakfast. They had been talking just twenty minutes, but he felt oppressed and weary. The world, overcharged with information, was hammering at them with guilts and fears. As if he, Frank, had just been used again as a sort of straw target for the moral archery of his brother's pride. He pushed the plate away.

The heat was on Frank's back. Birds twittered in the cotton-woods.

'You don't love Harvard Square more? Or sailing on the Zurich-see with Isidor and Pauli?' Frank gently tested him. 'Or Bohr's vision, or Einstein's? Or cosmic-ray work with Neddermeyer, or Plutonium, or Fermi's reactor?'

'That's behind me . . . it was almost easy.' Robert smiled simply, refusing to be embarrassed. Blue smoke filmed above his head.

'I can set up the maths of a collapsing sun in the mind's eye,' he went on softly. 'Like a landscape painter who's mastered the structure of sensation. Then add or change factors without losing the thread. I can see the mesons in cosmic rays as if they were stable, or anticipate a rare instability like U235.' Robert shaded his eyes. 'But this place and our friends here – Paul, Don Amaldo – always seemed so mysterious, Frank. I've loved it so much I wanted to change it. Build altars. Be close to death, passion, ruin.'

'The locals have already done it in the pueblos. And without Wall Street paying the bills.'

'Not that kind, Frank. Being close to a really great . . . break-through.'

The grass knoll did not have the correct feel. Robert began slowly circling the picnic plot.

'When you're up there for the first time, Frank. When you're completely alone with beautiful images?' Robert walked up and down, gesturing, and Frank saw the dust mark where the horse had thrown him. 'They're all yours if you can *possess* them, in some bastardly way, keep someone else from having them!' he went on.

Frank paused, stacking the plates and cups. He grinned.

'What about Kitty? You love Kitty more, don't you?'

Robert had stopped fifteen paces off, staring away. There was no answer. And for some reason Frank remembered a scene four years ago, across a continent. In New York overlooking the Hudson River.

Chapter 2

If a suite on Riverside Drive with central heating and later air-conditioning could be said to possess a climate, then the weather in Julius and Ella Oppenheimer's thickly carpeted West Side rooms was, season after season, warm and dry, and free of storms. Even the ups and downs of the clothing business through War One, and later the Depression, did not violate the cloister of Jewish family affections. From their German father Frank and Robert learned a veneration of scholar-princes, and from their lovely painter mother a rather morbid aestheticism. It was an immigrant household, and though there was no lack of patriotism, sometimes for the boys there was a loneliness in the rough new country. And it was this fear of not being loved which had attracted the pretty Berkeley Freudian Jean Tatlock to Frank's brother.

That was the one dinner Frank remembered the pretty wasp meeting their parents.

From the long table you saw nothing of the city. There was only the river, and across it the red autumn forest. The paintings on the wall were by Gauguin, Van Gogh and Cézanne, scenes re-inventing man's innocent state in nature. There was even a hot yellow- and blue-shaded landscape of Provence which could have been the New Mexico desert.

The family stood by their chairs waiting for Robert.

'Could the paper wait, Julius dear?'

Isidor Rabi whistled at Ella's pun. Frank and Jackie laughed nervously with Jean. Isidor had studied at Göttingen and Zurich, so he must be in on Robbie's wild European life. Julius lowered the paper, eager to please.

'Heinkel bombers over Madrid? What is going on over there?'

'Julius!' Ella gave a brittle smile. 'Any news, Isidor?'

'No word at all, Ella. The big fish swallows the little fish, und zat's zat,' Rabi said in thick Viennese.

'I'm sure your people are safe,' said Jean. From the first mention of Spain, the face under the cropped black hair took on a morbid gravity, as if the great fascist sin was hers to atone for. Even their mother, who cherished her withered hand in a velvet glove, was relieved to see Robert come in. He was absorbed in a thin green book.

'Julius, will you invite your son down among ordinary mortals?'

'New mathematics by Hahn, Isidor, on neutron rates for Uranium,' Robert hurried to his place. 'That black suit again.'

'If you do not think it cute, buy me another,' Isidor laughed.

'Robert's been too long in a clothesmaker's family. Robbie, you should keep in touch with suffering humanity,' Julius went on as they took their places, without noticing his son's humiliated glance at Jean.

'Oh no, Mr Oppenheimer.' Jean lifted her chin. 'Robbie knows perfectly well now. He's helped refugee Jews settle over here. He gives a lot to Civil War Relief.'

Their father stopped serving himself to stare at his son. 'Then I have a book which may interest you. A fellow who has spent time in Russia,' Julius said. 'But I still remember how you heard of the Crash only two years into the Depression.'

'Frank joined the Communist Party,' Robert offered.

Frank blushed. 'I lost my Party card in the laundry.'

Robert sent Jean a worshipful smile. During the last months he had spoken openly of marrying her, without knowing if Jean wanted him to. Seeing her confusion Robert was terrified that if

16

they did not, he might have thrown on his self-confidence the guilt of Jean's ruin. A moral panic had begun, a need to take in great breaths of freedom.

'It isn't such a terrible world, Papa!' Robert was saying now in a jump of excitement. 'There is so little we know. Human nature can do such great things. There's such beauty if you train yourself to look.'

'Take collapsing suns,' Isidor prompted him.

'Yes!' Jackie agreed. 'That is amazing.'

'Why not tell us, dear?' Ella's voice, warm, enveloping.

'Well, first forget any sentimental view of the Creation.' Robert had forgotten his food. He smiled up and down, fingers knitted.

'Thousands of light years from this planet are myriad suns, most of a far greater magnitude than our own. Spheres of staggeringly hot fires, energies bound by unimaginable force fields. These suns have life-spans. Alive, they may be a sustained, awesome fusion. But when they die?'

Robert shrugged, and there was a dreaming glaze in his eyes. No one stirred. Everything was fresh and new.

'There is a beautiful theory that they collapse in on themselves,' Robert said quietly. 'Such a sun, maybe a thousand times the size of ours, might in one single day collapse to a nuclear core the size of a boulder.'

'No one has Robbie's magic way of describing things,' Jean had whispered to Frank later, sitting on the window couch. She said it as if she, like the suns, knew the threat of collapse.

Their mother would never have contemplated Jean sleeping even in neighbouring rooms with Robert before they married. So Robert shared Frank's room. It spared him Jean's bedroom scene.

'Robbie?' Frank had whispered in the dark.

'What is it, old man?'

'Jean seems pretty devoted. Why not marry her?'

There was a silence.

'Frankie, how do you live with someone who wants you to be God?'

Now, barefoot at their picnic table in the New Mexico morning, Frank remembered their boyhood home. He felt the sweet suffocation of their mother's presence. All that had gone for ever. Yet

Robbie still needed things about him to be sacred. Wherever he stood, whoever he liked, whatever he said, it had to be his alone. It made you wonder who this woman was his brother had let so close to him.

Over the Rio Grande valley, the Mesa called Los Alamos, and the brothers' cabin above Sangre Pueblo, the overcast was burning away as Robert said it would. It was going to be another hot day.

Chapter 3

For twelve years the radical patrician Franklin Delano Roosevelt was president of America. It was the golden age of atomic physics, and utopian politics. The last free centres of science were in the obsessive midnight laboratories of the great universities: Columbia at the edge of Harlem; old world Harvard and austere MIT, back to back on the banks of the Charles; Chicago, and informal Berkeley on San Francisco Bay with its cyclotrons, Lawrence's great particle accelerators. And their faculties did battle for the master intellects as they fled to freedom from fascist Europe, bearing dark revelations from the high-energy worlds of stars and atoms, forebodings of power that gave anyone half up to date a sense of superiority to Hitler's slovenly world of heroic myths and legends. Nothing less than Reason could save men from their evil ways. Then reasoning Stalin signed a pact with the mythomane Hitler. And it was just next year Robert and Kitty were married. Then it was 1941.

A thick, chill, seaweedy-smelling Pacific fog had gathered on San Francisco, hanging through the cypresses and eucalyptus of the Presidio. But across the Bay at Berkeley, it was a balmy California morning. Spring fever pollinated the campus. A spirited young man of letters, with a reputation as the friend and translator of the French radical Malraux and as an adventurer of the high seas, was upstairs in Le Conte Hall, walking with some distaste along the high narrow corridors.

The intent, dreaming science students were in short sleeves. A faint reek of hot metal and sulphur stirred romantically in the air. Haakon Chevalier found a department head he knew slightly.

'Lattimer, I cannot find my friend Oppenheimer the physicist.'

'He's moved.' Wendell Lattimer looked up curiously. 'I will take you to him.'

Chevalier trailed the chemist's cigar smoke between the murky lab doors.

'You know, Doctor Chevalier.' Lattimer spoke slowly. 'Your friend is an unusual man, a very interesting study in human personality.'

'My friend is a friend. Therefore he is not a study of any kind.'

'Nevertheless . . .' Lattimer said significantly, pausing at a closed door. He stared at Chevalier's blond Norwegian beauty.

'Are his offices far?' Haakon cut the eccentric fellow off.

'Right there in front of you,' Lattimer wheezed.

Haakon rapped on the scarred door and opened it slowly. Among the far desks four grimly absorbed faces had turned to stare. Bob Serber was seated delicately upright under the blackboard, Rossi Lomanitz sprawled like a bad boy in the fifth row, legs on the next desk, and Weinberg like a plump bespectacled dentist. Oppy stood glowering against the radiator in a cloud of pipe smoke. Haakon felt his face redden.

For the last two hours Robert had been working numerical approaches to various field theories for the Coulomb barrier – the yoke-sac of the nucleus into which only the magic neutron was thought to have entry. He knew the purity of these three minds well, having taught them himself. He knew there were no technical limits in this room to breaking the most inscrutable code in the universe. And at first, as Oppy chalked up the sheet-music of factors, Sines and Cosines, they all felt the mad exhilaration of being up against the untouched, the absolute. But this morning there was no penetration, or resolution. As the minutes ticked away, instead of an all-illuminating simplicity the chalk marks sank into hideous complication. So the colleagues had tightened and willed their concentration against it, until they were hurting each other. And in that attenuated, sweaty struggle Robert saw Haakon's romantic smile in the rear door. With a happy laugh, he walked between the empty desks.

They embraced at the door. Haakon waved to the others.

'How good to find you here at last. Los Angeles is no place for angels.'

'So you're back, Haakon.' Robert let out his breath and laughed. 'How goes, you dashing fellow?'

'Well, Oppy. Very, very well.' Haakon hesitated, glancing suspiciously at his friend's crowded blackboard. 'But who is that terrible person with the head like an egg?'

'A caliban, Hoke.' Robert laughed. 'Every lab has one.'

'Ugh!' Chevalier shrugged. 'But, my friend, you have been making secrets. Or should I say, making babies?'

'So you know.' Robert smiled, pushing his notes in his satchel. He loved Haakon. He loved the subtle play of his European vision.

'Of course I know!' Chevalier protested. 'From Ernest Orlando. But keeping secrets from your best friend! Not only nasty, but dangerous. Think if I had not found out. Who would there be to celebrate with?' He lowered his voice. 'Tell me, how is she really, your Katherine? How did she get you?'

'Last summer she left her last husband and followed me to the desert.'

Haakon whistled. 'The German will, Oppy.'

'To me she is Andromache.'

'Ah!' Chevalier said, trailing his friend to the group closing shop at the front. 'Well then, leave this foolishness. Take me to her.'

'Right now isn't possible, Haakon.'

Robert had squeezed out a sponge. He cut black swathes through the chalk notations.

'I promised to meet an old friend of Kitty's from the Lincoln Brigade. Do you know him . . . Nelson?'

'Steve Nelson?' Chevalier was looking outside over the miniature cactuses and palm fronds. On the sleepy campus lawn, a group of blonde California girls in white bobbysox were curled primly. 'Then, do you know him well?'

'Indirectly.' Behind him, Robert heard Bob, Rossi and Wein fall silent. It was four against one.

'*Steve* Nelson?' Rossi laughed triumphantly. 'We certainly know old Steve, don't we guys?'

'I should say so,' said Weinberg.

'Throwing in with high-ups in the CP again, Oppy?' Haakon enquired.

'Oh?'

At the blackboard Robert pondered the last triangle of factors and frowned. His face was burning. The Party . . . the Communists. These four remembered how the cruelty of money to the helpless had shocked Robert in Jean's time, in the Teacher's Local and all the others. How had the cure seemed so plausible then, an absolute you surrendered all ambition to, and forgave everything? How did it seem to him both futile and alarming now? Rossi's effortless conviction violated Robert. Steve Nelson should be different though. Nelson hadn't just given money and bragged dialectic. He had been there.

Robert erased the last factors. 'No jumping to conclusions please.' He smiled crookedly. 'You can always talk to me about it.'

'But don't ask you to commit?' Rossi offered.

'Ad tedium, Rossi,' Bob Serber said softly.

'Absolutely. Now push along young gentlemen. Haakon and I have other commitments to discuss.'

'You knew Nelson was close to Joe Dallet? Kitty's Civil War-hero husband?' Robert went on when they were in the corridor, locking the lab door. There had been reporters snooping around. Robert was softening now. He felt utter safety in his fellow-exile's sensitive spirit.

'Okay, between friends no politics. *D'accord*?'

'*D'accord*. Here, have a Lifesaver.' Robert grinned. 'Better stop over with Barbara tonight. We'll celebrate.'

'I will meet Kitty. But you know, Oppy, I miss our debates on the Revolution . . . the great future.'

'You mean Stalin throwing in with the Nazis? More like the end of *all* debate,' Robert said.

They had wound in step down the crowded stairwell, and out on to the Le Conte front steps.

'Oppy, you simple booby! That's a beautiful coup.' Haakon threw up his hands. 'Think of Mata Hari, the Trojan Horse!'

'Bonaparte's alliances, Haakon?' Robert stood in the sun, head hanging. He felt a little deranged. 'Weiskopf is back from Russia,' he murmured. 'I told you about the solar-fusion man, Houtermans? The Communist.'

'Oh yes, yes.' Haakon waited eagerly.

'Apparently when he reached his friends in Russia, they tortured

21

him half to death.' The contradictions oppressed Robert, joining somehow with this morning's defeat at the Coulomb barrier.

'Mistakes!' Haakon hid his face behind his hat brim. 'The movement cannot stand this many mistakes!'

And so forth. Presently the friends broke up affectionately under the coconut palm. Robert put his charming friend from his thoughts, focusing instead on the man he was going to meet. The homely local Party chairman who had known his wife's great love, and fought face to face with the fascists. A man who had drunk, undiluted, the draught of justice and death . . . of loyalty and betrayal. This will be a test, he thought. Robert needed to know, he needed it to be solved.

Crossing the wide lawns, in and out of the shade that murmured with bees, sprinklers and students' chatter, Doctor Oppenheimer was very excited.

Chapter 4

The Santa Cruz mountains form the ridge of San Francisco Peninsula to Salinas and Monterey, dividing the shallow mud estuaries of the south bay from a cold surf that thrashes the kelp coves and cypress dunes, the Spanish fishing villages and rocky cliffs of the Pacific shore. Rising and ranging as the skyline leaves the city, they become a dry scrub wilderness of yellow slopes, spruce laurel and eucalyptus forest. Of glades and secret gorges where the craggy live-oaks, grey-green as olive trees, scatter their acorns and crisp sharp leaves. And over this range, fanned most of the year by a warm sea breeze, waits a soft and innocent stillness, a reverie broken only by the few deer, wildcats, raccoons and rattle-snakes which have always lived there. A hush like youth, or sleep, which knows nothing of history.

It was here Robert and Jean had sometimes driven on picnics, to a secret glade of live-oak streaming cobwebs of lace lichen they had mistaken for Spanish moss. Each of them terrified of not being loved, terrified the other was not immortal; Robert and Jean had been tormentedly in love. But there was a magic in this glade which made it, of all the places Robert Oppenheimer had been, most like Eden. It was to this special place Robert and Kitty drove the

Nelsons and their baby that afternoon. It had been Jean's place, but that was long ago.

They squeezed into the Oppenheimer coupé with Kitty's picnic basket. Both Nelsons sat in the back seat with the baby litter. They had left before noon. By one o'clock they had coasted through San José, which in those days was still a mainstreet town. They accelerated straight out on the flat artichoke fields along the narrow Los Gatos road. It was a breezeless hot day and the couples were happy but a little awkward with each other, so it was a relief to ride with the windows down in a roar of cool air.

Kitty was behind the wheel. Steve sat in the back over the drive-hump.

'If a cosmic ray came into Robbie's head, Steve, we'd all end in a field,' Kitty had explained before they set off, flushing with pleasure in both men. Her cheeks were already pink with the coming of their first child. Now, as they all sat in the dry wind enjoying the distances of spiked grey artichoke plants, Kitty's hard bright eyes glanced at the scarred face in the mirror. Subtle emotions played on her pretty face.

On her right Robert sat sideways. Sometimes he smiled back at Steve and his plain blonde wife. Sometimes he pointed to a tiny crop-dusting biplane racing over a field, or the straw-hatted Filipinos stooped among the artichokes. Kitty was conscious of the contained gestures of the man in the back seat. Joe's rough pure friend from the Pennsylvania anthracite fields certainly made a contrast with her bony, rather effete Harvard genius, Kitty thought. She smiled again. But she knew the men had liked each other.

Straight ahead now, the road disappeared in blue-hazed mountains. Steve had kneeled forward, his elbows on the seat back between Robert and Kitty.

Kitty held the steering wheel beside them. Her eyes glanced ironically from the two men's faces to the empty road and back again. Blasts of vegetable-smelling heat blew in their faces.

'I'm awfully glad you could come, Steve!' Kitty called. 'Today means a lot to me. To be bringing you two together – the two best people I know!'

The men were leaning close on the seat back. They exchanged

23

pleased, embarrassed grins. Ahead, the road was leaving the plain of artichokes.

'She means Joe, doctor,' Steve laughed.

'I should think she does.' Robert looked away, feeling somehow ineffectual beside the blunt modesty of his wife's friend.

For ten years Robert had heard people at radical gatherings talk of justice and revolution. But sitting next to this simple man, Robert felt justice, revolt and mankind very close. Close as these labourers, this hot dry wind, the food in their basket. Nelson was a fellow he would not mind being influenced by.

Under the windy coupé roof they exchanged excited grins. This was important, and they all felt it.

'I've left so much of it behind. Haven't I, Steve?' Kitty had suddenly looked around.

Steve was gazing ahead up into the mountains, chin on thick freckled arms. The two men sat close to her because of the wind.

'That's okay, Katie,' Nelson called softly. 'You put in your time back in Youngstown with the best of us. Bob, I remember Katie in Paris, after Joe. If I hadn't stopped her, she'd have gone straight to Barcelona. Lost cause or no. You'd have laid your life on the line.'

'Would I?' Kitty threw them an uncertain look, and saw Steve's quick nodding grin of admiration. Robert was listening. With a little frown, she stared ahead over the wheel. A deep flush mounted to the roots of her hair. 'Well,' she said indistinctly. 'I guess nothing's that clear to me any more.'

'Just on a hunch, Katie, I'd say you never had things so clear.' Resting his hand on her brown shoulder, Steve gave Robert a wink.'

Steve slipped back on the rear seat between his wife and baby and they all understood. There would be no talk of the Party or of ideology. In its blue canvas litter, the baby gave a few tentative gurgles without crying.

Not looking at each other now, the couple sat with their arms in the hot wind. Kitty absorbed herself in the winding mountain road. They enjoyed the wide rolling gold slopes of tufted barley, the forests of craggy, elephant-bark oaks. Finally they crested the Santa Cruzes, starting down a valley. Far ahead and below was the undulating distant rim of forests, and beyond that only haze – the ocean. They parked down a thick wooded fire-path. In the sudden silence, Robert took the picnic. Steve slung the sleeping baby on his wide back. All around them, the cricket sound pinwheeled in a zinging vibration. A short while later Robert was leading them down the valley, hearing the exclamations of the others at the huge live-oaks and their moulting cobwebs of pale green lichen. Even the meadow Robert remembered flamed with poppies. His legs weakened under him. Watching the knee-deep grass for rattle-snakes, Robert thought: It's because we're both utterly free of all the selfish living out there. Because Steve's renounced all interest in personal fortune. And you? Because you never had to care about wealth.

It was two o'clock before Kitty spread their blanket on a cool moss bed, by the stream under the spruces. She set out her roast chicken, iced tea, crab salad and stuffed peppers. Then the bottles of Rioja Steve had found somewhere. She thought how they had starved in Union days.

They were hungry now, and as they ate the baby slept. In the shady sage and wildflower-scented stillness of the place, it would have seemed ungrateful to say much. Or other than in lazy murmurs comparing family, children and ordinary things. When they had eaten, the baby gave small whimpering cries and the mother began unbuttoning her blouse. Kitty was very interested in this.

'You men can go off for a while,' she announced firmly.

Chapter 5

Steve took the light spinning reel. Robert stumbled upstream after him.

They explored along the pools. Presently coming to a low fall, they sat five feet apart on a rock ledge which formed the bank of a clear black pool. Away from Kitty, an awkwardness came over the two men. Robert looked out of the spruce branches across the brilliant poppy meadow. There was Jean's speckled lupin bed under the oaks.

'Good thing to get a few minutes away from our ladies. Don't you think so, doctor?'

'Robert. . .' Robert offered and felt embarrassed. He unscrewed a jar of pink salmon eggs. 'Yes I suppose it can be.'

'Say, not those. Periwinkles.' Nelson stretched face down on the rock shelf. His red face almost touched its reflection on the black pool.

'Periwinkles, Steve?' Robert repeated, trying to open himself further to this Croatian miller's son, fifteen years an organizer. Was he not a seeker after wisdom?

'Uhuh.' Steve slid his thick forearm under the water. 'See? They make these tough twig houses to cover up their soft backsides. Funny how you can turn the river against itself. You pick these periwinkles off the rocks, put one on the hook . . . presto you got a trout.'

'Easy as that?' Robert puffed his pipe.

'Yessir. I'd be dead in the mountains after Brunete if I didn't know that. Look! Over there.'

Nelson kneeled up by the pool. For a moment his eyes met the scientist's. They both watched his tiny bait snake out. It lit on the shallow rapids and swept into the pool.

'Doctor? I mean, uh . . . Robert.'

'Yes, Steve?' Robert struck a match and spread the flame in his pipe bowl.

'You know . . . I don't know the God damnedest thing about physics.'

Robert laughed nervously. He controlled a wave of his usual fear, almost hatred, in the presence of a common mind. 'If that were the only thing I didn't know the damnedest thing about. For instance . . . there's war.' Robert tensed at the alert glance the man threw him. Had his laugh left a conceited echo? 'I'll bet you could pass on a thing or two about the world,' Robert went on, experiencing a wave of self-disgust. 'Sometimes I think there's been far too much peace in my life.'

'Peace is a fine thing,' Steve said quietly. He lifted the rod tip to float the line on the surface.

'After what you've seen it may well be.'

There was a silence by the pool. Both men watched the floating line. High overhead in the California heat the spruce tops rustled. A red chipmunk jumped hesitantly along the facing pool ledge. It did not see them.

'Tell me,' Robert said presently. 'What sort of man was Kitty's husband? I guess you knew Joe pretty well.'

'Joe Dallet?' Steve said without looking away from the steady rod tip. His voice had softened, muffled in the water sound.

'Well, Joe was a very moral guy.' Steve thought this over. 'Sort of a fanatic, you might say. Didn't love life much, not like Kitty. He wouldn't have liked coming here to a place like this. But like her, he was a great one for causes. Spain was the best cause going, up until this war,' he said. 'If you knew Joe as well as I did, Doctor, you knew he came to Spain to die for the cause.

'Kitty's changed though. I guess you're the only cause she cares a damn for now.'

'I'm glad you think so, Steve. And what about you?'

'Damn! Missed him!' He reeled in the hook, and threaded on another periwinkle. The bait lit back on the pool and sank in the darkness.

Feeling Nelson's silence, Robert changed the subject. The coal in his pipe was burning satisfactorily now. Together they watched the line.

'Five years of Spanish Relief parties, Steve,' he heard himself say. 'What really went on over there?'

'I can tell you.' Nelson concentrated on the rod tip. He spoke so softly, the sound of the waterfall almost swallowed his words. 'Right from the beginning our people had the spirit . . . and it was quite a spirit. But the *falange* were a sick bunch of professional killers. And they had the armament. Think what that means, hmm? When it's your life on the line. The Party sent me to China too . . . that was worse.'

'What's it like fighting a tough fight on the losing side?' Robert pressed quietly, not knowing what he wanted to hear. He felt a craving for some brutal, irreducible truth in Nelson's words.

'It wasn't like that, doctor. But rough.' He paused. 'Morale was low . . . that's why I went to Spain. On the retreat from Madrid . . . oh, I was on other retreats, a lot of them. On that retreat I was the only Brigadier to come out. I lost twenty-five men in fifteen minutes. All of them were pretty close friends. Between the Heinkels and Franco's personal artillery . . . well. Funny thing though,' he said, 'the comrades didn't seem to mind that. I guess when you've always had less. . .'

Nelson seemed to speak to himself, his voice had gone so gentle and remote. Hearing the words spoken by a man sitting close, a thrill of violent indignation rose in Robert. Both men sat watching the rod tip above the black clear water. It was steady.

'I guess I didn't care at that point whether I was winning or losing. Do I make myself clear?' Nelson said.

'Very . . .' The tobacco in Robert's pipe had burned through. He put the thing away.

'You can accept anything if you forget yourself,' Nelson went on simply. 'The scared ones were always getting themselves cut up proving they could do it. Fraternity, honesty, they did mean a lot. They were all you had, if you even had them.'

The blunt man holding the rod roused himself. He sighed a little wearily, then he laughed and glanced at Kitty's husband. The dark oppression of Europe was lifting from Robert's mind.

'Well, just handing out a lot of the old mierda. Must sound like braggadocio,' Nelson muttered.

'Absolutely not at all.' Robert laughed eagerly. 'Out here we're a little detached from the acts themselves. Imagine how much violence there is in my life.'

The two men were still for a minute. They stared at the rod tip; it had dipped sharply. Finally Nelson stirred.

'Knowledge is a fine thing,' he said. 'Collecting it like you do.'

'Pleasant, I would say,' Robert corrected, and felt again discomfort of a common mind. But he was sure now he would not be misunderstood. 'Still, I think I'd rather collect an experience like yours.'

'Doctor, anybody can do what I did. There's only a few in the world who can do what you do.'

'Look at me, Steve. You really think I could do what you did?'

Steve gave the scholar's body and stringy neck a polite, thoughtful smile. But he was spared commenting. The rod tip had jerked violently down.

'You've got one!' Robert sang out.

Steve was already on his feet. He balanced against the pool.

'Damn!' he shouted. 'And it's a big bastard too.'

28

The rigid line raced, cutting the black pool towards the bouldered rapids. They both saw a muscular silver boil, a lunging tail.

'Away from the snag, there, I see him! Watch it . . . the line!'

The fish had tunnelled straight across current, into the rapids. Grabbing the hoop net, Robert trotted along the rock shelf. He jumped down in the water. Shoes and trousers cold, thigh-deep on the gravel bottom. For a moment Nelson saw Kitty's husband plunge up to the shoulders. Then stagger up holding the net, the wriggling weight a black crescent in it. And just for a moment Steve Nelson thought they were back, half starved, in the terrible, senseless fighting retreating along the Ebro.

Then they weren't. Steve was in the safe forest afternoon in the Santa Cruz mountains, with Joe Dallet's wife and her new physicist husband. Yes, Katie had found a good one.

'He's no shark,' Robert laughed. He shook out the struggling net on the rock shelf.

'Yes, well, they always look bigger underwater,' Steve answered gravely. Holding the three-pound rainbow in both hands, he snapped the panting head once hard on the wet stone.

Watching Steve and his fish, squatting against the spruce trunk, Robert heard Kitty's voice call somewhere in the summer heat below. A little pang of guilt shot through him.

But Steve seemed not to hear. Unsheathing the narrow fish blade, Steve poked the tip into the milt vent, then sliced the belly to the gills.

'Rob?' Steve glanced up speculatively. 'You asked about me.'

'Uhuh, your cause,' Robert repeated, and there was no distance between them. The wet clothes were wonderfully cool.

'Right then, I'll tell you.'

Steve paused from cleaning the fish. Squatting easily on one heel, he looked out towards the sun-drenched meadow of poppies. The crickets made a persistent sound like monastery bells.

'I'm glad you brought us to such a wild pretty place,' Steve said. 'Awfully glad. Joe was a fanatic, sure. I guess a lot of us went to Spain to die. And still today it isn't clear in my head if that was a kind of hope, or a kind of despair. But I tell you this . . . it was deadly honest. Your Katie's got that kind of honesty.'

'I know,' Robert lied. 'I know.'

'And so has a place like this. It's not the same back in the old world. They've had property too long. They'll never get rid of it. Not even when they think they have. But in the States . . . here, just a hundred years ago,' Nelson waved the knife around, 'it was all like this . . . free, naked. Untouched as your atoms, Doctor.'

The two men's eyes met, and Robert smiled. He was moved. He glanced down at Steve's quick motion on the rock. Two diagonal slices had freed the fishhead.

'This country, Doctor. It's a stolen country.' The soldier's rough face was intent. 'It was taken piece by piece from hard simple generous men, better men than you or I. And then still rottener men came to steal it again, and then again. And each time the thieves got fewer, softer, subtler and more arrogant,' he said. 'And the land beaten, layered, more into *property*. And the people who were there first, still there. But the ones low as the soil, sold with the soil into the bondage of *property*. The great American people, and them back in Europe, and the Russians too. All generations of thieves inventing property. And all the while,' Steve laughed with a bitter, pitying wonder. 'The owners of the property . . . getting poorer and poorer.'

'I know, I know,' Robert said, spreading out his long wet legs, feeling the freedom of this afternoon.

'Them who wanted to end the grief of it, going to bury their hearts in Spain. And then, Doctor.' Nelson examined Robert's face gravely. 'Those one or two long months of pure hope, of pure freedom from property! Christ, but weren't we rich in wilderness and freedom. Like this little valley. Then those like Katie who loved their lives so much, they gave up that freedom and hope. And it tore the heart out of them. To be so poor again.'

Squatting on the rock shelf close in front of Robert, Nelson ran his bloody thumb inside the trout's belly flap. In the speckled sunshade he wrenched and tossed the clustered guts into the river.

'As for me, Doctor?' Nelson concluded. He rose to his feet, standing over Robert. 'I don't love death as much as Joe . . . or life as much as Katie. I haven't given up my riches of pure hope yet. I haven't given up my life either. We're in for some pretty rough generations. But as long as you don't forget the way things once were, and could be again, as long as you come to places like this

30

today. There'll be a time when these layers of property will be rolled back, and people will be rich again. I believe that time will come, Doctor Oppy.'

From the river bank Nelson smiled at Robert over his shoulder. He bent over, rinsing the gutted fish in the clear cold current.

'Until it does,' he went on. 'I'm happy to be in and out of the real money, in and out of the country, that hope of freedom. Wherever it happens. Now, let's get back to the ladies.' He stood up with the spinning reel, the fish. 'I think I heard someone call you.'

Robert stood by the spruce trunk for a few seconds, refilling his pipe. The tobacco was still dry. Robert watched the veteran step slowly out of the cool river spruces into the sun. Then he followed out into the heat.

The two men walked back in silence, down through the knee-deep yellow grass and poppies. The seeds stuck to Robert's wet trousers. Both men were feeling delighted with each other, but each knew nothing more could be said. As Robert and Nelson cut back under the spruces further down, the two women were leaning close on the blanket. Their heads were bent over the baby. Robert saw the women were delighted with each other too.

Robert stopped Steve out of earshot. 'I never knew how poor I was,' he said.

'You're not poor,' Steve Nelson said quickly with a little embarrassed frown. 'You've got Katie.'

And looking just ahead at the two women sitting in the cool spruces Robert had a vivid impression of having been in this situation before. Was it just having in Paris seen Manet's picnic under the trees? Or some cursed memory of an Indian campfire?

It was hot late afternoon in the valley when the couples carried the sleeping baby and the lightened basket slowly back up through the mysterious oaks. Kitty steered the car down through the long coasting Los Gatos curves.

Chapter 6

Yes, Nelson was thinking, wondering why he had told so much to this wealthy scientist who would never join the Party. Yes, the great thing he, Joe and the rest learned, fighting beside peasants, was resignation. But one thing he would never get resigned to is a naivéte like this fellow's. And Katie? He looked in the front seat. The little woman's high cheekbone, her fine temples and blowing hair were profiled in the open window against the sunlit Golden Gate. Katie was crazy too. But somehow Katie's craziness did not make him indignant. Never mind, it had been a fine, careless day. It left him feeling strangely at peace with his past.

On the front seat, Robert was lost in weary reflection. He had just thought of tomorrow's lecture, and the dinner tonight for the Chevaliers and the Peters. How could he face them? With a pang of irritation, his mind went back to the serene privacy of his blackboard. To the lonely mathematics of heat in a collapsing sun.

But gazing out over the glittering bay to the jagged black profile of the San Francisco hills, Nob Hill and Telegraph, Robert's skin, flesh and breathing, his entire soul, were humming with the moods and sounds of the hours in the secluded valley. The strong emotions that had passed between them. He thought of Italy, France, Germany and Spain . . . civilized society in the hands of fascist gangs. And somehow it seemed less desperately gloomy. Feeling the pride of the freedom-fighter silent in the back seat, Robert stared out over the plain of artichokes into the warm Pacific sunset. And he saw with the eyes of some warlike conqueror. Of Arjuna, or Agamemnon returning from Troy, or Sherman come out on the beaches of Georgia. How strange these California gas stations, streams of cars, towns and bland fatuous faces seemed beside a truth like that.

The Oppenheimers had just time to drop the Nelsons at their rooming house then speed to their Berkeley mansion (already named in the Jack London manner 'Eagle Hill'), before Robert's German physics assistant Bernard Peters arrived at the door with his wife Hannah. Five minutes later, Haakon and Barbara joined them. There was no time for Kitty to satisfy her jealousy, and hear what Steve had told Robert to put him in such a mood. Seeing Steve and her husband come slowly down through the poppy field, Kitty had noticed on Robbie's face an excitement she did not recognize.

Through that warm evening they sat talking in the patio, while the moths flickered and the little brown bats tumbled through the still air. Kitty kept searching her husband's absorbed gaze. Strangely, no one else seemed to notice the host's secret excitement, or that Kitty had cooked him the fresh trout while they were eating cold cuts and guacamole salad. If anything, Robbie's calm was vaguely intoxicating, and Kitty at once got along with the talkative Chevaliers, and broke the ice with the hot-blooded young Peters.

Lost in thought at the table head, Robert was only aware of his wife and close friends through an exhilarated haze. Scarcely following their argument over German and French culture, he sensed the effect he was having. What was this emotion which had come to him like a sort of holiness that afternoon at his favourite spot? Whatever it is, Robert thought, you aren't going to spill it out to college intellectuals. He was not even sure he would try telling Kitty when they were alone. But it was strange. Robert could feel this happiness generate a sort of nervous control over Haakon and Bernard's moods. Mesmerism, Robert thought. Not very scientific.

At last the gathering broke up. Robert was walking Haakon through the dark hall.

'She's good Robert, very very good,' Haakon whispered. His arm passed through his skinny friend's. '*Enormément de caractère.*'

'I was pleased to see you two getting on so well.'

'That is natural!' Haakon laughed. 'You and I and the women we love will always get along.'

'Well, that's a very nice thing to say, Haakon.'

'*Et le Nelson?* What did you think?'

Robert halted his friend in the dark hallway. Kitty and Barbara were outside under the swarming veranda light.

'Quite a guy.' Robert stared away feeling a vague disgust. 'A very good fellow.'

'I'll find out from your Katherine.' Haakon, who was building his life around celebrated friendships, laughed triumphantly. 'And when we see you next, you'll be a father. A rather sudden father.'

'Think of that!' Robert smiled, giving some ground. 'I suppose I will. Don't forget to send a postcard.'

When Robert came in from the hall, Kitty was standing at the kitchen table mixing Bernard and Hannah iced martinis. There was a deep silence.

33

'How old is that man, Oppy?' Peters suddenly said.

'Dear!' Hannah Peters fixed her eyes on him. Oppy was their greatest benefactor.

'Why . . .' Robert smiled evenly at his young friends. 'Probably about thirty-eight.' His amused glance sought out Kitty's.

'Bernard doesn't think your friend Haakon is tough enough.'

'That is right!' Bernard grinned unpleasantly. His nasal voice went up a note. 'He is a romantic. He talks, yes . . . but not acts! For him the world is a pretty place with pretty ideas.'

'I think he's a nice fellow.' Hannah's delicate mouth twitched. 'I liked him.'

'Haakon's a good friend, Bernard.' Robert looked down. Studiously he puffed his pipe. 'These francophiles are always fruitily romantic.'

'It's the same with all the Party out here!' Peters's lean face brooded on in the circle of the hanging lamp, oblivious of the relieved laughter. 'All sentiment, no will! These California dreamers, they do not demand justice. They beg it!'

At the kitchen table, by the door opening on the warm dark garden ringing and bubbling with cricket, frog and cicada sound, the young German Jew looked provocatively through his spectacles at each of their faces.

'Beg . . . beg!' Peters shouted, the tone alien and strange in the balmy California night. 'You do not *beg* a state! You overthrow it!'

For this final indignation, Bernard had crouched forward on the kitchen chair. His eyes met his professor's amused gaze. In the momentum of his anger, Peters was suddenly aware of the older man's sympathy. And as if taken by surprise within warm waves of understanding, Bernard started out of it.

'Bernard . . .' Robert broke the silence with a fatherly interest. 'You came to Berkeley to do some quantum mechanics with me. You're my most gifted student. Hannah's the family doctor. We're all good friends, and Kitty will now make you a wicked martini. Do we need a violent revolution tonight?'

Hannah Peters was staring across at her husband's fine, clenched face. She was surprised to see it fall apart in a sheepish grin. Bernard was suddenly stammering like a boy. A mixture of smiles, frowns and apologetic shrugs.

34

'Listen, I fight brownshirts in the streets. They ruin my uncle's fruit shop. Fruit?' Bernard held out his open palms. 'I cannot sleep for thinking of killing just one of them.' He stood up and paced through the big American kitchen, making a comic strip confession of it full of ethnic shrugs and grimaces.

'Dachau . . . eh?' he muttered. 'Three years ago, ja? There is nothing but to hammer rocks and think,' Peters said intently, telling it in bewilderment now. 'You are still a boy, but you are sure to die. Nothing else but to wait and watch the way they treat the old ones. Then you got away from these bastards!'

Peters faced them by the blackened silk windows. His lenses flashed.

'How, Bernard?' Kitty said.

'Oh, I have a smart mother on the outside,' the young physicist muttered. He was suddenly nervous, shyly wiping his lenses. Without glasses his eyes were soft and gentle. 'It wouldn't be possible now.

'I'm tired,' he said. 'There are a lot of tired ones here in America. But with this Roosevelt we'll never go to war . . .'

'Enough! Stop this rudeness.' Hannah went to him and put her hand over Bernard's mouth.

Kitty's eyes flashed. 'No, Bernard, don't stop!'

'As Mrs Oppenheimer's physician,' Hannah said, smiling from Robert to Kitty, 'I must demand that you do not excite her. Come home, Bernard.'

Strangely, as Robert and Kitty said goodnight to the young couple by the front magnolia, instead of feeling shocked and awkward with the ugliness of Bernard's story, the sound of Robert's voice under the Pacific moon gave the friends a sense of eternal safety and good sense.

'Darling, they do seem to bring you the problems of the world, frankincense and myrrh,' Kitty said with ironic satisfaction, the minute they were alone in the darkened living-room of the new house. 'Now, tell me what you talked about with Steve this afternoon.'

Kitty held her arms around Robbie's neck. She leaned away to see this man's strange remote face. 'Oh, you know. Just men's talk.' Robert smiled unevenly, but without his eyes losing their intelligent alertness. 'Steve said,' he whispered in her hair, 'my soul will never be poor, as long as I have you.'

With a triumphant laugh Kitty swung on his neck.

'Oh, did he really? Did he say that?' she whispered huskily. And gratefully, Robert felt her will to make things work for them.

For some time after Kitty went upstairs in the early summer night, Robert puttered about the half-decorated rooms. Then he paced out in the moonlit back garden on the thick wet lawn. In the shadow of the giant cypress, Robert looked up in the tranquil sea of stars and nebulae. He was not thinking about heat gradients.

It must be dawn already in Paris, over Unter Den Linden, at Rastenburg, Robert thought. And morning in the Kremlin. But for the first time such images of monstrous evil did not oppress him with horror of the Old World. Through Chevalier's jealous emotionalism and young Peters's tormented outburst in the kitchen, Robert had stayed aloof on the feeling he brought back from the Santa Cruz mountains. Simply holding to that quiet belief by the shady river gave Robert the strength to overcome his friends' moral struggles. Yes, you made them all happy, and they are difficult ones. Did everyone have this faculty, or just him? What did it mean? And how should he use it? He felt an intense, slightly mad love of all things.

For in his garden that Pacific night, standing under the clouds and corridors of stars as a sick horseman had twelve years before on a New Mexico Mesa, Doctor Oppenheimer was testing the greatest power known to man. A power greater than Stalin's over the souls of two hundred millions; or of Hitler's to use tanks as cultural harvesters and execute death sentences on entire races. A power greater than Roosevelt's to be the most voted-for of men; of Stravinsky to concentrate the highest beauty; of Einstein's to see first the structure of time . . . a power to do universal good.

You silly, arrogant fellow! he thought as he turned back to the darkened house.

And thinking of the woman he had left waiting inside that open upstairs window, Robert was suddenly faint. Then he remembered she was pregnant.

36

Chapter 7

Soon afterwards Kitty Oppenheimer gave birth, and it was a son.

During the seven months following the afternoon in the Santa Cruz mountains until the baby was weaned, nothing new seemed to intrude on the bland routine of California campus life, a life of canteen hamburgers, faculty infighting and clambakes at Stinson's Beach. Through that summer Doctor Oppenheimer repeated some of his quantum lectures, and saw the eager trusting mid-western faces respond with the same unwordly excitement. Robert travelled east briefly for a conference in Schenectady where, at Arthur Compton's request, he offered a simple estimate of the quantity of Uranium 235 necessary to build an explosion. For, as a result of the Englishman Oliphant's visit, Lawrence was now convinced it was the Berkeley Labs' responsibility to keep America ahead of any Nazi project. And sometimes Robert was able to see Isidor Rabi, Hans Bethe, Segre, Fermi and other charming refugees from Europe. There was much awed excitement among the great mass about gas-diffusion and cyclotron development and dreams of fast-fissioning, even fusing nuclei . . . making suns. But there was too little money. The talk of a 'power-industry' bored Robert, and it hurt him to be one among many. Nor could the heavy autumn schedule in the Berkeley Science buildings absorb Robert's restless expectancy, or his sense of too-easy mastery. He pitted himself against more and more unresolved questions on the high-energy nucleus, and cosmic rays, scattering, deuterium-deuterium and as always, collapsing suns. He stuffed his mind on more Greek tragedies, the Ramayana, the Tang poets, Dante and Goethe and all of Donne's poems.

Robert knew very well these were the simplest, sweetest hours of his life. But conventional well-being only affronted the memory of times when he had clearly felt a sense of unique, tremendous capability. Surely this scholarly self-satisfaction was not what he had envisioned for himself on the Mesa, or up in the Santa Cruz. In his dread of being cut off from it, Robert assumed more and more tasks, duties and research in different fields. Recording and assimilating, until the slightest emotion in his life was intricately woven to precedents in the past. Yet the more that involved him, the more impatient Robert became with the banal routine of Berkeley life. Sometimes he even detected the first irrational sparks of a hatred for his well-being. A perverse longing for the old daemonic period of Göttingen and Corsica, which had nearly ruined his mind and body.

Such intimations – which he and Kitty only talked out in the privacy of their kitchen, and as a joke – so alarmed Robert that he secretly forgave Kitty for drinking a wee bit too much scotch. He absorbed himself even more deeply in disturbing affairs taking place remote from his blackboard and bed.

That June 22, on the other side of the world, history's most nihilistic hero had launched a faceless $3\frac{1}{2}$ million Teutons eastwards from Poland, thus betraying the dictator who had himself betrayed the Bolshevik Revolution. Into the immense, superstition-ridden, byzantine plains of Russia were sweeping three giant tank armies moving faster than the world had ever seen. And as the summer progressed, another name emerged in Jewish circles. Of a man called Heydrich travelling in the slave territories with a hardly comprehensible order: quite simply to murder every Jew on earth. Robert's Berkeley well-being was dwarfed by such a Babel-tower of systematic cruelty. It was as if all the good of three thousand years could be undone in a single summer or two. As if in Hitler, Civilization's conscience had invented a high-voltage cyclotron capable of perverting every human soul in its field. Amid the oblivious routine goodness of the Berkeley campus, Robert and his exiled friends, who had seen these far-off lands, followed all this obsessively in the newspapers. And they gathered frequently in quiet Pacific homes to hear themselves speak in depressed tones of the sufferings of the Russian people. They who were the experimenters in a future world of logic and brotherhood, without greed or selfishness.

Berkeley days now seemed not only too blandly good and aimless, but also grossly detached from hard events that would decide man's fate. The only connection Robert could detect between the enlightened quiet of Eagle Hill, and those remote monstrous sufferings, was the quiet slipping away of his science colleagues from the Radiation Laboratories to work on weapons projects.

Robert had listened with the others to Edward Murrow's broadcast from London during the great summer air battles. And it was no secret that Oliphant had travelled out to Berkeley with the news of some kingly bomb.

For Compton, Robert had toyed with it himself along with Allison, Breit and the others at the weekly Le Conte meetings on how such a bomb might be. Though without involving himself even as much as Fermi, Teller, Wigner and Szilard in their little Uranium Committee. In fact the theory disturbed him not a little. He could feel its violent mystery deep in nature like some great fish in the sea, but he resisted it. For a bomb seemed to Robert crude, and quite a degradation of their science oath to expand knowledge for the good of man. Yet what was he, Robert Oppenheimer, in his pleasant campus routine, doing for the good of man? While mankind was daily flying to pieces along a road to universal evil, what honour was there in the secluded happiness of the wisest sage? Now, ambling in a daze across the campus lawns under the foggy eucalyptus, giving concentrated lectures, or analysing the world moral crisis at occasional Spanish Relief Parties, alone in front of silent blackboard formulations for the mass of the universe, or with Kitty and baby Peter over a waffle at the kitchen table . . . now Robert recalled the strong sensations that had come to him more than once, of a strength in him greater than the power of any Hitler, Franco, or Stalin, or Churchill . . . the strength to do universal good. Now that strength, whatever it was, seemed to him stupidly insigificant, lonely and useless. Nothing had prepared Robert for the impotence of such an ethic. It alarmed him. It hurt his pride. But at least he was not completely alone. America his country, and its great childish genius, shared his inaction.

Then one wet day at the end of the Berkeley fall term Robert had come home early to lunch. He needed to be on his own. In the humid glass conservatory, Robert sat by the potted palm. Pushing away his wife's newspapers, he switched on the radio set. He knew what was in the papers. The Germans were almost in Moscow. Snowbound Leningrad was under siege.

The local classical station had stopped playing music by German composers, just as hamburgers now were called 'liberty-steaks'. Today Robert recognized Debussy's *La Mer*. He leaned back, eyes closed. The rain was letting up. That morning's lecture on the beta-radiation from tritium isotopes had felt unsatisfactorily flat. As the students watched alertly, the famous flight of inspired brilliance seemed to fail Oppy. Even man's mastery of an element had not seemed beautiful enough. Maybe it was time for a Christmas on the Rio Grande.

He recalled a line from a Tang poem: 'The sage stays limp and calm . . . the world corrects itself.' Well he was limp and calm all right, but the world was going to hell.

The music stopped abruptly. Robert heard the rain and Kitty's feet in the pantry. Upstairs the baby was crying.

'Fellow Americans,' began an earnest voice. A rustling of papers. 'Today, December 7, 1941, at 7:55 a.m. Honolulu time aircraft of the Imperial Japanese Navy attacked the American Pacific Fleet at Pearl Harbour, Hawaii. This report will be continued.'

Debussy resumed on the radio set, filling the conservatory with surges of eternal Mediterranean light. Kitty stood flushed in the pantry door.

For some reason her husband had risen unsteadily from the couch. Robert stared back at Kitty's wet face. So now it was to be this.

'Take off the coat, darling,' he said vaguely. 'Let me dry your hair.'

'Never mind my hair.' Kitty laughed sharply, throwing down her keys. 'We need a drink.'

Robert stood unsteadily by the potted palm. With a firm decision, Kitty set a whiskey bottle on the metal table. Then two glasses wide apart, like a Spanish bartender.

And quite suddenly Robert, too, experienced a rush of emotion so intense it almost blinded him, draining the past, choking all moral inhibition in childish abandon to the moment. Holding the cold glass, he watched the rainwater sway the black tropical vegetation outside. In all the millions of houses across the continent people would be hearing about this awesome thing and feeling these emotions. Then Robert felt something else. An even more violent longing, and a loneliness almost like panic . . . to be part of these great events. To be close to his fellow beings, to rush out in

the street and find someone, anyone, and ask, 'Have you heard . . .
do you know?'

'Must we listen to that?' Kitty said.

'There'll be more,' Robert paced aimlessly. *La Mer* sounded
absurd now, but somehow he could not turn it off.

'What more can there be?'

Kitty pulled out a green metal chair. She sat in her wet raincoat
staring intently at the drifting fog.

'Well I guess it's about time,' Kitty said. For some reason both
spoke in whispers.

'It feels awfully strange, doesn't it? Even having known.'

Kitty turned and gazed at her husband's pensive, non-committal
expression. Her wet hair streaked her brow.

'I'm happy about it, you know?'

'I suppose it's exciting. In a ghastly way.' Robert puffed his
pipe. They sat listening to the rain begin again, drumming on the
glass roof.

'Oh Robbie!' Kitty started pacing. 'I never made it to Spain.'

'They'd already gone under, Kate.'

'I must have been meant to go.'

Kitty's hand on the whiskey tumbler looked small. As she
emptied it the gesture was childish.

'Remember what Steve Nelson said last summer. You would
have laid your life on the line.'

'I would lay it on the line now, Robbie!' Kitty went on in a
strange husky voice. 'That's why I'm glad.'

'Pearl Harbour.' Robert repeated the pretty name. Kitty was not
listening.

'I didn't go,' Kitty went intently on. 'And all this time the Nazis
have been murdering their way out of the east. Now another lot of
fascists are half-way here from the west. This will be their first
stop. We're under siege like the Russians.'

'We haven't gone under yet.' Robert stared into the garden.
Clouds of rain gusted sadly by the giant cypress. He barely heard as
the Debussy soared mysteriously on. Kitty's hungry self-
examination sounded vagely foolish and crude.

'Exactly . . . not yet!'

Kitty had stopped close in front of her husband, leaning back on the glass door. She examined his face with a tender seriousness.

'If you don't go to Spain . . .'

'. . . Spain comes to you.' He looked up at her. The rain thundered like stampeding feet.

They had to raise their voices, like a conversation in a dream.

'What about you, Robbie?' Kitty was asking.

'It's always said that women drive their men to war.'

But Kitty's questioning face didn't smile. 'I'm quite serious, darling,' she said unhappily. 'Is your life on the line?'

The blood rushed to Doctor Oppenheimer's temples. He stared up at her for a long time. *La Mer* rose to absurd heights then ebbed. Quite suddenly the rain outside stopped completely.

'I don't know,' Robert said, his voice suddenly loud. 'That's the most difficult question anyone ever asked me . . . the philosophical, ethical implications. Why, the best minds . . . the prophets of religions . . .'

Kitty stamped her feet and shook her wet hair. Tears rose to her eyes. 'Oh, good God!'

As was natural for Robert during lectures when explaining the most difficult ideas, his voice now softened almost to a whisper. But he was speaking about himself.

'Well, Kat?' He took his wife's tense hand. 'Almost everyone up at the Lab now is on some weapons programme. I'm afraid I'll be taking over Breit's group myself any day now.' Even in the surprise of hearing himself say it, he detected a tremor of relief.

Kitty stared at him doubtfully. A deep silence had fallen through the house.

'From the Oval Office in the White House,' the voice on the radio continued, 'President Roosevelt has beamed a message to the American people advising them that he will request Congress to declare the United States at war with the Axis Powers of Japan and Germany . . .'

Soon after the President's message, the telephone began to ring. First Isidor called from New York sounding fatalistic. Then Lawrence, full of impatience with the Uranium Committee and excitement at having a war for his cyclotrons; then Chevalier from Harvard in a flamboyantly grim mood. Then the Uranium Committee's genius Enrico Fermi called from Columbia, covering his

42

nerves with cynical humour . . . and then young Edward Teller in a state of mixed anguish and hope. Then his brother Frank called, bewildered. And the energetic Leo Szilard, who had alienated the Yankee physicists from bomb work. Faculty friends from other departments called, and a lot of Oppenheimer's students . . . Peters, Melba Phillips, Lomanitz and Bohm, and half a dozen others. All these scientists, whose childlike inwardness Robert had shared, and sometimes wounded with his sharp mind, all seemed to need his advice and encouragement in the face of this human folly. It was the first time Robert felt how widely he was trusted by souls who had never sought public power or wealth, and who despised generals and politicians. The telephone went on ringing all that day and into the evening. A circle of university friends trickled into Eagle Hill, to join the urgent discussion in the conservatory.

This discovery of his growing authority as a philosopher king to the brilliant, the sensitive and naive left an anxious impression. Robert was half reminded of the feeling years ago, when he knew Jean Tatlock was expecting him to take her over. He had felt an unnatural suffocation. What had he said to Frank then? 'How do you live with someone who thinks you are God?' But this time it was harder for Robert to hold on to the emotion he had felt in the Santa Cruz mountains, or alone in the desert wind that day on the Mesa overlooking the Rio Grande, the impulse of humility before nature.

Through the first months of World War, as if confirming it, Gregory Breit, paranoid over Secrecy, gradually relaxed his grip before the expansive brilliance Oppy generated at weekly weapons-duty in the Le Conte attic. And Robert found himself at the blackboard of his excellent group of friends, resolving the neutron-maths to confirm his Schenectady prediction of 'critical mass'. He was, comically, 'Director of Rapid Rupture', with Lawrence and Compton in Chicago in overall charge of Uranium and Plutonium production, and Vannevar Bush handling the Washington end. It was the bomb-design group for the United States atom weapons project. And simply by shuffling up two flights of stairs, Robert was near its summit. And in May of 1942 anno dominii, Breit did stand down, and quite suddenly Robert felt himself bending to a force field not at all like Hitler's, yet something dark, hushed, immense, elegant, beckoning with such velvet ease that moral apprehension was blind, deaf and dumb, floundering in its tide.

One week in July the chamber group convened as usual in the bare sloped garrett, with its slotted balcony and wired windows. Using the sole key, Oppy locked them in: Teller, Bloch, his old friends Hans Bethe, Bob Serber and three others . . . a desk, an assorted half circle of chairs, and a blackboard. It was dustily suffocating, and these gentlemen were like summer boaters in their white slacks and shirts. An hour into a formula of heat-radiation at 300,000 degrees, Teller had finally broken in.

The garret air was compressed; there was so much Mind in these walls, it choked sensation, made them lightheaded. Long, creaking concentrations, broken by soft monosyllables. In the silence, Robert stood sideways before their abstracted eyes, chalk poised. And it was Progress. Then three spoke together, inching it forward.

A long silence. Through the balcony window came the 'clock' of a baseball bat, then tiny shouts. Robert's hand dropped.

'All right, Edward, what is it?' he said.

'Edward . . . it is not deuterium-fusion again?' Bethe looked up at the man standing beside him.

'Not so exactly . . . but why not?' Teller beguiled them.

'Doing fission for the government, Ed, is not at all our idea of entertainment,' Bob Serber said. 'Your solar-fusion business keeps holding us up.'

'No, no . . . this is grave, ver-ry grave. You will see!' Teller hurried forward. He began vigorously scatching up formulae, the chalk crumbling and squeaking. 'Excuse me, gentlemen, I have already done the factors. At this level of heat, look . . . here! And here! Not only deuterium-deuterium . . . deuterium-nitrogen.'

'Nitrogen!' Bloch squinted. 'A *nitrogen* reaction?'

Bethe was on his feet, his face very red.

'Edward, what are you saying?' Serber's limp, bland voice.

What was Teller saying? The charming face searched theirs with complete sincerity. Their concentration stretched out horribly in sheets of singing nerves, warped and flexed, until it felt their jaws would tear, eyeballs evaporate, and hearts burst out like springs.

44

And on all their secret faces, fortunately locked away from the lives of ordinary men, there was the twisted contortion of close psychosis.

'Bob,' Robert said at last. 'How much nitrogen in earth's atmosphere?'

'Point eight zero per cent.'

'All right gentlemen,' Robert's voice quavered hollowly. 'This meeting stops right here. Hans, better get to work on Ed's figures right away. I will go see Compton.'

'Compton is in Chicago!'

'Me? You are trusting me with *that*?' Bethe stared around at them.

'Who else is there to trust?' said Allison.

Next morning Robert stepped down from a train into the cool of the Great Lakes. Compton looked formidable, waiting on the village platform. With scarcely a word or smile, they drove to a rock beach on Lake Michigan. The sky was overcast, with scows planing back and forth through the whitecaps, and no one noticed the two stumbling gentlemen holding their hats.

'All right Oppy, spill the beans.'

'The beans are . . . a solar phoenix,' said Robert.

'What do you mean?' Compton screwed up his face.

'Teller's figures. Deuterium fusion could jump to nitrogen.'

'You mean,' Compton breathed, 'strike a match to all the water and air on earth?'

Suddenly the two men were too hideously embarrassed to look at each other. They stood side by side, looking out on the gusty lake. And it was like an endless sea.

'Arthur, what shall we do?' Robert said finally.

'Until the maths are a hundred per cent resolved, the project is off. There are limits to what we risk to keep Hitler out of the White House.'

'I'm glad.' Robert grinned. 'I see no other way.'

'Ninety-nine per cent anyway,' Compton corrected, just to be scientific.

Strangely, the moment Robert had unburdened himself the impression of monstrous derangement passed, like a dream. Once again at one with things, Robert struck a match for Compton's cigar. But when it flamed loose on the wind both men flinched.

So the fledgling freedom-fighter passed his first trial of fire. It even left a confident feeling of Robert's life being on the line, and of enlightened checks and balances to keep the whole messy business well under control. Finding Kitty, the baby and lovely Eagle Hill as ever overlooking San Francisco Bay seemed to confirm it. And Hans had very soon weeded out some errata in Teller's figures, and run the whole thing several times past a computer. Yes, Robert thought then, with numbers you could even restore the skies, the continents and the oceans all to their appointed places.

Chapter 8

In the most innocent possible way Leslie Groves of the US Army had always wanted to go to Washington. And because he was born American, Groves knew that, in spite of being fat and not very brilliant, he could do it. Once Groves was in Washington, he would be as slim and handsome and superbly intelligent as any man in the country. That was America.

For twenty-four years, Leslie Groves had stayed in the US Army and fiercely pursued the dream. In boot camps and bases all over America, depressing places of stale magazines, sadistic dentists and sneaky embarrassed friendships, places where lazy mediocre men cultivated the brutal application of force, Groves had tirelessly administered, reorganized and disciplined. He had implemented any order and accepted tasks men who were promoted over him would not. In this way very gradually, rank by rank, Groves learned to divide, conquer and forget his victims. He learned power. And then one day when he was pure enough in power, 'Greasy Groves', as he was remembered at West Point, went to Washington. Not only did Groves go to Washington but he went as the Colonel in charge of the billions spent on building projects for the United States Army. And not only that, but for the construction of a *Pentagon*. A supreme temple as generously proportioned as Groves himself, from which those even purer in power than himself would administer all the bases in the most pure and powerful country of all time, newly at war with Hitler and the Japanese Emperor. But in September 1942, just when Groves was beginning

46

to feel the equal of any man in the country, the army, instead of sending him into battle, again offered him a particularly unpopular task with a promotion if he accepted. Groves must drop all his dreams of the front line and return to the hinterlands, there to administer a corps of men more depressing, undisciplined, slovenly and unresponsive to the brutal application of pure power than any Groves had come across. Groves knew this could mean the end of his dreams, and the beginning of nightmare. But he did not feel so slim, handsome and superbly intelligent that he could afford to refuse the assignment. The army was his only road to the purest power.

So, one morning, Colonel Groves pushed into the back of his olive-drab staff Buick with the little American flag on the fender. His aide Lillie drove him from the War Department slowly across the Potomac, towards the sooty wood offices Groves most detested. Spectacled Lillie, who was very lean and pure and from Nebraska, tried a few soft-spoken comments about the morning. For it was a mostly clear September day, crisp with the poignancy of a new school year. But behind his moustache and dark glasses, Colonel Groves was in the urgent alert heartsick mood of a man frustrated on a glorious journey looking for a detour. As the limousine rolled across the great double grass expanse of the Mall and passed the White House, Washington and its mild bright-faced citizens in gay blue seersuckers had never seemed so sweet or so oblivious of him. Groves had never felt so tragically hot in his khaki shirt and pants, or so undistinguished in his life.

The car rolled up at five to nine by the steps of what had been the Uranium Committee building. Lillie, carrying the briefcases, accompanied Colonel Groves in past the security guards. The Colonel had assigned these as a matter of form. For if ever a technical sector had to Groves the smell of failure, it was the Manhattan Sector.

Colonel Groves and his aide were shown up into the director's office. Inside, behind a large desk, sat a cranky, neat little New Englander with a bow tie. He welcomed the army man with shy grins and some puzzled mutterings, and squeezed his pulpy hand. Groves forced himself into a wooden armchair.

'How are you, Bush?' he said in a slightly wheezy baritone. 'What? Speak up!'

'I welcome you, Colonel,' Vannevar Bush said brightly. 'Glad you are with us.' The fact was, no one had warned him of a Colonel's visit.

But across Bush's desk top, almost in line with the portrait of Bush's wife, the suffering, aged fat-boy's face was staring at the model standing on the desk like a large bug. It was made of coloured wood balls and dowels. There was a cluster at its centre, and other balls orbiting on stalks round it. Colonel Groves had never seen anything so nauseatingly senseless or sad.

Groves put the model down. In the silence, they both heard the wall clock ticking. Beginning to feel disturbed by the wavy-haired officer across the desk looking almost as if it might burst into tears, Vannevar Bush tried thinking of something to cheer the man up. On the desk in front of Bush lay a manila ledger. With the measured smile of a Brooks Brothers salesman, the director reluctantly removed a photocopied letter, and held it out past his wife. Groves stirred.

'All right! Let's get to work.' Groves took the letter. 'It's time we found out if this department really has something worthwhile for the Army.'

'This letter was written two years ago Colonel.'

'Hmm . . . to the President.' Groves held his narrow temples between his fingers as if to ease a headache. 'Yes, yes, I've seen this one. No I haven't,' he corrected. ' ". . . a hitherto unheard-of destructive force".' Groves reread the words, as if trying to find some niche among the painful realities of the hour for such a grandiose fairytale. 'Yes, I guess that's what we're all doing. And naturally the Germans being interested recommends it. A bomb, sir, that's what we're trying to build.'

'We scientists,' Bush hurried to say, feeling more and more oppressed by the cold hounded eyes across the desk. He was conscious of the panels of generals listening over this man's shoulders. '. . . we scientists prefer to speak of energy, Colonel, yield.'

'A very big bomb,' Groves went on, adding the withering edge to his tone he reserved for finicky civilians who tried to pull class on him. 'With a weapon like this, you understand Bush, we could crush the Kraut and the Jap in short order. And as for the communists, sir, we could make as short work of those sons of bitches as Franco did of the Republicans.'

Vannevar Bush's smile had become so strained it positively ached on his face. His impulse to cheer up this poor fat fellow had been replaced by an alarming impression of the Colonel's swollen uniform, his oily waved widow's peak. And of something else, something which could not be appealed to. Bush shifted his eyes to his wife's smiling face, then back to Groves.

'Yes, well,' Bush stuttered, tugging at his bow tie. 'We try to play down the applications with our people. You know, Colonel Groves, scientists are temperamental. One must coddle their talents . . . research, etcetera. A few thousand dollars here, a few thousand there.'

Groves sat wedged in his chair near the window. He watched the director with fascination. Maybe things weren't so bad, he thought. After all, so many eggheads thought the theory was promising. Maybe these characters simply needed discipline and they would make good army material too. Already the scroungy little offices had begun to feel like a place Groves could be comfortable in, a place of power. He had simply not grasped how fussy and feeble they were, and he felt his dream stir.

'Listen carefully, Bush,' he began. 'This department is small-time.' Clasping his hands together Groves fixed his eyes on the wood model of sticks and balls. 'But I'm going to put you all in the big time,' he went on.

Vannevar Bush, emperor of American science, sat back with his fixed, kindly smile. Groves had gone slightly pale.

'From today on, Van, let's not ever again hear talk of a thousand here, a thousand there. Do you have any idea what I've got to spend?'

'Perhaps a little idea,' Vannevar Bush said, and noticed that his own voice had a conspiritorial sound. The office air suddenly felt more charged than Bush could remember. And Bush felt a giddiness as if his nervous system was moving into the field of some immense voltage.

'Not thousands, Van, hundred millions,' Groves said, drawing his spit-polished boots under the chair. 'A billion dollars, maybe two. Van, I am going to put this office in the big time. In two years I am going to build that big bomb! And the Army is going to win the war with it.'

Across the papers in the quiet Washington office Vannevar Bush let go of his bow tie and lurched forward against the desk. At the mention of the inhuman sums of dollars (a wealth that humiliated all human aspiration, that seemed to evaporate the favellas of Rio, the lepers and beggars of Calcutta, the starving Chinese, not to mention the West-Virginia miners and the ragged migrant rabble of the Southwest), sums bearing only a dream relation to the one dollar necessary for the pen, ink and notepad to record $E = MC^2$, Vannevar Bush's vague alarm had grown to a certain terror.

The two men stared at each other across the model atom.

'But Colonel Groves!' Vannevar Bush grinned toothily and two locks of hair dropped on his freckled forehead like inverted horns. 'It is not at all certain the bomb can be built.'

'Not thousands, Van, *millions*.' The khaki Colonel in front of Bush exhaled from among the straining excesses of his huge bulk. 'No need from now on for those cheesy little laboratories, and monkey-cage offices. This isn't a hobby for cranky dreamers any longer. It's a war industry. Now you're going to see those eggheads work!' Groves laughed then with a considerable charm. The officer was suddenly aware of being under scrutiny in his new role. 'By God, you'll see them earn their bread!'

'Well that doesn't sound bad, I must say.' Bush joined in the Colonel's laughter. Sinking back in his chair, the director felt so heady a relief at being freed from his first terrible impression, he momentarily felt something like grateful affection for this fellow Groves.

'Well, Van,' Groves was saying, 'in three weeks now I'll be a Brigadier-General . . .'

'Congratulations . . .' Bush heard himself say, and it was like surrender.

'Then I'll make a little tour of the nation. Berkeley, Chicago, New York.'

Behind his desk Vannevar Bush sat speechless. Of course, what could he expect? But the dawning reality somehow overcame him with shame and horror. It was almost as if he had just thrown open the exclusive fraternity of his friends and colleagues to a circle of ruthless brigands.

'Colonel Groves . . . General,' Bush said with nervous apology. 'Lawrence, Compton and Urey are not easy men. If I may say so, sir, you will have to tread softly.'

'They want to serve their country, right?' Groves snapped. 'Anyway this will make war heroes of them. They'll come around. Now give me a run down of where we stand on the U235 processes.'

When Colonel Groves left Vannevar Bush's office an hour later, the scientist sat for several minutes in an exhausted stupour not unlike shock. Then he stood up and crossed to the dixie-cup dispenser like a giant transfusion bottle, and ran a trickle of water into the soft cardboard cup. Giant silver bubbles wobbled slowly up inside the water tank, joining the air trapped at the top with violent 'glug-glugs' that shook the heavy glass on its metal stand.

One of the director's telephones began ringing.

'Yes, the President at Harvard University,' Bush snapped, feeling like an unfaithful husband in his tormented eagerness to unburden himself. Another voice came on.

'James! Hello, James, is that you? I just met a certain Groves. Yes, all morning. And I fear we are in for a rough crossing . . .'

As Bush and Conant talked, Lillie was driving the transformed Colonel Groves in the olive staff car down Pennsylvania Avenue (Lillie had orders always to take in the White House). He had a meeting at the new War Production Board, where the unprecedented gearing-up of plane, ship and tank production was being designed. Groves had never felt so vividly as at that moment the Capitol's beauty. Through his sunglasses, the brilliant tree-lined brick housefronts were a rich green.

Half a century ago these planes, ships and tanks were unknown to man, Groves was thinking in the lofty excitement left by the meeting with Bush. Now they will give jobs to millions and make America great. In fact, Groves could remember almost nothing of the long technical discussion with Bush, but there would be time to pick that up. Brigadier-General Groves, in charge of the Atom Bomb Project . . . or should it be *Nuclear Weapons*?

Hell! You never know what damned thing will happen next in America, Groves thought, enjoying the cool wind on his swollen cheeks. It was God's country. How could an American like Doug MacArthur go around calling Stalingrad the greatest military achievement of all time? A bunch of Russian atheists. It made him sick. That was why it had been necessary to crack the whip a little with the scientist. There was nothing like a big budget to snap a snob to attention. He, Groves, knew a lot about snobs. He had been dealing with them most of his life. But he could tell from Bush's manner he had liked Groves quite well. He would make good military material out of them. He had done it before.

And turning all this over that September noon, in the back seat of the staff car, Colonel Groves felt surer and surer that he had already found his detour.

Chapter 9

In the first week of October 1942, Brigadier-General Leslie Groves climbed on the New York express in Washington with Lillie, his army engineer Ken Nichols and three subordinates. He was setting out into God's country. After meeting Urey and Fermi at the Columbia University laboratories the army men booked sleepers on the air-conditioned Twentieth Century, and set out to visit Compton's project at Chicago University. Then they carried their bags on to the Zephyr and rolled on West over the Great Plains, up through the Rockies, across the cruel Utah desert. Then a second night up over the Donner Pass into California . . . to San Francisco.

Groves and his aides made a drab, charmless group. But in the great national saga of the new World War, the 'team' glamour of their uniforms earned the younger men admiring banter and drinking companions wherever they went. Yet wherever they did go that American autumn, Groves and Nichols moved through friendly enthusiastic multitudes oblivious to the goings-on among the physicists, multitudes innocent of the tiny atom and what the Army might have in store for it. And this gave even Groves strange, sometimes quite complex sensations.

From the very first meeting, General Groves's journey into the hinterlands had been different. Like all military men, Groves would rather have been posted to the field of action. He had never in his life felt so far from the clear moral qualities of the battlefield, than in the absorbed, dusty silence of physics laboratories. One hour among these soft-spoken, irritable sleepwalkers brought on a yawning and restlessness in the fat general, like a child's boredom at a symphony that never ends. In these rooms of instruments, among the queer apparatuses, the eggheads apparently saw themselves in supremely heroic terms. Yet none of them, the haughty, humourless autocrats, the charming scatterbrains, or the enthusiastic overgrown children, seemed to find the slightest thing to inspire them in Groves himself. Nothing interested the scientists but refining Uranium to a purer U235, while what interested General Groves was to refine the eggheads themselves to purer military power. These scientists might be disappointing him, but Groves was acutely aware that he was disappointing them more. The physicists would not even condescend to tell Groves openly what they were doing. At the same time, these jokers kept speaking as if they didn't really know very much. Groves had already given orders that all Manhattan scientists should stop talking to each other. At least that kept them divided. Yet without being able to grasp the principle of power that governed the eggheads, he could not even begin making military material out of them.

But General Groves had already detected and was refining another power the scientists paid no attention to, the power that linked their work to ordinary people.

Alone at night, trying to hold his moist bulk still in the blackened pullman berth while his khaki uniform relaxed on a hanger, Groves was aware that he was still not able to remember what Urey, Fermi and Compton told him for more than a few hours after they said it. While they were explaining, it all seemed perfectly clear. Then, in the relief of being on his own again, Groves would be left with a pleasant sensation of Olympian clarity that lifted him far above the pathetically ignorant people of the trains and towns. But quickly the Olympian clarity would vanish from Groves's mind, just like invisible ink, and he would find himself back among ordinary people feeling ordinary emotions and unable to remember the differences between electrons, solids, mass and time, or between fission and fusion, whether they were all the same thing, and why it mattered. Groves was much too sure of his own heroic qualities to accuse himself of stupidity. And he certainly had no trouble remembering the mysterious superiority that lingered after the meetings. So Groves elevated his ignorance to a mystery and called that mystery Secrecy. Soon he was despising the scientists for underestimating it. And though the General would not permit himself to respect what he could not even remember for more than an hour or two, Groves certainly respected the secret sensations that so clearly divided what the eggheads were thinking from the innocent emotions of ordinary folk.

What if the Army could just slip between the eggheads and ordinary people? Groves lay awake thinking this thought as the train lurched and thundered through the innocent night. What if the Army took over that mystery . . . *secrecy*? If only he could find out what made these characters tick!

'What do you suppose it is, Lieutenant, what do you suppose it is?'

'Sir?' Lillie muttered weakly, trying to keep the milk in his glass. 'Well maybe cause they're not really Americans.'

It was the morning after Chicago. General Groves and his aide were sitting face to face, by the dining-car window. Both men automatically fell silent as the Negro steward set a bowl of a new-fangled bran cereal in front of the freshly scrubbed and shaved US General.

Groves stared down at the bran. Then he fixed his eyes mockingly on Lillie.

General Groves was a man who only trusted completely pure men. It was why Groves had chosen Lillie as his aide. But because he was so pure, Lillie was always guilty, and it satisfied Groves strangely to keep him that way. Right now, the aide did not even dare to glance out of the dining-car window, though these rushing autumn-red forests and glades of thick wildflower grass were Lillie's home state.

The train had just joined the winding thick forest along the Platte River, after Omaha. Huge peaceful flat-bottomed clouds paraded into the prairie distances. They were in the land of the great treaty meetings where Groves's Army predecessors had seduced Indian chiefs, as elusive and uncooperative as the physicists, into signing away the wilderness and its mystery. But as far as Groves was concerned American soil was a new country quite pure of all invasions. And he was going to keep it that way.

Lillie leaned cautiously forward. 'I mean, sir, most of them, the eggheads, sir, are from countries we're at war with.'

'Oh, Lieutenant,' Groves said with an especially horrible pity. 'It isn't that at all. It's just that intellectuals make lousy leaders, that's all. They don't have the slightest idea what keeps this country going.'

'That's for sure sir,' Lieutenant Lillie agreed hopefully, and they swayed together.

'Bunch of Jewish snobs!' Groves said. 'To think we're going out to fight for them!' Groves slowly retracted his head on his swelling neck, as if trying to free it from something.

'Well, sir, I'm sure you'll get to the bottom of things.'

'Lieutenant Lillie. . .' Groves leaned forward. The steward had replaced the empty bran bowl with a soggy stack of boysenberry buckwheat cakes. Groves gave Lillie a tough look so accusing the Lieutenant felt pressing down on him the guilt for every last American soul who was not like the man across the table.

'Lieutenant,' Groves said, 'ingratitude is a hideous thing.'

'Yes, General.' Lieutenant Lillie grinned back crookedly, setting down the milk glass. 'It's great to be able to call you General, General!'

By the time General Groves drove up outside the Berkeley Radiation Laboratories two days later – the officers climbing grimly out of two white-starred Army jeeps in their hats and sunglasses, making quite a stir among the fresh blond young bobbysoxers curled in groups here and there on the campus lawns – Groves had worked himself into a state. A deep depression over the scattering of cranky Jewish, German, Italian, English, Hungarian and Danish refugees, and truckloads of twisted pipes, gauges and old wire he had been provided to build the promised superbomb; the absolute power that would give American glory on earth. Groves felt as the finest sword maker in Japan might have felt, being commissioned to produce the purest, sharpest, best-tempered blade, a blade capable of penetrating steel armour, and shattering all other blades. And being asked to produce such a sword from a trash-heap of old box mattresses, crushed radios and corroded bicycle wheels.

Perhaps this explained the General's emotion that cool fragrant afternoon on finding himself welcomed on the Radiation

Laboratory steps by a tall, blond, well-tailored, mid-western enthusiast with a firm handclasp. Ernest Orlando Lawrence, all-American physicist and winner of the Nobel Prize for his cyclotron. Lawrence, who even now was dreaming of pushing the child of his ambition to a hundred million volts. They stood for a moment in the sun.

'I have heard a lot about you, Doctor Lawrence.'

'You're an important man for our country, General Groves,' Lawrence answered smoothly, and his spectacles flashed like semaphores.

Groves and Lawrence shook hands beneath the big California palm, among the little group of beaming officials. And it was as if not only their spirits came together, but that the hundred-million volts in Lawrence's dream vibrated with the hundred millions of dollars in Groves' cheque-book. For Ernest Lawrence knew, whether it was the best process or not, that it must be his cyclotron which would produce the fuel for the Atomic Age.

For the next three hours, in an unflinching prodigy of salesmanship, Lawrence walked General Groves of the US Army up and down the busy corridors and spartan laboratories of this place of learning. And somehow Lawrence was like an impostor with a big buyer, who would stamp 'for sale' on the books in a public library, the instruments of a hospital, a forest he does not own, or even the Brooklyn Bridge. Opening doors for Groves, hurrying to find little ways of showing the General a grateful obedience, Lawrence offered him all of it: the students, the teachers and their knowledge . . . the entire scientific enlightenment of man. And though General Groves was seeing the same handmade-looking machines and weirdly indifferent cranks, and hearing the same clear but elusive concepts he recognized from New York and Chicago, they all suddenly had a point. In these rooms the war was already being fought. From these instrument banks the world was already coming under American control. Sensing in Lawrence a man confident of taming the secret elements and prepared to sell, Groves's tough depressed face melted to an almost unctuous sweetness. Despite its perspiring bulk, the US Army seemed almost to tiptoe among the tables of instruments and vast machines.

'Good evening boys,' Groves called to the six technicians

crowded under the giant sixty-inch cyclotron in windowless room 203.

Frank Oppenheimer turned to stare with his assistants at the army man standing beside Lawrence, thumbs in belt.

Lawrence rescued them. 'Gentlemen, this is General Leslie Groves.'

Before anyone could move, Groves stepped up to the huge vacuum chamber. He gave it a friendly slap.

'Beautiful machine you have here, boys!' Groves grinned down. 'Boys, boys, you don't think you're going to feed this big baby's appetite with those effeminate little wires do you?'

'But General,' someone finally said, after a thoughtful silence, 'these are field-sensors for beam focusing.'

Groves's eyes watered. He gave the technicians a fatherly smile. 'Now don't you go telling me about electricity, boys.'

For just a moment under the bare hanging bulbs of room 203, Lawrence stood paralysed. From behind his glasses the famous man saw his place in the nuclear age wobble precariously.

'If you permit me, General,' Lawrence broke in, 'there are some installations down the corridor that will particularly interest you.

'Oh, you'll get used to them,' Lawrence laughed pleasantly, when he had Groves safely away in the warm evening outside the Radiation Labs.

Groves and Lawrence strolled slowly out of earshot along the unguarded campus paths, under the spicy eucalyptus. The earlier mood of high voltage and big money was back. Skilfully, Lawrence led the conversation to the crux of their ambitions . . . to build the most awesome weapon of destruction in human history. After passing on to Groves his useful axiom for dismissing any moral difficulties (that of course America, being good, would never use it), Lawrence came to his final pitch.

Groves listened carefully. This time, he was sure he would have no trouble remembering. In their piercing concentration, neither men paid attention to the splendid Pacific sunset.

'We've practically got the process ironed out already, sir,' Lawrence lied with sincere good nature. 'But designing the bomb and producing the fuel will have to be quite separate programmes.'

'Uhuh . . . sounds good.' Groves hung his head beside Lawrence's. He toed the thick-matted lawn with his trooper's boot.

'Otherwise, General, fuel production will outstrip bomb design.'

'How much U235 and Plutonium,' Groves said professionally, 'will the bombs need?'

'Doctor Oppenheimer and Doctor Teller are handling the theoretical end of it,' Lawrence confessed. 'I could drop you off with Robert if you like, General Groves? He's Coordinator of Rapid Rupture.'

'If you would, Doctor Lawrence, thank you,' Groves said easily.

But the truth was, the strain of promoting his huge, tightly-run Radiation Laboratory with its staff and cyclotrons, and the hours of making this fat uncouth Army fellow sound like a physics genius, had exhausted the famous man. Lawrence felt relieved to leave Groves under the walls of Le Conte Hall. And so it was that, panting heavily, Brigadier-General Leslie Groves of the Army's new Manhattan District, who had been fooled by none of Lawrence's performance but who knew the value of a salesman, rapped four times on the wire-grille door of an attic laboratory, and was surprised to hear a soft hesitant voice inside. Stepping through into the dusky orange light, Groves saw an indistinct blackboard covered with numbers and Greek. A tall rumpled figure was sitting motionless on a desk talking with four foreign types. And though General Groves had never felt further from battle-fronts and glory than in these bleak, grim laboratories, he suddenly found himself face to face with the most graceful, handsome and superbly intelligent man he had ever met.

Interrupted by the four loud raps on the attic's security door, Doctor Oppenheimer smiled crookedly, thinking of Beethoven's Fifth. Fate knocking at the door. Glancing over his shoulder, Robert saw a fat stranger in khakis, staring dumbly in the open door. The blood rushed to his cheeks.

Instantly he was ashamed. For during the months since Pearl Harbour, heading Compton's seminar on Uranium chain-reactions with his worshipful new disciple Teller, Robert Oppenheimer had been trying to be an adult and control the irritable, pompous side of his character which had let down poor, confused Jean, which seemed to hurt people more the more they put their trust in him. It was time he, 'Oppy', took responsibility for his strange effect on people. Increasingly he felt it as a moral failure to see anyone hurt.

Now seeing a look of helpless embarrassment on the face of this comically clumsy soldier, Robert hurried to make the fellow feel better.

'Doctor Oppenheimer?' the officer wheezed.

'Why yes.' Robert grinned nervously. He slipped off the desk. 'Come in, can I help you? Might you be the new Army man from Washington?'

'Yes sir,' Groves said holding out his moist hand. 'Yes, I am he.'

'It's a pleasure, how do you do?' said Robert. 'These are Doctor Ed Teller . . . Doctor Serber . . . Doctor Bloch and Doctor Hans Bethe.'

And to General Leslie Groves of the US Army, still intently groping for a principle of power (beyond Nobel prizes) that governed the physicists, and absorbed in the untapped secret which lay somewhere between what those eggheads knew and the innocent oblivion of history's masses, it felt so strange finding himself suddenly spoken to with a natural simple warmth, without salesmanship, contempt or fear, that for several moments he quite forgot who he was and what his business was with this man.

Chapter 10

Across the Bay from San Francisco the summer of '42 vanished into the fall term, and there was scarcely a change. In the *Chronicle*, millions of German soldiers had been repulsed from the suburbs of Moscow. And there were other rumours, of increasing savagery.

In Lawrence's laboratories Army work went dreamily on. But you could not feel a war. There was not even a real security screen. Only the dry baking afternoons were gone. Thick whispering fogs rolled in off the Bay, and the sun was not strong enough to burn them off. For Robert it was a good, exciting time. To satisfy a wife's wish to see you more committed you did not have to go to Madrid. You did not even have to give up advanced research. In the quiet Spanish mansion overlooking the Bay, the Oppenheimers teased each other about it. Robert had definitely come a long way down off his mountain of pure contemplation (Kitty called it his

'Mesa'), and been involved in the great issues and sufferings of his time.

It had only been necessary to relocate the long blackboard hours. To make a shift from the sage-like elusive migrations of cosmic rays through dark eternity and warps of time – the chamber music Robert was temperamentally attuned to – and wrestle with warm-hearted irrepressible Ed Teller over cruder fission and deuterium-fusion laws that governed noisy, Beethoven-like rendings of suns and solar systems. Teller was at his side fulltime now, since Robert helped him through a security snag to do with mother and father Teller still being in fascist Budapest.

The air Doctor Oppenheimer breathed was thickening with prestige. Large numbers of indistinct persons beyond the Oppen-heimers' intimate circle for some reason considered Oppy a neces-sary friend, available with advice on every detail of running civilization, from the religious origins of fascism to disciplining children. It was a strain. But Robert agreed with Kitty. Humanity must deal with its own affairs. You did not leave problems like France, Hitler, knowledge, parenthood and justice up to God. So Robert spread his influence wherever it was asked and tried to stay simple and good and modest. It did not matter that not many others thought like this. Conscience held him to it. Still, at each step, he had to fight a suffocating urge to tear himself from these moral parasites who sucked dry his happiness. He would long for the desert. And sometimes the subtle ones sensed this selfishness, and took Oppy's goodness for political guile. Sometimes you just could not be good enough to keep everyone trusting you. At least Robert did not have that problem with General Groves.

During the few hours of casual talks in front of Robert's black-board, Robert and the Army's man had agreed what a crude, ill-defined business this new atom-fission research really was. Groves hating it for not submitting to his memory, Robert needing to see it as a degrading sideline to a lofty scientific threshold. Soon the plump prickly General was showing a ravenous appetite for whatever truths Robert had to pass on. When General Groves listened to the polite charming New Yorker, this whole immigrant garbage-dump of conceited gibbering crackpots, corroded bicycle wheels and crushed radios called the Manhattan Project for the first time took on purity of meaning . . . well-tempered, sharply honed. The whole smell-less invisible secret of the thing began magically to submit to Groves's will. As for Doctor Oppenheimer, he could speak on Groves's level with so little effort he was barely aware the officer had a personality. Knowing nothing about Groves, Robert tactfully assumed there was little to know. And he was too committed to objective truth and spoiled by people's interest in him to contrast his ignorance of the man against the General's boyish fascination with every detail of Robert's own character and thinking. Since the afternoon with Steve Nelson, Robert had a romantic feeling about soldiers and freedom-fighters. He liked Groves being a tough man of action. And he noticed the General showed no discomfort or even interest in Robert's radical views on Spain. They both seemed equally shocked by the idea of Hitler with an atom bomb.

But those few hours of solidarity with General Groves became a commitment. Fat, graceless, patriotic Groves, who must never have had the advantages he had. Seeing Groves ridiculed by immigrant physicists, and the fellow's clumsy pride, even guiltily suspecting Groves might not be so good, Robert experienced a vague compassion. He felt it his duty to help the fellow. The advice General Groves was being made to suffer for was so easy to give. Quite obviously the Army's Project, and thereby the thresholds of human knowledge, could be made to advance faster if the best minds were locked up in one laboratory instead of competing in different faculties strung out across three thousand miles.

Not long after, General Groves and his officers left California. But approaching Chicago Groves discovered a terrible thing. Without Dr Oppenheimer's relaxed conversation, the General's simple, clear control over his new command again began slinking back into that dump of meaningless refuse. *Groves was forgetting again!*

So it was that Robert received an urgent telegram requesting him to rejoin the officers in Chicago. And as soon as polite, thoughtful Doctor Oppenheimer was back at Groves's side on the Twentieth Century to New York, Groves regained his memory and his power and they discussed the war like Yankee fighting men. Robert praised the incredible Russian sacrifice in front of Moscow, and Groves said nothing.

You and I, doctor, Groves thought under the train's night light, and he grinned quickly across the jouncing compartment at the effete young Harvard gentleman draped in a chair between scrawny little Nichols and his Intelligence chief. You and I are going to pull off a great one!

From that moment the General's trust in Doctor Oppenheimer appeared to redouble. And Robert hurried guiltily to save Groves's high hopes from being disappointed. Soon the soldier was confessing his intimate doubts and difficulties with the physicists. And Robert, retreating more and more dutifully into his guilty goodness, was politely revealing everything about the members in the club called high-energy physics. Soon he was even advising Groves in his selection of a scientist-prince to rule supreme over this powerful new 'Nuclear' Department of War. And this was an application of science knowledge Robert was not at all clear on.

Back at Berkeley Robert's daily schedule, his life at Eagle Hill with Kitty and little Pete, and the long Olympian sessions with Ed Teller and a horde of other laboratory responsibilities, went on without any more turbulence than in the balmy Bay-area weather.

And then one thing happened that Doctor Oppenheimer had not thought of.

Chapter 11

That Indian summer noon as Robert swung the car into the drive, there was no one in the windows at Eagle Hill. Something was strange. Shielding his eyes, Robert stood in the drive. He stared back down San Francisco Bay, towards Sausalito.

Far into the distance stretched an iridescent white bed of fog. It filled in all the outline of the bay and low-lying valleys; only the high hills of the city rose out of it. And from the pines, just below where he stood under the dizzying clear blue sky, to the tiny apartment buildings clustered like sea birds on Nob and Telegraph Hills, was a glaring white mat. Noting only that this scene so typical of dream's end, so oppressive and prophetic, so full of foreboding, was unusual for the season, Robert turned away. He shuffled in past the fig tree. The way Robert felt, every little impression was an aggravation.

Frank was already in the shadowed conservatory, standing round-shouldered at the open garden door. Out past the awning, the sun blazed. As Robert quietly set down his satchel and took out his pipe, Kitty came out of the kitchen with iced tea. Robert looked away.

'Here he is,' Frank called. 'So what's all the excitement?'

'What's happened, Robbie?' Kitty set out the wet pitcher. 'Is something wrong?'

'Thanks for coming, Frank.' Robert turned away, avoiding their eyes. 'Nothing's wrong I guess. Maybe a little out of hand. Look, let's go in the garden.'

'It's cooler in here.'

Kitty searched her husband's untanned face. She had never seen him look so sober. Suddenly Kitty was excited.

'Sit on the divan, you two!' Kitty heard herself chatter, curling sexily in a canvas chair facing the brothers. 'Heavens, this climate is too tropical for me. Imagine a hothouse seeming cool, it makes me think of snowdrifts and throwing myself into them with nothing on.'

'Sounds fine by me, Katie.' Frank smiled uncomfortably across the table at the tough little beauty with the emotional eyes. They both looked at Robert. The baggy gentleman sat very upright along the striped green divan, almost suspiciously, as if he did not want anyone to come near him.

Robert stiffly crossed his legs. Puffing the pipe, he stared intently at the rubber plant.

'Come on, Robbie,' Frank began softly. 'What is it?'

'Well . . .' Robert stared in his pipe bowl. He resumed puffing. When Kitty mentioned heat he had thought of the fog just below the house. 'Well, I guess I need some moral support.'

'Is it my Party card again?' Frank flared dismally. 'If so I'll resign before they can fire me.'

'No, no,' Robert smiled. 'Lawrence loves you.'

'It's your Army friend!' Kitty said apprehensively. 'Isn't it?'

Her husband flinched. Looking around, he saw his iced tea and picked up the glass.

'He chose me . . . I didn't choose him.'

'Why always be so nice to people?' Kitty snapped.

'It's a family trait,' Frank laughed. 'Well, what about Groves? They say he admires you a lot.'

'He must, Frank.' Robert grinned strangely at Frank, then at Kitty. 'He wants me to run the whole project.'

Kitty was incredulous. 'The Army's atom-bomb project?!'

'The whole Manhattan District, Robbie?' Frank sat forward with a nervous laugh. 'I mean, what about Lawrence or Millikan . . . Urey . . . or even Compton?'

'Frank.' Robert put the glass down untasted. 'It's your brother he wants. I recruit who I like: Enrico Fermi; Isidor; Hans Bethe; Ed Teller . . . Bohr even. The best metallurgists, ordnance people, mathematicians, chemists. Build a lab in some out-of-the-way place.'

'Robbie darling!' Kitty sat forward, her face flushed. 'What would it mean?'

'Gosh, brother!' Frank whistled. 'How do you feel about it?'

'Well . . .' Robert waved his pipe in a vague circle, smiling, crookedly. 'I suppose that I'd be a big name in history.'

'*Would* be? Robbie!' Kitty was suddenly passionately alert, almost as sober as her husband. 'What did you tell him?'

'I'd think it over tonight,' Robert reflected with a strange smile. 'Think it over tonight . . . tonight.'

Then Frank understood. The embarrassed man beside him on the couch, his brother, had just brought word of the most momentous thing that would ever occur in their lives. Frank felt his throat tighten, a little familiar stab of hurt. He seized Robbie's limp right hand in his.

'It's a great moment for you, Robbie,' Frank said. 'I'm proud of you.'

'Tell them you'll accept!' Kitty burst out in a hoarse voice. 'Call Groves right now. Tell him you'll do it!'

But sitting here in their shadowed conservatory, Robert experienced a wave of sickening loneliness. A solitude as if all life had just crouched its weight on his brain in vague fractured scenes of tragic throngs, nations, great cities sinking in fog like half-remembered images of nightmare. Robert stared at his wife's intently eager expression, then at his brother. Why can't they see? Robert thought. But he'd been working on it for months, and he didn't see it either!

64

Not until Groves offered him total control. From that moment only, he was alone in the ring with the truth, friendless on the ship's bridge, sinking without a lament from its human cargo. Even the silence around him crying for him to take action on humanity's behalf! Then, listening to the droning California afternoon and all the sleepy populace spread out beyond in its murmuring oblivion, an intimation passed through his consciousness, a signal brief and sharp as the shock of some eruption that will slow to a tidal swell. He as no man before him, now held the trust and future of all men in his hand. He, and he alone, must act morally . . . at once! He must *do* something!

But in his hushed, leafy conservatory, staring over the iced tea at Frank and Kitty's excitement, Robert doubted his senses. What *was* there to do? Wild thoughts spun in his head like bingo numbers in a cage seeking their tiny exit. He could simply turn the position down. But it was conceited to imagine that would moderate events. He could go along and sabotage the actual bomb as German physicists had promised to. But America was not Germany, and Roosevelt was not Hitler. For a moment, looking at his family's faces, so naively willing for fame, their pride in him seemed obscenely disappointing. And Robert hated them even as his heart beat passionately to go back to their simple view. But there was nothing conventional in the powers he might tap. *The fires of the sun!*

During these seconds of dying, the intricate argument tore through Robert's soul, and it took five puffs on his pipe. In his glass of tea the ice had almost melted.

'Kitty, I'm a scientist,' Robert said gently, looking thoughtfully at his wife. 'I'm not a Krupp.'

'Robbie!' Kitty objected with a slight shock. She leaned forward on her crossed knees. 'If you don't work for our side, it will be Krupp who does build it!'

'I don't understand, Robbie.' Frank was shyly hesitant. 'You want scientific knowledge to hold back or something?'

'I don't know!' Robert waved his pipe. He averted this strange gaze. 'Not . . . I don't know!' What was it, this strange urgent droning silence through Eagle Hill, out over the world?

'Well, I know,' Frank gestured with a gentle excitement, 'that deuterium-fusion work with Teller. And, why, the fission principle's practically a sure thing. They're the most basic direction in physics!'

Robert stretched back on the striped couch, crossing his bony legs. Nervously puffing, he looked over at them with a faint hunger. The inhuman pressure on his brain had just let up a little. The flow of words helped, this idea of just letting himself be carried away on the inevitable tide of knowledge. Like the Ark, bearing Noah up on the Flood.

'That's true, Frank,' Robert said. 'There's no stopping these breakthroughs.'

'To talk of holding them up . . .' Frank shrugged. 'That's playing God!'

Robert laughed nervously and heaved a sigh. The clock ticked on the brick mantel. Far away, a foghorn groaned.

'I rather thought,' Robert grinned, 'it was playing God to lead humanity into it.'

'For God's sake, Robbie!' Kitty laughed sarcastically, with a grateful love for this subtle sensitive man. 'Look at what humanity's already led itself into!'

But that is nothing like *this*, a voice blurted inside Robert's head. The evil weight was back, crushing down on Robert's brain. Frank and Kitty's eyes were fixed on him. Apprehensive, almost medical, not seeing the thing crouched inside him, once again the whole intricate mass of what Doctor Oppenheimer knew. But his soul only a sort of senseless floundering debris. And Robert saw himself already carried so deeply into the heart of the thing, somehow already buried in it. Compromised long ago, when he had let the philistine Hegelians at Göttingen confer the new knowledge on him. Like some licence to sweep away all the prophetic 'human nonsense' of Goethe and Shakespeare. Robert thought of his position here at Berkeley, and the wide circle of people who loved and counted on him. Of the grandeur of America, and the evil hosts that were arrayed against them all. Of poor Groves already deeply committed to gambling the future of the West on him. And himself, 'Oppy', alone nevertheless. A lonely goodness being borne guiltily forward, committed to struggle at the very heart of a faceless and unfacable terror, annihilation, what not!

66

Suddenly Robert could hear the silence of the world beyond. Humanity, all living things stretched out trustingly around him. Hearing them all, the old and young, the families, hopes and dreams, the highways farms towns, the rich and poor, lovely and plain. What *was* it, this silence of a California afternoon? Straining bravely to hear it, be utterly alone with it, Robert could no longer see the living people. The sunny afternoon was a plain blank ordinary silence. And Robert did not hear that it was *innocence*.

He sat with them stiffly erect on the couch. Say something! his crooked smile said. Anything that will save me from this!

'If you don't do it,' Frank offered, 'somebody'll do it.'

'If I don't do it,' Robert repeated in a strange listening litany, 'somebody else will do it.'

Trying to imagine himself turning back *now*, at this blind fateful hour, and so forever not being a part of such an immense collective importance, Robert knew he would do it. Oh, you'll do it all right, you hypocrite! Robert thought. And he despised himself and at once felt a humble flooding of relief. Anyway, he thought, I'm only a man.

In the room and the rest of the Oppenheimer house there was a profound, slightly irritated silence. Listening to these two soft lanky men going heavily, effeminately over and over the thing and seeing the crushed look on her husband's face, Kitty felt a sudden violent wish to see the matter set simply, heroically at rest. Couldn't these damned intellectuals trust themselves to take a moral position on anything, even face to face with Hitler?

'All right!' Kitty laughed, her voice high and musical with anger. 'All right, let's look at it differently.''

'The research will get done Rob!' Frank threw up his hands, for some reason feeling disappointed, as if something was slipping away.

'We're at war, Robbie!' Kitty's cheeks reddening. 'The damn thing will be built.'

'If it *can* be built,' Robert corrected, feeling himself slip back. Something beautiful, sweet and sacred was drawing away from Doctor Oppenheimer in revulsion.

'Then, Robbie, prove they can't!' Kitty taunted.

'You two don't see it!' Robert said with a last flare of self-disgust, for some reason turning to Frank. 'The way the world's built today. So much knowledge, so much state power. All I have to do is move my papers next door to Groves's office, and the world is sold out!'

'There is nothing you can do to stop him hiring someone.' Frank shook his head. He leaned back clasping one knee. Kitty glanced from one brother to the other, her flushed excitement back now.

'Darling, just take it!' Kitty said, her voice huskily rich. 'Take the power it gives you. Let it be you who brings the thing into the world if it really has to be. Use the power to keep it as moral and decent as possible.'

Frank and Kitty were back in their pride again, and looking at their happy intelligent faces, Robert did not clearly remember what it was five minutes ago which had stretched his sanity to breaking point.

'That's right, Robert!' Frank was saying. 'Let them finance the breakthrough.'

'Make a civilized event of it, darling . . . a hopeful beginning!'

It was only then, in the acute relief of letting himself be caught up in their pride for him, maybe even in these few words, that Robert suddenly knew what he must do. Relaxing back on the couch, he puffed his pipe, sipping his tea with a musing smile. They saw Robert's face was a healthy red. Everyone loved him. He was himself again, conscious of the hot vacant droning afternoon out past the awnings. Of orange moths racing among the marigolds, the watery reflections inside the cool conservatory walls. For at that moment, Robert's imagination had retreated from the dark poisoned terror of man's city, history and the civilized mind. Like a cripple he went again to the glorious full-souled happiness in the Santa Cruz mountains. And beyond, to a deeper holiness he alone had known. Small and grateful in the hot wind on his Mesa.

'Maybe,' he offered. 'Well, what if we did it in the desert?'

Yet the taste still in Robert's mouth of the thing that had seized him after Groves's call . . . the complete guilt. You fool, Robert told himself. Guilt is only absolute if you are God! Groves, the politicians and all the rest could take responsibility with him. The bomb should mean peace! Suddenly he was wildly happy.

'Yes,' Robert said, his voice resonant. 'I want to do it in the desert. Maybe even in New Mexico . . . in the pueblo country. In all that heat and emptiness. A community of superior scientific minds. I'll run an open laboratory without nationalisms or prejudice. We'll teach the government what enlightenment means. The world will share in what we find. . .'

The three figures under the window sat perfectly still. Somewhere a telephone had started ringing, someone answered it. Hearing his brother's words, Frank again felt somehow hurt. And something else.

'Always choosing the unbroken horse, Robbie,' he said.

'A government horse this time, Frank.'

'Well, I have to say, darling.' Kitty's face shone. 'Being your wife is not without its little surprises.'

'I could have told you that before you married him,' Frank said.

'Maybe I wouldn't have,' Kitty grinned ironically. 'Aren't physicists supposed to be quiet gentle creatures?'

'Well I don't foresee any changes.' Robert got up unsteadily. 'Let's eat. I'm hungry.'

Later, leaving for the campus after lunch, he paused again by the fig tree. He stood by the open door and shaded his eyes.

The strange, glaringly luminous fog was still there over San Francisco Bay. But it seemed disrupted and to have taken flight, as if something large had fallen through. It rose now here and there in vaporous mucousy tendrils, like some poison gas. But with a vague relief Robert noticed that his earlier feeling was gone.

Chapter 12

A few weeks went by. Finally Robert had telephoned Groves in Washington. He had politely accepted the General's offer. He even sounded quite eager to put on the uniform of a freedom fighter.

Already the Army man was constantly at his side, and Robert could feel his life subtly accelerate. At first it was a vague easing of the way, a loss, as when an explorer long in uncharted wilderness finds himself on broken trails. Then the trail widened and matted down, and Robert sensed around him the eyes of powerful officials who appeared to know him, all encouraging and seeming convinced of the course he was on. But still that moral rawness in the conservatory stayed with Robert. Still Groves did not make Doctor Oppenheimer's power official.

The General had been in charge of the Manhattan District one month. His aggressive, well-insulated khaki soul, cold, shrewd darting eyes and moist handshake, had left their ominous impression in every major American physics lab from MIT to Oak Ridge Tennessee, to Cal Tech. By now Groves had no further doubts that he was on to something very big. Something not only worthy of him, but which, handled right, could be the biggest thing in the war . . . even in history! It gave him vertigo even to think of it. He had the bankroll, and the moment seemed built for glory. Somehow, though, the scientists in the labs – most of them destined for miserable obscurity pushing chalk in front of dull students – were still rude about his money and ambitions for them. Groves could remember the desolate years of the Depression, the shanty towns and breadlines. He knew the sleazy emptiness of remote boot camps, and loneliness of puritan towns. What made the eggheads so special? It drove Groves wild with anxiety and hatred. But there was no time for that now. He must make the next move with the greatest, coolest judgment. For not only must he build the successful super-weapon. Groves must guard for America all facets of its mighty authority. Not only must the eggheads sell him their secret, but do so in such a way that its exclusive knowledge, which from the beginning Groves had felt as its most fascinating property – its power to lift him, for brief periods, far above the trusting ignorant masses of the earth (he always referred to *innocence* as *ignorance*) – should stay exclusive.

For in the General's frustration, finding himself at the limits of his power to master ideas and control men, an emotion like rejected love turned to a jealous hoarding of 'security'. If Groves could not grasp the eggheads' tremendous secret, then no one else was going to hear about it until he could shut them away like hens or whores, and squeeze it out of them in the form of a bomb. 'Oppy' as 'G.G.' now beamingly called his exotic recruit (perhaps in that military vein which seeks pet names for instruments of destruction), Oppy might be his key to unlock the mystery. The moment Doctor Oppenheimer had telephoned his willingness to help out the team, Groves hurried him for a trial spin. They were on the road again.

From Chicago to Nashville, quiet Princeton to the longer-haired Harvard labs, Groves and Oppenheimer rode the overnight pullman. Unseen by the sleeping nation (nobody had asked them if this was the fate they wanted), scarcely noticed on the train and keeping to football's 'Big Game' in the dining car, they passed through the sweet prairies and dream forests of the young country. They rode in a jolting compartment with the blind pulled down, in company with the boisterously dirty-joking Colonels. They sat up late over martinis and peanuts, somewhat criminal somewhat divine, discussing with romantic enthusiasm the great events of the age. The marvellous new era they all somehow could feel was upon them. And draped gracefully at their centre like some restful bird of paradise, cultivated, handsome, superbly intelligent Oppy seemed scarcely aware of Groves's close scrutiny. With satisfaction, Groves noted the way Oppy's sharp sophisticated honesty angered his Colonels, especially Nichols, but seemed to breathe a magic into the wooly irascible refugee faces in the laboratories; a magic causing even those faces which had closed to Groves's realism, with impatient twitches of contempt, to warm again with wonder and light. To all of them Oppenheimer spoke gently of the most fundamental goal of physics, to explore the energy of the sun which gives life to all things.

But still Groves hesitated in a state of jealous agitation, not being able to trust his luck. It made him feel vaguely suspicious that Oppy appeared not to know his power in having knowledge like *that* at this fingertips. He detected cunning in his protégé's elaborate guilty efforts to protect Groves's uncouthness and patriotic cause from disgrace. Could a man who had so much of everything he lacked really be so naive, modest and good? It was distinctly fishy. But then finally they climbed on the dinner express from New York to the Capitol. And there, Groves saw this obscure egghead from the west coast saunter without any change, as easily and gracefully as any president, through the hushed corridors of State. It was then General Groves remembered. Wherever he had been with Doctor Oppenheimer, it had felt like Washington. Now, quite suddenly, Groves understood. All he had to do was keep Oppy's goodness and the realities of the world secret from each other, and the longhairs would give Groves his bomb!

It was time to choose a site for the most secret of laboratories.

Chapter 13

So it passed, after checking some locations in California, that the new Director of the Manhattan District travelled with Groves and Ed MacMillan, father of Plutonium, into the New Mexico Desert. Deep among the silent red-dust canyons and Mesas of pueblo country, Taos, Acoma and Mesa Verde on the Rio Grande. Groves's party climbed discretely down in a cool orange dusk at the adobe village of Albuquerque, an ant colony clustered on a great scrub plain, under the footsteps of a towering sky.

As the unmarked staff car drove them on to pink Santa Fe up the rising tongue of the Rio Grande valley, Robert took off his wide-brimmed hat and smelled again the fragrant dry scent of juniper and alkali. Feeling the hot desert wind in his face, it was as if he had left behind the vileness of cities, war, the poor ruined world. Come here for the sake of all the lost hungry souls Groves so dreaded, into the Great Mystery of all things. Maybe, Robert thought smiling around the car at the circle of grinning sunglasses, just maybe, humanity will be given a last chance, as once you were.

That evening Robert tasted again tamales, enchiladas and tequila at the La Fonda Hotel, which is down the street from Bishop Lamy's pastel Cathedral. In the morning Groves's party drove out into the Mesas to inspect locations.

The last of these was down a parched scrub canyon. They jounced for an hour along a track of axle-deep red sand, between cliffs with Indian shepherd shacks built against them. Finally they came to a dead end.

'No, I don't think this is quite the place.' Robert leaned politely on the open door.

'For Lord's sake, Lillie! We'd die of thirst.'

Groves swabbed his cheeks steadily. This place had the feeling of an ambush. MacMillan giggled nervously.

'Listen,' Robert offered, muffling his excitement. 'I could show you some high ground I know up the Rio Grande. There's plenty of water too. And nobody there but a boys' school.'

'Okay, that's fine by me.' Groves motioned Lillie impatiently.

So it was that untidy Doctor Oppenheimer and starched General

Groves, allies against the undemocratic foe – one hating the fascists who were destroying his race, the other hating the Communists who challenged a fellow's free rise to personal power – found themselves banging and swerving dangerously ahead of a column of red dust, up a winding ledge cut diagonally in a cliff. The gorge below was dotted with cottonwoods and scrub pine.

Ahead in the windshield they all saw the rolling mountain plateau, and grey-white peak beyond. Above that towered a milk-white empire of cumulus storm clouds, rolling up in the deep blue.

It was this trail Robert knew best of all. He remembered the minute plodding of a paint pony bearing a sick student up this lonely promontory. In the grinding staff car the trail seemed very short.

'What's it called?' Groves shouted into the front seat.

'Los Alamos Mesa.' Robert leaned back not to raise his voice. It was getting colder.

He had Lillie stop the car at the Mesa's ridge.

'. . . of course, Oppy, your scientist friends,' Groves was saying as they all piled out on the rock ledge, into a silence that opened out, '. . . won't be too happy about the appointment. But I've been telling them you're the only man for the job. What are those mountains over there?'

'The Sangre de Cristos,' Robert said into the bitter clear breeze. He squinted away east under his flop hat. Then south over the Rio Grande valley, into the hazy-blue desert distance.

'What's that mean?' MacMillan pursed his lips.

'Blood of Christ,' Robert translated. 'Well, how do you like it?'

Groves stepped back from the canyon ledge and they turned together. Up past the sedan stretched the wide pine-forested plateau of the Mesa.

'Quite a spot, Oppy!' Groves was getting more and more tough and excited. 'Secretest I ever saw! Say look! I could build our town right along that knoll. No leaks, no spies. Everyone in uniform. Say, are those *kids* in shorts over there . . . a school? Never mind. We'll requisition the damn mountain and clear that forest.'

The officers stood together by the automobile making a tiny group on the bare yellow knoll. Their pant cuffs snapped at their slim stockinged ankles. It was then that General Groves too had a vision.

The hat on his shaved head looked curiously like an army tent perched on an inflamed world. Groves pulled it off. Beside him, Robert stood gazing happily up at the distant peaks.

'You men know,' Groves began, 'this wild country of ours was tamed by Army men like you and me. Free men . . . pure men!'

Lillie and Nichols half turned to stare at the General. He blinked in the wind. MacMillan raised his eyebrows and giggled.

'Men,' Groves went on, his voice trembling, 'who no matter where they went, or how barbarous the enemy, never forgot they represented the Constitution back in Washington. Knowing that kept them true and good. When they built a fort, why, men, that fort stood! And where it stood the land it influenced all around submitted to our Constitution. Now our whole land, why the Constitution itself, is at war with a world-wide barbarism. And on that spot there, I am going to build a final fort with a world-wide influence. Yessir! If you like, a Fort Los Alamos that's going to spread the power of our freedom-loving Constitution all over this untamed globe! Look, men, right on that hill over there, we're going to build the first World-Fort. Bugle-reveilles and all!'

The mysterious breezes of the Mesa instantly snuffed away the sweatily inspired officer's words.

'What do you think, Oppy?' Groves called, suddenly aggressive.

The lanky, thoughtful figure was slouched by the car grille.

'Oh? I guess that's about it, sure it's so.' Robert smiled around at them awkwardly, as if not quite returned from some distant thought. 'Though you'd best not let the science fellows hear about the bugling!'

'Maybe so,' Groves grinned. 'Anyway the science fellows are your bailiwick.'

During the weeks before Christmas 1942, Robert set out without Groves through the University laboratories of the East, South and Midwest to recruit his staff for Los Alamos. But everyone had heard of Groves, the 'uniforms' and the bugling. What was Oppy trying to do in that wilderness, a place from which no one would be allowed to return?

Yet Robert went among the cities in a strange intoxication. He bore tidings of a lonely mountain fastness to which the best intellects would go, as to some Acropolis or Vatican, Court of Brandenburg or Bauhaus. Leaving behind the torments and security screens of the war, the unrest of industrial cities and petty intrigues of faculties. Where in the simple freedom of untouched nature, with the finest equipment, they would stand face to face with the fundamental laws of the firmament. Then, with these absolute powers, restore Reason to enlightened ascendancy over an evil age.

Meanwhile, Groves caught the train to Washington. Back to the pleasant realities of the War Department, the Federal Bureau of Investigation and Senate sub-committees. To the discreet brick Georgetown homes of influential persons where Groves's honest cynicism was appreciated. That is, to the panelled halls, corridors and busy offices where power was practised and refined. Places where people liked to sport their 'Security Clearance' by speaking in undertones. And in all these, Groves was already known as the head of the Government's most top-secret project, a project so secret it could only be discussed openly before the President and Joint Chiefs. These were Groves's most inspirational hours as a purifier of power. Since, known only to few, the whole endeavour was Oppy's design and dependent on him entirely, Groves had first to push through Oppenheimer's security clearance, despite FBI files on Oppy's sinister, even vaguely threatening, circle of revolutionary friends.

Then G.G. had to make quite certain the eggheads had no power of their own. Vannevar Bush and Harvard's President James Conant were firmly shifted under Groves's authority in the Manhattan District. Finally, Groves must build an escape-proof fort to lock the recruits in where no one but Groves – above all not the eggheads – could gain a hold on the forces they set loose. And so Groves began to write cheques. Cheques written in fountain pen, very slowly and neatly with an even hand. Cheques on Treasury accounts twenty years of grovelling, dividing and conquering had made available to Groves. Sums greater than those used to purchase the original territories of the United States from Indians and trading powers. Cheques for hundred millions.

Of all Groves's inspired Washington activities during those weeks, the new Director of the Manhattan District had only a passing awareness. Robert had already recruited thirty friendly apostles of his creed, many of them famous names of physics – Fermi, Bethe, Teller. And Robert's little notebook was thickening.

As for the desert mystery up Edith Warner's Mesa, three thousand Special Project Army engineers swarmed on to it before Christmas. They bulldozed a broad reddish gash along the mud plateau. Had it not been for Micci Teller they would have levelled every last tree. By April 1943, bachelor and married barracks had been built of green pine. One large administration office, five laboratories and half a dozen smaller shops and warehouses, connected by a parody of Venetian foot bridges.

There they stood, tactless and temporary on the mysterious plateau. In command of the tremendous vistas of the Sangre de Cristos, the valley of the Rio Grande and distant Albuquerque desert, looking not at all like a town or factory or resort, let alone a temple of unflagging enlightenment. Implausible, impudently out of character and charmless, appearing to bear no relation, spiritual or practical, to anything in the huge spaces from which it was visible. Looking in fact like nothing so much as a space station established on earth by a race alien to our universe, a race who had only stopped by curiously for a short stay. Aliens who cared nothing for the sufferings of miserable human life.

It vaguely disappointed Robert when he first saw his utopia completed. What did you expect, Ictinus? he reflected. He thoughtfully avoided any comment to an inflated Groves the day the two men returned from their separate journeys. They held a brief private celebration on the red cliff ledges from which Groves had made his 'final-fort' speech.

'Sonofabitch!' Groves fumbled. 'Forgot the corkscrew!'

Oppy, Nichols and Lieutenant Lillie stood smiling. They held their tin cups in the overcast early spring warmth.

The bottle in Groves's pink hand appeared to have frost on it. The General had strapped a nickel-plated revolver around his huge waist for the occasion. Tugging it free, he hit the neck off the bottle. It spun tinkling in the void. The three men held up their spilling cups.

'To our bomb, Oppy.'

'To the end of all wars,' Robert said softly.

It was the closest they had come to disagreement.

PART TWO

Chapter 1

New Mexico, April 15, 1943. The US Army's top secret science laboratory on Los Alamos Mesa was opening for work.

Soon a new sun would come to the valley of the Rio Grande. But today the old one rose as usual over the black rim of the Sangre de Cristos.

Long before the whistle broke the silence, waking the hundred 'Smiths', 'Bakers', 'Malloys' and 'Mr Joneses' asleep with their wives across in the green and black tarboard barracks, Doctor Oppenheimer was up, standing by himself in his hat and baggy tweeds by the cottonwood knoll that is halfway from Main Tech to the security fence. He had given away his solitude to the assault on nuclear fission. This was the only hour left when the desert was still his. As he eagerly puffed his pipe, the desert dawn felt cleanly lucid as a planetarium, with Robert as its multi-lens projector of stars, elements and seasons. Shifting his shoes on the red dirt, he could almost hear music.

Now the first hot, yellow rim edged over the facing range. Across the great silent plateau a billion brushes, too quick and delicate for eyes, inked gold shafts along the red ledges of Los Alamos. They stirred a faint cool air rinsed clean by the dew, even of pinion and sage. Behind Robert's lean shoulders the night was deep lapis blue. Then very quickly it was gone and the sun was at full intensity. A bluish heat-haze filmed the distant plain, a hot hardness was against the red stone canyons. And the Mesa's immensity was hard and final, as some great printing block of all the souls who ever lived on it. The sudden whistle cut Robert's solitude to the bone.

Soon a little cheerful murmur came down. On the Mesa the Smiths, Malloys and Joneses were awakening, even General Groves, who had made the trip from Washington. And in Santa Fé town and Albuquerque, the hidden agents of Colonel John Lansdale and Peer de Silva were probably awake, and beyond them, Colonel Boris Pash at Berkeley. And then Army and FBI counter-intelligence — right up to the Pentagon, and the President. And somewhere beyond, already half-way into the working day, was occupied Paris, the Nazi physicists at enchanted Haigerlöch and Trondheim in Norway, and the Polish death camps.

For weeks the Smiths and Bakers had trickled in unnoticed through the country, the best of them from far beyond. One by one they swung open the screen arcade door at 109 East Palace Street, walked through a tropical Spanish garden into an adobe office, to be met by Dorothy McKibbin, given their aliases and oath of secrecy, and assigned to local ranches. Guiltily eager to see that the faithful thinkers who had followed him to his Mesa were not disappointed, Robert had entertained them in his jeans, boots and heavy belt, organizing horse-treks and barbecues. The valley was soon like some dude ranch for long-hairs, a Calgary Stampede of Göttingen atom-gazers. For now there were more of the magic Göttingen circle on Robert's Mesa than under Hitler.

One by one they left their pasts behind, churning by jeep up Robert's canyon horse path into the Jemez mountains, on to the Pajarito plateau, to wooded Los Alamos. They carried their bags into the tarboard shacks called 'pacific hutments', shacks more truly like stalags since Groves had spent none of his hundred millions on the immigrant-eggheads' comfort. If they were so holy, let them live like beggars. Then they pinned on Lansdale's white security badges. The compound gates swung shut.

Who in pueblo country knew what they were, these distracted scholars and bohemians in desert clothes? At the poor Indian and Mexican goat farms in canyons around Santa Fe, who had heard such accents before? Who could understand the words these Mr Smiths were muttering, even the American ones? 'Mesonspinnin . . .' they might be overheard saying. 'Dorae X process . . . excited Indium 115 nuclei . . . betatrons; deuterons; dipole character of meons.' Who could fathom that these were the planet's most rarified intellectual magicians? Or why? Or what, if anything, their magic had to do with moral life among men? More truly, these polite beings on the Hill seemed more like aliens indifferent to the New Mexico soil, come to colonize it for reasons of their own. For who, ambling unintroduced up the muddy, ramshackle mainstreet of pleasant faces under the iron footbridge, would have recognized around him the high divines of modern science, the conquistadores of the invisible atom?

From England James Chadwick would come, discoverer of the neutron, with woolly Otto Frisch, among the first to elaborate the Hahn-Strassman fission theory. W.G. Penney the ordnance man, Manchester proletarian Tuck, and avid, hunted Emil Klaus Fuchs. (His and Robert's mutual teacher Max Born in Edinburgh had refused all war work.) Also exiled from Germany were Rolf Landshoff and Hans Bethe, Oppenheimer's second-in-command. There was conceited, weird Edwin McMillan, discoverer of Elements 93 and 94 – Plutonium. From Italy the shy little Nobel Emilio Segre, and Bruno Rossi, and the supremely brilliant, charmingly ruthless Enrico Fermi, who just months before had burned the first slow-fission under Chicago Stadium with Leo Szilard, and who was as fanatical a sportsman as Niels Bohr. From occupied Budapest was the mathematics freak John Von Neumann, and boisterous, soulful Edward Teller. From Austria came Victor Weisskopf and Robert's Göttingen comrade Isidor Rabi, by way of Boston. There was the labyrinthine Renaissance mathematician Stanislas Ulam of Poland. And out of Russia, the volatile ordnance star George Kistiakovsky, now of Harvard. The Russian's colleague, the dour Navy Admiral Bill Parsons, was Robert and Kitty's neighbour and friend, the third-in-command of Los Alamos. Not to forget Urey, Compton and all-American Lawrence, running the Chicago, Tennessee, Berkeley, and Hanford Uranium and Plutonium plants – the reactor piles, cyclotrons and gas-diffusion centrifuges. And there were dozens of lesser-known even younger ambitions. There was thick-spoken Rudolph Peierls, the McKibbens, the Graveses, and Bradbury and Allison from Berkeley, Manley and Robert's bird-like student Serber. There was the waspish slow Luis Alvarez, Ken Bainbridge (he would control tests) and Condon. To say nothing of Critchfield, Hornig, Froman, the Canadian Christy, Joe Bacher, Seth Neddermeyer, Lee Du Bridge, Kerst, Lavatelli, Hughes, King, doomed Harry Daghlian, Dick Feynman, Sam Weissman, Kennedy, Morrison, Higginbotham and Nick Metropolis, and scores more. Their average age was 29. A good age for apostles.

Yet many on these secret canyon walls this morning still did not know why they had come, or what they would do with the cyclotron, accelerator, chemical and cryogenic equipment. And there were hundreds of others without white badges, who would never fully know. Simple labourers and engineers like the coarse young Army machinist David Greenglass, who had spent his whole life in New York struggling to survive the immigrant sweatshops of the lower East Side, crosstown from the Oppenheimers' princely Riverside apartment.

Only Doctor Oppenheimer knew completely. On this Mesa a few dozen Newtons, Galileos, Copernicuses and an Einstein or two had assembled under a presiding Da Vinci. Minds hard as billiard balls, clicking off each other. And from their racked concentration (ignoring Spengler's warning that final decadence was the reliance on strict causalities), Robert would gather a solid moral summit of ideas. And he would lead them up it, and seize what even Leonardo would never have dreamt of. The forces in the sun. Creation . . . destruction.

Chapter 2

Robert angled up through the early morning, passing a low windowless warehouse. A crowd of his friends and colleagues, most still in city clothes, had formed groups outside the Main Tech door. Theatre Two. Robert's shoes trailed a faint cloud of dust.

Then the jealous volatile atmosphere closed around him, of powerful egos compressed into an abnormally small space. Isidor Rabi left a noisy group centred on Fermi and Teller, and hurried toward his old friend in his Homburg and rabbinical three-piece suit. The new Director slowed his walk, composing his face in a mild patient smile. From that moment they must set a strict egalitarian tone. His Mesa was no place for rivalries, selfishness or gross ambitions. The holiday was over.

The friends shook hands before the steps. Robert gazed past him.

'Well, everyone seems here . . . shall we get going?'

'We certainly are all here, my friend!' Isidor laughed nervously. 'Your chariot is hooked to wild horses.'

Robert took off his hat and squinted in the sun. What a lot of European gentlemen they seemed, walking about in this wild scenery.

'Look, there's Groves.'

The friends climbed the steps, and in an excited press of colleagues went in the rough pine entrance. A second door led into low, shady Theatre Two.

The scientists arranged themselves down the slope of folding chairs and along the walls. Then General Groves's formidable khaki person loomed at the far end against the wide blackboards. The Army man's cornily patriotic speech stirred some restless clapping.

Robert stepped hurriedly from the second row to cut short the impression poor Groves was making. At once a rapt hush spread over the ranks of intelligent, bespectacled faces, a concentration so powerful it seemed intent on penetrating these pine frame walls, on rejoining the dry hot prehistoric stillness outside on the Mesa. Behind the podium Doctor Oppenheimer blew his nose delicately. He folded the handkerchief in his jacket pocket, then unfolded his notes. Even from far back in the room, Hans Bethe saw the dreaming glitter in his friend's eyes. The silence deepened.

'Welcome to Los Alamos.' Robert cut the silence, speaking simply and modestly as the emotion permitted. 'My thanks to all of you who have come. Especially so, as to many of you it may be a mystery why you are here. But now we are here, and no one will be leaving, it is time to speak openly . . . speak freely. And after my few words, four or five others will cover the ground at length, and in depth.

'I flatter myself I know something about almost everyone here. For instance, that there is scarcely a place in the world someone here doesn't come from, or hasn't been. So, if it is a mystery why we are here, it is no mystery what the fascist rulers of Germany and Japan are doing to civilization. Nor is there any mystery by now about the high energy to be exploited in fissionable material, or its possible military use. As you know, Enrico Fermi and Leo Szilard, who we have here, proved that five months ago in Chicago.'

Robert stood through the rattle of respectful applause.

'As men of science,' he went on very softly, 'none of us can help feeling this knowledge will soon be ours, or that it may be corrupted by warlike nations. My friends, colleagues, that is why we are here in this peaceful place, in this moderate peace-loving country. Working together in enlightened democracy, as it were, a tribe . . . we will attempt to tap forces so, well, so mighty they can only be spoken of in terms of our sun's heat factors . . . the genesis of our planet. Our end product will be either one of two kinds, or both – 'explosive devices' General Groves calls them.'

A burst of nervous, eager laughter gusted around Robert.

'And gentlemen, I sincerely hope our bomb will be the world's first. For if it is not, there might be no check on the forces of evil. The future will seem dark indeed. But with the kind of minds I see here, my hopes are with us . . .

'. . . two f.f. bombs,' Robert wound up minutes later. 'One fuelled with U235 to a critical mass of 25 kilos, the second fuelled with Plutonium to a crit of 5 kilos. The Plutonium bomb is an unknown quantity. To test the f.f. principle using Plutonium we will have a test firing as soon as possible. Meanwhile we must explore the readiness and excitation levels of the available isotopes to react with protons, deuterons, electrons, neutrons, alpha particles and gamma rays – and of course every kind of device to trigger that reaction. Well, that's it. And if at any time anyone here has any doubts or ideas, consider it my responsibility to be available. Now Bob Serber has something to say, and he's a hell of a lot less shy than I am.'

Robert had already turned away, folding his note sheet. A second ripple of excited laughter rumbled through the bare pine building. Everyone knew Serber was one of the shyest pilgrims on the Mesa.

Hearing the alert willing rumble of laughter, Robert walked unevenly back to his chair between Allison and Ulam. The little assembly had caught his mood and accepted what he had said, and he had enjoyed the sensation. Oppy's words gave their specialized knowledge a tragic fate in the legend of their time. They would trust his completeness.

With the lunch break for hamburgers and sauerkraut under the trees, the first conference on the Mesa lasted most of the day. There were several long, magical debates in the auditorium, debates between men who had lived their entire lives by the same obsessions in different cultures across the earth. Now again they were elaborating similar elusive ideas with the same shy, excitable passion. It was a global hall of mirrors; reflected in each mirror was the power of the human imagination to imitate nature. The spoils of conquest awaited them. Reputations would be made.

At dusk, they stumbled out on to the muddy mainstreet, elated and wonderfully tired. The distant Albuquerque plain looked stormily electric. In the crowded shadows Enrico Fermi fell in beside Robert, hands clasped behind him. They walked in silence, neither caring to break the feeling in the air.

'Well, Mr Farmer, how was I?' Robert joked softly.

'Splendid, my friend! Splendid!' Fermi waved his arms, shaking his head solemnly. 'Magnificent . . . even frightening!'

'Frightening, Enrico?' Robert stopped with a gesture.

'Of course I am scared!' Fermi laughed genially. 'When I plan something frightening I am scared. But those in there? No! And you are not scared, Oppy?'

In Robert's stomach something stirred. 'It is a tremendous responsibility.' He smiled vaguely.

'You will be scared, you will see.' Fermi took Robert's arm under the pine branches. 'Now let us speak of food. *Che scandolo*, it is necessary to make *reservations* at your Edith Warner's. Will you and Kitty meet la Laura and myself there tonight?'

'Why thank you, we accept!' Robert called after the shadowy figure.

As the festive assembly splashed away noisily among the trees, Groves had lingered with young Colonel Landsdale outside Main Tech.

'Well, General.' Landsdale grinned boyishly, examining the older man's heavy restless face. Tonight the boss looked almost relaxed. 'You surely have bought yourself one pandora's box of a laboratory.'

'Thanks John,' Groves muttered sotto voce. 'And we are going to damn well keep the lid on. I'd say we've got every angle pretty well sealed off. Except the sky . . . except the sky. My God, what a place this would be for an airborne assault!'

And as if it had just arrived from Mexico to blow over the Mesa a flotilla of German, Japanese or Russian parachutists . . . like dandelions, or sugar plum fairies . . . a damply cool breeze began to stir the branches over the two officers' heads.

In the wild desert evening the scientists rolled out from Main Tech, questioning and discussing. They were all feeling very excited, so excited that soon they were clearing Fuller Lodge for a Glen Miller dance and beer party. It was necessary. They had never felt so heady or intoxicated in their lives. 'Must be the altitude!' they told each other. 'Must be the altitude!' But most of all, it was what Oppy had told them. His heady, gently spoken words had infected everyone with a vivid pride . . . as if their lives were on the line. Suddenly, after the secrecy and bitter feuds on the campuses, to be released all together into this complete and generous freedom! To feel, not their vulnerable isolation, but this fusing of their souls into a single soul, their minds into a single mind. Was it real? Could it be true? Was it really happening to them? It did not feel like building bombs.

The excitement went on into that first evening, long after most of them forgot Oppy's exact words. The older ones, the Europeans, did not forget all of it. But the younger ones, being just men, and incomplete, remembered only the exalted emotion they had felt. As, seven month earlier, General Groves had not been able to remember the obscure concepts that had lifted him above ordinary men, this evening the excited scientists on the Mesa, even Fermi, could not recall the epic poetry which had raised them above being mere technicians. Like some invisible ink, the all-responsible morality that had invented their fate vanished, leaving only the intoxication, the spell.

But words or no words, any man who made them feel emotions like that was worth following. All they had to do was trust him.

Chapter 3

Robert and Kitty left the shantytown of frame huts, stooping under the ranks of sagging clotheslines, and walked down to the car. They could hear the phonograph up the hill, and laughter. The soft moan of swing saxophones made a small dreamy pulse under the desert stars. It was like college dance weekends and Indian camps, and they walked hand in hand. But the drug of concentration in Robert's head was too strong for him to notice Kitty absorbed in something she wasn't talking about.

'Just Molly and me,' a voice crooned. 'And baby makes three. We're happy in my . . . blue . . . heaven.'

Very little had changed down at Edith Warner's little peach-coloured adobe ranchhouse with the cramped wood tables. Tileno was more sun-wizened and like a medicine man. Edith, propped by the stone hearth in a red serape, more the dowager frontiers-woman. There were people he didn't know, and more Navajo blankets and pottery Edith was trying to sell for the pueblos. Going in to eat, everybody had to pass her.

She pulled Robert down by the wrist. 'Well Mr Opp, it's about time! Say, I heard a story you're building a spaceship up there, or some such tomfool thing.'

Rabi, Kitty and Fermi stood grinning unnaturally. Tileno got up and went into the kitchen.

'Something like that,' Robert laughed. It was strange, old Edith not knowing their young men. Groves's security make-believe. 'Edith, I'll sell you the first ticket to the moon.'

'Oh no you don't. I came here to stay!' Edith croaked. 'Anyway I've been holding that last table over there for you. Don't know why. I suppose you gents are furreners too?'

'All Americans, Miss Edith.' Rabi squirmed, and his jowels trembled.

'I only used to be!' Fermi made a face.

'Well, you're Americans now. Sit down over there and eat.'

Robert stopped at Ed Teller's crowded table, breaking in on his monologue about American Indians in German literature. He muttered something with a grin to Victor Weisskopf. The others were pushing behind the corner table under a Mexican tin crucifix. The air around the men still crackled with the resonant clarities of the afternoon, but they were outside the security screen. There would be no nucleonics.

'Wonderful, Robert!' Enrico leaned forward on the table with his foxy penetrating smile. 'I feel so American.'

His three friends burst out laughing at Fermi's sincerity and thick accent.

'Sounds like the classic move to the right,' Kitty drawled.

'Now that I am feeling so American,' the Italian grinned at Kitty, 'there is no left or right! Only sometimes a belladonna.'

Rabi struggled to control an attack of giggling.

'In English, Enrico,' Robert explained, 'belladonna is a poison.'

'Naturally,' Fermi went on, 'in Italian also. But there is no such "English" from now on, only American!'

'I felt like that, first coming up here,' Robert said.

'Yes, it is most primitive, most primitive,' Rabi riposted.

Kitty had just returned Edith the menu. She turned with a quick intensity. 'That's what I like about it, Isidor. I hope we don't change that.'

'Now that I am feeling so American, it is clear!' Enrico bantered on. 'This is the answer to all the craziness back there. Soon the whole world will be American. It will solve everything.'

'Oh, we have a problem or two over here,' Kitty boasted cynically, though she could not help a slight flush of pride.

'Purgatorio, only purgatorio!'

The couples were crowded close around the table. Fermi was inspired, his mocking eyes softened with a beatific light. The table candle jumped in his breath.

'As for the Inferno?' he laughed. 'We Americans will do it away.'

'There is some fine poetry in Hell, Enrico,' Robert said. He felt Kitty's eyes on him. 'Though that's a thing of the past.'

'You know, Robbie.' Rabi lowered his voice, glancing at his friend. 'It really does feel like being in the future . . . up there. It is something very remarkable.'

Robert gazed thoughtfully at the warm circle of faces. His glass of water did not stop the burning of the *enchiladas diablos*.

'We'll have to make it,' he said, holding his voice low, 'the most enlightened place in town. We're training a future aristocracy.'

'Aristocrats?' Fermi looked surprised. 'Aristocrats, I would not say. Most are not so special. Bright boys and girls, yes. But aristocrats?'

'You'll have to make a choice Enrico,' Kitty said. 'You can't have Americans and your kind of aristocrats too.'

'An aristocrat is an aristocrat!' Fermi raised his eyebrows mockingly.

'All Americans are aristocrats,' Robert said quietly. 'They are responsible. Everyone knows what we're doing. The meaning will get shared around.'

Fermi looked disgusted at this serious turn. An impish glitter jumped from the candles into his eyes and he laughed. Anything left ambiguous repulsed Fermi. But when he could laugh at it, a thing was simplified.

Before Robert could escape, Fermi's arm reached over the fresh round of tequilas. He squeezed his friend's gaunt cheek.

'Oh you are so innocent, such an American, Robert.' Fermi grinned devilishly. 'You are so sweet I want to pinch your cheek!'

Then the Italian sat back while the others laughed until tears came to their eyes.

Chapter 4

Robert and Kitty walked from the car in silence. Home from now on was the requisitioned headmaster's house.

A full moon had risen from the Sangres. It sailed slowly, never touching, through an atoll of iridescent clouds and shed an unreal distanceless glow across the flat remote desert, making crumpled shadows of the canyons. The forest Mesa was breathless and dark, and the mud across the clearings slippery.

As they passed near the main guardbox Robert was glad to be alone with Kitty, the rebellion in her, the needing to be free. He felt a lightening of desire.

In the moonlight, they saw clearly the tough bony sargeant.

'Evening Doctor, Miz Oppenheimer! Full moon tonight.'

Robert's right arm was around Kitty. He pressed the corner of her breast. 'Good evening,' they called together. Holding to each other, they climbed slowly along the muddy knoll.

'How do you feel, darling, are you happy now?'

Robert heard what she meant. Under their feet the mud was flattening out.

'I feel like your lover.'

'You are my lover, darling, when we're on our own.'

'It's not very prepossessing, our hideaway,' Robert admitted.

'Don't say that!' Kitty said quickly. 'I love it up here. It's life.' She reflected deeply. 'Like being migrant workers. Like my old Youngstown days. It'll keep us all honest. Only Robbie . . .' Kitty turned to him.

'What's that?'

'I don't have to be social chief hen, do I? I mean they're awfully sweet girls, but . . .'

'No more than I'm going to be chief rooster,' he said. 'Don't tell anyone. But we're running a commune up here.'

Kitty balanced up on the flat mud to reward him with a kiss. 'Will you have any time back home for us?'

'Berkeley?' Robert held her. 'We'd make time. It could be your last trip out of the Mesa.'

'Me and all my secrets,' Kitty laughed.

'I'll tell you what I think, Kat,' Robert whispered in her ear then. He let go, stopped to face past the last of the blackened huts.

The moon had taken a wrong turn behind a cloud. But far out, the Albuquerque desert drifted in pearly glow. Two or three lights were still on. Robert kept his voice very low.

'Up here,' he said, 'I've never felt further from the . . . the coarse crowded stupidity of this world. Closer to the ones out *there*, who are being trampled down. All these thousands going into the camps. Wretched Paris. All of Europe, half Russia under forced labour! Kat, it's too big to think of, to hold in your mind.'

In the chill opaque American night, Robert felt Kitty's hand in his. He squeezed hard.

'But now . . . this thing we're doing on the Mesa,' he went on, 'it's just as big. Big enough to reach out and rap the knuckles of all the thugs and the gangsters the world can throw up. We're on the side of the angels, Kat.'

Robert's voice had thickened. He cleared his throat. 'I keep seeing barbed wire, miles and miles of it. And behind it . . . eyes, starving forgotten faces staring. Hundreds and hundreds and thousands of them, Kat!'

'Yes I know, Robbie.' Kitty stirred without touching him.

'But now?' he went on. 'We can look them in the eye. And say, my friends, my brothers and sisters, just wait! It's not much longer now.'

'Is the invention really that sure?' Kitty said thoughtfully. She heard with interest the new mood in her husband's voice. 'It must have gone well this afternoon.'

Robert and Kitty stood waiting for several minutes as the moonlight came out again on the plateau. They were not ready to go inside yet. Low voices droned over in one of the hutments.

'Did you let some of the others talk out your ideas again?' Kitty asked quickly. This had always worried her about Robert. All of him must belong to her.

'Knowledge belongs to everyone, Kat,' Robert said, half-wanting her to cut him off.

'Do the security men think so?'

'You mean Landsdale and de Silva?' Robert was impatient. 'They're good guys. They have a point about security. It's why I let Ed Condon go.'

'Good guys?' Kitty's voice choked. 'Robbie!'

The droning voice among the hutments had stopped. Robert and Kitty stood together tensely on the open mud.

'They make my skin crawl,' Kitty whispered hoarsely. 'They're so full of spite and venom. They don't have to say anything, I can feel the greed ooze out of them. The predatory instinct! They're no friends of yours, Robbie. Or of any of us up here!'

'Katie . . . Katie.' Robert laughed. He felt for her strong little hands in the moonlight. 'They just have funny feelings about us, that's all. So was Groves a little scared in the beginning. With *our* background, we have to make them feel at home with us up here. They'll get over it, you'll see.'

'Shut up out there, will you!' A muffled voice was cursing among the darkened shacks. 'Can't you let a guy get some sleep!'

It sounded like Leo Slotin. Slotin had seen adventure and death in Spain. Now he would be managing the lethal final assembly under Otto Frisch.

With a thrill of panicked embarrassment, Robert and Kitty pulled apart. Then they hugged, balancing on the indistinct mud. Kitty trembled with all the strange new powers on the Mesa. She threw back her head and nervously kissed him.

'Oh, Robbie!' Kitty said against his mouth, and in the hunger for his triumph was a frightened note. 'Where is all this going?'

For this desert night, the full moon was as different as when a man has been turned inside out. Different as the classical sun Doctor Oppenheimer was leading mankind out of, and the murky distance-less night they would enter. And face to face with barbed-wired

Old World multitudes – as the moral centres of a mind reach to the body's broken bleeding limbs – Doctor Oppenheimer was a long way from a dawn on the Mesa with his paint pony fourteen years ago. When he had chosen the desert, to begin again in freedom, feeling quite sure all that was left behind.

Chapter 5

The Pullman berths for Doctor Oppenheimer and his wife were reserved on the night train from Albuquerque to Stockton, California. The carriages were crowded with brash gum-chewing boy marines bound for the Pacific, Guadalcanal and the Solomon Islands.

It was the Oppenheimers' last trip together down from the mind-god on the Mesa. Already it was a strange feeling for the couple to be among ordinary people, to be free and alone, heading for San Francisco and Eagle Hill. Until they were clicking again across artichoke fields, with the hazy Santa Cruz mountains far off to the left in the soft, tender Pacific morning, the burden came with Robert. They were like spies among these everyday lives. This was satisfactory to neither of them, as it was to General Groves.

So it was very good to be sipping a martini again in the cool conservatory at Eagle Hill. Good for Robert to surprise Frank at the Radiation Labs, and with Lawrence in his office to run through the intricate itinerary of their two projects. Like nervous fathers agreeing on the wedding day of strange children.

Robert found Ernest Orlando Lawrence much changed by the hundred millions of dollars Groves had given him, a gilded wealth to build batteries of even huger Uranium-producing cyclotrons. As they cracked crab at a window table on Fisherman's Wharf, it seemed to Robert that Groves had touched off a craze in the great all-American. As they talked through the war project, keeping their voices down as they dug the last meat out of the shells, Ernest Orlando was a one-man Gold Rush for U235. There was no further talk of the lonely delicate borderlands of knowledge, but only of Ernest's giant new calutron plants at Hanford in Washington, and Oak Ridge, Tennessee. Regiments of mammoth, glistening high-voltage doughnut coils, whirling up beams like the forges of

Vulcan to fulfil a Dark Age alchemist's dream, perverting elements to dominate the greedy souls of men.

But it was Compton's Plutonium reactors Lawrence longed for. Element 94, scarcer, and more precious than either gold or platinum, beside whose weight gold and platinum were flimsy. Plutonium, infinitely more poisonous than arsenic. Cry the lost innocence of mere gold and platinum, from which men did not even make bullets. Tremble before the virulent spawn of Element 94, whose first property is a perverted hatred for natural living things. As once the dog soldiers raided the Black Hills of the Sioux and then the Sierra Nevada for the yellow metal, General Groves had despatched Compton among the elements in search of high-purity Plutonium, to be thrown in the enemy's face as children throw mud pies.

For the rest of that day Robert and Ernest Orlando kept their obsessive minds locked together in this exhausting hyperconcentration. Amid clouds of pipe and cigar smoke over Le Conte laboratory's weak coffee, they laid plans for the wedding rites of their difficult children, the Mesa's unborn clockwork sun and the few handfuls of vile loot from Lawrence's patriotic gold-rush.

The technical discussions were routine, but left Robert feeling disturbed at his old friend's loss of charm, his new barren intensity.

And what might all this earthly power do to *you*? he asked himself.

Robert leaned to clear a patch on the car's misted windshield. He was racing back to Eagle Hill past the Grocery Mart, through a tropical spring shower. He'd better watch himself pretty closely. That was the trouble living with the trust of so many people you could see deeply into. Their changing, changed you. Well, the Radiation Labs might be off to the wars, but the Humanities Faculty was still at full force. Suddenly Robert was looking forward with a kind of spiritual thirst to seeing Haakon and Barbara Chevalier. He was starved for human talk. They would cloud-walk with Li Po and Pushkin, and speculate splendidly over Goethe, Dante and Shakespeare's love-life. At least Groves's security rules would make it easy to keep off the kind of subjects he'd been over with Lawrence. To Haakon he would be just the same old Oppy of the fine passionate debates. The romantic of Local 349. What if

Haakon treated him as some sort of hero? At least he'd seen his best self. He could count on Haakon to put the poetry back in life, Robert thought, as a parent does who expects the innocence of a child to keep him honest.

The car skidded neatly between the magnolia and thick bamboos. Robert remained inside the car's fogged windows until the drenching gust blew on. Then he climbed out.

Far away over San Francisco Bay, a huge electric storm trailed an unmoving screen of rain. The bay surface below seemed beaten flat, and to dissolve. And for just two moments, Doctor Oppenheimer thought he saw trapped ocean being sucked in great slow billows, up into the white-topped cloud. Before Robert could turn and walk up the wet path a second downpour began. Kitty found her husband absorbed under the veranda shaking out his sodden tweed jacket.

Chapter 6

A little later, the Pacific sky turned deep blue. When the doorbell at Eagle Hill rang punctually at seven thirty, it was Robert who hurried in a fresh shirt and well-pressed jacket to let in Barbara and Haakon. Kitty met them in the hall, looking dangerously Mediterranean in a lemon summer dress, her damp hair brushed back.

'Haakon, it's nice to see you,' Kitty said a little haughtily. 'And Barbara, always so soignée!'

'And you too,' Haakon laughed, touching Kitty's pointed chin. 'But these are not Stinson's Beach sunburns, alas.'

'You will come to the beach house?' Barbara followed them, cool and red-headed.

'We only came for two days,' Robert shrugged. 'We're off in the morning.'

'Back to Post Box 1663, Sante Fe?' Haakon laughed, falling back on the conservatory couch. He tugged out a pack of cigarettes.

'Aha! So you're keeping up with our social life.' Robert began filling his pipe bowl with a sigh of satisfaction. There was an electric excitement among them. Already the mention of the New Mexico desert had less effect on him.

94

'Sit down all of you!' Kitty drawled. 'Let's start things with some martinis.' She left the two men alone.

'Yes! And if that is so,' Haakon added with feeling, 'then there is not a moment to waste. My God, there is so much to say. And you too!'

'You two excuse me?' Barbara gave her husband a significant glance and stepped back out to the hall. Robert sat regarding his attractive friend over the glass table.

'That's your first mention ever of God.'

'Oh, God is fine for a curse.' Haakon smiled fondly. His gaze wavered, slipped around the overcrowded conservatory.

'No Parisian is all atheist,' said Robert.

'American ones perhaps. Anyway,' Haakon shrugged, 'I have outgrown the embarrassed little nihilists of the cafés. Alienation . . . *tout ça.*'

'When there is something,' Robert agreed, 'like the lifting of the Siege.'

'Ah, Leningrad!' Chevalier cried softly. He drew himself up on the edge of the couch. 'Leningrad! That is a great one against the fascists.'

'For Communism, and for the Russian people.'

'Perhaps, little Robbie.' Haakon laughed. 'You know my friend André speaks of liberating Paris this way.'

'That's quite an idea.' But tonight better keep off history. The secret of his Mesa was an immense superiority.

'You know what Malraux's working on?' Robert asked.

Haakon awoke from the sober emotion of Leningrad. 'Over the telephone, Oppy, you asked about Sartre.'

Kitty had come back in with the martinis. She curled up beside Haakon. It was getting dark, but nobody thought of the lights.

'I have not seen *L'Etre et le Néant* yet,' Haakon said excitedly. 'But there is a young Algerian called Camus . . . Albert Camus. It is said he leads in the Resistance with André. Good! So I must tell you about his first book, *L'Etranger!*'

'The Stranger, Haakon?' Robert puffed his pipe. 'Let me hear.'

Barbara had rejoined them. So they were all together at last in the California conservatory. A romance hung in the bland California dusk. The evening lay out ahead, and it was already a special

95

feeling between them. Maybe the tone was so charged because they shared a civilized grasp of the great and tragic times. Or maybe because tonight, Robert seemed to set aside his irritable science aloofness and spoke to Haakon equally. Which in turn made Haakon modestly assured. They were closer and glad to be together.

And so the evening began, very ordinarily. Later in the next room, conversing through Kitty's dinner, nobody noticed the food or Napa wine. How well we know each other, each of them was thinking at some point as they performed for each other. A fine trust thickened between them. The chaste flirtation between handsome married couples having much in common. Then it came to dessert. Barbara left the table. Haakon had returned to *L'Etranger*.

'Of course it has much to do with colonialism,' Haakon leaned forward on his elbows, speaking intensely. 'With the desert, the sun and heat. Camus's sense of the absurd. The hero in the book, he murders the Arab and then scandalously neglects to feel the correct guilt, contrition and fear of death. He is in a way caught between two worlds. The *pied-noir* bourgeois . . . and the ancient brutal heroism of the desert people who live close to death. Who are drawn to the toughest truths.'

Kitty was alert. She examined Haakon's face closely as if to discover his secret. 'That's a cruel philosophy, Haakon,' she said with admiration. She wanted to be a part of it.

'It is all around us, Kitty.'

'What if a generation is influenced by such a nihilism?' Robert mused. He leaned back, loosening some strands of pipe tobacco.

'Somehow it is not nihilism.' Haakon sat forward eagerly. 'Somehow it is a ruthless, even far-reaching . . . *honesty*! Strangely, Robbie, you have a sadness for the man's hopeless rebellion. He has no Sermon on the Mount to deliver. But he refuses to succumb to the accepted life of lies. You see?'

Suddenly the dining room lights blacked out. With playful comments they turned to watch Barbara push through the swinging door. She was carrying something looking like a coffee-coloured plum pudding with little candles.

'Gosh, Haakon!' Kitty laughed unsentimentally. 'What's that?'

'Barbara made it,' Haakon said. 'It is Russian.'

Barbara laughed. 'It was quite a trick smuggling it into your refrigerator.'

'Wonderful! But what is it?' Robert leaned forward and examined the frozen dessert. 'It looks more like an Indian *kulfi*. A going-away cake.'

'It is a sort of frozen cheesecake.' Haakon looked at Robert. 'But it was not for going away. Will you be at Box 1663 so long?'

'The shortest time possible, Haakon,' Robert said with conviction. 'Barbara, I must know the Russian name for this creation.'

Barbara clapped her palms to her temples, turning red.

'My God, what has happened to me? Haakon, I have forgotten it. Oh, how stupid . . . damn!'

'Barbara, try hard to remember,' Robert urged impatiently.

For several seconds they all sat waiting as Barbara shut her eyes, trying to remember. All of them were caught up in the vague failure of the misplaced word no one else in California could tell them.

'Darling, why must you know everything?' Kitty suddenly came out. 'The dessert will taste just the same. Better! Our Russian mystery dessert.'

'All right,' Robert said. 'Russian mystery dessert. Champagne, good cheer.'

'Champagne, Oppy?' Haakon brightened. 'Is there champagne?'

'Why not? I'll get it.'

Haakon waved his arm. 'I will come too.'

Chevalier followed Robert through the swinging door. In the brilliant kitchen, Haakon leaned on the formica table. He watched his friend rummage in the big California ice-box.

'Oppy?' he said presently. 'I must ask you a question.'

Hearing the melancholy gravity in Haakon's tone, Robert looked around. 'Anything you like, Haakon. Go ahead.'

'Post Box 1663,' Haakon said. 'It is very secret. Very important?'

'I guess in some respects.'

'The truth is, Oppy,' Chevalier said soberly, 'I have been told it is so.'

'That's hard knowledge to come by, Haakon.' Robert straightened and turned. Very suddenly both friends were acutely conscious of each other, of the alien brightness in the kitchen. Forgetting the open ice-box door, Robert struck a match and sucked the flame into his pipe bowl. The familiar house was silent.

The invisible hydrangeas teamed with frog-sound through the open garden window.

The last hours of charm and friendship had dispersed the unnatural hold of the mind-god back in New Mexico, blown away the poison of Lawrence's pursuit of the elements. Now all the fine heady friendship of the evening felt just a sham. Robert had put it over on Haakon with the security rules. He felt a panicky guilt for both of them towards poor General Groves. Groves had nothing creative to give the fission project but this security system he was so proud of, and which he and Haakon had just broken. Robert felt the emotion of someone caught spreading evil gossip about a close friend.

'Listen, Robbie,' Haakon whispered, 'I'm torn by this thing. You must help me!'

Smiling tensely, Robert noticed his friend's forehead glisten. Frozen vapour poured from the ice-box behind him.

'No no, you are so intelligent.' Haakon threw up his hands and took a deep breath. '*Still* you do not understand? People. Well, ones you know, our old circle.' Suddenly a stubborn pride hardened Haakon's handsome face. 'They wish you to share with them, would be interested to hear the details of what you are doing. They asked me.'

Every trace of light and affection had left Robert's face. The two men faced each other in the kitchen with drawn, solemn stares, stricken, crushed by what suddenly they were doing. Hearing the women burst out laughing beyond the kitchen door, they unconsciously lowered their voices.

'Oh? Well, to what end?'

'You know George Eltonton?'

'The English fellow at Shell Oil?' Robert frowned, tugging his ear. Hearing his friend's formal tone Haakon turned pale.

'They know a microfilm expert at the Russian Consulate.'

A giddy trembling had started up from Robert's knees. He leaned back on the open ice-box.

'The others?' he whispered. 'How many are in on it?'

'Many . . . most of them. Your brother knows.'

'Steve Nelson?' Robert's murmur sounded in his ears like a rumbling of boxcars.

Haakon swallowed. He blinked helplessly. 'Yes. Steve also. Steve most of all.'

'And they know you are asking?'

Haakon nodded. 'But it is the Kremlin,' Haakon said. 'The International that requires this, the information.'

'Haakon, think what you are saying!' Robert heard himself mutter. He repeated it. 'That is high treason!'

But at the word 'Kremlin', Robert's concentration finally broke tether from the dense affections of the evening. It flew out in desolate loneliness across the naked face of the sloping world.

Impressions attacked him, vague but acute, out of an awareness that had been growing on Robert for months, like some fungus whose sheer weight could bear him to the ground. Impressions of the hot sun and low fog on San Francisco Bay. Of General Groves's cunning glances. Of their reaping of the poison Plutonium, and the piercing, unnatural clarity among the geniuses waiting for him back on the Mesa. Of the awesome, humbling mystery of what they were planning. So now *they* are beginning too, Robert thought, and remembered the old romantic solidarity. The simple outrage of the people he and Haakon had worked among on the unions. That day in the Santa Cruz with Steve Nelson. What good men Robert and Haakon had been then.

In the refrigerated breeze, staring into his old friend's too-handsome face under the wicker light, the flesh of Robert's illusion fell from his mind. The bones stood clear. He was Dr Oppenheimer, head of the US Atom Bomb Project; answerable to the President in Washington, but with a moral commitment to the poor and helpless of the camps, the world revolution. The mind nerved to the splintered bleeding limbs. He, and he alone, known, drawn and strung both to Roosevelt in the White House and Joseph Stalin in the Kremlin. And such a power . . . like being a tiny clapper, tethered inside heavy vibrating walls of some huge ideological gong. A small figure on a great open plain between two silent waiting hosts.

Abruptly, Robert was back in his familiar California kitchen with Haakon Chevalier. He turned and lifted the cold French bottle from the wire shelf. The grapes for it had grown in a free France. Robert swung the ice-box shut.

'Knowledge isn't property, Haakon,' he said as in a dream. 'You can't fight over ideas, or steal them.'

But the solidarity of their friendship tugged at Robert. It confused his thoughts. He fought down the waves of angry suspicion, the disturbed emotions that rose in his mind and flapped horribly. Spy . . . traitor . . . electric chair. Words you could not speak aloud between friends. They were at the limit.

'And the International,' Haakon shrugged questioningly. 'Are they not in a death struggle with the fascists?'

'And aren't we their allies, Haakon?' Robert was methodically setting out crystal champagne glasses. The last one vibrated on the Formica. 'Isn't that enough for the time being?'

'Robbie . . . the establishment over here!' Haakon smiled doubtfully and Robert felt his face burning. For a moment he thought he might faint.

'Listen, Haakon.' Robert heard his weakest voice. 'You have roots in France. I am American. You must not speak to me about these things, not like this.'

The two men stood tensely face to face. Little beads of perspiration like the condensation on the champagne bottle.

'Good! Excellent!' Haakon suddenly said with guttural feeling. 'Our friendship must not be used in such a way!'

'I know, Haakon. I know.' Robert let out his breath.

'You understand, Oppy? I had to be sure. I had to be sure.'

'It's certainly not easy, Haakon.'

'I have not upset you, Oppy? Promise you are not upset.'

'I am not upset,' Robert said. 'Now let's go back in and not spoil it.'

Suddenly Haakon gripped both Robert's arms. A wave of relieved emotion passed between them.

'Oppy my friend, truly you are an honest man.'

'Haakon,' Robert softly laughed, 'I told you no Frenchman was an atheist.' By this he meant that Haakon had set personal feeling over absolute reason. 'Now take the glasses.'

As the men pushed back into the dark Berkeley dining room, the women's smiles were lit from the kitchen. Robert and Haakon had been out of the room five minutes. Their faces were red and tipsy-looking.

'And what took *you* so long?' Kitty taunted.

'The Russian mystery dessert is melting!' Barbara said tragically.

The two friends exchanged looks and they laughed. Haakon was setting out the glasses.

'Good thing too,' Robert said under his breath, and popped the wired cork. He poured the yellow wine through the spume into the glasses.

'A toast to honest men!' Haakon said firmly.

'Then, to simple men,' Robert observed and they clinked glasses.

'And to Oppy and Kitty's new home,' Barbara said. 'Wherever it may be.'

'Wherever it may be,' Kitty agreed.

As they drank the cold champagne, a silence fell over them.

'I'm not sure I trust Oppy,' Barbara Chevalier told Haakon later, as her husband steered their old car down towards the Bay shore.

'Nonsense, Barbara,' Haakon said gravely. 'You must not say that of a friendship like ours.'

And that was the moment in the life of Doctor Oppenheimer when belief in his wisdom was at its highest tide.

Chapter 7

The night train southeast from San Francisco, bearing Dr Oppenheimer and his wife back to Santa Fe, was half empty.

Long after midnight, after Flagstaff, Arizona, with Gallup somewhere ahead, Robert lay perfectly awake on the top bunk staring at the weak red bulb. He was conscious of Kitty's warm body asleep on the berth under him. Of the sleeping world, lying at peace out beyond the obsessed jostling click of the trucks.

Robert's tired body and spirit longed to be alone in it, to join in rest. But the mind resting on his crossed palms stayed brilliantly alert, as if the man was bound by columns of unnatural light, great rays of unextinguishable hyperconsciousness, out through the dark to Göttingen, Harvard and Cambridge. To Lawrence's army of sluice-box cyclotrons. To all the fronts and cultures of the World War, with master beacons to Groves and the secret mind-god on the Mesa. And back home to his shock during their dinner with Haakon and Barbara. As if some fierce moral light, which had not left Robert at peace in his old loneliness until he had poured it into the material ambitions of his life, the immortal children of his mind, now must stream back in magnified reciprocation. As the first unfiltered eye under an astronomer's telescope might burn out under the sun the instrument was built to reach. As if the over-charged human mind had rebelled from the animal limitations of night and gone off in unending sleepless days.

Trying to free himself, Robert twisted in the airless compartment. Then for a long time his body lay, in the submission of someone buried alive in rolling catacombs. His mind raced on.

The further the kitchen at Eagle Hill fell behind, the more guiltily secret the talk with Haakon seemed. At the time it had felt like a victory to come away undying friends. But it was a hard secret to carry around, and that was strange in someone who kept most of his life secret from the world. Haakon's secret had lodged in Robert's conscience, along with Groves's secret of the Mesa. Yes, though it was a corruption to have blocked the spread of knowledge, and to an ally like the Russians. In particular it had been a humiliating betrayal of the people he had worked beside, a taking sides with the anti-Communism of the security paranoiacs. On the side of property . . . property, and his country. Well, it was a mistake either way, and Haakon should not have made it. Kitty was right about that. Well, he would file them with the other few important mistakes . . . like Jean. You are getting into this pretty deep, he thought. But as long as he did not lose track of the mistakes and unmade them when the time came, he could keep his morals straight. But what of the guilty feeling, leaving his friends up on the Mesa while he went out hobnobbing scot free?

Strangest of all was discovering yesterday how happy he was to be going back. The visceral things of the world were still a bit too much for him, weren't they . . . was it that? Or was it the power? Or even worse than that? What would those fools from the Por-cellian and Fly Club think of him now? No, it was not power. Power was no substitute for strength. Kitty had given back his strength, thought Doctor Oppenheimer, forgetting the desert. Since Kitty there had been no looking back. The old feeling of ethical suffocation was gone. Or was it some attraction to violence that freed him? None of these things. It was the moral commitment to the World War and the pitiful, doomed, beseeching faces the mystery on the Mesa had at last brought him within reach of. No, he did not want the old morbid sensitivities back now, though it was dangerous to feel disgust for his true self. It spread to disgust for other things. No, he felt just the same. But the world out there was reorienting itself around him. And because he trusted his motives, Robert trusted the effect he was having.

He would just have to be tough, Robert thought, lying awake somewhere after Arizona. And keep close track of the mistakes. Back on the Mesa, with all the brains organized and focused, with enough fellows left over to track down the wilder, more exotic line of research . . . they would have a fast-fission by Christmas. Nine months or a year was not a lot to give up: to settle fission, and free the camps. Then they would all go back to the universities, and he would sort out the mistakes and contradictions. You could not get in that much trouble with yourself, in a year.

So wide awake in his bunk that he forgot he was not asleep, Robert propped his head against the jolting bulkhead. Gazing tenderly at the weak red bulb, Robert ran through all the names, faces and personalities waiting for him on the Mesa, until he knew them as well as himself. Until they *were* himself, all inhabiting the same soul – the way the things and people he had possessed by loving them or loved by possessing them, even his cars and houses, had names and rôles, as in some mysterous childish game. For everything in the natural world fell into patterns, like chess. Everything but good and evil, love and hate, and justice. Now, feeling the power and beauty waiting for him on his Mesa, where Oppy had named even the buildings and laboratories – the most dangerous, 'Omega' – a mystery lurked deep among the elements. How would it *be*, what would it look like when *it* came on the face of the earth? For the first time in his life, Doctor Oppenheimer's innermost soul and mind were at rest. He was committed to something bigger than himself.

Feeling at peace, Robert was suddenly asleep. The only wakeful thing was the faint red glow from the little emergency bulb.

Chapter 8

The stiffly gallant de Silva had himself driven Oppy and Mrs Oppenheimer from Santa Fe up the muddy Mesa trail into the security net.

The last section was by jeep. De Silva grinned genially at the lanky Director, now absorbed in the steep view of the canyon. The jeep motor ground whiningly in the deep mud. De Silva was very conscious of Mrs Oppenheimer listening in the wind behind.

'Glad to be getting back, Oppy sir?' de Silva shouted.

'I certainly am, Peer,' the Director called back. He gave the young West Pointer his sharp mysterious smile. 'How are you fellows getting on up here, everybody cooperating?'

They wove around a bend of pine roots, and De Silva steered for the hard dry mud. As always in the presence of Oppy's friendliness, de Silva experienced a violent inward alarm.

'Off the record, Oppy sir.' His stiff smile reddened. 'I'm not always sure the scientists learned their manners the same place you did, sir.'

De Silva knew how to grovel when he had to grovel. Beside him on the shuddering bucket seat, the tweedy director laughed.

'Well, off the record, Colonel Peer,' Oppy's soft voice confided, 'there are some pretty big egoists on the Hill.'

The Colonel's impression of something mysterious and weird in the seat beside him intensified. He kept nervously changing gears.

They had come out on the flat plateau near the barracks. De Silva yanked on the emergency brake. He jumped down on dry ground. With a chivalrous grin at the pretty woman staring ironically, de Silva lifted the Oppenheimers' bags out of the jeep. He disappeared between the clotheslines.

What had caught the Director's attention was the lack of activity inside the lab compound. Leaving Kitty to collect little Peter, Robert stumbled up over the red dirt toward Main Tech. The low green buildings had an abandoned look, like a campus out of term.

Did he only dream it, Robert thought, and felt an old panic. The great minds of the world here on his desert Mesa? How quickly it went cold on him. The Mesa never felt like this, packing up here on the paint pony.

But upstairs in his big pinewood office, Bethe welcomed Robert with a relieved outburst of gossip. There had been angry exchanges. The general level of jealousy was high.

General Groves had worsened this before he left for Washington by taking aside a dozen physicists, even Fermi and MacMillan, for day-long lectures on what they were forbidden to say to each other. Heavier locks were put on the laboratory doors. But the scientists could no more keep knowledge secret than lovers could hide their feelings. How did they expect men about to unlock the forces of the Creation to be disciplined by a Yale-bolt? The locks had been broken off the same night. The lawless physicists had gone back to their drugged moonlight passion; to the little groups plotting over work-benches like revolutionaries, arguing in front of blackboards, sitting in cold, delirious trances for hours in front of meter banks like an all night jazz band improvising a completely new music. Nursing his pipe, Robert listened nervously at Hans's desk.

But by morning Colloquium, the excitement of complete moral and technical freedom had returned. As the overcast burnt off, everyone knew Oppy was back.

Out of the spring of 1943, through the hot dry summer into the autumn yellowing of cottonwoods across the plateau, each sunrise Robert was up before the others to smoke his first pipe. And every morning all the scientists on the Mesa crowded eagerly into Theatre Two.

The tormenting impression left by the Berkeley trip quickly receded, along with the rest of the mundane world. A crackling lucidity was released in Robert's mind. Now the minds behind these gentlemanly, gazing faces – with a compounded power like that of X-rays to see through flesh, or neutrons to pass through matter – were focused into the seventeen-foot *Thin Man* fuselage, seeing a bright-green Uranium apple with the core punched out. Witnessing, inside that isotopic apple, the unseeable particle charges that held its substance in uncritical suspension. And seeing deeper inside these, the micro-instant when the balanced charges would be tripped. And beyond that, a rending of forces at a heat and violence no man had ever seen, could see, save in these quiet blackboard notations, like those of a deaf and blind composer.

Then it seemed to Robert that at last he was hearing the lovely music of the spheres. Ultimate violence, separated from him by a million light years of airless space. And this auditorium of scholars laughing and debating on folding chairs, jumping up to solilo-quize, were the superb instruments of his orchestra. Men deliver-ing orations on his secret Mesa the likes of which the holy desert had never heard. While the sparrows fought in the pine branches outside the window, charming tumultuous Teller, standing like some Aristophanes to make cosmic jokes about gods and geniuses; Von Neumann, sleepily running out formulae no one could follow; Stanislas Ulam, stately, sad and serene, full of old world civility. A talkative, urbanely friendly master like Fermi, or shy puritan dreamers like Neddermeyer, at first too daunted by the famous presences to speak out. And their ambitions all subsumed in one, so that truly it was like Plato's robed circle debating in inspired indolence on another Mesa, seated on the long cool stairs of the new Parthenon.

Yet sometimes they seemed only a faculty of privileged professors without students to think about. And among their ranks a few loveless ones, like hollow-eyed Leo Slotin, who knew already their student was mankind and the lesson being prepared. His was the Final Assembly.

The six hundred morning Colloquia were what all of them remembered long after. Still, there was one morning that first spring that Robert remembered best, a morning when a number of revelations came in less than two hours.

Chapter 9

One blazing canyon day had followed another. This morning in Main Tech, the faces, upturned with relaxed attention to hear a single guttural voice, were deeply suntanned. Through the pipe smoke over the podium table, they looked to Robert like a tight-knit commando of intellectual freedom fighters. At this hour, two or three of the youngest ones were still contemplating the fine French toast and Vermont maple syrup the army had inexplicably provided for breakfast. But the rest were listening alertly to Edward Teller, at present leaning on Fermi's chairback tuning up on the thermonuclear problem for some eventual fusion bomb.

It was getting very hot in the low pine room and many jackets had already come off. The dixie cup tank in the far corner was so empty you could not see it was not full.

Teller stood in the third row of chairs to the left of the podium, where the élite tended to gather. The swarthy face addressed Oppy formally, twisting sometimes with an explosive giggle to take in the crowd of uplifted faces. Robert gazed across thoughtfully at his civilized friend and protégé from Le Conte attic days. Seeing the Hungarian's theatrical grin fixed on him with a sort of presumptuous trust (like a child who expects to be adored simply because it trusts), Robert experienced an unmistakable stir of irritation. Why did Edward always have to rush off beyond the tedious technical struggles to a level of pure inspiration, to leave the music all of them were composing together and compose alone? What was this artistic longing for intellectual ecstasies? Keeping this great creative obsession to the work at hand was like gathering mercury from a broken thermometer.

Now, standing waist deep among the throng of men he knew respected him as the most powerful questor among them, Edward Teller fixed his eyes lovingly on the most gentle spiritual face in the room. Today he was feeling free and open and raw, and ideas erupted splendidly from his unconscious like some Ninth Symphony. Yet somewhere behind this sentimental charm of Budapest and Danube beer gardens, Edward Teller was thinking as he always thought. He, Edward, knew as well as any of these here what bloody antisemite beasts the Germans could be. Were not his parents in danger at that moment? But because he had grown up in Pest and Buda, on the doorstep of the Bolshevik Revolution, Edward Teller knew that Communism was the real enemy. Were not all of them here in this room practising German science? Was not the music they loved German music? Did not Teller remember the crushing of the civilized classes in Russia, the purges by Stalin, the disgusting executions of the entire Russian folksinging tradition in the Ukraine? Yes, he understood the romanticism of these folk-loving Americans. But to Edward Teller, civilization was sacred. Its future enemy was Russia, and the West must always have the strongest arm. Teller would see to it.

He shifted his feet heavily, blinking in the morning sun and smiling sweetly. He was thinking of the Superbomb.

'So we see . . .!' Doctor Teller continued gutturally in the profound silence, like someone telling a fairy tale to children, though in fact he was describing the unthinkable hell of heat and violence at the birth of a man-made sun, a power man had made no moral words to resist.

'So we see, the rate of heat transfer to the tritium shell incr-r-reases as T cubed! But the radiation pressure on the shell incr-r-reases only as T squared.'

On the pine auditorium wall, the clock ticked. The black arm jumped another minute. 9:17. In the corner, little Segre pulled his bony nose and raised his eyebrows. Bethe and Ulam both stared fixedly at the ceiling. In front of them Kistiakovsky nodded without seeming to hear, and smiled around at no one in particular. A little rustle of guarded excitement spread up the ranks of chairs. The electric silence deepened still further, neutron background to the focusing pressure of minds.

Doctor Oppenheimer was doubtful. He inspected his pipe bowl, then struck a match. 'On the thermonuclear problem, Edward, we invariably formulate back . . . back to the temperature factors.'

'No! No, there is no impossibility on this thing!' Teller's zest increased. The best part of the tale was yet to be told.

'Let me give you all my thoughts in unqualified factors. Clearly there is a term in the temperature distribution incr-r-reasing as an exponential factor of T . . . while the maximum shell velocity is linear.' Teller held up his thick finger triumphantly. 'Thus a singularity in the mean energy must occur!'

He beamed around him, eager to collect his reward of astonished adoration before going on. But Fermi and Bethe were avoiding his eyes. Feeling a crevasse of absurdity opening, but too excited to sit down, Teller turned hopefully to the face at the head of the auditorium.

The Director stared back dreamily at his friend's sensitive, stricken face. All right, he was thinking, Edward had laid his queen open, and maybe Robert should be kind. But if the game was for discipline of the laboratory and every day precious to help the Russians and beat Hitler to the draw, then Edward was losing a queen.

'You're the expert in this area, Edward,' Robert said politely, then giving his pipe three fierce little puffs. 'And this idea of using qualitative factors is a very promising approach. But do you think we should go so far as to treat the speed of light as unity?'

Behind a patient smile, winning the struggle against a giddy rush of pride at the perfect genius of his joke, Oppy watched Teller's blanched face smile back, alone above the level of the other faces mirthfully reddening under their tans. Up the crowded auditorium passed a little cruel chuckling ripple. Somehow reassuring that such a vaguely mad piece of cloud-walking close to their technical nemesis had not gone unpunished. Ignoring it, Dr Oppenheimer briskly switched the topic.

'All right then, if there is no objection?' Robert puffed vigorously. 'We'll give the rest of the morning to problem number one. Plutonium seems our most promising fuel . . . how best do we trigger it? George?'

For thirty tedious minutes, Fermi, Bethe and MacMillan debated restlessly with Kistiakovsky over the way neutrons might look entering and exiting nuclear orbits converging at different velocities. The Director impatiently broke them up.

'Would anyone care to inject some factors here? Seth?'

Even before Oppy had stopped speaking, a tall gaunt figure rose awkwardly against the sunny rear wall, which is the row the most timid students take, and where they are most visible to the teacher. The Modigliani face, solitary and remote as a crescent moon, stared over the plain of curious colleagues. It was with Seth that Robert had discovered mesons.

'I was just thinking,' the American said in a rather flat nasal voice.

'Louder, Seth!' Bruno Rossi called up, dropping the h. It was the first time this obscure American had opened his mouth.

'Well, I guess this is going to sound silly.' Seth's pale eyes travelled sightless down over the rows of heads, resting on Robert's forehead.

'But your explosive gun is only one dimension. Maybe two dimensions, three dimensions, would be better. Maybe you could make your Plutonium sphere critical by compressing it with an explosive gun. In three dimensions, I mean.'

For the second time that morning, a small spasm of anguish fluttered through the auditorium. Feeling himself out of his depth, Neddermeyer awoke with a shrug. He picked up the ripe persimmon from breakfast.

'I mean . . . well, if you push this fruit from one side . . . or many sides . . . well, the mass is going to escape. The fruit will splatter. But if you explode it simultaneously and with equal violence over the whole surface . . . the mass would not escape. Explode it violently enough? Maybe the nuclei would be compressed closer together. And if this fruit were your Plutonium sphere, then you would have a critical mass. Not explosion . . .' Neddermeyer frowned down at the overripe persimmon on his palm. 'Implosion.'

Down over the auditorium spread a rustle of sympathy. Outside, somewhere high above the Mesa in the New Mexico sky, an aeroplane droned fitfully. The sound seeming to waver, jump and percolate in the desert sky.

'Interesting!' Kistiakovsky burst out. 'But you know about explosives?'

'Not much,' Neddermeyer said, almost hopefully.

'And haf you ton ze maths?' Von Neumann enquired.

'Well a little. No, not really anything exhaustive,' Seth apologized.

'O.K., we'll think about that one,' Oppy's voice cut in.

The many male voices of Theatre Two orated on toward noon, while outside a military policeman stood at ease on the wood steps of Main Tech.

Chapter 10

'Seth, could you come up to my office for a minute?'

'Thanks prof, I'd be delighted.' Neddermeyer pushed politely after the rumpled figure with the thick bundle of papers, shyly shouldering the noisy crowd of world-famous faces grouping in the hall.

Seth had been one of Robert's first students in Pasadena days. Due to this coincidence he was now on this desert plateau where great names would be made. Seth felt better when the rumble of voices cut off behind the stairs.

Priscilla pulled the office door shut behind them. Through the open windows in the far-off haze, the Albuquerque desert was greyish yellow. The two men faced each other over the wide desk.

'Prof, I haven't had a chance yet,' Seth muttered awkwardly, knitting his fingers and drawing up his shoulders, 'to tell you what a wonderful experience this is for me.'

Robert leaned back in his chair. His eyes gazed evenly into Neddermeyer's.

'Quite a bunch, aren't they?' he reflected. Both men spoke with an unaffected warmth. Seth had known him long before Robert knew power. 'Things will get much harder,' he added.

'Nothing could be harder,' Neddermeyer said with feeling, 'than imagining myself back in Washington. Hope you're not going to fire your old student for shooting off his mouth down there?'

Across the stacks of documents the Director raised his eyebrows. The irony in his even stare deepened.

'Seth, we have quite a few problems to solve up here.'

'Most of them critical.' Neddermeyer drew in his shoulders.

'And instead of getting fewer,' Robert frowned, tapping his teeth with his pipe stem, 'each day we seem to have a few more. Now you bring me, not a problem . . . a whole new conception.'

Suddenly sitting here in Oppy's spacious office, Seth Neddermeyer was feeling light-headed in a way he did not quite understand. In a way Vannevar Bush at the Uranium Department in Washington had fathomed better the previous autumn, hearing General Groves speak of hundred millions. A way Robert Oppenheimer had understood less well, frowning at the fog over San Francisco Bay from his driveway at Eagle Hill. Forgetting the mountains, the far-off plain and towering sky beyond his old teacher's head, Neddermeyer was concentrated on the serene gentle face by the portrait of President Roosevelt.

'Oh, that was completely nutty!' He licked his dry lips.

'Seth, I'd like you to take all the men you need. Find out all there is to know about implosion.'

'Two or three, you mean?' Seth muttered.

'A dozen or more, Seth.' Robert waved his long fingers. 'Of course the concept's probably useless for the war. But we're up here to expand knowledge . . . and who knows? So be aggressive, take a lot of minds and work them hard.'

'All right Prof, I'll do my best.' Neddermeyer sighed heavily and flushed, rocking slowly back and forth in the chair. The reflection from someone's spectacles below fluttered over the pine wall. In those few moments of shocked silence in Neddermeyer's life, a storm of ideas, possibilities and theories boiled up in his head. And more pressing than any of them, including implosion, came an idea that had been spoiling his sleep for the last few days.

'Can I . . . maybe it's not the moment.' Seth was suddenly mumbling. 'Now you *are* going to fire me!'

And Neddermeyer groaned, feeling his new rôle already slipping away. Abruptly the thing could not wait. Another minute would kill him.

'Go ahead, Seth. No one's firing anyone.'

Neddermeyer was already forward on the chair edge, elbows on the desk.

'I'll fire *myself* for this,' Seth said hurriedly, keeping his voice down and looking at the door. 'This is just so insane. And of course it couldn't be, or none of us would be here! I mean, I can't think about it and keep on behaving normally.'

Oppy crossed his arms on the desk, puffing his pipe nervously. He glanced at Neddermeyer's greying temples.

'I'm so sorry, Seth,' he said. 'Are you seriously ill?'

Neddermeyer laughed painfully. He licked his lips. 'Sick! Oh gladly, gladly!'

'Out with it then, old man.'

'This is going to sound so nuts . . .' Seth took a deep breath. 'Okay, well, I've been toying around with the mathematics.'

The two physicists broke it off. A knock had rattled the office door. Immediately Fermi's face appeared, grinned impishly at Robert then at the despair on the young visitor's face.

'I am interrupting something, I hope.'

'Avanti Enrico,' Robert said. 'I'm giving Seth a crew for implosion.'

'Oh yes, that was very nice,' the Italian said. 'Not sublime. But a little neeftee, eh?'

Fermi took a chair. He peered at Seth's miserable face.

'Go on, Seth,' Robert said. 'It's all in the family.'

Neddermeyer's drawn face was now tinged with green. To say what he was about to say, before the world's greatest Nobel physicist after Einstein! Seth hid his face from the expectant eyes. He fixed a gaze filled with longing on the tips of the pines outside the window.

'. . . toying around with the mathematics,' he went on hollowly. 'The maths of . . . well, the heat an uncontrolled fission might generate, taking nitrogen reactions into account . . . well the heat figures ran . . . ran out to infinity . . .' Seth's voice trailed away, swallowed in total, universal darkness.

'Bravo! Bravo, Neddermeyer!' Fermi interrupted enthusiastically, slapping his leg. A little cloud of dust rose over the desk. Fermi emphasized his delight by squeezing the American's shoulder.

'Robbie, you see? He has found out how our bomb could make a phoenix and incinerate all the water and air on earth! Bravo, Neddermeyer, you are only the second recruit on our magic mountain to work it!'

The sick alarm had vanished from Seth's face. He sank back in the armchair staring at them in a wondering paralysis.

'If we will do that . . . I mean, excuse me,' Seth said quietly. 'Then what are we doing on the Hill?'

'Oh, Teller came up with these figures, Seth, last summer at Le Conte,' Robert said pleasantly. 'He had us all a little worried. But we've refined it down to a slim possibility.'

'Two? Or was it five in a million chances?' Fermi philosophized 'It is curious, however. The major decisions of my life, they were not made by numbers. Our planet is not such a bad place, despite man. I particularly love Taormina – in Sicily,' the Italian added for Neddermeyer.

As Fermi made this last comment, the office door opened again. Hans Bethe stepped in. He hesitated, delicately dignified.

'Do I interrupt?' Bethe said slowly. 'Aha. Enrico, I hoped to find you in Oppy's office.'

'Well, Seth,' Robert grinned playfully, poking the air with his pipe. 'I hope you'll sleep better tonight.'

'I guess so.' Neddermeyer got quickly to his feet. He was suddenly feeling a quite unscientific need to be out in the open air. Alone, away from these giants of physics.

'Thanks for everything, prof. I guess I'd better get to work.'

'Keep me posted,' Robert said vaguely. 'Oh and Seth, keep off the solar-phoenix theme with the others. We haven't the time.'

'Oh . . . sure,' Neddermeyer called back through the open doorway.

'The door, Neddermeyer, the door!' Fermi shouted gaily.

Hans Bethe reclined elegantly in the chair Neddermeyer had left empty. He smoothed back his long hair with both hands. The office door banged shut. The director of the American atom project was alone with his great German and Italian colleagues.

'Well, Hans?' Robert made a face. 'Is it Edward again?'

'Teller absolutely *will* not do what he is supposed to!' Bethe began sadly. He and Teller were close friends, but such incurable obsession could weary any friendship.

'It is a stupendous ability,' Fermi mused, suddenly serious.

'We need him to work on fission rates,' Bethe went on. 'Instead he hides down in Y-Lab whipping his disciples into ecstasies over solar-fusion.'

'Has the bomb gotten any smaller?' Robert said sharply. 'After all, couldn't we use Klaus Fuchs instead?'

'Absolutely no smaller,' Bethe mused. 'A whole beer-vat full of refrigerated Tritium.'

There was another loud banging at the office door. The three gentlemen looked around and saw Teller's heavy flushed face poke in with a genial grin. Seeing their sober faces it started to pull back.

'Oh, Edward!' Robert half rose behind his desk. 'Edward, please come in. We were just speaking of you.'

Teller came back through the door. He gave a guilty apologetic giggle that left no room for them not to forgive him. Slipping playfully behind Robert's chair, Teller sat on the windowsill. His dusty shoes dangled.

'Gr-reetings . . . greetings!' he said. 'Oh ye of little faith!'

'Ed,' Robert broke the strained silence. He fixed the Hungarian with a bemused stare. 'What we are here to do is to build a bomb as quickly as possible to end this war. Your bomb might be bigger.

But the people dying in the camps cannot wait twenty years.'

'I know, I know!' Teller burst out with feeling. 'This is so true and very tragic, Robert. Okay, okay, then, you must tell me very seriously. How long do I have to make the Super portable?'

Robert's pipe smoke had filled the office. He reached over and pushed the window wide open. The sound of children's voices came to them out of the spring hush. Fermi and Bethe exchanged looks.

'No time, I would say.' Robert looked evenly at the thick kind face begging playfully not to be chastened. '. . . no time at all, Edward.'

But as Oppy, Bethe and Fermi all watched their strange friend's on and off smile, half hurt, half not listening to them at all, all three had the same disconcerting premonition. An impression of something too mercurial, too vast to be harnessed, a primordial ambition it was futile to waste words on.

Downstairs, the Main Tech entrance hall was still crowded with debating sages. No one noticed Neddermeyer pass among them, out the open doors. On the steps, the gawky Englishman Tuck was ribbing the young guard about the MP stencilled on his white helmet. The Yank had never heard of Parliament.

Seth pulled on his flop hat. A hundred yards from the buildings, he stopped on the red dirt outside a circle of shady pines. With a groan, Seth breathed in deep the dry spiced air of the Mesa. Two months ago, he thought, I was an obscure social servant with no future. Just now, I was lifted among the great names of physics.

Fixing his pale eyes hungrily on the hazed horizon of the Albuquerque plain, the American felt himself slowly shrink back to a healthy insignificance. But instead of feeling happy with himself, or moved, Neddermeyer kept asking himself what he had just heard up there. What were they saying? Had the old friend and teacher, whose completeness he had never doubted, just told Seth Neddermeyer not to speak openly of the 'burning up the earth' theory?

And remembering the heady mood back in the Director's cramped office, Neddermeyer felt a horrible guilt before the naive magnificence of the day and great sleepy blue sky. It was as if he had been conspiring against them.

Chapter 11

By that summer the shanty town of tarboard barracks, laboratories, warehouses, hutments and even trailers had taken on the character of a chosen hamlet, in which not quite everyone knew everyone. Even General Groves, having called up the very ghost of all those remote, depressing boot camps, could not keep from flirting with Oppy's mystique of an enlightened crusade and quite unsoldierly enthusiasm for hardship. They were a frontier camp of revolutionaries, not at all tragic or spent like the Indians at the pueblos of Taos and Acoma, soon the dark forces of Europe would feel the wrath of their elements. Yet even with its mainstreet shops and cinema, Los Alamos was a hamlet without surrounding farms, without church, banks or official brothels, bars or bums or soda fountains, or even a through road for trade or travellers to stray along. The fable of a community but without a community's sustaining human body.

And up in this secret shanty town only Oppy seemed to know what that fable was. More than Bethe or Fermi, Ed Teller, Groves or anyone else, Oppy generated every aspect of the Mesa's functioning, its philosophy and ethical place in civilization and the universe. And somehow Robert and Kitty were finding it increasingly necessary to stay aloof, and keep a certain part of each day for themselves. Usually it was in the hours between nightfall and ten o'clock, long before the thinkers in the all-night laboratories, trekking obsessively into the mysterious new continent of unexplored elements, were finally overcome by sleep.

They lived with little Pete and entertained in the heartbroken headmaster's one-storey stone and log house, facing south. Groves had ordered that not a cent of the Army's hundred millions should be spent on the smallest comforts for these conceited eggheads, so the Oppenheimers' bare rooms were relatively grand.

Leaning on the open windowsill one moonlit night in the first week of June, Kitty was watching the iridescent mist drift over the forest tips, the distinct greenish light and shadow of the river canyon below. Beyond that was a flat ghostly sea, the great desert Kitty could only tell from a plain of snow by the warm air on her

116

bare arms. Over this scene of peace were fixed the brilliant desert stars; presiding among their twinkling legions, the near-full moon. Its familiar tantalizing patches were like the faded islands of some mediaeval treasure map.

Following the slow descent of a flashing red light between the stars, Kitty smelled the sweet scent of English pipe tobacco. Over towards the plywood barracks, she heard Teller's piano suddenly break into a rippling passage in the Emperor Concerto.

In his chair by the weak reading lamp, Robert stirred.

'Say, Kitty, listen to this,' he said. 'I'll translate.' Held open on his knee was the short Bhagavad Gita, which records the battlefield debate of Prince Arjuna and the Hindu demi-god Krishna, more than three thousand years ago.

Kitty turned quickly from the window without smiling. Tucking her nightgown behind her knees, she curled in the facing chair and stared critically at the gentle face bent over the book. She had noticed Robbie reading more and more books recently, especially religious ones.

'Remember, Kat.' He looked up at her. '*Knowledge* opens the infinite . . . *love* evolves and transforms everything to light. This is Krishna!'

'All right darling, go ahead.' Kitty lit a cigarette and watched him.

'If . . .' Robbie translated quickly, forgetting his pipe. 'If the light of a thousand suns suddenly arose in the sky, that splendour might be compared to the radiance of the supreme spirit.'

There was a deep silence in the living room. Robert rustled the page.

'. . . and Arjuna doubts himself,' Robert muttered, the veins standing out on his temples: ' "Reveal thyself to me. I adore thee and long to know thee, for I understand not thy works." Now listen, Kat! Krishna answers Arjuna: "I am all powerful *time* which destroys all things, and I have come here to slay these men. But if thou doest not fight, all the warriors facing thee shall die!" '

Robert glanced up. Kitty was smiling ironically.

'That's pretty good, darling. But isn't there enough religion in the Old Testament?'

'Which?' Robert's left eye twitched impatiently. Didn't she see

117

it was the justification of their bomb-quest?

'You're just thinking,' Kitty said, 'of Moses getting his Ten Commandments. Remember? Moses wanted to *see* God.'

'Well, we're certainly going to see something along those lines!'

'I wonder if it will be God, darling.'

'God's a lot to live up to,' Robert smiled. This time Kitty had kept up.

She lifted her martini from the magazine table with the blue envelope. The ice in the martini had melted.

'The Eleventh Commandment,' Kitty lowered her voice, 'ought to be not working for governments.'

'Another from Jean. I haven't opened it yet.'

'No need to, darling,' she said. 'Somebody else already has.'

'They can't make an exception for us, Kitty.'

'Doesn't it disgust you, Robbie?' Kitty's lowered voice was suddenly husky with throttled rage. 'They are all over the hill spying, listening, dressing as carpenters. How can *we* trust people like that?'

'What fools they are!' Robert twisted irritably. He added, with an apologetic smile: 'Still, I'm no dictator.'

'Who's the boss up here?' Kitty objected, eyes glittering.

'I am not going to push anyone around.' He leaned forward close to the small woman. 'We'll all have to live with the thing.'

'And what about your girl friend,' Kitty whispered. 'It's her fifth letter. Jean doesn't seem to be living with very much.'

Hearing someone's shoes trip somewhere out on the hard mud, Robert and Kitty were both whispering. Kitty's face hardened with temperament.

'Psychiatrists . . . turning to religion? Robbie stared at his hands. 'Jean sounds at the bitter end. I guess I'll have to see her this trip out.'

They were by the open window, knees touching. He felt Kitty's breath. The Los Alamos night closed around their lonely dim words.

'While I stay up here under guard.' She raised her eyebrows, her hands around her locked shins. 'We're captives, isn't it silly?'

'Only nine months more,' Robert promised, and an angry excitement came into his eyes. 'Think, Kat, this Army machine can free the camps! For *them* in the barbed wire, every day counts.'

Kitty searched in her husband's face with a little astonished laugh, following his hands curiously. Robert had put down the Sanskrit and picked up a magazine.

'Haakon sent this review. There's a new poem in it about you.'

Robert glanced in the woman's glittering dilated eyes.

' "His anima liked its animal," ' he read suggestively, ' "and liked it unsubjugated. So that home was a return to birth. Desiring fiercely, the child of a mother fierce in his body, fiercer in his mind, merciless to accomplish the truth in his intelligence." Wallace Stevens.'

Robert's voice trailed off. He laid the review under the lamp, Kitty grasping his free hand. She met his look with a mocking light.

'What a strange good man you are,' she whispered, lifting his hand to her mouth. 'What a wonder.'

'Goodness again!' Robert laughed. He saw her bare arms stretching under the lamp. 'What is all this talk of goodness, not from unsubjugated you?'

Beyond Los Alamos in the night, the red light Kitty saw flashing among the stars over Santa Fe had come to earth. General Groves, Colonel Landsdale, Nichols and Lillie were already approaching the Bandelier road in a jeep.

As Kitty switched off Robert's reading lamp, the jeep lights were jiggling nervously up the canyon flank.

Chapter 12

The whole bumpy flight out from the East Coast by Army Dakota, Groves and Landsdale had argued their way through the thick bundle of secret FBI reports and photostats concerning the Director of the Army's Atom Bomb Project.

Now both officers were exhausted and depressed. It was the first time either man had seen this new file, and both had come to the not unliterary conclusion that Doctor Oppenheimer did not look the same in the flesh as he did on paper. Landsdale was a southern Academy gentleman with a Harvard Law degree, who had conducted a purge of Spanish Civil War volunteers from the Army. He had also made a study of the Berkeley Communist circle. But tonight he was frankly shocked. Was the global balance of power between America, Russia and Germany really resting in such enigmatic hands? Groves, who was more familiar with the flesh and blood of Oppy and with his guilty goodness, was trying to imagine how this Project that was making Groves famous might look without its mastermind. But apparently bureaucracy required that the human mystery at least be cleared up. 'Made legal,' Landsdale called it. So the officers agreed to meet again. Next morning in de Silva's office, while the eggheads were occupied with their Colloquium.

At nine o'clock sharp, General Groves and the baby-faced Southerner sat down facing each other. The desk was bare save for a thick manila folder. One hour ticked away.

'All right sir,' Landsdale began again in his gracious drawl. 'Let's run it through again. First, the meeting with Steve Nelson.'

'That was three times!' Groves frowned indignantly. 'And two years ago.'

'Well sir, we know for certain Nelson is spying for the Ruskies.'

'Not up here he isn't.' Groves took out a Baby Ruth candy bar. He began peeling the waxed wrapper. God, but he hated these Harvard types! Of the two, Groves now felt sure he preferred Oppy.

'Well then, sir, shall we consider?' Landsdale drawled on with leathery graciousness. 'The Federation of Architects . . . Friends of the Chinese People . . . Teacher's Local 349 . . . Consumers Union . . . Committee for Democracy and Intellectual Freedom. There are Communists in all of them.'

'Architecture and intellectual freedom doesn't sound too bad.' Groves chewed imperiously.

'A quarter of the man's income to the Lincoln Brigade? And his brother Frank a Party member . . .'

'Frank's an even bigger child than his brother.'

'His old flame Tatlock a Red?'

'Tatlock's gone religious. And our man's married now!' General Groves parried bitterly. He could feel the very foundation of his career being pounded at.

'Mrs Puening Dallet Oppenheimer was a Communist,' Landsdale thrust home politely. 'Why sir, she was at the heart of the Party with fellows like Gus Hall. Kitty's practically an apparat-chik!'

Groves' sun-pinkened face went pale. He spoke gruffly: 'Hoover's a filthy-minded SOB if there ever was one!'

'Fine, Leslie sir.' Landsdale leaned back, chin on fingertips. 'I don't care too much for this junk either. But let's see where the Doctor's loyalty lies. The country can't afford any accidents at this level.'

The officers' bated voices trailed away in awkward silence. For here General Groves too was at a loss. When Groves was at Oppy's side, the Director's honesty and patriotism seemed inspired. But when Groves was alone again, he no longer remembered what Oppy's passionate patriotism consisted of, any more than what a 'meson' was. Where *did* Doctor Oppenheimer's loyalty lie, Groves thought? And he felt an emotion like that of a lover who longs to possess even the religious life of the beloved.

'Robert Oppenheimer is the most discreet man I ever met!' Groves swore suddenly, with a sort of threatening indignation, and he swallowed a mouthful of chocolate and peanuts unchewed. 'Just who do you think, John, rounded up all these crackpots in the first place? Do you think they'd listen to anyone else?'

'Then you wouldn't mind, sir, if I put our man under close watch?' Landsdale murmured thoughtfully. The Southerner swivelled his chair. His cold blue eyes shifted from Groves's sweat-beaded bulk to the view over the magic plateau. He had shot grouse and puma in country like this.

'For Lord's sake, General!' he mused. 'That man comes and goes . . . lonely and free as those little desert clouds out there. Say, what's that banging? Target practice?'

'Fellow called Neddermeyer blasting tin cans,' Groves muttered glumly.

'Do we pay him to do that?' Landsdale shook his head disgust-edly. But suddenly he sat forward at the window. 'I thought you said the Doctor was in the auditorium!'

'Always at this hour,' Groves stirred impressively.

'Well, there he goes! And he's got a suitcase.'

Landsdale swivelled to the desk with a weary glance at Groves. He lifted the telephone.

'Hello? . . . Landsdale here!' He controlled his voice. 'Give me section 5 . . . 5!5! Goddam it! Oh, good morning Henry. I forgot to mention . . . Dr Oppenheimer has been assigned a bodyguard for this trip to the coast. Understand? Yes, he just left. Pick him up at the station.'

Colonel Landsdale delicately put back the receiver. His round cheeks were very red.

Chapter 13

That long summer night Pullman, clicking back West into the everyday world of men, Robert, for whom neither physics nor Kitty's rebellious background were secrets, experienced an intensifying dread of seeing Jean Tatlock again. Robert was quite glad to have the company of the young, half-breed officer from Montana, who had overtaken him on the Sante Fe platform. It amused him to be travelling with an aide-de-camp, like poor fat Groves himself. So he bought young Charlie some drinks and dinner, and they talked for a while about his farm boyhood and conditions at Crow Agency, and how Navajo Indians were being used to transmit secret messages in the Pacific war zone. It was good to have the constant Mesa dust off their shoes.

But through the next days, letting Charlie chauffeur him around the Bay Area marshalling eager scientists and contractors, his sidekick's vague awkwardness did not relieve Doctor Oppenheimer's impression of the burden of himself on ordinary men. He felt it more without Kitty's sexy confidence. The membrane of public ignorance they had noticed on Kitty's last trip down, which divided the mind-god of the Mesa from the friendly faces Robert saw in the street, was gone now. Oppy was no longer the inspired thinker alone with the forces in the heavens, he was their emissary. He carried the desert experiment with him, scarcely remembering its awe. And somehow Jean was feeling his power. With her heart fixed on Robert, Jean was still disintegrating.

Keep calm. Don't be nuts! Robert repeated irritably to himself. He even forgot to light his pipe as Charlie steered him up past the White House display windows and Saint Francis Hotel awning. Robert had kept his last evening free for Jean before he caught the night-train back to Sante Fé. She couldn't know what he had been doing! Somehow, though, Robert could not rid himself of an impression that in some way Jean did know. In this oppressed mood, it almost seemed that everyone else knew too.

All day a sultry fog had tenderly mantled San Francisco and the Bay. But to Robert it was like a poison mist. Now Charlie was inching the black Dodge uphill, behind the narrow-gauge Polk Street cablecar, its running boards overhanging on both sides with businessmen going home. Robert wished morbidly he was one of them, not going where he was going.

He climbed out on a steep street corner, thanking Charlie with a vague gesture. He would find his own way to the station.

'See you back at site-Y, Doc!' Charlie stared out uncertainly.

'Don't worry,' Robert laughed, 'I won't get in trouble up here!'

The car u-turned then plunged, steeply vanishing in the fog. The Director of the Atom-Bomb project lingered dreamily on the corner pavement. But it was good to be on his own after so many months!

Tucking his London raincoat against the ocean-smelling mist, Robert remembered to light his pipe. Then he strolled in his distracted, flat-footed way along the half-empty sidewalk, along the white clapboard houses of Telegraph Hill. You certainly saw a lot of handsome high-collared white Navy uniforms in the streets. No one was paying attention to Robert.

Four short blocks further, Robert's steps slowed. His stomach tightened. Three porches along, between the palm and the cactus, was the Tatlock house. In the mood of that afternoon, needing to see her saved by her feeling for him, Robert jumped nervously up the steps. He pushed the bell. Other steps were running toward the door.

Abruptly an indistinct face was in front of him.

'Oh Robbie . . . Robbie sweetheart!'

'Hello Jeanie, hello,' Robert said. The slight young woman was pressed familiarly in his arms.

As the door shut behind them they moved, clutched awkwardly, across the silent hall carpet, and Robert felt her surprising wildness. The guilt began to lift, poisonous mists to clear from the city. Jean held him back. She was in a pale velvet sheath.

123

'You've come at last,' Jean whispered.

'Yes Jean, I'm here,' Robert said with equal relief. Jean's hair was longer, her pretty face more animated. *Of course she knew nothing at all . . .* he was free!

And for a moment, Robert tasted again what he had never known he was forgetting: the sweetness of bachelor days, when he had been a bright vulnerable Harvard romantic about San Francisco, with money and the prestige of his European physics, and uncluttered by family. When he had beaten his past with Jean, working for nameless migrants, and all the hordes who lived forgotten and undefended. The flavour of that discovery came back now in warm waves, with the lonely streak of mesons in the winds of space, the wierdness of quantum jumps, and biblical awe of collapsing suns. In that vivid happiness, as Jean pushed a second door to draw Robert into a small dining-room with New England furniture, he felt strong enough to deal with her.

'The suntan suits you,' Jean said.

Robert grinned from Jean's stylish dress to the polished oval table, precisely arranged with crystal and silver. Two candles were already flickering. No, Jean would not suffocate him any more. Then remembering wartime San Francisco spread out promisingly under the Pacific night, Robert thought he might show off.

'First let's go to the Mark,' he said.

'Anywhere, Robbie, anywhere at all.'

Their view from the candlelit room-lounge at the Mark Hopkins Hotel was a planetarium upside down. The coloured lights and necklaces of the Golden Gate spread out around. There were Jap submarines somewhere out there. But in the lounge full of Navy men, it was too noisy to satisfy Robert's curiosity about Jean. What was this certainty she was finally in love with him, now he was married to someone else? After three martinis he took Jean home to Telegraph Hill. As soon as they were alone, he was sorry.

'Now you wait here,' Jean said when they were back in the narrow Tatlock dining-room. Her voice was suddenly strange. Jean took nervous steps over the carpet to the swinging door. 'That's your place there,' she pointed to a chair with its back to Robert. Glancing at him, for some reason not meeting his eyes, Jean went out. The bright kitchen lights swung on and off.

Robert waited, awkwardly alone in the windowless room. He listened to the privileged silence through the Tatlock house. Were they sitting down to dinner right away, with no sentimental catching up on each other's lives? Robert remembered then the obsessive letters, and the psychiatrists. Abruptly, each thing that had happened since he walked through Jean's door seemed unnatural and fear-ridden. In an instant, the heroic mood of the last hour was spoiled. His old guilty chaos rolled back over the city.

Rubbing both bony cheeks, Robert gave a little agitated groan. He stepped to the polished table and sank on the chair. In the sickening hush, the legs wobbled.

'Where are your parents?' Robert asked.

Jean had come from the bright kitchen, balancing an imitation Ming tureen.

'They've gone, sweetheart.' Jean rested the hot dish on a straw mat. Her eyes met his over the ladle, and Robert felt his worst impression confirmed. He tried to concentrate. Their conversation was halting.

'Staying with friends in Marin.' Jean tilted her head brittly. 'Turtle soup?'

Fear started up from Robert's stomach, his cheeks burned.

'Oh yes,' Robert laughed, 'your soup.'

Jean was sitting forward, wrists on the table edge. Seeing him watching her, she drew her knees back from him.

'Robbie,' she said, 'why are you so cold to me?'

The veiled silent walls closed secretly around their little table.

'I could never be cold to you, Jean,' Robert answered quickly, taking out his pipe. 'I feel, I just am not sure what to tell you.'

Jean let out her breath. She stared at his hands with a nervous laugh.

'Sweetheart, you don't have to tell me anything.'

Jean looked up in his face with the threatening certainty Robert had noticed back on the Mark. Now he felt like an impostor at someone else's party.

'I understand everything,' Jean sighed. Lowering her eyes she began hurriedly spooning her soup. 'Robbie, it's been like this for such a long time.'

'What has, Jean?' Robert felt for his spoon.

'Everybody's life is so sad.' Jean licked her lips and went on. 'This war, sweetheart. The poor and the ones being crushed, always so. The rich will always lie, and pretend not to enjoy the suffering of others. Everywhere there'll be cruelty, death.'

In the horrible silence, Robert heard the failure in her words. He stared through the candles at her averted face. Whatever was in him, which had been a power to do universal good, was crushing Jean to death.

'My cruelty, Jeanie?' Robert's voice as unnatural as hers.

Jean examined his face triumphantly. 'Never you, you could never be cruel.' Her voice had taken on the humourless pity he remembered. 'Behind that arrogance you're as gentle as a lamb.'

'I'm no lamb,' Robert laughed hollowly. 'The soup's wonderful.'

Across her parents' crystal, Jean watched every motion he made. 'My God,' he suddenly heard her voice saying. 'It's death to live without you. How did I ever think I could.'

'Jean, I'm married!' Robert heard himself. 'I'm married.'

The face under the black bangs tilted, as if he had said something very bizarre.

'*She*'s been married three times, Robbie!'

'We've settled down, Jean,' he insisted, defending Kitty back in their little barracks overlooking the desert. Here in the raw intimacy of the Tatlock house, he was floundering in this absurdity. Or was she trying to embarrass him? For some reason he laughed.

Jean abruptly stood up. And seeing her sensitive fingers lift the bread basket, then put it back, Robert was suddenly desperate to see Jean saved. Kitty, the Mesa, his friends and his life's work all fell away.

'You can't love *her*,' Jean said with gentle patience.

'In many ways,' Robert held it together, 'she's very much like you.'

'Your wife is not at all like me!' Jean's voice broke, she shivered. 'No, positively not at all.'

Sitting back on the wobbly chair, Robert went pale. 'Perhaps not very much,' he said stiffly.

'Robbie, you can be an awfully cruel man.' Jean's eyes flashed scornfully. 'All cold reason. Not an ounce of feeling.'

You mustn't let her treat you like this! a voice told Robert. But the poisonous accusing mists were pressing him down. 'That's not just,' he said, spiralling in guilt.

Jean had sat down in the shadows.

'Of course it's not, I'm so happy you're here.' She laughed chokingly. 'Can you imagine, happiness? After a whole year of misery, my only love is back.'

Robert got up. Knees weak, scarcely trusting himself to keep his balance, he went unsteadily around the table.

'"You'll stay with me?' Jean had gripped his wrists. 'Won't you? You'll stay with me?'

'I wish that I . . .' Robert touched her hair, dead feeling.

'You won't?' Jean groaned. 'You can't leave me alone, not in the night!'

'If I could convince you, tell you.' Robert rambled numbly on. 'If you could only see as I see.' Then abruptly, he was speaking more sincerely than he had spoken of anything human, since a glorious noon in the Santa Cruzes. Her madness aroused him. 'That despite everything, Jean . . . life's worth it!'

Forgetting her tears, the girl beside Robert gazed fixedly. She moved, and Robert felt his face crushed against Jean's collar buttons. 'That everything regenerates, comes back,' he went on against her white blouse. 'what you can't do is allow yourself doubt.'

'Sermons!' Jean groaned. 'Sermons and sermons!'

'Don't, please don't!' Robert said ruthlessly. And at that moment Robert felt his will reach a deep accusing knot of misery where his world was disintegrating. 'Please Jean, please! I won't leave you alone, don't worry.'

Holding each other clumsily in this room where they had been alone with human disaster, Robert gradually felt her sobs dwindle away. But after being demolished with guilt, he felt a vague disappointment, how quickly Jean recovered. He certainly hoped the Tatlocks stayed away.

Out in the wet garden, night had come in. A fog smelling of kelp absorbed the delicate colours of the rhododendrons, and darkened imperceptibly. Far out past the eucalyptuses of the Presidio, in the moonlight under the stars, the fog lay piled in great drifts about the Golden Gate bridge. Hidden under the fog, cutting the long cold

Pacific swell, a wolf pack of three submarines was slipping out to the war. And one by one as the cruel deckless boats reached open water, they silently ran under. Carrying little sealed worlds of men down into the dark.

In the sultry overcast California morning, they sat like two ageing college lovers in the Tatlock kitchen.

But when Jean told him soberly that this was her last chance and asked him not to leave her, a bitter warning she did not quite understand hardened on Robert's face. Feeling herself guilty and condemned, Jean drove him without a word down the marshy Bay shore to San Mateo for a flight to New Mexico.

They kissed goodbye outside the noisy aerodrome building, muffled in their raincoats. Neither smiled. Jean took a step back and gave him a strange look.

Well, Doctor Oppenheimer was thinking, as he hesitated by the gangway to smile crookedly and wave to the little figure alone at the wire fence, it *is* your country, isn't it? After all, to save Jean through the night, hadn't the Director broken his solemn word to Groves not to risk flying? And suddenly Robert felt vividly the crushing power of that efficient machine of human enlightenment waiting for him. He stifled the beginning of another guilt.

As the circling aircraft climbed over the south bay, bouncing and swaying, Doctor Oppenheimer stared down at the underwater patterns. They were invisible from the ground.

Chapter 14

The same afternoon, Oppy was back in time to hear the latest excitement over neutron background from Bethe, Fermi and Ulam. No one seemed to notice any flaw in his mastery, and Robert found no reason to upset Kitty or anyone else over the night he gave poor Jean. It was another of the little deceptions Doctor Oppenheimer was allowing himself. White lies to ease the burden of staying good in time of national sacrifice.

Several days after Oppy had resumed his usual place, conducting the instruments of pure reason in the music of the spheres, there was another Colloquium on Cottonwood plateau, one which no one mentioned to the genius of the Mesa. It was a meeting which belonged to the secret catacombs of mirrors and bureaucratic mazes General Groves had built under his science hens on the Mesa, undermining, dividing and securing every inch of the barnyard they strutted, so the eggheads would deliver to him alone their mysterious power, the child of their minds. The absolute egg of their obsessions.

Colonel Landsdale was almost finished tightening the security screen around Groves's camp of gossipy eccentrics; of Jews, quasi-revolutionaries, fuzzy-brained idealists and other such foreigners. The Southerner was about to leave for Washington when someone appeared at Los Alamos to see him.

By now there were almost five hundred strangers swarming among the cottonwoods and shanty towns. No one took notice of this officer, who had set aside his post at Berkeley to pay the secret Mesa a visit. The stocky Chief of 9th Army Counter-Intelligence was in khakis. But he had little else in common with Landsdale, who was of good Maryland stock, nor with the dashing West-pointer de Silva. In fact, this jowelled person with the light-blue staring eyes had only received a few weeks' training in spy-hunting upon joining the Army three years ago. If this did not seem scant reason to consider Landsdale's visitor a fit expert on virtue among the physics' geniuses, it was worth contemplating the man's curious background as a physical-education instructor and relief-worker in Russia. And if anyone still doubted their visitor's authority as a voice on American innocence, one last fact clinched it. Colonel Boris Pash, Landsale's guest at the secret meeting in de Silva's office, was a second generation Russian. The son of a typical Russian émigré family, dedicated to the tradition of a lost golden age before the Bolsheviks introduced the proletarian lie. Of an uprooted class, still steeped in the Byzantine social intricacies of Czarist times, and of Russians generally; and vain of their talent for detecting (sometimes also producing) the Kremlin's agents. And seeing darkly beyond all such intrigues, the bolshevik Satan incarnate, Joseph Stalin.

Colonel Pash, who had the solemnity of a much older man, placed his fingertips together, his expression not quite smiling, not quite evil, but very knowing. He leaned forward, and an American voice came from his lips.

'Those lights I saw at four this morning, John?'

'Those must have been the laboratory sheds.'

Landsdale arched his eyebrows questioningly. Los Alamos was more in Groves's jurisdiction than Pash's. Anyway this fellow was his social inferior, and a dangerous ally.

'The brains work late,' the southerner added. 'Sometimes right up to sunrise.'

On the chair to Landsdale's left, his back to the locked door, de Silva flinched at the sound of Pash's laugh.

'Without getting overtime?' The visitor laughed again. 'Whose little trick is that? The General, or Oppenheimer?'

Pash's soft, toneless voice trailed off menacingly. A vague insinuation was left hanging in the airless room. Indeed, in the ten seconds silence, neither Landsdale or de Silva could help a feeling that something *was* sinister in what Pash had observed.

'Perhaps they enjoy working, Colonel.' Landsale's face creased.

'Fame and glory, eh?'

Pash took out his cigarettes. He struck a match, then perfunctorily leaned forward to offer the pack.

'Let's hear your urgent matter, Boris.' De Silva accepted a cigarette.

Pash took out the match and smiled with voluptuous anticipation. First at de Silva. Then at Landsdale. For apart from his passionate hatred of Communism, Boris Pash felt a quite sincere loathing of bureaucracy and delighted in infusing it with human mystery. That is, with gossip.

'Well, Colonel,' Pash muttered, pausing to pull his chair closer. 'The spy ring at Berkeley we're unravelling . . . this mysterious intermediary Steve Nelson, Weinberg and Lomanitz.'

'Get to the point, Boris!' de Silva broke in waspishly, almost as if he knew what was to come.

Pash lowered his voice still further.

'It all suggests a source,' he confided. 'A source here at Los Alamos. Lomanitz and Weinberg have been talking to the Federation.'

Landsdale released his breath. Leaning far back in his swivel chair, he ignored the ironic grin de Silva threw him. The three

130

khaki-shirted men sat smoking. For several minutes, no one spoke. Then Pash sighed deeply. He blew a long column of bluish smoke into the sunshine.

'Tell me, John . . .' Pash gazed steadily at a large earwig worming down the pine boards above the Southerner's bare head. 'Where do you think our Director spent his last night on the Coast?'

Behind the thickly stacked desk facing Pash, Landsdale's heart jumped. Suddenly he was preternaturally conscious of every sound. The rustle of their uniforms. The pleasant, far-off note of collective laughter from Main Tech. It was an emotion Landsdale had felt before in his life. On a hunt the instant he first saw a fresh spoor, each detail mortally significant.

'He checked in up here on schedule,' Landsdale finally said with great caution.

De Silva covered himself. 'We had a tail on him.'

'All night?' Pash tilted his chin. The earwig was out of sight behind Landsdale's head.

Pash shook his head genially. Abruptly he leaned forward. On his uncreased vanilla-coloured features there was an expression of sober wisdom.

'The subject,' he whispered, 'spent that night with an active Communist.'

'Nelson?' Landsdale's confusion was well disguised.

'His old girlfriend Tatlock.' Colonel Pash pointed over Landsdale's shoulder.

De Silva whistled softly as Landsdale turned, disgustedly slapping the earwig off his uniform.

'In my studied opinion, Colonel sir . . .' Pash paused until his young superior had composed himself. A number of expressions were competing for a place on Pash's smiling face. His eyes blinked rapidly behind his spectacles.

'In my opinion our subject is a spy, sir. An agent for the Soviet Union. He should be de-commissioned from government work right away.'

Landsdale felt the expectant looks of both officers on his burning forehead. He made a face, stalling for time.

Landsdale had never liked Oppenheimer. He had often asked

himself just such questions. Still, the obscenity of hearing the accusation spoken out loud provoked in the young lawyer a strange humiliation. For a moment an image passed through his imagination. The gentle, gangly scholar in a striped suit, his wrists and ankles manacled to the San Quentin electric chair, the electric helmet clamped over his frail brilliant head. It was too barbarous for a gentleman to contemplate. Landsdale twisted his leathery neck to look at de Silva.

'I don't know about spying, Colonel,' de Silva encouraged. 'But the Doctor sure is a tricky gent if you want my opinion.'

Landsdale swivelled his chair and swung his boots up on the open window frame. Putting on his tinted flying glasses, the lawyer absorbed himself in the little stationary fluttering sweeps of a sparrowhawk, hunting at the level of the cottonwoods.

'Anything else, Colonel?' he said indifferently.

'Yes sir,' Pash said, not in the least underestimating the effect of his words. An expression of byzantine subtlety had won the struggle for Colonel Pash's face. 'The Subject must know damn well. We're going to make him a big cheese in history one day. A man like that should be reminded what he owes the Army. You'll see, Colonel. He'll break off these friendships right away.'

'All right, Boris . . . you go on back to Berkeley,' Landsdale said presently. He looked over his left shoulder, to examine Pash's surly repose. Then he gazed back gratefully at the hawk shimmering over the trees. 'I'll pass on your recommendation to the General. Meanwhile, Peer.'

'Yes sir?' De Silva's chair scraped. 'What do you want me to do?'

'Close surveillance,' Landsdale said. 'No more . . . no less.'

Watching the hawk dip down in the cottonwoods, then flutter up, trembling on the dry Mesa air, Landsdale felt de Silva's ambition through the back of his neck.

'What? Telephone . . . shadows?' de Silva said with professional satisfaction. 'Bugs in the bedrooms?'

The Texan made a face. 'The works. Only don't let them catch you. This is supposed to be a civilized establishment.'

'You betcha! John . . .?' de Silva began.

But Landsdale had suddenly kicked down his boots and lunged out of his chair. The two officers watched him clump lazily around the bare walls behind Pash. He paused with his sun-blackened hand on the flimsy door. Suddenly the Security chief looked surprisingly tall and stately.

'Thank you, gentlemen.' Landsdale made a slight gracious bow. 'I don't want to miss my train.' His boyish blue eyes fixed on Colonel Pash. 'By the way, Pash, who spotted the Tatlock thing?'

'The Bureau,' Colonel Pash said a little too hurriedly. 'They had two gents in the bushes outside all night.'

Landsdale stared hard from the door, until Pash stirred nervously. He frowned and hesitated. Then he closed the door behind him.

Outside the Army's offices, the desert sun was broiling. The dry breeze carried an odour of wild thyme. Landsdale sauntered over the mud past the ugly green buildings, on the way to collect his bag. The scientists were gathering genially outside Main Tech. The Security Chief automatically redirected his steps to avoid them. Well, you sure found the damnedest people in the Army. To say the least of these brains. Still, Groves had himself a pretty place. Maybe he'd do some hunting up here some day.

But right now the Hill had an unhealthy feeling to Colonel Landsdale. He could scarcely wait to leave its problems behind and be back in Washington.

Chapter 15

Long after, Oppy would suspect that the local nicknames of their two creations – 'Thin Man' and 'Fat Boy' – became currency among the witty little society on the heights of Cottonwood Mesa with himself and poor Groves in mind. But it did not matter, the bombs' shapes were inseparable from their hidden function.

The Uranium invention was a sixteen-foot cannon barrel, with its critical bullseye bolted on the muzzle, built to tolerances as exquisite as those Oppy had used attaching the physicists' minds to their task. The Plutonium invention would not transmogrify into the ugly, boiler-shaped tub called Fat Boy for another year. It too was still a Thin Man. From that summer of 1943, until the winter of the new year, it had seemed that Robert's prophecy would come true. They might all still witness and thus prove the Frisch-

Meitner fission theory, and the Oppenheimers be out of the desert, all within the year.

These were the glorious days of Light on the Mesa, when Robert was confident the Great Mystery would be brought into the world amid the ceremony of Civilization. The phase began with a brief August visit to a certain Colonel Pash at Berkeley to clear his conscience about what his friend Haakon had told him in the kitchen last winter. He also summoned his hot-blooded disciples Lomanitz and Weinberg to his office, and warned them to stop talking fission techniques to friends in the Party. The time of Light ended with some news Robert had gnawingly dreaded since his flight from San Francisco.

For General Groves in Washington, this phase of almost incredible personal success also began with a tortured decision. For the catacombs of Army 'security', which General Groves had conceived nine months earlier with all Groves's genius for purifying power, were by July threatening to swallow up his whole project. Secrecy was all very well. But should he not rein in Security until the eggheads could hand over their bomb?

Groves made his decision deep in a suffocatingly humid Washington night.

Reaching the Pentagon at ten. after a Joint Chiefs' reception, Groves first locked the door of his plush new office. Then he folded his heavily braided and decorated dress-jacket neatly on the facing chair. Only then did Groves spin through the combination of his wall safe, swing back the door, and take out the letter in its pink manila folder. Groves also took out a short flat frilly box. The design on it was of Quaker forefathers tilling cornfields. 'Fancy Chocolates' it said on the lid. Groves knew tonight was certainly no occasion to hurry over . . . but perhaps the most important decision of his career. That was one of the advantages of living a life devoted to the cultivation of power. You certainly knew it when a moment was important.

With a sort of agitated ceremony, General Groves squashed himself behind his desk. He switched on the spot lamp, then arranged the unsigned memorandum squarely in front of him. Choosing a chocolate cream from the box, he began softening it on his tongue. Finally, with a gesture not unlike Robert's when first sensing Jean's madness, Groves agitatedly pushed the cushions of fat up and down the sides of his face. He read the document through.

'As Army commander of the Manhattan District,' the memorandum concluded, 'it is my firmest opinion that J. Robert Oppenheimer's services are indispensable to the success of the Atom-Bomb project. All files and reports tending to question Dr Oppenheimer's loyalty to this country are to be disregarded.'

Behind the luxury of his desk, Groves leaned back and shut his eyes. Then he opened them, and looked grimly beyond the circle of light into the dim depths of the big room. If Groves did not sign this memorandum his Oppy would almost certainly be dismissed from the Manhattan Project, under suspicion of spying for the Kremlin.

One hour thus ticked by in the hushed Pentagon office. The box of chocolate creams was almost empty. Now in a sultry Washington night, Groves seemed to see the world stretching out, a glory that never slept. Somewhere out there, the tide was turning in the most magnificent war in history. In the Emperor's Pacific theatre, in the Gilberts and the New Guinea of the head-hunters, triumphant MacArthur was wading ashore on tropical beaches. In London Eisenhower was banqueting with Churchill. Meanwhile, pearl-handled George Patton roared like some Carthaginian down Sicilian farm roads ahead of Sherman tanks, being showered with flowers by heavy-breasted peasant girls. And somewhere out on the Russian Front on the huge salient around Kursk, Zhukov was at that very hour claiming victory over the dictator Hitler in the biggest armoured battle of all time.

And what of Groves? Groves was sitting ignored here in Washington. The huge, godlike explosion that would announce Groves's presence had not yet taken place, existed only as a possibility to a few thousand college snobs, scattered through a billion dollars' worth of boring laboratories producing smears of green paste! Groves did not even understand how it worked, if it worked at all. Yet if it did not work soon, the war would be over and the whole damn project would vanish into oblivion without even a puff of smoke, *as if it had never existed*. And Groves would vanish with it.

Then Groves saw an apparition. And this apparition was of all his lonely lost camps and desolate commands, and the passionate ingenuities with which for twenty years he, 'G.G.', had swallowed his lament and purified power, raising his unprepossessing self through the American system to the threshold of immortality!

Only then was General Groves able to think clearly about Oppy and his guilty goodness. Handsome, graceful, superbly intelligent Oppy. Oppy who loyally, thoughtfully and without a complaining word had orchestrated the whole Los Alamos project, and was putting in Groves's hands the power to erase whole enemy cities. All that without even asking for thanks! And thinking of Dr Oppenheimer, Groves experienced a wave of the most chaste, bitter and exalted love. The love we only feel for those who mirror our weaknesses, and for whom we have made every sacrifice. Could Oppy really be a Soviet spy? Of course he could! Yet why then would he have created the whole thing from the beginning? But what if he really were, and Groves was responsible for installing a Russian agent as head of the whole US atom-bomb project? Yet even at this excruciating thought, Groves was still sure that if Oppy was a spy, it was only his subtle goodness that made him that way.

Oh Lord, why couldn't Oppy just have been more like him, Groves thought with a bitter love, perspiration pushing out on his face. Or was it that the man had just been going along with the Army, and would sabotage the thing the moment it was done? But what could that matter now? It was at this terrible moment, sitting alone at his Pentagon desk in front of his exhausted candy box, Groves experienced a thing few men ever know. Sitting there pitifully alone, Groves heard a faint chiming laughter. And it was the laughter of the gods.

Suddenly very cool, very calm, Groves picked up the pen on his desk. He signed the letter.

Chapter 16

Beyond the Capitol's moonless night the young land lay west, marked in the black void by a phosphorescence of towns.

On the top-secret New Mexico plateau, remote from General Groves and his air-conditioned decision, as Church from State, the seekers after truth had also put their faith in Doctor Oppenheimer's goodness. They had renounced the high wages, eternal cities and comforts of human society. Oppy would take care of the world below. In the black night, that flickered with electricity, the pioneers clustered under naked bulbs were just sitting down to their vigil at the instruments registering the unknown powers of the universe. For these glows and noiseless beams, these twitching needles, streaked cloud-chambers and smoking gold screens were the first signals out of a great mystery. And in their hundred temperaments, cultures and tongues, the thinkers were as one. Only Doctor Oppenheimer stayed aloof from their passion, even when the shanty town hummed with news of the great Bohr's escape from Hitler.

For the last weeks, the memory of Jean Tatlock standing alone by the wire fence outside San Francisco Aerodrome had tormented Robert almost as much as the host of condemned faces behind the miles of fascist barbed wire. And this guilt Robert could not talk out even with Kitty.

On this humid August night, the laboratory Director and his wife were dining on the Rio Grande, at their corner table in Edith Warner's tearoom. Edith was sick, and the others were abandoning her to stay up in the labs. For some time Kitty watched her husband swallow his cold soup. Then Robbie sat frozen with his dead pipe, eyebrows knitted. His large teeming eyes stared past her at the maze on the red Navajo wall blanket.

'You know, darling,' she said, 'when I was a young girl, it specially scared me to see a couple with nothing to say.'

It was so still between Edith's whitewashed walls, Kitty had almost whispered. Dinner was the only time they spoke now. The man in front of her only frowned without looking back. Kitty lifted her brown hand and took the pipe from his mouth.

Robert looked at her quickly.

'Sorry, Katie,' he said. 'Yes the . . . well, the custom with Spanish peasants. It is bad form to talk over meals.'

Then, staring at her husband's abstracted face, Kitty had a sensation of great masses in motion, like the stone monoliths sealing a pyramid. She had invested everything in this man.

'Why not tell me?' Kitty snapped. 'I don't know you like this.'

'Well, maybe . . .' Robert's eyes evaded hers. 'I don't either.'

'Tell me then,' Kitty persisted. 'Is it that business with Haakon?'

'Partly, it must be partly that.'

The Director examined Tileno's blank face, as the Indian set down plates of enchiladas and frijoles. Tileno was the Governor at San Idelfonso pueblo. He never commented on what Dr Opps had brought to the sacred lands.

'All right then,' Kitty went on coldly when they were alone. 'Let's run through it again. We're going to settle this.'

Robert's tanned face darkened. 'The security fellows are making such an effort for Groves. And if Haakon wasn't exaggerating,' he whispered, 'the old gang, some on the Federation too, are snooping around Ernest's calutron. And are curious about up here.'

'And being up here's like taking sides?' Kitty sat, chin on knuckles, her eyes full of female danger.

'I don't know which is worse.' Robert's voice rose. 'That letter the President sent me about secrecy, or the Russians snooping.'

'Well, I do!' Kitty said.

Suddenly there was a feverish wave of hostility between the Oppenheimers, hot and sharp as the chilli on the beans.

'Kitty? Maybe I should get out of this, now.'

'You can't,' Kitty said flatly. 'Everyone says there's no one else. Anyway we haven't got anything else.'

'Thanks.' Robert stared at her.

The Director and his wife sat in strained silence through the rest of dinner. Yes, the simplest decisions were taking on a feeling of concrete permanence. Power made the atmosphere of living almost viscous, like water on its way to becoming marble.

'I know which is worse,' Kitty tried again, when they were back on the hill.

They paced slowly back to the house, along the familiar path. This stormy night they kept to the open mud they could see between the blackened cottonwoods by Ashley pond. The mountains were a darker shadow out to their left. Directionless gusts muffled their voices and blew Kitty's wavy hair in her face, reminding her somehow, tragically, that she was a woman. The warm humid air felt like tears.

Suddenly Kitty clutched Robert's hand in the dark.

'Once a secret's out, Katie . . . The Russians have sold their souls to the fascists once already.'

'Wouldn't *you* want to know what your ally was up to?' Kitty said. 'For all the Russians know, we'll throw in with Germany.'

'I wish there was someone up here to make sense of it!' he said bitterly. ' "Let Oppy take care of it." '

'Because he's such a success,' Kitty teased a little sadly. Their arms brushed in the blackness.

'What good's a success like this unless everyone's successful with it?'

'That's why the Russians are snooping, Doctor!'

'Well, Katie!' he laughed. 'Then tell me what I should do.'

The man and woman had been stumbling along, whispering in the dark, past the laboratory windows like Japanese lanterns in the night.

They had paused at their favourite lookout. But without the stars you did not feel the enchantment. The canyons below, the great river and mountains beyond, were only different shades in a mysterious shadow that was drawing them all in. Even here, among an élite of friends in the bosom of God's country, Robert and Kitty felt their loneliness.

'Well *you* certainly aren't making the decision to tell the Russians,' Kitty spoke close by him. 'But they ought to be told.'

'Neither can I go around not telling our fellows about the snooping!' Robert muttered, listening to the fir branches.

'Robbie, go ahead and tell them!' Kitty said with decision. 'That fellow in Berkeley?'

'The Colonel . . . Pash?'

Robert felt his wife abruptly face him. She pressed against him, infusing him with her restless craving.

'Yes, tell them!' hurried on the only voice Robert Oppenheimer trusted to the depths. 'But tell them you think the Russians should be in on it!'

'The Russians will do the research themselves, anyway.'

'Tell them that too,' said Kitty.

'But Katie!' Robert whispered half hopefully. 'Katie, what about Haakon, and Frank?'

'Haakon hasn't done anything wrong,' said Kitty quickly. 'Not knowing what you're doing up here. He can't expect you to keep a secret like that!'

'Secrets and secrets and secrets!' With a flooding of relief, Robert held her fierce little body. 'My secret's I love you.'

'See what a useful wife you have?'

'A very useful and very brainy wife.'

'I just know what I believes in,' Kitty exulted. Robbie had never called her that before.

'Mmm. What do you believe in?'

'I believe . . .' Standing close in the dark, Kitty suddenly felt her cheeks burning. She was laughing. '. . . tonight you're not getting your p-js.'

So it was that on his next journey out to California, Doctor Oppenheimer stopped briefly by Durant Hall on Berkeley's sweltering campus. There he made his first polite effort to influence government policy.

The Counter-Espionage Chief gave the Manhattan Director a familiar welcome. Somehow, though, Robert did not feel the same cool certainty of right and wrong, here in this campus office face to face with Colonel Pash. Robert's own voice sounded odd to him when he sketched out the message from his 'professor friend': how a circle of Russia's west-coast enthusiasts wanted to help out with details of what her Yankee ally was doing at Los Alamos. Would it not be wiser, Robert muttered clumsily, if Roosevelt was simply open with the Russians? The security man seemed interested only in the 'professor's' name. And so instead of rewarding such openness by trusting Robert, Pash burdened him with a fresh load of guilt. Oppy was covering up a friend's name. He caught the Sante Fé train and arrived back on his cottonwood Mesa in a guilt-ridden depression.

So, month after month, the passionate conquest of nature continued, everyone in camp trusting 'Oppy' to stay strong travelling the laboratories of America's vast atom underground, through the growing feud over Uranium production. Yet like all innocent men Robert had not yet learned to stay strong without his conscience free.

The thought of Jean and Haakon went on troubling him. Were their lives in his hands?

Chapter 17

Eight months after the Mesa was sealed, the last refugee from Germany's broken scholar-circle came to the red canyons of the Rio Grande, to begin again.

For ten years, as Hitler and Stalin refined their Old World empires of lies and death, slow, wilful Niels Bohr had protected his little Institute of tolerant truth-seekers at No. 15 Blegdamsweg, Copenhagen. But this September, during the migration of the eels, Bohr fell back at last by small boat over the icy moonlit Oresund, to Sweden. At once the knowledge of the universe carried in the physicist's big head became a prize for power states.

Robert had entertained the noble Dane twice in California, in '37 and in '33, when Bohr invited Lawrence to introduce his cyclotron in Europe. The first time he had met Bohr, in 1926 as a student in Cambridge, Robert had told the great teacher that he was in trouble both in maths and in experiment. Now Robert was conducting the most tremendous physics experiment of the ages, and Europe's sage was coming to Robert's sacred domain on the desert Mesa. But he was not thinking now of the restless fantasies of a consumptive boy come to these lonely canyons on a paint pony, or how they had come true. He felt sicker and lonelier now, and in need of guidance.

Dorothy McKibben personally drove the charming Danish gentleman up the canyon, into Groves's security fences. That evening, there was the usual witty banquet in the schoolhouse by the amateur stage. And as the brash young minds of the shanty town listened to Bohr's throaty whisper describe life under Hitler, a civilized Old World subtlety and tact spread among them.

Robert sat, shoulders hunched, gazing at the heavy, thick-lipped Nordic face. He could detect not a single scar from where his guest had just been. When the dinner broke up at ten to go see Clark Gable and Charles Laughton in *Mutiny on the Bounty*, Robert led his guest on a long stroll in the desert night, out where Groves had no ears. For some minutes they stumbled uphill in their overcoats, keeping a polite intimate silence. Both men felt the significance of the moment.

That afternoon, the clear frozen air had abruptly warmed forty degrees. Sooty snow clouds formed to the north. The night air was pungent with melting mud.

'Well, Doctor,' Robert softly opened. 'How do we seem up here?'

Bohr took Robert's arm. 'Necessary, Oppenheimer!' came a guttural whisper. 'You know Heisenberg came to Copenhagen?'

'I heard something.'

'The man was never my favourite student,' Bohr whispered with a sigh. 'But I believe he will give Satan this weapon.'

'Then we're on the right track?'

'Tomorrow, dear fellow,' Bohr whispered, not to hurry their muse. 'I will examine the solutions of Fermi, Bethe and Neumann.'

The old European fell silent with another heavy sigh. And as they walked bundled arm-in-arm under the darkening stars, Robert felt the strained excesses of his own mind and troubled soul shrink back, until no part of himself claimed ascendancy over the greater order of things.

'Truly Oppenheimer, *this* will be an experiment!' Bohr suddenly said out loud in the blizzardly murk, with a sort of restless gravity. 'But you know, my young American friend, these laboratories of Urey, Compton and Lawrence. I must say, I am taken aback! They are monsters, my God! None of us had any idea!'

Robert fumbled with his pipe. Hearing a new note of equality in the great man's voice, he felt his panic again.

'The atmosphere is so different up here.' Bohr stared back toward the shadowed Rio Grande without releasing Robert's arm. 'Those calutrons you require bicycles to explore!'

'The US is the mother of money,' Robert said apologetically.

'But you see, Oppenheimer,' the whisper went on in an intimate sing-song, 'it is *permanence*!'

'After the war,' Robert offered. 'Peaceful uses?'

'Perhaps that is so, dear fellow. But you know Heisenberg. That means our veil of mysteries, this hymen over nature.'

'The whole thing will come out in the open.' Robert shook his head soberly.

'Let us hope, let us hope!'

Bohr's indignant growl left the two men standing alone together in a penitential silence, three hundred yards up the cleared ground. The reflection of the moon appeared, trapped below them among the trees of Ashley Pond. The papal vigour of this old man brooding in the wintery night was so calming that Robert felt an impulse to kneel on the mud and kiss one of the old hands.

'Oppenheimer . . .'

'Yes, Doctor,' Robert mumbled to the old man, who had turned to face him. Two or three snowflakes stung their cheeks.

'Oppenheimer, you are bringing a religion into this world,' the Dane whispered with a heavy delicacy. 'Up here, Oppenheimer, you have made a paradise!'

Robert stood with his head bowed in the dark. He thought of the power he had once felt in himself, the power to do universal good.

'These up here, spoilt children in paradise. But down there, Oppenheimer. The fires of damnation.'

'I know!' Robert muttered. 'What are we to do?'

'Dear fellow, you will bring a new religion into the world.'

Bohr's guttural sing-song was by Robert's right ear now, as they ambled towards the snow clouds.

'The forces of history,' the voice rose and fell. 'The way men rule and are ruled, even the sea the human soul belongs to. All will be altered beyond recognition.'

'Yes!' Robert suddenly saw it. 'Humanity is in the balance!'

'We must be worthy of this thing, you understand? We must preserve it as a scholarly experiment,' Bohr whispered. 'The free peoples must be seen, *generously*, to share this new knowledge with our friends. Not hoard it for domination.'

Robert stumbled forward in his galoshes. He had a sudden vision of Groves and his security myrmidons.

'Naturally,' Bohr lifted both his hands, 'we can expect nothing from these military persons. One of us – possibly yourself – must speak to the supreme rulers of the world.'

In the patchy moonlight, they had reached the north security fence. A fine snow was falling. Bohr turned and held both Robert's wide baggy shoulders.

'You think they will need advice?' said Robert, whose stomach was too weak for so much evil.

'Think, Oppenheimer!' Bohr murmured in excited tones. 'If

this ceases to be a great work of scholars!' Only *think* . . . if the jealous rulers imagine they can win such a race for brute force! We will never have again this opportunity.'

The blood drained from Robert's head. If Bohr had not been holding him, he would have staggered.

'I don't know if I'm built for that sort of thing,' Robert laughed. 'Look! It's started snowing . . . they'll be missing us.'

'For myself, Oppenheimer,' Bohr whispered thoughtfully on the walk back to the schoolhouses. 'Perhaps I am only built for the society of my English Tube Alloys. But at the first opportunity I will chat with Roosevelt. Also perhaps to Churchill. They must be told, this race has already been lost! Lost before it is begun!'

'Please keep me in touch.' With regret, Robert felt the old sage release his arm. 'Anything I can do.'

Stumbling down over the darkened mud, the two men were nearly back in Robert's science paradise. In the main street, there were figures and falling snow in the lights under the bridge of sighs. Bohr's hand restrained him.

'This opportunity cannot be lost, Oppenheimer!' Bohr's whisper came close to Robert's ear. 'You must go down from this paradise. It is the lesson of our time, the great morals await us in Hell . . . not utopias!'

'Yes I know, yes,' mumbled Robert. He was forced to imagine the fires stolen from him, as African tribesmen in their dance seize hot coals to devour them. Bombs myriad as the cities of man! But that was too unthinkably ugly. It demolished his soul. Robert suppressed such paranoia.

But as Bohr came back to Los Alamos from Roosevelt and Churchill, with word that hired physicists were apparently not trusted to make prophecies on history, it was not the old sage's warning Robert liked to remember from that winter walk. It was his own sense of absolution. The scholar's Olympus was not dead. Its demigods were forgiven everything.

Ten more obsessed months slipped by on the Mesa. It was January 1944. The behaviour of high-energy isotopes and neutron backgrounds had been mathematically tracked, and refined to a constant presence in the machines and mass spectrographs. The Uranium and Plutonium triggers had both been designed. Still the sensation of weakness would not free Robert. An impulse was growing on him, to tear his goodness loose from the innocent world below, to let his country and colleagues carry him toward their final devouring by fire.

Late one night without sleep, Robert noticed an envelope under the living-room door. A clipping fluttered out.

TRAGEDY ON TELEGRAPH HILL

Yesterday the body of Jean Tatlock was found by friends at the home of her parents, Professor and Mrs John Tatlock of Berkeley University. Miss Tatlock had apparently taken her life, after what was described as a long period of disturbance and psychiatric treatment. Professor Tatlock, who is a Chaucer scholar . . .

Robert folded the neat clipping. He walked to the open window. Gazing out over the cottonwood tips to the distant ghostly moon haze adrift on the Albuquerque desert, his throat tightened. For Jean, and for himself. Now he could never be free. Jean had made him her God.

And for the first time in his life, Robert felt something neither his childhood nor ethics had readied him for. He was at the exact frontier of his capacity to suffer for his fellow beings.

Chapter 18

The first new Plutonium from Compton's Chicago reactor piles had arrived on the Mesa in an Army courier's valise. And soon everyone knew about it including MacMillan, who had discovered it. There was no more time to think of the humanity below.

Manmade Element 94 . . . heavier than lead, more precious than gold, more virulent than arsenic, whose first property is its malice towards all living things. Compton's tiny batch of Plutonium 239 had arrived. And it was violated by an even more hideous isotope of itself, P–240. Unseparated, this double Plutonium molecule had a neutron background so feverish and independent it made rashes on the Mesa's spectrographs. The computations of Von Neumann, Segre and Fermi proved it. No projectile known to man was fast enough to make the stuff's contagion critical before it vaporized itself. It was as if the Plutonium bullseye and Plutonium projectile were lovers who ejaculated on sight, who would have to be rushed together at impossible speeds so that penetration and fertilization occurred in the same micro-instant. Soon everyone in the barracks and labs knew it. And at Chicago, and Berkeley. 'Thin Man' had scarcely enough U235 from Lawrence's calutrons. 'Fat Boy' *was no good at all*.

During that week, the Director of Los Alamos became aware of his tall self shedding weight. At first Robert wondered if it was cancer, and he had himself examined. But no, it was as if even the desert air had grown so thick and dense around him, the force of gravity so strong it was pulling, flaking the flesh off him into the parched soil, like the little stacks of bones he used to see riding his paint up the lonely Mesa trails. Knowing now that he and Kitty would not be off the Mesa this year, nor Europe's condemned saved from Hitler, Oppy was crumbling like some cubist portrait. He could find no trace in himself now of the bland scholar's reverie that had tormented him back at Berkeley. The Director's face was getting bony and brilliant-eyed, as the faces behind the barbed wire in his dreams. All of Robert was up against the absolute mystery. His life was on the line.

Finally Robert telephoned Groves in Washington. And two days later, a meeting convened in the Director's bright-lit Main Tech office. Bethe, Teller, Parsons and Ulam were already exchanging gossip when Groves walked in. The General saluted and limply shook hands. Then he squished in the corner chair behind the Director. Little Fermi stood tight-lipped at the blackboard, vigorously formulating the P239–240 molecule.

'Greetings Gr-roves,' he said, puckishly ·elegant. 'Aha! This Yankee salute is so fine. I must pick it up . . . eh?'

'All right, Enrico.' Robert gave Groves's face an absorbed glance. Putting his pipe on the desk, he took out a pack of cigarettes.

'Oh yes!' Fermi assumed his oracular pose. 'Well, dear boys, here is the troublesome molecule again. Shall we have a look at it? And what a cute little number it is. Look here.'

Since Tuesday, an unbroken downpour had attacked the Mesa.

Groves's voluminous khaki trousers were splattered to the knees with mud. His wet face looked pitifully childish, beads of moisture trembling on his short eyelashes. Groves kneaded his hands and tilted his swollen head. He watched the excited Italian's performance from the corner of his eyes, feeling too disgusted and miserable even to pretend he understood the egghead's words.

Groves had sensed something in the air for days. After hearing Oppy's long-distance voice, the train ride from Washington had been like a one-way journey to obscurity. Groves noticed Oppy saying something.

'So this seems our position.' Robert delicately puffed his cigarette. 'We have a Uranium bomb with not enough Uranium left over to test. That one could fizzle. Then we have the . . . the Plutonium bomb. We've worked more than a year on that. And, contradict me please, we have only disqualified any conventional trigger.'

In the Director's office, there was the longest, most realistic silence Groves had ever heard in his life. Only Teller looked comfortable.

'Somebody say something!'

Groves stared at Parsons. Parsons was an officer like Groves.

'I would regard that sir, as a quite complete picture.'

'You understand, General, it is quite thorough,' Ulam said with mournful emphasis.

'Things could look better,' said Fermi with his tight-lipped grin. He chalked a line through the sketch. 'Or worse, however you see it, ha ha!'

The grateful rain thrashed the glass behind Groves's head, and it was the only sound. Groves recognized this silence, staring in absurdity on his billion-dollar dreams of glory. So it was ending here . . . so *this* was failure! And for a moment, Failure was more excruciating than the General had ever dreamt. Then there was a 'click' . . . and it was not so bad.

'Well, thank you gentlemen,' Oppy was saying genially. 'I'll have something definite for you after lunch.'

Groves had forgotten his terminal despair. A mad hope lifted him out of his chair. His boots clunked after the eggheads as they bustled out the closing door.

'Hell's bells, Oppy!' Groves turned back. He crumpled in

Teller's chair. 'You can't just let them walk off, they're a bunch of geniuses! I thought they had all the answers.'

Over the stacked desk, Oppy's gaunt fascinating head watched Groves without smiling. There's nothing to be accomplished by getting steamed up, Robert's gaze said. And for the first time, Groves' suspicious eyes saw no guilt in Oppy's look. They were in it together.

'What will they say back at the Pentagon?' Groves began menacingly.

'I'm more worried, General,' Robert gave the Army man a melancholy smile, 'what they'll say in the concentration camps. This delay is costing twenty thousand war dead per day.'

Five minutes later General Groves in his huge rubber poncho was downstairs, clogging the regulation entrance to Main Tech. Lillie stretched with an umbrella. Oppy looks consumptive, Groves was thinking, having gratefully remembered his old instinct to reorganize. He would look for a replacement. Only then the strangest thought came to Groves: But what if no one else could do the job?

There was such a quagmire of snow in Mainstreet, Groves had to climb back upstairs and cross the second-floor bridge.

Chapter 19

Reflecting in his office scented with pine and wet cotton, listening to the desert rain making tearing sounds on the glass, Oppy was not at all tired. It was only Groves and Ed Teller, and even his old friend Fermi who wearied Robert with their insoluble human foibles.

But just now he had forgotten Groves. The old good feeling was very close. Robert had summoned Neddermeyer, and he was excited. Pure, modest patient Seth, who was more American and almost as old as Robert himself. Innocent Seth, whose mind Robert had trained to a free-ranging vision, and who first detected a new particle in cosmic rays. Now the best minds from Old Europe had come up with a dud. Only his first student's great American idea still stood, vital and alone.

Past the big window the canyons and sky were lost in slow-descending rain. The General was scarcely visible as he crossed the catwalk, his aide struggling to fold an umbrella. Robert was so absorbed in Seth's hour of glory, he nearly missed the gentle 'rap-rap'.

'Oh Seth! Come in, come in!' Robert swivelled his chair. A fragrant smell of tobacco lingered in the office. The new secretary, Anne Wilson, smiled usefully.

Neddermeyer poked his head round the door and glanced around the room, then stepped in and carefully pushed the latch shut.

'Hi Prof,' Seth said quietly, and he sat down on the chair nearest the door. Fishing out a half-smoked cigar, he looked briefly at the brown face smiling above the stacks of papers. The desk phone lay off the hook.

'Dickens of a week,' he said. 'Like the flood.'

'Like the flood,' Robert agreed. And he looked at Seth as if Seth were Noah.

Sitting behind the empty chairs, half of Seth's awkward smile slipped away. Never would he forget his feelings in this office, hearing his old teacher and the Nobel heavies scoff breezily at burning the earth's air and water. Seth would never let himself forget that.

'What's cooking?' he said.

'How's implosion coming, Seth?' Oppy smiled brilliantly.

'Well, our guys took some pretty good photos,' Seth began carefully. 'You can see the metal inside the pipes we imploded collapsing in uneven wobbles.'

Seth had begun obediently. But taking in his old teacher's impatient smile, his voice trailed off. His cigar had gone out again. Rain must have got it.

'Fine, Seth!' Robert took it up serenely. 'You know the others have just about wrapped up the maths on the projectile for the new Plutonium?'

'No good, uh?' Neddermeyer offered sympathetically. But he felt a vague stir of hope. 'So we'll only make the one bomb.'

'Wrong, Seth.' Oppy leaned on the desk, his forearms crossed. Seeing his old teacher's expectant smile, Seth experienced a sensitive alarm. He waited, a warning irony in his eyes.

'It means,' said the Director, 'we're going to ignite the new Plutonium by imploding it.'

Before his old teacher's dreaming voice could reach the word 'implode', Seth's word, an alarm shot up Neddermeyer's spine. He glanced towards the frame door. Then he tried to concentrate on the wall portrait of Abraham Lincoln, and the inscription: 'The world cannot exist half slave, half free.' And after implosion? Seth's thoughts raced. Will the world be free? Or will it be all slave?

He suddenly felt an uncontrollable impulse to jump up and run with his lonely idea out of the Director's office, down through the innocent rain and the cottonwoods and throw himself, panting and grateful and humble, face down on the warm red desert mud. Seth Neddermeyer abruptly rose in his muddy boots.

He stumbled across the floor to the water dispenser, and filled a soft paper cup. The glass tank was full to the brim, and Seth flinched as a large silver bubble appeared. It wobbled up, bursting with a sickening 'glug' that shook the metal stand.

When Neddermeyer turned back, his old teacher was watching with a benevolent amusement. Seth sat down and grinned uncomfortably.

'Seth, I'm putting everyone on the Hill – that is, except Edward – on implosion. All this country's labs, the hundred millions in Compton's reactors, and in Los Alamos. The two or three years of everyone's work. All of it. We have no alternative to making implosion work. And you're in charge, Seth.'

'Why me, Prof?' Seth asked him.

'You can't think in terms of months any more, Seth.' Dr Oppenheimer smiled encouragingly. 'Get cracking.'

'No, really.' Seth drew in his shoulders. He frowned. 'That ain't my style.'

Without warning, a flame of extreme anger leapt up from the Director's stomach. He had just then felt his old student's suspicion of him.

'You're forgetting something, Seth!' Robert's voice choked. 'There are people dying out there! Their only hope is this country saving them.'

'Sure Oppy. Anything you say.' Neddermeyer retreated quickly, guilt in his troubled gaze.

150

After the two old friends had run politely through a schedule for implosion research, Robert stood for a long time at the streaming window sucking his pipe. If only he could see the cottonwoods and the Sangre de Cristos, and the towering blue penitential sky. They were somewhere out there in the murk. But he had to face the grey, whirling-down clouds of rain.

Well, there it was. Neddermeyer the protégé he always felt so good about, whom he brought to this physics utopia and just offered a great role in human history. That same Neddermeyer unmistakably saw something in Robert he didn't like. And remembering his own display of temper and Seth's guilty secretive look, Robert felt a deep sick hurt. For the first time, for only an instant, he turned over the idea of letting someone else lead the Mesa. But before he could go any further, Robert saw it clearly. The whole Mesa had become, and would go on being, the child of his mind. The world thinkers had followed him here and trusted him, as did Washington and the tortured world. There was no time left in history to turn back. Neddermeyer's great idea was going forward – with or without Seth's love.

The week-long rain screened Doctor Oppenheimer's view of the desert distances. It kept Kitty from her restless drives out to the adobe farm villages, up the Jemez and Sangre de Cristos canyons where she had met old Jed Holmes. It was on one of these drives Kitty had decided her second child would be born on Robbie's cottonwood Mesa. But this rain kept her in the biology lab, or with little Pete.

The rain fell. And as it thundered on the desert below it sluiced the dry soil, the bones, the bleached twigs and rattlesnake skins. It made roaring red mud rivers of awakened seeds that cut the canyon walls, and laid bare the roots of trees like age, and turned the main street of Los Alamos into an ankle deep bog. It glutted even the insatiable desert plains past Albuquerque, sorting out prehistoric underground waterways and pans, and turning to lakes places blackened by an infernal heat. And in the dry mud-floored farm huts of El Rito, Taos, Chimayo, San Isidro and Coyote, and on the fortress Mesa of Acoma, the few Mexicans, Indians, farmers and shepherds who battled this cruel meagre land, scarcely more comprehending than their fathers of the hundred millions waiting in

Washington to back the Army, patiently watched the rain flood down, and they were happy. For these rains were liquid of the sun, and the other half of growth.

The spring rain fell steadily, and its green sweetness reached even to the heart of desolation two hundred miles south of Sante Fé, where the helpless earth is beaten to black metal under a lidless sun. And it freshened the little dead sea by the poor border town of Alamogordo, and brought life to the most evil lava wastes of all, which the people call *El Jornada del Muerte*, meaning the Journey of the Dead.

It was this place Doctor Oppenheimer chose to test Implosion. And he called it *Trinity*.

Chapter 20

Suddenly it was 1945, and month after month the inspired schedule of the Mesa's enlightened colloquia had been cutting deeper into Seth Neddermeyer's original American idea. But still Seth would not be accelerated in his scholar's contemplation. Understanding his student's feeling, Robert suppressed his irritation at Seth's subtle mistrust of him. He encouraged his student patiently to rise on the tide of his idea.

But the four thousand daily war dead weighed on him heavily, went on stripping flesh from his bones. A proud bitterness arose between teacher and student. And Robert grew ruthless with Seth, and there was no friendship between them.

When still Seth was not shaken from his quiet science, the Director cut slices out of Seth's beautiful idea, and turned them back over to the European masters. Overall control passed to Hans Bethe and the Canadian Christy. Typically, Edward Teller refused flatly to join the theoretical section with Fermi. So to the other Hungarian, that Merlin of numbers Johnny Von Neumann, Robert turned over the mathematics work on heats and pressures at the instant of violence. The Englishman James Tuck was asked to theorize on explosive outer rind to focus an evenly converging shock on the Plutonium. As for the explosives . . . that went to the passionate Russian, Kistiakovsky. Robert had wanted and needed it to be Seth. But in the end, there was nothing left of the teacher and his enlightened dream of the lovely Mesa, but the bones. And the bones were pure Power.

And as the Director forsook the last of Bohr's absolution to concentrate on the Test – that hour drawing nearer until he could almost hear it in the Mesa's huge vacant blue sky, like the advancing steps of Hamlet's father – so Groves and his nationwide security net concentrated on Doctor Oppenheimer. And Oppy was *their* great mystery.

Robert had never found his life very obscure. What secrets had he to hide? The true mystery was out *there* in the glory of nature, and they would all meet it at the Test, which *was* nature. So Robert taught again and again from the podium in Theatre Two.

That last autumn, the illustrious morning debates of the Mesa's scholars drew together in a single will, set free from the ordinary passions below, like mountaineers who tense for the assault on an untouched summit. While Seth sat silenced in a corner, and Teller brooded over his ultimate exterminator. But alone on a winter night, while Kitty groaned shallowly in her dreams swollen with their second child, and the Mesa's sheds crackled with pure intellect, the Director lay awake, abandoned by Bohr's words, and tormented by the faces of Jean, Haakon and Seth. Even as his conscience arrayed against these the hosts in the concentration camps, Robert seemed to see in himself an amoral ambition. For weeks he fought the gathering cold-whiteness with readings in epic religious poetry . . . Sanskrit, Blake, Donne and Dante. But as his powers of love for what was just and human petrified, the suspicions of Landsdale, Pash and Groves grew to an obsession. Again tonight, Robert was like a convict raking them with his fingernails, searching them for a way out.

With every intimacy you honestly confided, the security men discovered a deeper guilt. A chain reaction of guilts! Robert got out of bed and went to the kitchen where he could turn on the light. They were all Americans working together. You just had to trust these strong fellows not to mistrust dreamers like Haakon and Frank, just for being dreamers. America should learn a little loyalty to Lincoln, Emerson and Thoreau, and its own revolution. It was more than a year ago, on a trip back East in Indian summer, that he had dropped by Groves's Pentagon office for that chat with young Colonel Landsdale.

The Russian Army had been engaged bloodily with Paulus's Sixth Army at Stalingrad. General Mark Clark was preparing to assault Kessering's stronghold in Italy. But it was a soggy hundred degrees by the Potomac.

Inside the Pentagon building, the meat-packers' air conditioning attacked Robert's perspiration. The walls in Groves's huge office whirred softly, producing cold.

'Well sir,' Colonel Landsdale smiled graciously. 'You are probably the most intelligent man I ever met.'

Across Groves's wide polished desk, with its two slack flags and little schoolboy's model of an atom, Robert had lowered his eyes and busied himself with his pipe. He was too absorbed in decoding the impression of shipboard security in Groves's powerful building to fend off this man's crude probes at his vanity.

'And if I can say so,' Landsdale grinned, 'your wife is a remarkable woman.'

'Thank you Colonel,' Robert said and his large sad eyes met Landsdale's. 'Kitty certainly has been making me behave myself.'

The officer laughed and his face reddened. He had given Kitty a lecture on security. Now the Southerner sat sideways in Groves's huge leather chair with one ankle on his knee, the leg sharply cocked.

'Sorry about that, Doctor,' he drawled graciously. 'But how *have* you been? I sort of hoped you were going to clear up this "Professor X" business.'

'You're just going to have to trust me over this,' Robert had answered with an inward shame at the boredom these tedious fellows made him feel. It made Robert treat them more politely than people he liked.

'In my judgment,' Robert stammered, 'Eltonton's the only man who'll persist in snooping.'

Landsdale's pale eyes examined Oppy's enigmatic face. 'But how do you feel, refusing us a name? The name of someone who has approached you for classified information in wartime on behalf of the Soviets?'

'I can't say I'm overjoyed about it,' the Atom Director answered simply. 'But there's nothing you can trust in a person if not character. I trust this person's absolutely.'

'Well, if you won't sir, you won't,' Landsdale grinned. 'Don't think I won't ask again.'

'You may Colonel,' Robert said. 'Now what's this about my students?'

'Forget Lomanitz, Doctor . . .'

Their voices droned hollowly, back and forth.

'What have you done with him?' Robert had persisted.

'Drafted him into the 25th Division. He kept up contacts with the Berkeley ring . . . and we're looking into Bernard Peters.'

'Bernard?' Robert leaned back wearily in his deep chair. 'Bernard's a wonderful guy and a brilliant physicist.'

'His politics?' Landsdale inquired earnestly.

'Oh, Bernard's quite a red,' Robert had confessed ruefully. 'Talks very wild.'

'And a girl called Jean Tatlock?'

Landsdale's eyes met Oppy's vaguely.

'Oh, I think Jean drifted out of the Party.'

Tonight in New Mexico, lying awake on the frame bed in the cool desert night, listening to the rain thunder outside drowning Kitty's breathing, Robert struggled to remember. That had been Washington. But what had he told Pash out in California that so fascinated them all?

'Well, the Soviets being our allies and fighting for their lives,' Robert had explained helpfully. They were back in Pash's Berkeley office. 'The fellow who contacted my two associates about the microfilm man in the Russian consulate is in a sense implementing US policy.'

Those embellishments, Robert reflected sucking his dead pipe in the dark, were not quite true. But they conveyed the sense of something worth investigating. The whole Haakon episode was so distasteful, it had scarcely been worth mentioning.

'Well, I'm not being persistent.' Pash had looked toward his assistant, Johnson, then back at Oppy with steady bespectacled blue eyes. Robert recalled now the exact scholarly smell of old paper and ink in that little Durant Hall office. Even Pash licking his lips.

'And of course,' Pash hurried to say. 'We can promise you on oath, your rôle in any information getting out would not be leaked.'

'You *are* being persistent,' he had cut Pash off, defending his soul from so gross a suggestion. 'And that is your job.'

'But,' Pash's glassy eyes had scrutinized Robert's face, as if it was an exhibit for the prosecution. 'Now could we know through whom the contact was made?'

'That would only mislead and be unhelpful,' he had explained patiently.

Suddenly Robert had felt an insufferable need to get away from these dull witless fellows, back into the innocent free air of the campus and his own thoughts. But what if the poor fellows realized how crude they were?

'It is the *tone* that is crucial,' he had laboured on. 'Not whatever silly thing is said that might sound technically treasonous. But which is confided with respect and sensitivity between friends.'

The conversation with the Intelligence Chief had spoiled Robert's day, and stained his spiritual tone for weeks. But he had put his guilty goodness in their hands, and they would not let him go. They had their kind of discretion and he had his. What was theirs? State integrity. What was his? Love for his friends?

Shortly after Niels Bohr, General Groves himself had visited the snow-covered Mesa. The soldier had come directly to Robert's office in Main Tech, for some reason wearing a fur-ruffed arctic jacket. He paced nervously up and down.

'Now, Oppy,' Groves had begun, in the gravelly insincere voice of someone who has prepared a speech. 'When you helped us out five months ago over Eltonton, I promised to . . . to trust your judgment of the intermediary.'

'Yes, and I promised.' The Director followed the red averted face. Even wanting to help out poor stumbling Groves, he felt humiliated by their suspicions. 'Promised to give you his name if you ordered me to.'

'Well, Oppy.' The man had trundled to Oppy's desk and thumped his chapped fists so hard Kitty's and Roosevelt's portraits fell over. 'Now I am ordering you!'

'I'm sorry it's come to this.' Robert puffed his pipe, gazing mournfully out the window at the icicles stuck along the metal framework. 'Though my friend has nothing to hide. I only hope you fellows are not hiding anything?'

'No problem, Oppy.' Groves's little eyes flashed and bugged out. 'Don't you worry.'

'Well, my friend.' Remembering his words tonight, he for some reason thought of his lovely mother and her wounded hand. 'The fellow I mentioned – and my brother Frank knows about it – the man's just a literature professor, and a very nice and honest fellow called Chevalier.'

Now one year later, still perspiring in this desert night with the wound of nightmarishly accusing faces – Haakon, Jean, Frank, Peters, Lomanitz and Seth, the people who had trusted him – Robert must have slipped off into a troubled sleep. Because he was suddenly being woken by the seven o'clock camp whistle, 'Oppy's whistle' the ambitious fraternity on the Mesa called it. He had missed his hour in the cottonwoods alone with the desert sunrise! Then Robert remembered yesterday's intelligence report. Was it true. Had the security problem really gone away?!

Yes, somewhere far back in the ruins of Germany, that same Colonel Pash had this November captured the fabulous cliff-top village of Haigerlöch with shocktroops and found there the last remains of Göttingen. The Nobel, Heisenberg, and Teller's friend Von Weiszäker. They had been spending Hitler's money building a reactor and playing Bach toccatas on the local organ.

They had kept Nature's veil of mysteries. There was no German project to speak of.

Chapter 21

He bounded youthfully out of bed. From the pillow, Kitty's eyes followed as her man padded in his pyjamas to the open window. Robert drew the blinds.

He was thinking as he had not thought in two years. None of that ugliness mattered any more. In a few months they would be through here, and these shacks would be torn up. The war was closing down. There would be no more talk of General Marshall's eight bombs to end the war: even these two would probably not be necessary. The Army would have spent a billion and a half dollars to finance the greatest adventure in pure science of all time. It was quite a victory! He could forget Bohr's dark warnings. What they had mastered on this Mesa would be a fire of hell to warn future Hitlers. To remind men of their mortality.

Standing in the schoolmaster's window, his very pregnant wife now pushed against his back, Robert held up his arms. He contracted his wasted chest luxuriously. Making fists of his slender fingers, he stretched like a boy in the morning sun.

'What are you so excited about?' she whispered.

'I just had a thought, Kitty. Maybe everything will work out.'

'Well you better make sure the damn things go off, darling.'

'You worry about your kid,' he teased her, 'I'll worry about mine.'

But in the morning Colloquium in Theatre Two, and shuffling between the projects and conferences scattered among the Mesa's labs and briefing rooms, Oppy found everywhere the signs it was true.

All through the Mesa's parched ant-nest of familiar floor spaces and cubbyholes . . . of specialized metallurgical, chemical, mathematical, ballistical, theoretical, experimental, of dangerous and innocent projects, visible and invisible reactions, of argument and focused silence, and which were linked to Vulcan's cyclotrons, calutrons, reactor piles, gas-diffusion plants scattered from Hanford Washington to Oak Ridge Tennessee, and thence to Commonwealth African Uranium mines, through Slotin's Dragon room, Fermi's little reactor, Y-lab and the chilly cryogenics repositories (all except Ed Teller's thermonuclear effort) . . . floors were being swept, equipment checked through. And gradually all they had invented was gathering and concentrating in the hands of Slotin and Kistiakovsky. And it was a single thing.

For days, Ken Bainbridge, Allison and McKibben had been with their test crew two hundred miles south in the desert, the lonely place called the Journey of the Dead. In a sleep-walking satisfaction with the success of his new patriotic role, Oppy even twice wrote to Washington, enthusing generously about the thousand-time greater power Teller's thermonuclear work might produce.

All of it, all the labyrinthine inspirations on the Mesa, and

158

science curiosity for thousands of years, now drawn together in a single perfect shape. A ball-shape in heavy metal: the size of two clenched fists held not quite together in a frame of miniscrews adjusted to tolerances allowing for no error. This whole singular thing, weighed to the very critical threshold. And, yet to be clamped over the Plutonium hemispheres, an explosive womb, sculptured to deliver the poisonous embryo within an even convergence of pressures. And this spherical, heavy handful was the apple of absolute knowledge in God's perfect garden. But it was an apple without seeds or growth or even lust, an apple artificial, inedible: a mere distillation of man's old hunger for a stature equal to that of the humiliating universe, to restore Eden's innocence as crib to the cosmos. But would it go off, the thirsty scientists asked themselves? Would it be a boy or would it be a girl?

Now their creation lay in front of dozens of dry-rimmed eyes on Slotin's work-bench in Omega, intricately sprouting ignition wires and looking like a brain attached to an encephalograph. The mind-god.

The war would soon be over. They would be left guiltless to live through their moment of forbidden knowledge.

As the well-fattened bear goes into hibernation in his cave, Robert now went into complete moral hibernation from the human world outside. He slept in the moment lying ahead . . . the mid week of July 1945 anno domini. And as Robert's body continued to waste under the weight of Groves's hundred millions and his colleagues' anxiety, his soul was fat on prophecy.

When, on April 12, tidings came that America's thirty-second President was dead, the young men and women drifted from the labs, aimless as dories left by a sunken mother ship. Oppy gathered them again, bareheaded on the dusty space between the half-masted flag and the budding cottonwoods. In a low quick voice, he spoke of the great unifying voice of mildness and peace and of doing no harm or hurt, which spoke through all religion. Of the divine will that flowed through all things, mastering even such an Egypt as Roosevelt had lead them out of. His words floated free on the midday heat, simple and light as seeds.

Soon Robert received word that Haakon Chevalier was translating at a Charter Convention in San Francisco's Civic Opera

House to create a new 'United Nations', with Alger Hiss as its first Secretary-General. Then finally two weeks later, the tidings that Hitler's body . . . the invincible butcher of millions . . . had been burned in Berlin, like garbage in the Chancellery garden.

Then it was June. All of Robert was concentrated in spiritual sleep on the hour ahead. In his little vegetable garden, Joe Serber had to ration his own water to keep his plants from dying of thirst. But Robert scarcely noticed the Mesa's drought. For this would be the new knowledge, and they must go to receive it morally cleansed.

Chapter 22

In July, as the cottonwoods snowed white fluff over the Mesa, the Oppenheimer brothers left by car for the Journey of the Dead. The remaining thinkers would come later, in camouflaged buses.

The Army men came for Oppy before dawn. Kitty had been up most of the night with her baby, Kate. He dressed his wasted body in the baggy English tweeds and slipped out without waking her.

Robert was still shivering and a little jerky as he stumbled between Farrell, Groves and Lillie past the dark buildings dreaming under the stars. Frank was waiting in the moonlight among the cars. He had a thermos of hot coffee. From now on, each motion they made was rehearsed. But the unprotected feeling of being woken up stayed with Robert.

The three cars filed under the darkened guard barrier, wound down the back canyon, crossed the Rio Grande and joined the road down from the Rockies to Sante Fé, Albuquerque and the desert south. The moment they left the Mesa, Robert's queasy feeling was back.

In Europe, the living remains of the camps were free. The mysterious hour ahead was Doctor Oppenheimer's alone, he knew that now. He would not be released from it until it was over, and he and all the world *knew*! Kitty had teasingly accused him of being Moses wanting to see God. But Robert thought more of Arjuna's words: 'Reveal thyself to me! Who art thou in this form of terror? I adore thee oh God supreme.' And Krishna's answer. 'I am all powerful time which destroys all things . . . even if thou dost not fight, all the warriors facing thee shall die!' Well, that was quite splendid and a fine excuse at a distance. But as 'Time' came near, the luminous phrases were like free air thickening to marble. A marble song, which was there but inaudible. And as the hours intensified, Robert wobbled sickeningly hot and cold. In and out of hearing and believing it . . . and believing he heard it.

Well, whether you hear it or not, he thought, one thing is clear: it is your moment of truth. Anyway, didn't Krishna sound a little like Frederick the Great shouting to his fleeing soldiers: 'Fools! Do you want to live for ever?' Probably it wasn't very reliable, quoting fellows like Krishna, even if they were gods. What had Melville said? 'Art is but the effort of the mind to keep the open freedom of its sea.' Yes, maybe this experiment was such an effort of the mind.

Robert laughed to himself and some of the hot coffee from the thermos went up his nose. He was a little happier, feeling himself in command of the ideas.

The little convoy was leaving the opalescent glimmer of Albuquerque, over on the slope to the right. The road went straight, flattening on to the great desert of the Conquistadores. Dozens of the great minds from Oppy's Mesa must already have taken this road, but it was still empty. Their headlamps kept freezing jackrabbits, and sent scorpions skittering.

Abruptly the man behind the car's wheel was having trouble focusing his thoughts. His body in its rumpled tweeds went on as usual, but his stomach sent up little flutters of alarm. Suddenly he was like some young soldier dreaming of heroic feats, first approaching the field of battle. And as the soldier nervously re-oils his gun, Robert absorbed himself in the technical problems of the test. No one ever had broken his will. And neither was this going to!

Holding the wheel against the glow of the child-like car instruments, Robert held out the empty thermos. He felt his brother take it.

Between Tularosa and the San Andreas mountains that run to the border at El Paso was the great circle, eighteen miles across, on the Jornada's red-streaked, grey plain of baked mud, sand and lava. Hushed, unobserved save by the sun's eye, and somehow like a target for its cruelty. At the circle's centre was Point Zero, a hundred-foot, steel-frame gantry with a platform hut on top. And by its base, the crumbling mud floor ranch hovel, where the cleft Plutonium egg would lie at last in its explosive womb. Six miles from the tower was the backward-facing control bunker where the thinkers would hide their flesh; laid out here and there for miles around Point Zero, the monitoring meters, camera points and dugouts. They seemed to the Director in the depression of the dawn drive as solemn and obscure as the slabs of some giant modern Stonehenge. Yes, and in all the Jornada's senseless desolation so much precise measurement, such a subtle navigation, did have about it something of wild faith, like some scattering of an electronic faithful gathered for a Second Coming. Robert flinched.

'Hey Robbie!' Frank was shouting. 'Take it easy!'

The Director looked down, then in the car mirror. Eighty-five . . . Groves's lights were far behind. He lifted his foot and wound down the window. A blast of warm moist desert air mussed their hair and his tie fluttered in his face. A first purple aurora had spread over the east.

'Well, Francis O.' He licked his lips. 'I guess I'm rather eager to be there, and get it over with.'

'You'll still have until Sunday night,' Frank offered as the wind died.

'That's just it,' Robert smiled, feeling the strangeness of human conversation. 'There won't be much for me to do. I wish Kitty could have come. No I don't.'

'Anyway, you've got me.'

Robert had to turn and look at his brother's face, scarcely recognizing him.

'I'm sorry to put you through it. Thanks Frank.'

'I only had to look at you. The whole thing's on you Robbie.'

'It wasn't supposed to work out that way,' Robert said with a sudden irritation. 'That part hasn't been much of a success.'

'If you ask me, Robbie . . . now the war's nearly over?'

In the yellow dawn light Robert glanced twice at the hurt worried face by the window. The automobile was coasting.

'All right, go on.'

'Better if this part doesn't succeed too well either.'

'A few of the others feel the same,' the Director said dreamily, thinking of the resignations.

'It should be unanimous!' Frank said. 'After the job everyone says you've done, no one would ever try again!'

'Your brother would have a lot to answer for.'

'Maybe someone will baulk.'

'Don't let the General hear that.' Robert's face was alert. 'The army calls that disloyalty.'

They were almost stopped on the empty desert road, the eastern horizon getting too bright to look back into. Only the few strongest stars were still there. In the rear mirror the Army cars had pulled up close. Robert could make out Groves's red face, bug-eyed in the windshield. With a guilty grin and a wave, Oppy started them off again.

Moderation made the Director think gloomy thoughts. Such as Seth Neddermeyer bitterly refusing to come watch implosion tested. He longed to forget the Army cars, to set out full speed down the straight road, to race the wind. At least the bad moments coming down from the mountain were past. He had begun enjoying the way; with every slight rising and falling of the desert road, the vista ahead was subtly different.

At Tularosa, the convoy stopped at the one Chicano gas pump. The passengers stood uncomfortably together and perspired in the hot dust. Even little General Farrell had little to say. There was a vague humidity and an electric rumbling to the west. Then they were in Alamogordo, filing right between the pitted pink stucco housefronts on to US 70. And soon, out there far ahead, were the vague blue masses of the San Andreas range, mingled with low white clouds. They passed two bow-legged Indians in flat-brimmed black hats, walking the other way.

As Robert slowed for the Army roadblock, a brown biplane came overhead from behind. It sideslipped off to the left, settling out of sight over the ridge. The moment they were through, back inside the roadblock and the saluting MPs, the Director had back his full hold on his great patriotic duty. He was very excited.

Now the cars wound slowly right. Then left, up a blackened lava ridge. As they came out on top Robert pulled over. The engines died and doors squeaked open.

The soldiers and scientists huddled jealously around Oppy in a bare-headed group, in the vast suffocating hush.

Chapter 23

'Gosh, Robbie!' laughed Frank, who was new to his brother's domain and had not learned its cynical wit. 'Gosh, what a place!'

'Hmm, those clouds again.' Doctor Oppenheimer gazed disapprovingly. He pulled on his wide slouch hat.

'Never mind the clouds!' General Groves panted and grinned toughly. He mopped his brow. 'What are a few clouds? There's no one out here.'

'Well there's Albuquerque,' Robert said with a glance. 'Amarillo.'

'Albuquerque!' Farrell laughed eagerly. 'That's half way to Denver.'

But the Atomic Director was surveying his world from under the wide felt brim. From where they were standing, an immense whitish sand and lava waste stretched out, as far as they could see. Until finally it dissolved in yellow heat waves, traced with alkali dust from an invisible jeep.

Resting a hand on Frank's burning shoulder, Robert held out his arm. Frank blinked in the glare. He rubbed the sweat out of his eyes and could see, way out, a small building with cars. The biplane was parked off to the left. Then much further off was a little black dot. And then, (he tried to focus in the heat waves), Frank though he saw a vertical shape wavering in water.

'Of course,' Robert said thoughtfully, 'the effect will be different at night.'

'Ask the dispatcher for one of our jeeps, Doctor. Look around the place for yourself,' said Groves.

After hating, disciplining and rationing the conceited eggheads for two years, the General had come halfway to believing what they prophesied. A few hours of largesse now would erase all that.

There was a muffled snorting of motors. Everyone piled back in.

Twenty minutes later, the Director's party climbed down in front of an unpainted barracks. Offices, a bird-house bulletin board standing outside, and white flagpoles. A water truck and some jeeps stood parked randomly, as if confused by the absence of any roads. Healthily sunblackened scientists came and went

164

expressionlessly, in short sleeve shirts, shorts, white jumpsuits or light pants. Bedrolls were piled here and there. In his disorientation, amid the threatening desolation of the scene, Frank was somehow surprised to see faces he recognized from Berkeley.

But something was strange in their expressions. Some dreaming exultation.

There was nothing but this little village and the remote mountains. Outside under a shed roof, half a dozen men stood absorbed over a table. As Oppy stepped out of the first car, business came to a halt. Klaus Fuchs was listening attentively, looking less withdrawn than usual. Something had been gotten off his mind.

'Perfect! Robert!' called a familiar voice filled with Viennese charm. An elegant person dressed for the Sacher Hotel in a three-piece suit, Homburg and umbrella came out of the shade towards the brothers. The alkali dust kicked from his shoes.

'Well, Isidor!' The Director shook his friend's hand in both his. Feeling Rabi and their old Zurichsee days close by, the guilt of Seth sulking back at Los Alamos receded.

'But what do you think of our spa? Only it is a spa with absolutely no water. Above . . . or below!'

'I will find water,' laughed Isidor Rabi. 'My bumberchute never fails!'

Frank hung back with General Groves. Fermi was walking forward into the sun, shading his small face. The Italian magician had been tearing scraps of white paper to measure atmospheric pressure, opening circus tricks for the betting pool on yield.

'A dowsing rod, Doc?' Farrell was joking. 'Begad, I remember we had a dowser back in Kildara.' Everyone was unnaturally talkative.

'No no! Dowsing will spoil it!' Fermi seized Robert's hand with a thoughtful grin. 'It is a sufficient dryness here to cure all the tubercolo in Europe!'

'Doctor Frank, you too? Excellent!' Isidor stepped over. He patted Frank's shoulder encouragingly. 'Oh, you will get used to it here. I have been here ten minutes. I am already used to things!'

But Frank could think of no words to say. He only smiled, hanging back in the sun. Shade surrounded the crowded table. Frank had never felt so strange in his life, hearing the oblivious tones, the bursts of giddy laughter. Seeing his boyhood friend at their centre, dreamily haughty as some prince. Everyone spoke loudly, as if to fend off the crushing silence.

'Doctor Enrico Fermi? Doctor Rabi?' Groves was holding court in under the latticed shade. 'May I introduce General Tom Farrell. Tom will be standing in for me, here at Trinity.'

Even the Director, staring thoughtfully out over the white sea of heat waves at the mirage of mountains and clouds, looked around. In two years, no one had heard poor Groves speak to a scientist without tortured servility. Or to a fellow officer without condescension.

'Pleased, I'm sure.' Fermi bowed with an impish grin.

'Tom,' Groves went on expansively. 'Enrico here's been in fission from the beginning.'

'That may not be such a good thing of course,' Fermi said with cheery modesty, not releasing Farrell's hand which began tightening and closing in his.

'You see, General.' Fermi stepped close. 'I am by no means convinced the human r-race will survive.'

Farrell had leaned forward to hear the famous Italian try his hand at a joke. Very abruptly the rosy-cheeked officer glanced up in Fermi's perspiring face, and his hand went limp.

The Italian dropped it without interest and walked around to Robert and Isidor. The old friends, in their wonder at finding themselves here with the others from all over the world, through some obscure logic of civilized thought, were standing almost affectionately on either side of General Groves. Frank waited uncertainly, not quite apart.

'Good, my friends!' Fermi was in the swing. 'So we are here for the great occasion. And the newcomers must place their bets on yield. *Faites vos jeux, mesdames et messieurs*! Eh? But Robbie, I am disappointed with this game of yours. Most unscientific. A limit of 20,000 tons! What in science is limited?'

Standing in the little cluster of Project leaders, watched jealously by everything within a mile, Robert shifted his dusty English shoes in the red dirt of the pueblos. He smiled thoughtfully in Fermi's face, knowing what was coming.

'Your mathematics on that is a horror,' he said.

'No no! This yield game is a bore!' Fermi stood his ground by Groves's darkening shirt with a sort of good-humoured urgency, as if trying to tell him something. Fission could trigger a sun, and blow up a universe. How did you sanely talk of strict limits on a precious speck of dust like Earth?

'I propose a more objective game,' Fermi went on. 'Bets please: on whether we destroy all life on this globe. Or simply life in New Mexico?'

For fifteen seconds, the little group stood in weird silence. Their pleasant grins clung to their streaming faces, like the ruins of great civilization. No one heard the whine of advancing engines. Groves's swelling grin sickened reproachfully. The more he believed in the eggheads, the more excruciating their tasteless sense of humour. He had dropped his sodden white handkerchief.

With the General's clumsy movement to pick it off the sand, his companions turned to a sedan and escort of jeeps just parking near the flagpole. A faint white cloud of alkali hung in the distances of windless heat.

The sedan door creaked open. Leo Slotin slouched, tall and narrow-shouldered, towards the crowd of officers and civilians near the shed. He stopped by Frank Oppenheimer, and Morrison came up. Slotin's burnt-out eyes, sunken in two bruises, passed over Frank's bony face incuriously.

'I've got the hemispheres,' Slotin addressed the Director in a slack nasal voice. 'Where do you want me to put them?'

'Klaus! Joe!' Oppy called over to the group gathered like sheep in the shade by the table. 'Could you help me for a moment?'

Suddenly feeling not at all shy or awkward, Frank chose that significant moment. He stepped up to his brother.

'Listen, Robbie. Maybe I'll take that jeep, go have a look around.'

'What, Frank?' Robert glanced around. 'Oh sure, better check the map.'

Frank felt as if he had left Santa Fe a month ago, had been standing with the Director's little élite by the headquarters shed for many hours. Clashing first gear, Frank started the jeep straight out over the lava flat as fast as he could make it go. Not even pausing to think.

Presently he glanced over his shoulder. The headquarters was only a black speck far back in the heat waves. Frank almost shouted with relief. Only then did he see he was heading northwest, straight at the wavering shape his brother had pointed out.

'Tower of Babel!' Frank muttered and wheeled the jeep so sensitive to his freedom . . . ninety degrees west, towards the river mountains and few advancing clouds. And only then, staring ahead, eyes wind-watering over the wheel, over the Army's white star and the flat sand expanse racing at his wheels, could Frank face the knot of impressions he had picked up back there.

The last summer weeks by San Francisco Bay, now the war was ending, Frank had time to learn some new flute pieces, and tune up his soul. Feeling very happy in the new peace they were all coming to, Frank had sincerely looked forward to visiting his brother among the great minds, in the cool of their mountains on the Rio Grande. He would be at his brother's side at the most dramatic experiment in science history, even if it did turn out a grandiose flop. But this was not what Frank had imagined.

All at once, Frank had sensed Robert's feeling of unreachable superiority. He remembered the thinkers' cruel humour, their jealous glances and the unnatural emotions behind gentlemanly smiles. The uncouth greed of the Army men (tensed with Groves's two billion unproven dollars, and President Truman at Potsdam with Stalin, waiting for news). And Frank was humiliated for himself, and for humble living things. As if he were the last free being amid the violence of this place. Holding the vibrating wheel, feeling his soul parched and burnt as if it had been crawling for days across this wasteland without food or water, Frank felt drops of water on his face. Looking up he saw the grey underside of a raincloud, floating cool as a jellyfish in the vacant sky. As the big warm drops began to rattle on the hood, Frank swung the jeep gladly toward it.

Back by the little headquarters where the Plutonium hemispheres had just arrived from Los Alamos, Oppy too had felt the raindrops in this place where it never rained. He began coughing again. A storm cloud could carry radioactive dust and rain poison on Albuquerque. Behind his pensive stare, the Director felt panic stir. For he was bound now to Point Zero by a Gordian Knot. Only some great blow could release him.

Then, two days later, Robert, like Groves, heard the chiming laughter. That was Saturday.

Chapter 24

On Sunday evening, the Director climbed in a jeep alone. He drove out to the restricted zone at Point Zero to see what there was of the last sunset. Since yesterday the Plutonium embryo had been resting in its explosive womb on the platform up Trinity Tower. And it was as if the skies had been weeping.

As Robert climbed out jerkily by the canvas base tent, the sad warm drizzle had stopped. There were tangerine-hued gaps in the overcast, and a faint cool breeze. After the trauma at Assembly, he felt better here, almost alone. Away from his short-tempered, suffering scientists, now arguing and playing chess in their monitoring dugouts.

'Hello Joseph!'

He called to a shadow huddled by a steel pylon. How quiet here, remote from the international press gathering at Control.

'Evening Robert!' said a voice. 'Seems to be clearing.'

The sleeping-bag did not move.

'Seems to be!' he answered and looked politely at the Jornada's wide low horizon.

Yes, here was probably the one most dangerous place on earth. Maybe that had ever been, if you ruled out volcanos and coliseums. But Robert was feeling tired of people. Tired of all their trust, and their jealous love, and the blame and resentment it earned him. Maybe God was not tired. But he, Julius Robert Oppenheimer, was tired. In his life so many millions had died so pitifully, so hideously, despite all his old conviction of a power to do universal good. Now thousands of brilliant men, his country, his President, and the captives dying in the Japanese camps all trusted him to make a success of it. Who could tell. Perhaps there would be no more wars, and the whole world proud and free as America? Right now, Robert *did* want to fight the guilty panic Frank and Fermi and the rest made him feel, with their doubts, their heaping of responsibility on *him*! Did they really expect him to suppress knowledge? Was he supposed to sabotage the truth? Now in the cool, shuffling past the slowly flapping tent, Robert felt close to moral law, remote from the sinfulness of man. Goodness had to be a success. But the final assembly had shaken him, was it only yesterday?

First had come the call from the Mesa announcing that George Kistiakovsky's intricate explosive lens had failed its test, and Robert had disgraced George in the canteen. Then Bethe had telephoned saying poor Kisty's moulds might be all right. But Assembly had been worst.

Shortly before, Robert scarcely noticed General Groves, Nichols and Lillie drive off south from the suffocating base-tent and tensely absorbed scientists inside. Their Army jeep had faded in a plume of alkali.

When they were clear of the tower, Lillie drove as fast as he could. A week earlier, lightning had set off the conventional bomb on this tower. Now wallowing on the bucket seat beside Lillie, the General went through his press briefs. Over the last three days, Groves's belief in the eggheads' words had grown religiously. It was seeing them scared. Fear meant power was around, and Groves knew that power was truth. Suddenly just being near that silent tower made Groves's flesh crawl. The wind spattered sweat on his papers.

'Nichols!' he shouted. 'You think I should draft another release?'

'I don't know sir!' You son of a bitch, Nichols added fondly to himself. 'It depends.'

'What's the biggest we've got here? Let me see.' Groves held up a memorandum.

' "Doctor Robert Oppenheimer," ' Groves yelled, grunting when Lillie steered over potholes, '. . . and fifteen other prominent scientists were killed when an ammunition dump – uh! – was accidentally set off while they vacationed at Dr Oppenheimer's ranch near Santa Fe. I think I better – uh! – do a more extensive one . . .'

'General sir!' Lillie was glancing over at the General so urgently he swerved the jeep off the road.

'What is it, Lillie? Well, out with it!'

'If it's any more extensive, sir. Well, you'll be fried too!' Lillie was careful to be modest about his own life. But the jeep lurched violently and they jumped through a cactus. A red prickly pear bounced off the windshield.

On Slotin's bench back in the walled McDonald ranch shack Louis had just, in a tense silence, tuned the cleft in the little Plutonium egg to its critical threshold. Now he was securing the thing in its capsule. Klaus Fuchs paused shyly in the door with the initiators to have his photo taken. Farrell, Isidor and Oppy stood looking on. It was cooler inside, but Farrell's shirt was soaked. Robert began nervously coughing. Bacher asked him to wait outside.

'Okay, General.' Slotin regarded Farrell ironically when he was done. 'Don't I get a receipt?'

'Oh yes. I guess you do.'

Farrell took out a slip of Army paper: 'One atom-bomb received from Los Alamos Laboratories for Army testing July 14, 1945,' it said. Flattening it against the shack's pitted wall so it wouldn't flutter in the breeze, the officer wrote his name on the dotted line.

'Is that all I get?' Farrell grinned nervously.

'Why not touch it, General?' Slotin showed his teeth.

Farrell's pink fingers stretched over the gleaming mechanism. Seemed to have difficulty reaching.

'It's warm!' Farrell forced his smile.

'It's always warm.' Slotin grinned back.

Now the ugly black boiler was dangling from a chain pulley inside the tower tent. On a stand between the tower legs, the explosive womb lay open. At various distances in the shadowy heat, fifteen perspiring scholars waited, strange-hollowed with concentration. The Army psychiatrist was looking more disturbed than his patients. Bacher and three well-rehearsed assistants eased the chain-tail. This was the last and simplest performance of the Manhattan Project.

'There . . . there,' Oppy's voice said. 'Joe, a little more . . . there.'

They had all jumped at the sound. The metal shapes on the table were being guided into final union. Faces gaping, everyone had seen the capsule pause halfway into its hollow. The pulley chain sagged. *It was not going to fit!*

Oppy took off his hat. He shuffled two steps to the stand,

between Bacher and Kistiakovsky, and stared down at what had just been the power of the universe. And now was only four pieces of dumb rebellious metal. Suddenly he was seized by a violent guilt, hope and terror. He heard, like Groves, a soft chiming laughter. Why, it was all a hoax. Mankind had been tricked! What had he believed in anyway, God, or pure reason? Or had the scientists tricked the Army? But in five seconds, this madness had subsided.

Murmuring without emotion, Oppy and Bacher worked it down to a schoolboy's problem – temperature contraction. The explosive rind was still cool from the high Mesa, the Plutonium egg heated by Trinity. Five minutes later, there was a sound like the clicking of billiard balls. Soon their hearts beat together as the black tub rose and rose, flickering through shadow bars, to its final bed a hundred feet over their heads.

Now on this last sunset, Robert stood alone smoking thoughtfully, tasting an emotion like some cosmic surgeon who had just abducted a child of nature, operating while nature sleeps, and sewing all the wounds without nature having woken. Well, perhaps here was the most dangerous ground on earth. But Robert was tired of people, and he felt at peace with what was waiting behind him on the tower. The only thought left now was not harming anyone in Albuquerque.

He watched the sun reappear as it set in the low band of cheerful blue along the San Andreas range. As the sun grew warm and kind at the very rim of the world, the steaming raindrops began again. They wept tenderly on the pattering dust. An inexpressible sadness stirred, among the few forgotten mesquite and cactuses rooted here and there into the distance.

When Robert looked back, the sun had slipped behind the mountains. And very quickly it was dark. The stage was set.

When the Director climbed back in the jeep, some time after midnight, lightning flickered in the humid suffocation. Joe McKibben was lying deeply asleep in his bedroom under the tower. Helmeted soldiers carrying machine guns slowly paced the perimeter. Bainbridge would come for Joe one hour before the test. Together they would withdraw from the bomb, switching activators. As for Robert, he wondered if he would feel like sleeping ever again. Light-headed and rolling slowly, he began the long drive south to Control.

Slowly, again and again checking his watch, four hours went by. Crushed, deformed hours. Robert was fully concentrated on the mysterious hour closing on humanity.

At 4:50 a.m., Oppy was back, standing outside the crowded concrete command bunker, not noticing that Groves had fled still further away. He was staring at the blackness to the north, when the distant tower suddenly blinked into focus. It was like some floodlit summer stage. Three pairs of headlights slowly divided from the glow.

There had been a delay for weather. Groves and Oppy had walked up and down through the puddles, arguing whether to forget the citizens of Amarillo. But now the detonating sphere holding the cleft Plutonium egg was armed. The jeep lights came slowly in over the flat. Hearing an excited voice beside him, Robert turned and stared thoughtfully. It was poor Kistiakovsky again. The Harvard professor had ambitiously mastered the detonator. Now like a mystic aghast at a mechanistic world, like some holy fool, the Russian had begun pacing up and down. He was babbling contradictory arguments about heaven and hell, innocence and sin, church and state, revolution, saving the world, redemption. Robert looked in Kistiakovsky's pallid saintly face through a veil of numbness. They were in the dark beyond the bunker door-light.

'This is silly, George,' he said. 'Calm yourself!'

Kistiakovsky's voice subsided in stunned silence. Robert shuffled out from the blockhouse to meet the three jeeps pulling in from Point Zero. For a moment in the whispering shadows, he stepped very close to Bainbridge, McKibben and Allison. There was resignation on all three faces.

As Robert stood staring up at the stars, he heard Allison's kind voice in the bunker. The night was clearing.

'Twenty minutes to ignition, and I am counting.'

Outside the bunker door, the Director stood almost alone. He was finishing his cigarette. It was very crowded with famous people inside. All of him was focused on the great solitude across the flat. In the distance, the holy framework of light outlined a crowd of cactus tops.

'Zero minus five minutes, and counting . . .'

The Director threw his cigarette coal in the dark. Was it his last? You don't care a damn, he thought, sniffing the cool dry air. Wondering momentarily about Kitty far away in the Mesa cottage and the long rich dream of his life, he looked out again at the very real gantry. Then up at the hosts of twinkling desert stars. Well this was it, this was Trinity.

He stepped back in the phosphorescent light, through a door. In the crush inside, there was scarcely a sound of breathing. Some whispering. Restless scrapings.

'One minute to ignition . . .' Allison's voice said without emotion.

A horn blew, somewhere back toward base quarters. In his mind the Director saw Frank, Isidor and the rest throw themselves face down, soles towards Point Zero, in their sunglasses and sunburn cream. Mortal men averting their eyes from the magnificence to come. With his hat off under the low concrete, Robert imagined all the hidden cameras and instruments, whirring, tuned for miles around. And he was shaken by a blinding exaltation so intense he thought he would faint. He scarcely noticed strange faces glancing around at his in the instrument glow. Or some young man's face chattering insanely about shutting the whole thing down.

'. . . six . . . five . . .'

And he could feel it now, moving near on the Jornada's great silent loneliness.

'. . . three . . . two . . .'

Standing in the door frame, shrunken wasted and pure, Doctor Oppenheimer felt *it* coming: unity of all things. And in his heart a tender welcoming cry rose up.

'. . . one! . . . zero! . . . minus one! . . .'

Allison's voice was consumed in a rending, thundering double shock that bumped the air. Robert lurched hard against the post. Then drew back his hand and looked.

And backwards out the bunker door, glowing south in the night as far as you could see, was a strange new light. Brighter, whiter, younger than any day. Lighting the cactus mesquite and far away San Andreas slopes with a black-and-whiteness beyond pigment. With the thunder now rolling in his ears and hearing shouts and cries behind him, hands hitting and tugging him, Robert thought in a dream: But no one saw it, no one saw.

Pulling loose, he stumbled out on to the white sand. Into the new white world.

But when the Director turned, where *it* must have been – Point Zero – was a spirit-swelling fireball. A ten-mile high purple incandescence, rising from the great shock-column of smoke.

'By God!' someone was shouting. 'You long-haired boys have lost control!'

'Twenty thousand tons!' Fermi called from his paper scraps.

Boiling ponderously up in the night with a faint hiss, a violence rose to drift slowly over the fading desert. A beautiful tragic shape, like bubbles exhaled by some titanic diver.

Later, after the sun did rise again, Doctor Oppenheimer stood with triumphant Groves on the baked, intricately cracked waste-flat where Point Zero had been. And they smelled the sulphurous never-before reek of fission heat. And worried about the never-before villainy called 'fallout' . . . now drifting coyly east-northeast, as if starting back to Europe. Then, finally, Robert made the strange long drive back to the cottonwood Mesa from the Journey of the Dead. But Robert would never forget, and he knew no one would ever forget, the way he had been that last moment. Face to face with the new light. Absolute Zero, in the bunker doorway, when he thought: No one saw! When the great positive had become the great negative, and you could not think about it.

Soon the sun rose again over the Rio Grande. It burned through that day, as if to assert its old dominion over the limits of lesser things. But to everyone at Trinity who had seen a world bleached bone-white, this pleasant sun felt wearily sentimental. It was all over, everything was over. The unknowable was known. With whispers and sighs the thinkers gathered their instruments.

At sunset Frank Oppenheimer drove his brother back to Santa Fe, back up to their boyhood Mesa. Isidor was stretched on the back seat asleep. His brother yawned persistently.

'Go ahead and sleep Robbie,' Frank said. 'Don't mind me.'

'Thanks, Frank, I want my own bed. Say, isn't that Enrico?'

An Army car was pulled over ahead, by the empty desert road. A man stood beside it.

As Frank drew over, the man looking east did not move. Robert climbed out. But this Fermi was not the old witty sceptic and master. He was a subdued, sickly, disoriented Fermi. A Fermi standing powerless like someone who commits a crime of passion, then loses direction.

'Too much excitement, Enrico?' Oppy said. 'Come along with us.'

'Oh . . . Robbie! Never mind, no need to wait.'

'You're all right?' Robert clasped his friend's shoulder.

'*Dio mio!* Who is all right?' The Italian looked away. '*La terra a perduta la sua virginita, guarda ti*! And this *ignorante* Gr-r-rofes will go cook thousands of poor Japanese. *E tu*, you are all right!'

'That's very pessimistic, Enrico,' the Director muttered in the hot evening breeze. 'We have done something quite unequalled.'

'You think perhaps they will behave themselves. Truly?' Fermi grinned at him hopefully. They both knew the decision. They had helped to make it. *If a bomb were used the target would be civilian . . . without warning*. Now all that was less clear.

'Thank you, Roberto. Perhaps you are right.'

'Well, I hope I'm right!' Robert said, suppressing a yawn. 'There is no other way.'

So Oppy climbed back in, and Frank led their Army escort back on the empty road. Then like a miracle, many many hours after Robert had felt his nerves and mind shredding with exhaustion, Frank was steering them in the moonlight, up the muddy Mesa road. And feeling chilled and clammy, the Director recalled then another pilgrim years ago. An Oppenheimer come home sickened and limp from Europe, riding a paint pony up this same haunted canyon trail. Robert knew he was even sicker and wearier tonight. It was as if he had been awake for three years. Now at last he would sleep. He would sleep, and it could not matter if he ever woke again.

Then he was walking among the pines, along the path he had walked so often with Kitty. Many ages later, he was on the darkened cottage porch. He pushed the flimsy pine door. And the first thing he saw in the bright inside was Kitty looking at him in the window chair. As in a dream Kitty put down drink and book and came quickly to close the door. She stood very close, holding his arms.

'Well, tell me quick! What happened out there?'

'I'm awfully tired Kitty . . .'

'Just tell me darling, now!' Kitty shook him gently. Suddenly she leaned up and whispered in his ear. 'Quietly, the room is bugged.'

Robert shut his eyes. He rested his sunburnt cheek against the woman's hair.

'It was this morning, Katie,' he said. 'At five-thirty.'

'Yes, well?' she whispered hoarsely.

'Well, I guess we have sold General Groves the sun.'

Opening his circled eyes, Robert saw on Kitty's face a triumph, awe and fear. And quite unexpectedly, he found the strength for a wave of angry bitterness towards her. But taking this for the pride of a returning hero, Kitty pushed her husband down by the open window. She brought him a double martini.

'Good . . . good,' she said, in a quick intent whisper. 'It will give you quite an influence. But now let's get away from this unreality. Let's get away from all these egoists before they destroy us! Let's go back to our life at Eagle Hill – the fascists are beaten, at least for now. We'll make a new beginning.'

Robert sat by the reading lamp, watching his wife with a sort of twisted absorption. For, listening to this woman's musical whisper, and seeing her energy and stomach for life, he could feel nothing in himself but a longing for eternal sleep.

Chapter 25

On the shanty heights of Los Alamos Mesa above the red canyons of the Rio Grande, it was a cherry-blossom time. The meandering breezes bore clouds of cottonwood fluff. But the drought would not lift, the tufts vanished on the dust.

Days went by after Trinity, and still Robert did not have back his brilliant moral light – the dreaming sensation which told him what was beautiful and what was ugly. It was as if, once his soul had strained to receive the new white light on the sands of Trinity, its moral iris was to stay dilated, as if even ethics had been bleached of all passionate distinctions. These crucial, complex days moving up to August were the first since the Creation in which Atom violence was in the sway of human destiny. Yet in the absence of the usual smells, atmospheres and impressions which once made Robert's affections vibrate with correct answers, the Director was having to run Los Alamos with his mind. There was only one answer he was sure of. Katie was right: the new knowledge of fire had come much too near history's authoritarian forces. It was time for free thinkers to pack it away and go down to their peaceful scholarship among ordinary folk.

From the beginning, Groves and all the hundreds of others had chosen to trust Oppy's voice with full responsibility for giving them their moment at Trinity, and even now were subjecting him to their confusion and angry debates. Yet Bohr had already failed with Roosevelt. Doctor Oppenheimer did not need to ask himself how much he would be listened to. One thing America did not need anyway was its men of knowledge becoming science-dictators. You had only to look at Washington.

Weeks before Trinity, Doctor Oppenheimer had been involved in a secret debate back east, at the Pentagon. What should be done with Little Boy, as Thin Man was now called? Already the cruiser Indianapolis had sailed the untested Uranium-weapon to the Pacific island of Tinian, where it was met by Luiz Alvarez and the gentle gardener, Joe Serber. Fat Boy was still here in the Mesa's bomb lab. In the devotional silence of his office, Robert concentrated on the fires of Hell.

It was not easy to end a war, especially when people seemed to prefer mass suicide to admitting they were beaten. Now that Fat Boy was tested, the problem was no less complicated. Robert knew something of the haughty cruelty that had made the Japanese the most hated race from Manchuria to Corregidor. And he knew something about *bushido*, which was harder to crack than the German will. Thousands of Americans would go on dying every day for quite a while until all four islands were bloodily invaded . . . one million, Groves had promised. Even firing Thin Man for a witness of the Emperor's (this in the petition by James Franck of Göttingen days with Szilard, Seaborg and Rabinovitch) might not make the Japanese submit. And what if it should fizzle, and a million lives be sacrificed? It was best for America if no American

178

should ever use a fission bomb. But whether they did or they didn't use it, far more important to humanity was that these should be the last bombs anyone used ever. Who could tell if using the bomb once would not bring that about?

That was a decision Doctor Oppenheimer felt more happy leaving in the hands of expert men of action.

Chapter 26

Three days after Trinity, letters and commendations began reaching Santa Fe PO Box 1663, from the new President Truman (who had only just heard of a new weapon), and everyone else cleared to know what had happened in the Jornada that dawn of July 16th. But the Mesa's drought went on.

The Director had drifted off early from morning Colloquium in Theatre Two. For now, in the bone-bleached sensation left by Trinity, last month's Franck Report was taking on a darker character. It was another hot day and his nose felt dry. As Robert crossed the catwalk to his office, he was thinking back to how it had begun in June.

The shady office passage had been empty. But the instant Robert closed the door, there had been a violent knocking. Anne Wilson held the door for an agitated Teller.

'Oh hello, Edward.' Robert stopped behind his desk. 'Come on in!'

'Szilard sent me this,' Teller had muttered at once.

As he fell into a chair, Teller pushed across a thick-folded paper. He managed to look excited, self-important and grief-stricken all at the same time, and was panting as if he had run the whole way.

'We need your signature,' Edward exploded. 'More than all others!'

Across the desk, sunk limply with his pipe and first new pouch of English tobacco, strung taut by the test ahead, the Director had felt a wave of bitterness tighten in his throat.

Robert swivelled away. He stared at the waterless, overcast New Mexico sky above the tarboard roofs.

Teller again! Edward whose security clearance Robert had arranged, but who had refused his order to help the others on either of the Army bombs. Teller, who for two years had stubbornly kept his team slaving on an unnecessary thermonuclear bomb for murdering a thousand times the number of human beings. Now this same Teller was playing the moral champion against the little unproven atom bombs? Was it just *power* Edward wanted? Or was it the Hungarian's sentimentalism about special treatment for highly civilized people? Or was it just to preserve public innocence, so he could push on to bigger and bigger superbombs? Who were these Hungarians to deliver jeremiads to the American government?

Anyway, Robert reflected, controlling his irritation, these issues were too ethically far-reaching to turn on personalities.

'Edward, we've all been going over this for months. Here and in Washington.'

Robert had turned from the window and watched Teller's face thoughtfully. The air was so parched it reddened their eyes.

'Actually,' he went on, 'I agree with Leo's petition. Let's hope Groves, the President and the rest end up not using the thing.'

'Then, Oppenheimer, you must sign!' Teller said emotionally. 'You are the only one who could persuade the government men!'

'Thank you, Edward!' Robert smiled, feeling a twinge of guilt that he might have some exclusive influence. 'I feel quite strongly though, science by itself does not give us an absolute right, or make us competent to persuade anyone at all.'

'You truly think it?' Teller sat forward with a sudden warmth. In his mournful eyes was suddenly the trust of someone driven to give himself in total belief.

'Edward, put your trust in this country's founding fathers.' The Director's subtly teeming eyes examined the Hungarian across the table. Even in shirtsleeves, the office was hot.

'Don't worry, Ed.' Robert shifted his pipe to the other side. 'The matter is being dealt with on a higher level.'

But during the incredibly ordinary days after the Trinity firestorm, there was time to wonder how the 'higher level' was dealing. Still, Oppy knew better than to let himself stray into cynicism. That had been a luxury of Harvard days. Too many people trusted him now. To succumb to Bohr's huge vision of evil would spoil Robert's simple hope for the better world waiting just ahead.

Now, this morning, the Director puffed his pipe and looked at

Lincoln's kind fatherly face. He watched the hurrying cotton fluff drift through the open window, settling on the pine floor. The talk with Teller had certainly left Robert feeling eager to escape from the project. But he could not leave this office now, not without giving away these desert canyons he loved. For the 'two were become one. He would never be free of the security screen.

Just a few days after Teller, another Hungarian had come to Los Alamos. Tweedy little Szilard himself, with his thick wavy hair.

'Of course,' Fermi had shrugged with Roman irony. 'There is this thing of the Navy Under-Secretary . . .'

'Yes . . . Bard! Yes!' Szilard tenderly rolled the 'r'. He sat very primly on the edge of the chair. 'Bard has resigned in protest. Japan is beaten, Robert! Yet this new Secretary of State Byrnes, he understands nothing! I went all the way to South Carolina to see him.'

'As Bohr went to see Churchill,' Fermi laughed cynically.

'Still, the war drags on,' Robert had reflected. 'A million lives.'

'But gentlemen!' Szilard exploded tragically, glancing from Fermi's resigned expression to Oppy's. 'You do not face the significance of this weapon! This is the last chance sane, rational men will have to say no! No! No!'

'Leo, Leo . . . you become over-excited,' Fermi had said, his mind as fixed to mechanical possibilities as any general's. 'We cannot boast of our great weapons. Not when the thing may crash on main street like . . . how do you say? . . . a heap of junk. Better drop it without warning.'

'They told me truly at Chicago!' Szilard had muttered then. 'The people here at Los Alamos live some fantastic dream. Yet believe me, my friends! You will see! This thing is no weapon to make utopias with . . . it is a mass psychosis!'

Yes, since Trinity, how like children's their adult voices sounded. Playing at statesmanship, confidently singing history in a dozen foreign accents. So like children . . . America's children! For somehow the thing was settled and the opposition silenced. And cities called Hiroshima and Nagasaki: selected to be delivered their splendid inventions just two weeks from now. But this morning in his sunny Main Tech offices, Robert recalled Enrico Fermi's disturbed face, standing by the empty road home from the Jornada.

Back *then*, before, had not words had a different sound? It was as if, on July 16, they had stepped through the door of a single day into some new world. A world of subtly, yet completely different, rules.

And now, for the first time in three years, Robert was acutely aware of poor fat Groves.

Taking a pad from his desk, Robert sketched Groves a hopeful cable: 'Hope cost of going through understood by you.' Just three hours later, a reply returned from Washington. A cable from someone named General Leslie Groves.

'Factors beyond our control,' the decoded message read, with the politeness of a once abject lover now set confidently on a divorce. 'Cannot consider other than to go ahead.'

Sitting in the office chair from which, for two years, he had led the enlightened utopia of the Mesa in a supreme adventure of the mind, holding Groves's cable in one hand, and his pipe in the other as the cottonwood fluff gathered inside his open window, Doctor Oppenheimer felt then the savage bite of real Power.

That same night, by his reading lamp and box of Swiss cherry chocolates in his darkened Washington office, Groves too was thinking about America's famous sons of action, about the glorious liberating heroes of Normandy, Midway and Guadalcanal, who had their offices just down the air-conditioned Pentagon corridor. But Groves was thinking about them with loathing.

For almost all of them, especially General MacArthur, had had their triumphs. Now they went around saying Japan was all but licked! At least, Groves had been able to use the instrument of State Secrecy he had so lovingly detected and refined to prevent most of those slim, dashing American heroes from knowing very much about his fat bomb. Suppressing Szilard's circulating petition had been easy. Groves had simply classified it . . . and there were no Army couriers available. The fact was, since Roosevelt's death, Groves had been able to keep practically everyone in Washington from imagining the violent thing he had seen at the Jornada del Muerte, even the new President. And no one was going to drop the Japs leaflets warning about radiation-sickness. No one was accusing G.G. of using poison gases! Groves even managed to keep much of the general opposition *inside* the security screen away from the new President. Anyway, Truman had the ignorant American public clamouring for revenge on the Japs. He would never have the guts now to call off the Hiroshima raid. Tonight the Supreme Commander was away at Potsdam. Tonight Trinity was Groves's own fat uncouth devilish secret, with which he would announce his presence to the world. But the war was running out. The public triumph, which alone could satisfy a lifetime of dividing and conquering, was balanced on a matter of days in a waning war.

The cable from his Oppy out in New Mexico had been brought to his office by the night dispatcher. Groves scarcely had time to linger over the most elegant of all his purifications of power, that of having so completely stolen the power of world domination from the Nobel eggheads *that Groves would never again have even to listen to a word they said*! He had almost been tempted to leave the error in his draft answer to Oppy that made it read: 'Factors beyond *your* control . . .' But Groves never left tracks.

General Groves's lonely sleepless anguish, on the brink of fulfilling his wildest dream of success and glory, was prolonged only two more weeks. Arriving back in the White House after meeting Attlee and Stalin at Potsdam, having made no serious peace petition to Prince Konoye, Harry Truman at once gave his permission for the nuclear age to begin.

Chapter 27

From the beginning of his love for the mysterious Mesa on the Rio Grande, Robert never was much concerned with the vast money system that cushioned his family and then his colleagues from the harshness of life.

Now, very secretly and quietly, an Army truck had taken Fat Boy from the bomb lab to rejoin Little Boy. And as the Great Mystery the scholars had stolen from the gods rolled slowly down the canyon road, it too was become Trinity.

Already Groves's two lonely secrets were far from the Mesa, at the bomber base on Tinian in the Marianas. So it came to pass, that when the failed Kansas haberdasher gave his permission for the nuclear age to begin, the first Trinity was shackled under Paul Tibbetts's silver B29. Along the flanks of his machine Paul had painted the name *Enola Gay*, for she was his mother. Before dawn, August 6th 1945 anno domini, at the hour Oppy was leaving his Colloquium, Paul Tibbetts controlled the *Enola Gay* down the airstrip. She rose heavily, banking out over the coral reef, and levelling northerly. The sister bombers *Great Artiste* and *No. 62* fell in, flanking her. Suspended in the bay behind the boy flyers was Trinity. Beside it, Oppy's friend Bill Parsons, who would arm its fires. Fifteen hundred miles across open water was a second Jornada del Muerte. And it awaited his coming.

Only this second Journey of the Dead was no lava flat. There was no tower at Point Zero, no concrete control bunker for thinkers to hide their flesh in, and no Stonehenge encirclement of subtle instruments to record the magnificence of Trinity's coming. No careful rehearsals to make sure no one got left on Point Zero. For this Journey of the Dead awaiting Paul Tibbetts, his mother and his Trinity, was a lake of innocent living man-woman-and-child flesh, stretching for miles of little one-level wood garden-houses. Of markets, schools, shops, shrines and temples, and headquarters for the Emperor of Japan's humiliated Southern Army.

It was over the red tile roofs of this ancient town, this sea of human flesh and intricate whispered human loves, that Paul Tibbetts's silver dragonfly appeared in the 8:15 summer morning sunshine.

A veil of woodsmoke hung over the rustling town. The street-cars, bridges and business districts were filling with hurrying tradesmen and air-raid workers. Hundreds stopped to stare up at three more very high Yankee aircraft, droning over like winged messengers. Many saw the parachute flutter loose, white as a cherry blossom. And many childish eyes watched it come quickly down toward the Ota until it was nearly among them. And no one who did ever saw anything again.

Abruptly, in a rending rush, the new white light was back on earth.

And in one quick flesh-splashing breath, the centre of Hiroshima lay down. And it fell away like a maze of cards. As one hundred thousand lips parted to scream, an alien wave of molten air raced out, filled with a hatred for the things of paradise. And again for only an instant, the new white light was there on the tranquil Inland Sea, bleaching all pigment and daylight for miles. Then as all the anger in Hell's last circle rushed up in a pillar to the sky, the air blackened and the Japanese earth was fired rust red as the Jornada. In this pitch darkness, instantly boiling with giant flames, the bewildered tiny screams of a hundred thousand voices lifted in the stifling heat of Hiroshima.

Then, through the rubble of burned and skinless bleeding flesh which had once been the streets of man's city, were scrambling twenty thousand faceless, eyeless, hairless demons that had been people, their skins flapping wetly around their wrists and ankles. In place of the love that had bound them was a shrieking pain and lonely terror of the unknown thing which had ruined their flesh. And as a hundred thousand of what had been men, women and children in the flaming wind shrieking abjectly the names of children, mothers and fathers, sisters and brothers, wives and husbands they could not see or recognize. And as minute after minute went by in the flattened red streets of piercing pain, in the sulphur-reeking blackness of flames and whirling ashes and bloated lacerated carcasses rotted alive, dying in blood-hiccoughing waves, there was no humanity in the world. And the eyeless, naked demons too crazed to think of death, flapped and scrambled toward the one idea . . . and it was the great water of life. And they raced through the streets, past standing corpses and monsters with burnt-out eye-sockets. By the thousands, from the smoking banks and splintered bridges, the pitiful dying man-, woman and child-monsters of Hiroshima threw themselves in the river. Hour after hour, as huge piles of grotesque maimed shredded and irradiated flesh, from which the souls had fled in horror, mounted outside the emergency stations in the surrounding third of Hiroshima – the distance from Point Zero the hero Groves had hidden at – the tidings went out through mankind: of a new hell and shame on this earth beyond the telling of it. And in England at Farm Hall, the captured German physicists Heisenberg and Von Weiszäcker who had kept Nature's veil of mysteries heard of it. And Otto Hahn, the father of radiation, was wild with despair.

Under a blood-red sunset, by another river in New Mexico, Oppy's whistle blew, to call the men of reason to Main Tech.

There was a tense silence in the crush of Theatre Two. Climbing on the wood podium where he had conducted the most inspired moments of the last two years, Doctor Oppenheimer stood soberly stuffing his pipebowl. He did not look up at the five hundred trusting, expectant young faces focused on him. Nor at the two sullen ones; Seth's because his old teacher had let the war trample pure science, and Slotin's because Oppy had refused to let him examine the truth of Hiroshima in flames.

Then the Director of the Mesa looked up at last.

'Congratulations to all of you at Los Alamos.' Robert spoke in a hollow, unnatural voice. 'This morning at 8:15 Tokyo time, the instrument we designed together struck a blow for demo-'

Oppy's voice was drowned in a thundering tramp and shouting. As the rumbling pandemonium went on, Robert could do nothing but exchange glances with the faces of friends in the crowd . . . Bethe . . . Fermi . . . Ulam . . . Rabi. Suddenly, and for the last time in his life, Robert felt again, all at one time, the subtle distinctions and gradations of the superb intellects in the room. How he had led them under the vast deep mysterious emptiness of the universe to man's first moment face-to-face with absolute Light. And at that moment Oppy was quite sure he had done all he could do for his country, that he had struck a blow against fascism far more effective than Steve Nelson had in Spain, a blow to repay the Guernicas and gas chambers and torture camps.

And knowing in his heart he was the obedient slave and prophet of Progress, the legitimate child of his time who had just brought an end to traditional warfare, Robert put down his pipe. With his back shadowing the sponged blackboard on which the new light and flesh-splashing violence of the Jornada had been chalked out, Oppy clasped his hands above his gentle ironic face. And he shook them like a triumphant charioteer.

In Washington, General Groves scarcely had time to celebrate the end of his obscurity. Fat Boy was waiting on Tinian for the flight to Nagasaki.

It is said that when Japan surrendered, the 'holy fool' Kistiakovsky set off a ring of explosive flares for the two-day triumph. And in the desert night, the shantytown on Cottonwood Mesa was again like some colony of aliens come from another planet.

Chapter 28

One month later, the quickest he could arrange, Robert Oppenheimer and his young wife left his lonely Mesa for ever. For its mystery was sold to General Groves.

The five hundred thinkers in the shanty town had rallied an association to lobby for immediate limits on human power. Oppy knew now what he had helped poor patriotic Groves do with his utopia and with the world. He had just spent several days in Washington representing the Los Alamos Association with Conant and Bush. Old Langmuir had told Robert of Kurchatov and Kapitza's work in Russia, how the Communists could easily exceed the Americans (and Truman scarcely accepting the Russians had scientists at all!). Before Oppy could even lead his physicists down from Groves's bomb factory, Harry Daghlian died horribly of a radiated hand and two others were blinded.

The afternoon before they left – the evening of the Oppenheimer's farewell dinner at Edith Warner's, and Robert's speech in Theatre Two – Kitty drove to the hamlet of El Rito to say goodbye to Jed Holmes.

During the year her husband had been bearing down on Seth and his great idea, Kitty had been aware of an impermanence on the Mesa. The visionary light had been dimming. The mind-god on the plateau had lost its divinity, the timelessness gone out of it. Was Los Alamos really no more than an Army bomb-factory?

The sense of moral squalor at the supreme height of their success disturbed Kitty's sanity in a way good friends could not help her with. It was the few visits to the adobe farm Jed Holmes had made with his own hands that did her most good. Jed was her secret.

On one of her restless drives, the old gentleman had helped Kitty with a steaming radiator outside the El Rito village store. Later, they enjoyed drinking tequila with each other, sitting in the little low-ceilinged white room with the scarred guns on the wall, and shelves lined with Thoreau, Melville and Emerson.

Kitty had only been half listening, one day seated in the cool at his round table, as Jed muttered some tall story. It was about a local man who, as a boy long ago in Pittsburgh, had lied his way into the

Northern Army, played the fife in Sherman's campaign to Atlanta, marched up Pennsylvania Avenue after Lincoln's assassination, and come west ten years later with General Howard to fight Apaches. This fellow had seen three wives die, and his nine children lived now in the canyons between Sante Fé and Pueblo de Taos. A month later, Jed Holmes told the nervous young woman licking the salt of the tequila glass that the man in that yarn was himself.

Kitty's embarrassment was so intense she did not go back again for four months. Then one day, testing cultures in the bio lab, Kitty realized with a shock that this was because she had not believed a word of the old man's story! In the conceited atmosphere of Robbie's Mesa, Kitty simply could not conceive it. Could such a life truly end up accepting obscurity in a mud hut living on beans and tequila? How many Jed Holmeses might America hold? Why, she had not even believed the old man's satisfaction in the simple things of his farm!

Kitty had driven over that afternoon to El Rito, despite the curious security guards. The old man showed no surprise when he saw her standing by his low mud gate. She had never felt embarrassed with Jed again. A half-dozen more times they had sat on the small low table by the open doorway, in the heavy silence of the noon heat. And Jed's lazy drawl would undo the knot in Kitty's stomach, coming on with her husband's depression on the secret Mesa. She always left El Rito with a fine rich feeling of life.

This last afternoon, Kitty steered left at the one-room El Rito Post Office. She squeaked down the flat-winding hard mud track. Her sophisticated embarrassment was back. Glimpsing the white adobe ranch and fig trees, Kitty pulled up on the weed bank.

Wouldn't it just be easier, Kitty thought, not going back.

A cloud of dust billowed through the open car window. That way their friendship would keep its timelessness. No, that would be dishonest.

She left the car door open and stepped quickly along the wall to the low mud gate. The grey-bearded old man came slowly from the dark door. Jed was in clean trousers, a starched shirt and string tie. His engraved boots were polished. A red neckerchief was tied around his grizzled hair. It was as if he knew.

Jed leaned on the wall at Kitty's elbow. The afternoon was big and still, with a metallic smell of sage and dust. From another shack came a faint cheering from the world-series game.

'You're not stopping for a drink today, little lady.'

Jed's creased blue eyes moved over Kitty's face, bitter and secretly discerning. Flushing, Kitty turned to lean back on the wall. They faced together, out into the flat valley. The Sangre de Cristos were a remote haze.

'I thought that last rain might have washed out your house, Jed.'

For a long time the wasps hummed in the arbor over the door. The old man waited for Kitty to leave the fence.

'Yes, adobe's a funny thing,' Jed said jauntily, and a sadness passed between them. 'Mud around here's got natural oil in it,' he went on. 'Got a theory there's a belt of oily mud right through. Mexico, Sahara, Persia, India, Explains all the mud houses.'

'That's a nice theory, Jed,' Kitty laughed.

Leaning by him on the low mud wall, Kitty watched Jed's sunspotted old fingers take a cigarette. He must be ninety-five. Kitty took one herself. His grey beard tickled the hollow of her hand as she held a match for him.

Abruptly Kitty was aware of the cool simple rooms waiting under the droning arbor. The tightness loosened through her. Suddenly feeling very loyal to this old man puffing the cigarette beside her, Kitty hated the intellectual passion back on the Mesa. Jed Holmes's life was unknown up there. She guessed how crazy Jed would have considered the physicists and their evil inventions. And how crazy and boring too the people on the Mesa would have thought her interest in this strange old man.

Yes, Kitty mused, picking tobacco off her tongue, she was carrying a double secret, like Robbie's Plutonium hemispheres. Each half had a crazy hatred for the other. And when they came face to face the world would go mad. At that moment, Kitty knew she preferred the hatred of knowledge to the hatred of life. Leaning on this wall alone with Jed felt as much an adultery as if they were young gypsies.

'Jed?' Kitty hid her face. 'I can't stay long.'

'Too bad, little lady. Still had a thing or two to tell.'

'I know you do, Jed.' Kitty frowned. Why had he let

vulnerability show through his formidable wisdom? Jed didn't own her. But the feeling of something in the balance confused her. In the wordless hush, Kitty heard the old man's boots crumbling mud clods.

'Well, okay ma'am,' he was saying. Hearing his dignified indifference to her, Kitty felt a little hurt.

'I guess it's been a pretty fine time.'

Kitty laughed. 'I've never heard of such a fine time, Jed.'

'Wouldn't mind if the kids thought so.'

'They're fools if they don't!' Kitty said.

'No, little lady,' Jed reflected coldly. 'They can't ever have what I had, way back.'

Kitty looked around a little haughtily at the sky-blue eyes focused into the haze. Jed's ancient skin was charred and creased as an Indian's.

'Uhuh. I gave 'em the only things still worth having in this country.'

'What are those, Jed?'

Kitty was having more and more trouble concentrating on Jed's soft slow speech. Her blouse was sticking to her.

'Failure, little lady,' he said. 'This land too. It can save their souls.'

Jed turned over on his elbows. They leaned back to back against the wall.

'They don't forgive me,' Jed added, as if Kitty were no longer there. 'But I know it was right.'

'I'm not ungrateful, Jed,' Kitty lied, her voice heavy. Just then she had felt the old man's strength. 'I'll never forget you.'

Standing away from the wall, Kitty rested her hand on Jed Holmes's shoulder. Then seeing the old man's ironic stare, the light withdrawing in his eyes, she drew it back. A wave of inadequacy and failure swept through Kitty.

'I better start back,' she said. She hid the angry tears as she stamped out the cigarette. 'I'll come back some time.'

'All right little lady,' Jed laughed. 'If I'm still around.'

Kitty stood to shake the old man's dry hand across the hard mud wall. She was glad when Jed Holmes turned away his pitying eyes. He walked slowly back under the arbor, into the dark door.

But twisting on the front seat, looking back from the rise in the road driving out of El Rito, Kitty saw the white beard and red bandana by Jed's gate. How did that happen? she thought. How did you get into that? It was as if she had condemned him.

By the time Kitty Oppenheimer crossed back over the Rio Grande, and was winding in the twilight up the canyon wall, she had somehow forgotten failing Jed Holmes's urgent old age, having sounded not quite sincere. And her life felt so dense with the good feeling of Jed's bare adobe rooms, that Kitty despotically asked the curious guard to babysit.

But Kitty had told Jed the truth. She never would forget the old man.

Chapter 29

It was the Director's last night on Cottonwood Mesa. The breathless, fiery sunset of Indian summer lay spread over the desert of the pueblos, and the Rio Grande was all blood-reds and chilly blacks. The mystery which could madden the world, lying somewhere between these ramshackle Army buildings and the adobe farm of Jed Holmes, was not yet breached.

The last weeks in Washington, Doctor Oppenheimer had been discovering the failure of ordinary men to take responsibility. Trapped inside Groves's security, the giant laboratories of California, Illinois, Tennessee and Massachusetts had become hives of moral agitation. But still Robert held them back, hoping the senators and generals men would shoulder the weight of reason, the nuclear lesson of Hiroshima – *that they had only to fear themselves*! But in Washington, the victors had earned the right to cherish themselves and to blame everyone else. Already Robert felt his faith weaken in the good of his life, and man's loyalty to the innocent land.

In those days, as the world went back to peace, Robert began fighting for it. For if they lost this fight, no one would ever leave Los Alamos. They would all be chained to the Mesa and their livers picked out by disillusion.

Later tonight in Theatre Two, the Director would speak to his five hundred scientists for the last time. Now, folded neatly in

Robert's baggy tweed jacket, as he waited in Edith Warner's tearoom with the Fermis and Isidor, Hans Bethe, Frank and his sister-in-law, Edward Teller and Niels Bohr, was his typed speech. A double warning in which Doctor Oppenheimer would counsel the minds of Los Alamos: it was no time for them, they who had called down on earth the terrors of the universe, to forget their solidarity with their fellow men. And he would make a prophecy. If leaders turned these stolen fires into weapons and added them to the arsenals of warlike peoples, their fellow men would one day curse the names of Hiroshima and Los Alamos. The words folded neatly on four sheets of paper.

Kitty had slipped in through Edith's kitchen, just as Tileno and the old woman were lifting a very big pumpkin pie from the wood stove.

'Well, Tileno.' Edith grinned. 'That's the last of the durn things. Hi Katie, better go rescue your Bob.'

Kitty laughed happily, sniffing the good smell of lamb and wood smoke. She bent over the molasses-coloured pie. Under the kerosene lamp, Kitty looked clean and tanned with the desert. Her wet hair was pulled back in combs.

'That sure is a pie, Edith,' Tileno said in his velvety poker voice.

The old woman laughed, the laugh turning into a deep tubercular cough. But she laughed again.

'Don't worry old friend,' Edith gasped. 'I'll save you enough to go whoop and a holler on.'

'What an unbelievable pie Edith!' Kitty said. 'But Thanksgiving's not for three weeks.'

'Not Thanksgiving, dear?' Edith turned to Kitty as the Indian picked up the pie and headed for the dinner tables. 'The war's over. That's quite a reason for thanks, I'd say.'

Kitty stepped after Tileno and the old woman into the darker dining room. The dozen candles and the white walls made it like a Mexican shrine. Kitty always thought of Spain here. As the group at the corner table turned, Kitty saw they were all eager to celebrate life too, all except Robbie and Edward. Seeing her husband's face, like a suffering saint, Kitty remembered the frozen gulf she had to cross now to reach him.

The pie was set down on the table. Everyone made appreciative sounds.

'I'm sorrier than heck,' Edith dropped her eyes, 'you young folks have got to leave Los Alamos. You've meant a lot to Tileno and me. You've helped us a lot.'

'They never could have lived without you, Edith my dear!' said Isidor, his puckishness intensified by sangria.

'Thanks, rainmaker,' Edith lifted her head. 'What's the matter, you forget your umbrella today?'

Rabi pulled a pickled face, and the circle laughed with Edith until they heard it turn to coughing. Tileno watched her patiently until the bout passed.

'Say . . .' Edith leaned on Fermi's chair back. 'Now you're pulling out, tell an old lady what you've been doing up here all this time. This spaceship business.'

With a grateful glance as Kitty pushed in beside him, Robert leaned into the circle of their friends' faces. Hadn't Edith heard?

'Inventing a newfangled sauce,' said Robert. 'To compete with the French.'

'You know, Tileno and me got together t'other day,' Edith went on. There was a smile fixed on her wrinkled red face. A little stir of ungrateful impatience went around the table.

'Uhuh, we made a few guesses. One of them was, that you were working on that bomb . . .'

The wrinkled old woman searched the faces around the table. But strange to say, though Groves's secret desert laboratory had been given headlines in the world press, not one of the guilty boys' faces around the table broke Edith's silence. Even her favourite, Dr Bohr.

'If that's what you were doing,' Edith continued, as she began handing the dirty cutlery to the Indian, 'I'd have been sorry for you. I wouldn't want to hear. Anybody who could put together a thing like that . . . why, I don't give a damn for whatever half-baked reason . . . well they've done their brother men a real disservice.'

Tileno left the old woman standing over them. Her smile passed kindly around their faces. 'Thank God, in a few more years I'll be gone,' she began coughing. 'I won't have to live with the thing.

'Anyway don't let an old fool like me hold up your dinner. You get on! Set to that pie, while it's still hot.'

'Thanks, Edith!' Kitty called after the old woman. No one around the flickering table had said anything. Teller squirmed.

'Will people get so hysterical about this thing?' he lamented.

'Anything's possible, Edward.' Fermi laughed pleasantly. He began vigorously cutting the pie. 'Maybe even you will become hysterical. It is so much more fun to work on than to live with!'

'Oh *dio mio*, these American pies! I am sure they will cure the accent in my vocal chords.'

'Yew will newer,' growled Bohr in his thick Danish, 'be Yankee!'

A little burst of relieved laughter passed around their table. They were still the world's greatest minds inventing their splendid theories. That meant something.

'Yes, Edward.' Robert took it up. He leaned forward with a tactful gravity, and Kitty sensed this was the earlier argument. He stared at the Italian's neat pie-work.

'That's why I can feel it in my bones,' Robert smiled, 'all of *us* – the really creative ones – must go back to the universities. This desert is a . . . a place of temptations. Temptations to bigger and bigger inventions. Temptations to grab for power.'

'Temptations?' Teller giggled explosively, then he looked tragic. 'But what about the next phase? This Tritium is no problem . . .'

'This is not the place, Edward.' The Director held up his hand with a painful smile. He was very conscious of Bohr.

For seeing the Hungarian's turbulent emotions, Robert remembered his impressions of Edward across the last four years. Of this primordial ambition, this irresistible jealousy to stand alone at the forefront of knowledge. This affectionate selfishness, like a child's for toys. The passion Robert had always felt himself: to stand alone with a beautiful idea, and possess it! But the passion was even more intense in Edward. And his friend was doing nothing to control it. It would only take one passion like Teller's, defying Robert's prophecy, and the world might one day face an armada of super-bombs. Robert could not think of it.

'This world is not the place, Edward. Go back to quanta . . . light theory . . . collapsing suns.'

'But there is nothing like fusion!' Teller objected soulfully.

'Edward, my husband's done enough,' laughed Kitty quickly.

'What more could anyone ask of you?' Frank agreed.

'Better listen to him, Edward,' Hans said heavily.

'That's a question,' Robert muttered across to Frank, 'I've asked myself a lot.'

'Do not do something rash, Robert!' Teller made a last charming plea. 'That is all very well. But imagine! We have only just begun to tap this force.'

'Edward . . . Edward!' Hans Bethe laid his hand tenderly on Teller's shoulder. 'Robbie needs some time to think. None of us have had the time to think these last months.'

Seeing Edward Teller's face soften with a chastened shrug, his friends around the table felt he would accept their advice. At least for the time being . . . But it was the most insecure feeling Doctor Oppenheimer had ever known.

Outside Edith Warner's adobe house, as the celebration went on, the young American continent sprawled out in the moonless night, clad only in its glow of cities. Among such hopeful gaudiness, the few lights on Los Alamos Mesa were no more than the tiniest sequin. And as the five hundred scientists in the shanty town left their fascinating machines, ambling toward Theatre Two to hear Oppy speak for the last time, they were like intellectual revellers sated by an orgy of knowledge, ready for a period of austerity and restraint.

At their centre, in his exhaustion, Doctor Oppenheimer was possessed with hope, eager to go down forever and find the lost thread of his solitude. And the desert Mesa was not beautiful to him.

PART THREE

Chapter 1

So Doctor Oppenheimer went down from Los Alamos. For the last time, with Kitty and the two small Oppenheimers, he rode the night Pullman away from the Rio Grande and out under the Arizona stars. With him into the world of men, Oppy carried Groves's ultimate crime.

Braced in the top bunk by the red emergency light, while his little family slept in the bunks below, Robert had a dream. A dream which continued when he woke, as if dreams were trying to fuse with matter.

In the dream Eagle Hill was a feverish place without shade. Out below over San Francisco Bay, so thick that only the lifeless apartment tops of Nob and Telegraph Hills rose above it, drifted a bank of white fog. Only it was a poisoned fog, and the world was bleached white. And in that new white light of the Jornada del Muerte Robert saw the streaming multitude of Man's splendid cities, bloodied, eyeless and skinless as heretics; an auto-dà-fé that cloaked the world in fire. And his own soul burnt in the lonely long hours of his nightmare.

Now, in the sweet orange California morning of artichoke fields and eucalyptus, Robert was humbled by the ordinariness of things. And he could not even speak to Kitty about it.

So Robert Oppenheimer's nightmares were delivered into the sagehood of college life, to his mild meditations on mesons and collapsing suns. He lost himself in a double lecturing schedule, travelling between San Francisco and Los Angeles. He struggled to draw about him the old happy circle of affections he had betrayed on the Mesa. But Jean Tatlock had put herself beyond the reach of love. And Haakon was translating at the Nuremberg Trials, where Europe too was trying to forget its criminal past and putting itself politely on trial. Many of his students had moved on, and Kitty let herself get drunk three times in one week.

Among the willing visionaries of the Mesa, inside the security screen, the Director had come half to believe in a new enlightened world that would face its own crimes. But awakening strangely free in a sea of ordinary souls, Robert and Kitty found an America gone happily back to peace. At the usual faculty gatherings, Robert listened with shock to the gossip of some act of God off in Japan, which had somehow made America a safer place. They were all marked men, but no one was involved. Groves's crime felt vaguely legitimate, as if Robert had belonged to a famous gang.

In Washington, some moral restraint had been building; even idiots could see that a philosophy must be created around America's godly fires. An Undersecretary of State, Dean Acheson, and David Lilienthal of Roosevelt's Tennessee Valley Authority were designing a thesis on sharing atom knowledge with the Russians. It was what Robert had tried telling the security man Pash two years ago. Unknown to all but a few men human enlightenment still hung, month after month, balanced between universal Good and universal Evil. That winter, Robert took the Washington flight.

What *if* America shared the peaceful uses of nuclear power? Robert was thinking grimly as he gazed below at the labyrinth of barren red shapes which is the Great Divide. That might still prevent a scramble of savage beasts. A race like that America could not win, not without losing its decency. It was a wild beautiful hope. He would fight for it if it killed him. He had the Power now, if he did not squander it.

So once again, as three years ago with Groves on their patriotic crusade, Oppy went on the road, this time with the stately Acheson and the patient, visionary Lilienthal. At an accelerated pace, the three men toured Groves's giant new war laboratories across the victorious young land. The people were returning to their country clubs, wealthy campuses, their football stadiums, movie houses, sleepy towns, their bars and jazz clubs, back to their safety and prosperity. To their unheard-of success, beloved of its own barbarous innocence.

Oppy was again sipping martinis in train compartments, speaking with his old flair of the new world, a world where all men were bound to their fellow creatures. He spoke of the subtle new line dividing their choice between a difficult paradise and an inconceivable hell of sleepless fear. Acheson and Lilienthal not only grasped but seemed to share his urgency, and Robert's sickened hopes revived. Soon they rose to a passionate intensity and he was sounding more arrogant than ever. Imagining a Washington, Moscow and Europe free from greed, ignorance and suspicion, Europe's old enlightened circle of scholars risen from its grave, the sadness went out of the towns and farmhouses. The rain, which since Trinity had seemed like weeping, was cool and fresh and cleansing.

And so Robert felt again the old mystery. A power to do universal good.

Chapter 2

After the Adviser had been back in Washington a few inspired days, giving ethical breadth to Lilienthal and Acheson's proposal to the Kremlin, the Undersecretary drove Oppy to see Harold Truman in the White House.

So for the second time, Doctor Oppenheimer was shuffling in his freshly pressed tweed suit under the portraits of Presidents. A warm winter sun shone into the Oval Room.

All was just as when the Director had come during the war to see Roosevelt. There was the same brushing past of glancing aides, and secretaries clutching sacred folders of State. But as he stepped behind Dean up to the President's door, Robert suddenly felt something very strange. He was feeling the shame of what he knew. Wasn't he as shabby as some witness come barefoot, smeared with the dirt and blood of Calvary? As the two men came into the big office, three aides left the side of a familiar, nondescript figure.

Truman waited firmly by the window. The unnaturally large eyes behind the spectacles fastened on the gaunt scientist's uncomfortable face.

Then he came forward to meet them with such a brisk confidence that Robert faltered in his tracks. Was this official with the subtle handshake not Kansas City Boss Prendergast's failed haberdasher? Instantly he sensed the mystical confidence of all honest insignificance when it has heard the roar of Convention crowds. A confusion came over him.

'Well, Doctor, this sure is a pleasure,' the politician began with an automatic flourish of geniality. The three men were settling around the big desk.

Truman sat squarely, pressing together his fingertips. 'This country owes you quite a debt, sir. How many men can say they ended a war almost single-handed? You've given America an advance no one will compete with.'

Robert stirred impatiently. 'I had little to do with it really. A lot of scientists . . .' Was it possible the President of America did not grasp *that*?

'Come come,' Truman blinked at him. 'A lot of guys I respect have complimented you, in a way that would almost make me envious.'

And so forth. But as the famous minutes went by and they got down to business, the President became aware of a vague hostility. And for a moment Truman troubled himself to wonder: was the father of the atom bomb too good for a President's praise?

Across the desk of desks, Robert Oppenheimer sat, trying to stay urgently focused on the innocent multitudes who depended on his eloquence. This official's neatly barbered, grey-flannelled ignorance had a hundred and fifty million Americans massed behind it. All Robert had behind him was a bleak devastating truth which might still save mankind.

Ten minutes had passed. Oppy was listlessly outlining his proposal: to offer the Russians Uranium fuel for peace, in return for a joint ban on missile development. He was aware of his silver lighter. It was trembling over his pipe bowl.

The President had suddenly twisted in his armchair. With a questioning glance at Undersecretary Acheson, Truman pulled down the drooping tip of his nose. He gave the gentle suffering face across his telephones a tough smile. Was this weak, gawky boy the famously brainy Doctor Oppenheimer of the crackling eloquence?

'Okay! You think the Russians can get the bomb,' the President interrupted. He had felt the stirring of an unpleasant awareness, and he mistook it for contentiousness. 'When will they get it?'

Robert crossed his legs. He overcame a wave of revulsion. 'I can't know that,' he said numbly.

'Well, I know.' The President leaned over his knotted fingers.

Robert stared back at Truman's huge, stony grey eyes. 'When?'

'Never!' Truman was not smiling. 'Doctor, is something worrying you? You don't look too happy.'

'Yes, Mr President.' A tasteless accusation rose in Robert

Oppenheimer's throat, mixed with hope. 'In fact . . . I feel we have blood on our hands,' he blurted.

Truman gazed over the desk top, his knuckles whitening. The gentle, accusing eyes stared back.

'I wouldn't worry,' snapped the Kansas City haberdasher. 'That will come out in the wash.'

In a few more minutes, this disturbing audience ended. The Undersecretary lingered behind to gauge the damage and make soothing excuses.

'Thanks Dean, that was pretty interesting.' Truman vigorously adjusted his glasses. 'But keep that guy away from here. Who does *he* think he is? I'm the guy that dropped the damn thing!'

Robert rode a grey limousine with Acheson through the snowy Washington avenues. Twenty minutes later, they were sitting in the crowded lounge of the Cosmos Club.

Nothing in his life, not even the extermination camps, alarmed Robert like Truman's failure of imagination. Sure, it was a long shot, making deals with Stalin. Molotov had already showed James Conant in Moscow what Uncle Joe thought of any moral panacea. But there was no choice, Robert's thought went on. After all, it was Hitler, not Stalin, who broke the Pact of Steel. The Russians respected strength and shrewdness. How would Stalin react to threats and hysteria?

Acheson vigorously lightened the mood. The Undersecretary's bristling moustache twitched as he handed his gloomy neighbour a chilled martini.

Even in the prosperous bonhomie of the Cosmos lounge, the scientist's mood exerted an astonishing power on Acheson's emotions. Oppy's depression now was as infectious as the brilliant enthusiasm of their last days on the road. It seemed to the Undersecretary to thicken the leathered lounge air, to darken the cozy lighting, as if someone were winding up the dial on the earth's gravity.

'Never mind,' Acheson said discreetly. He avoided the curious glances at their corner from neighbouring tables. 'The Plan's a masterpiece: "No monopoly is possible . . . no restrictions on peaceful research . . . fraternizing of scientists through the world's laboratories." It's a very inspiring solution.'

'Dean?' Robert drained the martini, for some reason unable to meet his companion's eyes. 'Who will present the Plan to the UN?'

'Well, Robert,' Acheson began haughtily. 'I was about to go into that!'

'Better tell me.' Robert stared ironically, gathering the last of his courage.

'Bernard Baruch.' The Undersecretary frowned. 'Byrnes says Bernard Baruch.'

The two men's eyes met, and Undersecretary Acheson was privileged to be the first to see on Robert's face a quite new expression; quizzical, ironic, pitying, scathing and infinitely patient and gentle. A look of someone who has accepted something. At that moment, amid the self-satisifed murmur of the most powerful senators in history, nothing else mattered.

'Baruch will never agree to give up our monopoly,' Robert commented, very simply and softly. 'Therefore the Russians will not accept it. And so I will not be associated.'

At that same hour, in a gabled brick house not far away, the model Washingtonian Billy Borden was at his desk. Flying a bomber on a raid over Hamburg, neat blond Borden had nearly been run down by a German rocket bound for London. Now the war was over. The Nazi boy missile genius Von Braun had brought his Programme to America. Borden could pour out his strange insecure heart in a book. The theme of Billy's book was that newly victorious America would shortly face a nuclear Pearl Harbour, that the domestic affairs of the American people were trivia beside the urgent need to provide US military men with a missile armada. A silvery host they could instantly launch into the heavens whether or not Congress was in session.

Unlike General Groves, Billy Borden had always been in Washington.

Chapter 3

Working on as if nothing had changed, far from Washington, another heart as tuned to violence as Borden's was also at work at General Groves's ramshackle war factory. For Louis Slotin, Oppy's squeamish refusal to let him see the dead and maimed of

Hiroshima had left incomplete the Mesa's quest for Trinity. Slotin had learned in Spain to suspect commanders who could not stand the sight of death.

That late spring morning, Louis was bent over his work stool in Omega lab. Just in front of him on the dented table, the little Plutonium hemispheres of General Groves's new test bomb stood in their miniscrew mounts. Hitler had been dead a year, but Groves was not satisfied. Bombs must stream like Buicks from an all-American production line. This Bikini Island test bomb would announce Groves's growing presence to the world. Far away in his Kremlin, Stalin would be humbled.

In Omega lab, gaunt Alvin Graves and five other excited young men held their breath, pressed like white-smocked interns around the table. They watched Slotin's screwdriver shaft slide steadily under the shining sphere. Over their heads, the desert rain drummed on the leaky tarboard.

'Where did you get your nerves, Lou?' Graves whistled. He watched the red ink in the neutron-counter climb as the hemispheres eased closer. Graves was thinking of what had nearly happened here to old Frisch.

Eyes fixed like surgeons, the others let their breath out. A half-smile tugged Slotin's bluish lips.

'Guess these test bombs just bore me . . .' Louis was saying. 'Damn! Go! Go!'

A blue glow radiated from Slotin's bench. The running men banged against the pine walls. Before his stool hit the floor, Slotin was half lying on the bomb, fingers wedged between the hemispheres. The blue light went out. Leaning on the shadowy workbench, Louis straightened. He looked around.

The six scared faces gaped back at him. Outside there was only the drumming rain. They were alone with what had happened. Slotin was the first to move.

'Okay . . . quick!' Slotin walked around the bench and stood at the blackboard. 'Each of you back in position!'

But Slotin was urgently hooking a tape measure to the Plutonium mountings. Now as each of his friends got back in place, Louis measured his distance from the hemispheres. Quickly he chalked a plan on the board. Then for a moment he relaxed his forehead against the blackboard.

'I guess you covered it for us,' someone said. 'Didn't you Louis?'
Slotin straightened. He faced them with a mysterious grin.

'Should be okay. Alvin, maybe your eyes . . .' Slotin grinned,
then he laughed almost proudly. 'Naturally I don't have a chance.'

One hour later Klaus Fuchs, and two doctors who were fast
becoming the world's first experts on radiation sickness, were at
Slotin's blackboard trying to work out what had happened. That
same week, Louis's hair started falling out. His blood began to
break down. Ten days later, his campaign came to an end.

And when the bomb which had killed Slotin became Groves's
Pacific firestorm to scare Communist observers, the Cambridge
physicist still captive outside Moscow protested publicly. 'To
speak of atom-energy in terms of these new bombs is to speak of
electricity in terms of electric chairs!'

At once, Stalin put Peter Kapitza under arrest in his English
country house outside Moscow.

Chapter 4

For San Francisco Bay it had been a cold winter. In the mornings
you could see your breath, and some days there was even frost
around the sprinklers on the lawns.

Back with Kitty at Eagle Hill, commuting to lecture quantum
physics at Pasadena, Robert concentrated on gathering the strings
of his old happiness, his old strength. But it was the other Oppy,
the Oppy chained to a desert Mesa, who was gaining in stature. It
was as if there were a Louis Slotin in every soul Robert met, one who
longed secretly to experience the new white light at Point Zero, to
see for himself the violence of Hiroshima. As Robert sharpened his
grasp of the new nuclear morality it was the fame of the *other*
Doctor Oppenheimer chained to a Mesa for giving fire to Groves
which gained in influence. And it was this injustice in people's
weird new interest that sickened him most.

But as the train rolled back in from Pasadena one spring evening,
in time for the reunion with Haakon and Barbara Chevalier,
Robert was feeling very excited. He remembered well Haakon's
first letter after Hiroshima. Haakon knew him at his best and
truest. Haakon would never confuse him – their affections were

free of it. As Robert stumbled off the train steps with his swollen satchel it was a lovely spring dusk. Dozens of monarch butterflies fluttered under the platform roof.

Suddenly he felt his old friend very close. Pausing by the news-stand, Robert smelled again the sharp spicy smell of eucalyptus. The rich seaweedy Pacific air was like wine, and his stomach tightened with a sharp little ache of hunger. But he could not resist buying a *Chronicle*. In the taxi to Eagle Hill, Robert looked at the headline.

'Baruch Plan Vetoed by Russians,' said the heavy black words. It was part of Doctor Oppenheimer's prophecy. America not sub-mitting its single phallic power to rally humanity . . . and therefore the Russians degenerating in antithesis. Yes, part of their blind-ness to his life. Like a logbook of some disaster, with all the coordinates necessary for a return to a golden age. Robert clung to his brilliant emotion back on the station platform. Ten minutes later, he was standing in the gravel drive in his flop hat and baggy tweeds. Robert frowned out into the orange sunset blackening the San Francisco skyline. Then he lugged the heavy satchel up past the magnolia.

The front door was standing open. Excited voices bantered with Kitty's in the kitchen. Robert forced off the crushing darkness.

In this dusky kitchen where so much had happened, where they had known each other so well, he embraced Haakon and Barbara emotionally. They were safely returned and like veterans together.

'You have cut your hair short, Oppy!' Haakon held his friend's shoulders with a kind of hesitant pride. 'But why so serious?'

Robert held up the newspaper for them. Kitty's eyes traced the large print. A bitterness hardened on her face and she laughed cynically.

'Ugh, the filthy thing!' she said. 'People will be here in a minute.'

'Exactly,' Barbara agreed. 'Friends before politics.'

Standing around the kitchen table, they all looked at Oppy's short hair and he felt an alien, disturbing note. But he was willing.

'You said it!' Robert laughed spontaneously. Setting his satchel, hat and newspaper by the swinging door, he turned to them with a playful charm.

'But first, Haakon, I want to hear about Nuremberg.'

Taking each other's arms, the two men walked ahead of their wives down to the dark conservatory, the plants and creepers melting into the garden outside. The circle of sky was a deep mineral blue. Chevalier was as blond and dashing as ever.

'Well, try to imagine it,' he said with a grave irony as Robert mixed the martinis. 'Think of it, Robbie! There they were, the rotten devils . . . horrible! And fascinating.'

'You saw them?'

In the weak light of the bar, Robert searched Haakon's face. He was remembering the exact emotion he had felt in the door of the Trinity control bunker, that first second of the new white light. The two women were listening.

'Yes, in a sort of jury box,' Haakon gestured at the panelled back wall. 'It was unbelievable . . . like walking myths! Naturally Hitler, Himmler and Goebbels could not be invited.'

Robert laughed strangely. 'They made their getaway into the history books.'

There was a long silence through the conservatory. With a shiver, Barbara Chevalier realized that her husband was telling this for the first time.

'Yes!' He walked away and turned. 'Like walking myths, pretending to be men. There was Goering, and Frank, Raeder, Schleicher and the rest. The doctors of the camps too. And Rosenberg and the exterminators. The king was dead but the knights of the Grail were there . . .'

'I understood,' Haakon's expressive voice hurried on with unnatural clarity, 'Nikitchenko wanting only death sentences. These imitation human beings should have been erased. But the English and Americans wanted to keep them for civilization.'

The hall door had begun chiming. There was laughter and voices.

'Come on, Kitty,' Barbara laughed nervously. 'This is too much for me . . . let's go talk about babies and books.'

'Yes.' Kitty made a face. 'Let them get it out of their systems. Remember, you two!' she called back from the steps. 'This is a party, not a wake!'

'Not me, Haakon!' Robert began, when they were standing alone at the glass door with their martinis. 'I can't understand the Russians at all.'

'Do you mean it, Oppy?' A sort of nervous expectant discomfort came over the writer.

'Why sure!' Robert threw up his hands. 'I tried listening to Adelson and Pinsky over at Frank's. But look what it has cost the movement to trust the International. Stalin wiped out their best people, made deals with Hitler. And now they've locked up half of Europe. *We're* more revolutionary than that, old friend!'

'I respect your judgment, Robbie . . .' Haakon brooded.

'Haakon, listen! If the Kremlin cared a damn for solidarity, cared for the defenceless mass, they should have discussed the Baruch plan with whatever stupid amendments.'

'The Party's a different matter.'

'They have some fine visionaries, Haakon.' Robert shrugged. 'But these conspiracies, paranoia and loyalty to the International!'

'Oppy, Oppy!' Haakon lifted his hand. 'I am so sad to hear you speak like this. 'Paranoia . . . look at Washington!'

Hearing his friend's distress, and again the alien uncomfortable note, Robbie forgot his anger. He gripped his friend's broad shoulders warmly.

'But the things we worked for are vital!' said Robert softly. 'I would rather hang on to them – *alone*! – than see them used as excuses for greed and brutality.'

'The class struggle is a reality,' Haakon said firmly.

'It would be a meaningless reality,' said Robert, 'if we let it become a struggle for power in a nuclear age.'

In the long silence, the two men heard the repeated chiming. From the living room came a festive rumble and clink of voices. Suddenly Robert was aware of his friend's embarrassment.

'Robbie?' Haakon said quickly. 'Maybe it is better if I speak to you . . .'

'Are you two coming?' Kitty called from the lobby. 'This is a little rude.'

'In a minute, Kat!' Robert called. 'Haakon, shall we behave ourselves?'

'Robbie, tell me now!' Haakon persisted. 'Do you know a Colonel Pash?'

Twisting back to Chevalier in the shadows, Robert gripped the door-handle, groping the martini on to the table. He knew that the lofty trust in their friendship was gone forever. He remembered poor Jean, standing alone and defeated in her pale raincoat at the Airport fence.

'Let's go in the garden.' Robert hung his head. 'I can't believe this!'

'I'm afraid I believe it, Oppy,' Haakon said as Robert unlatched the glass door. 'I have no choice.'

Outside it was cool and the lawn was spongy underfoot. As the men walked in the dark, Kitty's festive living-room window drifted past.

Haakon broke the silence. 'I am told they are unenthusiastic about spies on the Faculty.'

'Tell me the whole thing.' Robert heard his agonized voice.

'And your position too,' Haakon said coldly. 'Robbie, they seem curious to know why it took you eight months to turn in my name.'

'You were . . . *are* my friend,' Robert said quietly, walking faster. But before he could hear the answer he needed to hear, Kitty's voice was calling from the kitchen steps.

'Robbie!' she cried. 'Haakon! This is very rude!'

Robert stood still. Violent little shivers ran up his spine.

'For Christ's sake!' he called angrily in the dark. 'There are more important things than parties! We'll come in when we're damn well ready!'

Kitty looked very small for a moment under the door light. Then she was gone.

'Calm down, Robbie.' Haakon shifted uncomfortably.

'Listen, Haakon,' Robert began with a desperate brilliance. 'At first I only felt you were right to ask. Russia was our ally! Then they talked of spies at Berkeley. Like a fool, I thought maybe things could be opened up if I showed them it was natural curiosity. Then the mystery professor . . . you, Haakon . . . became a security obsession. It was distracting them from serious things.'

The two men were passing the big cypress for the third time.

'So you told them,' Haakon groaned. 'Do you know how serious this is?'

'I just don't understand! What do they mean by it *now*?'

Haakon laughed sharply. 'They do not respect our beautiful souls. I was questioned for ten hours, over at the FBI office. They had George Eltonton at another place. We were checked against one another. A gentleman with a coffee cup running in and out every ten minutes to telephone answers. Fortunately, our two stories were consistent.'

'It's absurd!' Robert swore softly. 'That was wartime.'

'Maybe it is only my job which is over.' Haakon stared up in agony at the Pacific stars. 'Or maybe our dreams . . . the electric chair.'

'But the War Department sent you to Nuremberg!' Robert said incredulously.

'Perhaps you could write a letter?' Haakon said hopelessly. 'Or some such thing?'

'You don't have to ask, old friend,' Robert said quickly. 'But I wonder if these people believe a thing I say.'

'Maybe they do not understand you.' Haakon was bitter.

'They must understand me, Haakon,' Robert said. 'They simply have to!'

The two men stood in light thrown over the lawn from the crowded window. Robert threw away his fourth cigarette. He took his friend's shoulders.

'Whatever you think of me, Haakon,' Robert whispered. 'Remember this! You can't know how high the stakes are, the tremendous dangers of the road humanity is on. How absolutely essential we keep ourselves clear.'

'Barbara is coming,' his friend whispered.

'Wait, Haakon!' Robert went on quickly. 'You *do* understand how this thing has happened?'

'Does it matter?' Haakon said. 'Those foolish fellows do not.' He changed his tone. 'Now go be nice to your poor Katie. The ones who love you Robbie, they have delicate lives.'

The two men crossed the darkened lawn in wounded silence, towards the press of familiar faces, laughing in the bright mothy window over the bushes.

The kitchen-screen banged behind the friends. In the sudden brightness, feeling too drained to look in Haakon's face, Robert walked on through with a crooked smile. He moved into the press of friendly greetings. Kitty was beside Frank with a little group at the piano, listening to a haughtily talkative Lawrence. But instead of turning to her husband with her old breezy irony, she who was always stronger, Kitty looked drunkly chastened.

Robert bent by her ear. 'Katie, that wasn't too nice. Shouting at you out there.'

'Yes, darling.' Kitty pressed against him with a slurred, nervous laugh. 'Be gen'l with us helpless creatures.'

He stared down at her pretty, bleary face, at the orchid someone had put in her hair. And again Robert swore to himself: If ever it came to a choice between humanity and those close to him, he would stay at home like the Chinese sage. And let humanity correct itself.

Chapter 5

But not long after the friends' conversation, Professor Chevalier was dismissed. Doctor Oppenheimer became Washington's Chief Advisor on America's top-secret new dominion over the fowl of the air, the beasts of the land, and fishes of the sea.

Still Robert clung to the old happiness, to his vision of the one river of moral truth and the one humanity. But, retreating from his earliest impulse to share openly with the Russians to the diplomatic sharing of the Undersecretary's Plan, Oppy was driven back to a mistrust of any concessions at all. As the war-battered Russians disintegrated into further antithesis before America's unyielding nuclear power, Oppy too was disintegrating. As he lost his grip on the utopian dream, it was like retreating from his love of humanity. Often now Robert would escape from this unhappiness into the other official, ever more respectable 'Oppy', accepting it as himself. Like Groves long ago, and then the new white light at Trinity, Robert was going to Washington.

The morning of March 8, 1947, Representative Osborn took over Representative Baruch's Atomic-Energy post at the new United Nations. That same hour, Chief Adviser Oppenheimer arrived at La Guardia Airport on the night flight from San Francisco. He insisted on a meeting.

The two strangers spent that weekend at the Representatives' mansion over the Hudson River. Then, by the great picture window, Doctor Oppenheimer guiltily retreated still further from his old happiness. The experiment in world solidarity had become too dangerous, he advised, free men must not expose their flank to a clandestine monolith. The last and most desperate hope left was to guard Humanism against any future nuclear Kremlin. So Oppy lectured Representative Osborn, as once he had lectured his Professors at Göttingen.

Then Robert flew back west to San Francisco Bay. Again he tried to gather the affections of family life at Eagle Hill and concentrate his being on the mysterious transmutations of atoms travelling in inter-galactic space.

For in this compromise with his old intellectual rebellion, there was a kind of middle-aged peace.

Chapter 6

Still, there was something about today. A few mornings later, Robert left the house very early. He ate hotcakes with the janitors in the campus canteen, and was at his office in Le Conte Hall by seven-thirty. For some days Kitty had not been drinking. Today Robert did not feel the guilt of his retreat.

The Pacific sun over the campus lawns, not yet dotted with bobby-soxers, was chilled to white wine. The dawn besieged Robert with its brightest colours. Below the windows, little orange butterflies spiralled over the grass.

Taking off his jacket by the miniature cacti in the window, Robert lit his pipe and leaned back on his desk. If it was not quite the same old translucent mind it once was, he mused, it was pretty well back together, with only the occasional cloudiness.

Then, as if his concentration were the great mirror of an astronomer's telescope, Robert trained it away from squalid Earth, up free among the black, unknown tracts and solar winds of the universe. Dreaming about the little high-frequency cosmic rays flitting out into light years, Robert felt the old excitement stir, the desert thrill of being alone with what no man had ever known.

The office door rattled. Half expecting it to be fat Groves come to invite him on another great adventure, Robert looked over his shoulder.

'Leo, for heaven's sake!' Robert frowned, his trance evaporating. 'I scarcely expected you.'

'Greetings, Oppenheimer!' Szilard pushed the door quickly behind him. 'Well, young American, you are looking very quiet and dreamy!'

The two scholars shook hands warmly by the window. But Robert had a sinking feeling. Here was blustery Leo Szilard who long ago (was it only eight years?), had written Einstein's letter to Roosevelt. Szilard, who had worked in Groves's Project but circulated the petitions against the dropping of their bomb, and since then noisily opposed further developments. Leo's remaining hair was almost all white.

'Yes!' Robert began excitedly. 'You see, I think there is a sweet solution to this business of atmospheric ionization . . .'

'Oppenheimer . . . Opp-enheimer!' The little Hungarian licked his lips, cleared his throat and adjusted his spectacles with both hands. 'I am not on the Coast for physics!' he laughed nervously. 'I am out here about the future of mankind!'

Robert knocked out his pipe. He had been concentrated so far away from mankind that for five seconds the word had no meaning.

'That is not so sweet a solution,' Robert joked.

Leo turned disgustedly from the view of the lazy campus lawn. 'But this is serious! The Pentagon eunuchs are down at Bikini. They shoot off bombs like a Chinese New Year. In Washington, they talk of "more bang for the buck"! Meanwhile, Robert, you know our little Federation, they are in one tiny room . . . ha, like Moscow poets!' Szilard's voice rose, filling the quiet Berkeley office with unthinkable guilts. 'Our frightened men go to see all the Congressmen . . . no one listens! But you! You are American and a clever politician. "More bang for the buck", imagine! And our friend Ed Teller . . . Oppenheimer, he is so close to financing his superbomb!' Szilard exploded. 'Finally he will burn up this planet!'

Robert stood listening, his eyes cast down in a bemused, melancholy smile. He could feel his final hold on happiness weakening. 'The Super has to go through our Advisors,' Robert offered presently. If Szilard so mistrusted American government, why had he written Roosevelt the original letter? Of course, Roosevelt had been different.

The Hungarian paced angrily up and down. 'Yes, yes, Oppenheimer! But what is all this out here?' Szilard flapped his arms. 'Go back! You must go back . . . you must sacrifice yourself in Washington!'

'That, Leo,' Robert reflected, 'is like trying to steer an iceberg . . . all compromises.'

He twisted open the window. In their long thoughtful silence, Robert heard the tone of early voices across the lawns. He had been wrong too often not to listen to Leo now. People still were not believing in Trinity.

'Well, they just offered me the Advanced Studies Institute at Princeton,' said Robert, thinking of the *other* Oppy.

He was thinking too of the snowy European end of America, the bleak Institute buildings like some sanatorium on a New Jersey hilltop housing the high priest of physics, Einstein. The old man belonged to Leo's Federation too.

'Then why wait?' Szilard stopped very close in front of Robert. 'Nowhere in Washington can you hear the voice of moderation!' he was suddenly shouting. 'Nowhere do you hear the voice of sanity! They are building castles made of Edward's superbombs! They do not listen to Szilard . . . I am always angry! They call you the Father of the Bomb, Oppenheimer! To you they listen, no one else! And what do you do about your hor-rible child, hmm? Dreaming of sweet solutions!'

The Hungarian shrugged miserably, leaning on the desk. He looked around for a new aisle to pace. 'You are exceptional, my friend! But this is wasting time. If you won ten Nobels! What difference? When they become accustomed to this idea . . . to *use* these things we gave them! Hmm?' He was back at the desk.

'I know, Leo.' Robert shut his eyes. 'I know only too well . . . we are losing our freedom.'

Szilard straightened himself. Tugging at the front of his sports jacket, he squinted out at the brilliant Pacific sun.

'Days and weeks go by, Oppenheimer!' Leo Szilard sighed as a man sighs who unburdens himself of a great load. 'Maybe years will go by. But you and I, we know! A time will eventually come . . .'

'All right, Leo,' Doctor Oppenheimer said softly, and their eyes

215

met. 'You've made your point. I'll have to think about it. I'm sure
. . . I'm afraid you're right.'

To hide his angry tears, Robert turned his back on the deep
Pacific sky. He began sliding the felt eraser gently through the
numbers clustered on the blackboard. When the long board was
blank again, Robert stepped around Szilard. He stood puffing his
pipe at the open window, staring bitterly over the warm campus
lawns. The paths were crowded now with students.

Yes, you have been proved wrong, and wrong again! Robert
thought, feeling bitter towards the world. But you have not inten-
ded evil. And you are not going to defend yourself to anyone,
whatever they make of it.

His worried eyes followed a blond boy and girl walking hand in
hand. The boy carried the girl's books. Abruptly remembering the
disturbing emotion years ago, driving home from this office after
General Groves's offer, Robert touched the hot glass. Well, from
now on that out there is not for you, he thought. And neither will
this in here be.

Oblivious of the two boring old profs watching them from the
science windows, the young students called and joked with a
splendid hope and trust in their lives. The great mystery was still
before them. For they had done nothing wrong. So why should
they be punished?

It was the end of Robert Oppenheimer's twenty-year dream of
the West, as once it had been of Europe. He was going home.

Chapter 7

Back east on the Potomac River, dominion over Point Zero passed
from the celebrated General Groves in January 1947 – that is Year
2, anno nuclei. It was called the Atomic Energy Commission, its
Chairman was Roosevelt's man Lilienthal, and its offices were as
makeshift and impermanent as a desert camp. Szilard's and Einstein's 'frightened scientists' of last year had already abandoned the
Federation for the glamour and excitement of the top-secret
weapons programme. The mass population beyond had taken its
oath of lies in order to become future splattered flesh at Point Zero.
It was America's golden age of Security.

The same spring weekend Oppy had spent up on the Hudson River giving UN Representative Osborn his expert philosophy on the Kremlin, in Washington the new Atom-Commissioners were in Lilienthal's warm bright office holding an embarrassed conference. As the minutes ticked awkwardly by, the five statesmen and their witnesses were trying, as Groves had long before, to make something of the much-admired scholar who was the Advisor-Chief over America's godly new powers of destruction.

Who then *was* their friend? Oppy, who had conjured the violence of suns, beside whom all of these mandarins had worked intimately? Already Lilienthal and Lewis Strauss had caught themselves doubting they knew anything about the man. In the golden age of American Security, it was a very insecure feeling.

Lilienthal stopped patiently behind his polished desk, fingertips propping his high bald temples. Across the stacks of folders sat the ex-Czar of science, Vannevar Bush, with a pursed grin. Their old friend James Conant, Atom-Advisor and President of Harvard, gazed soberly up at the blowup of Los Alamos on the wall. Standing at the gloomy venetian blind was Admiral Strauss, austere, imperfectly-educated, Lewis Strauss of Kuhn Loeb bank, now Commissioner with Lilienthal, Sumner Pike and Bob Bacher of Point Zero, in dominion over the violent mystery of the Jornada.

On Lilienthal's desk were stacked the Bureau files on Oppy.

For four years, General Groves had protected these secret files for his own use. Now Groves's triumph was secure, the file had passed to Chief Hoover, with a recommendation that all those of imperfect patriotism should now be eliminated. Hoover had passed the file on to Commissioner Lilienthal. Lilienthal and Strauss had summoned the others. So each day, Oppy's friend Joseph Volpe, the AEC lawyer, dropped off the confidental file with the Commissioners. Each day, the five powerful men had handed page after page along the table, reading of Robert and Frank Oppenheimer's imperfections, as a man might read detective reports on the girl he has married. And like Landsdale long ago, they were experiencing the not un-literary differences between Oppy in the flesh and Oppy on paper. It was unnerving for the most excellent men in the land. They needed their strength about them. And no one here was more trained to be sensitive to this insecurity than the prosperous statesman standing at the window, Lewis Strauss.

Banker Strauss felt quite certain the criminal hell of future Trinities was cleanly locked away in his new Commission. But it was not so easy to lock away the power of Oppy's hypnotic personality. The vileness of Hiroshima was too remote to dirty the vaults of Strauss's Commission. America had suppressed the Japanese films of human suffering.

But the equally unimaginable, low-class union offices and shoddy little California flats, where young Robert Oppenheimer had mailed pamphlets to defend alien farmworkers, rebel teachers and talked of changing society . . . those were on American soil! The worst, though, were the tapes of Steve Nelson, Adelson and Pinsky. When they thought no one was listening, those Reds talked as if they owned Oppy.

Lilienthal's scruffy classroom of an office was dry, and well-heated against the chilly rain veiling the capitol dome. Each of the nation's finest men was wealthy and decent. Each had been to the barber, and was shiningly shaved. Their button-down shirts were freshly laundered, their shoes polished, and their generously tailored Brooks suits lovingly pressed. When the Commissioners spoke it was with a vigorous mutual politeness that locked together giant issues like blocks in a Chinese puzzle. In short, there was nothing between the drab wood walls to betray the faintest hint of monstrous crime, or of social change.

'Of course Oppy told me that there was, uh, derogatory information . . .' Commissioner Strauss's voice trailed off. Over the last two days he had recovered himself. But it was time they decided.

'I can't believe it!' Conant frowned hotly behind his spectacles. 'I still cannot believe it's being raked up.'

'My feeling precisely, sir!' Bush snapped across the desk. In Strauss's vaguely obsequious tone, Bush had just heard a hint of Oppy's survival.

Chairman Lilienthal shifted slightly, steering the discussion. The fate of hundred millions of Lilliputians crushed down on every word.

'What still strikes me as significant,' Chairman Lillienthal repeated painfully, 'is that only *now* does Hoover send this over!

218

He keeps calling over here. Where has this new material been?'

'Temper of the times, David!' Vannevar Bush inspected the toe of his shoe with satisfaction. He thought of his first meeting with General Groves. His own influence had certainly outlasted the fat officers'. 'In those days,' he added, 'Groves kept Hoover's wolves at bay.'

'It seems what we are being asked to judge, gentlemen . . .'

At the venetian blind, Commissioner Strauss turned from his sly contemplation of the little raincoated figures outside under the trees, running in the downpour.

'. . . is the loyalty of Doctor Oppenheimer. And *that* is a shocking state of affairs!'

'Uhuh,' Conant nodded. 'Our top Advisor.'

'To sum up, gentlemen . . .' Lilienthal thoughtfully exposed his gold cufflinks. 'This file is indisputable evidence that the man primarily influencing American nuclear weapons policy does have a long record of Communist ties, and could possibly have concealed a Communist spy while directing the Manhattan Project.'

Vannevar Bush sat up. 'This is absurd!'

'I hope, Vannevar,' said Lilienthal, who idolized Oppy, 'that J. Edgar agrees with you!' All four men felt themselves sink into the darkness of moral ambiguity. 'Personally,' Lilienthal cocked his lofty forehead to the other side and gazed at the ceiling, 'I find this stuff worrying as hell. Our man's behaviour over Chevalier is utterly beyond belief!'

The Adviser, James Conant, recrossed his pin-striped legs. He had just remembered Moscow, and his attempt to touch Molotov's moral nature, and the cold indifference on the Russian face. What did the Communists know?

'I don't think,' he said drily, 'anyone in this room can claim to follow the reasoning which leads Robert to do what he does . . .'

'Exactly!' Commissioner Strauss cut in unctuously. 'It's an Advisor's continued loyalty which is the issue. If Robert were disloyal, the Russians would have a bomb. We might still be at war with the Japs.'

'Of *course* Robert's not a security risk!' Vannevar Bush burst out irritably. 'Surely we're agreed on that much!'

'Agreed? Fine.' Lilienthal's eager brown eyes made the rounds of the other faces. 'Then Robert will have his Q-clearance button. What's good for America in 1943 should be good in 1947!'

'Wonderful!' At the misty streaming windows, Commissioner Strauss let out his breath. For some reason this bald unattractive person felt a need to shake the other men's hands. He had needed their reassurance. 'Then there is no question either over Oppy's position at the Institute?' he continued.

'Sounds a little like worship sir,' Bush ribbed the touchy Commissioner.

'Maybe it is,' banker Strauss reddened behind the heavy glasses. 'Yes, maybe it is.'

As the four successful men talked on casually about paying Hoover a visit 'for safety's sake', talking to unwind as it were, they were all strangely relieved.

Though the Commissioners were (or was it precisely *because* they were?) the sole beings on earth responsible for all future Journeys of the Dead, in their hearts all of them except Conant found it excruciating to confront, face to face, the passionate cloud of moral riddles and cultural nuance surrounding their friend Oppenheimer. It was almost as if a human embodiment of the truth at Point Zero could not be looked deeply into, any more than the blinding New Light at Trinity. It was enough to have protected Oppy's prestige. Robert would deal with his bomb.

But the most satisfied this afternoon was Commissioner Strauss. As he made some notes and filed his papers, the banker felt the emotion of a man who receives a detective's proof of his fiancée's virginity. As if Oppy's Q-clearance was some high credit-rating granted an account which made Strauss's bank easily more powerful than the rival bank the Supreme Soviet called 'the state'. As for the big stake little Cambridge in England had in the nuclear secret, it was pleasanter to forget that. The exclusive vaults under Commissioner Strauss's personal influence already held the most ruthless instrument of intimidation known to man. Now they would contain the most brilliant, charismatic Chief Advisor, also the Director of the Institute of Advanced Studies.

It was a successful comfortable feeling, the kind of feeling to which Lewis Strauss was accustomed.

Chapter 8

In the autumn, when the forest from Maine to Delaware is a rolling sea of blood orange, Robert brought Kitty and his two children back east, to New Jersey, and to Olden Manor among the sanatorium of brick houses, on a sterile Princeton promontory called the Institute of Advanced Studies.

Here where there were no students, no great city, no desert or westward ocean, Doctor Oppenheimer began again gathering the gentle scholar-circle the fascists had splintered in Europe. Here came Einstein and Bohr; Kremlinologist George Kennan; child-psychologist Piaget; the young physicists of the new Japan, master mathematician Marston Morse, Panofsky the art historian, T.S. Eliot; Norwegian mathematicians, English poets and logicians, the Communist Browder's mathematician son Felix; Slavic physicists; Austrian, Hungarian and Swedish biologists; political and cultural historians. A hundred thinkers from all the world's isolated tributaries of language, race and specialization, sharing only a passion to be face to face with the Unknown. Humanists made the pilgrimage to this brick promontory across the great barriers of nature and ideology. They came to expose their intricate, diverse selves to an amiable chaos that ethics might overtake. It was a more open utopia than Los Alamos had ever been. But to Chief Advisor Oppenheimer of the Capitol's top secret dominion over living things, the Institute was a sham Mesa, his shanty town of rationalist boy freedom-fighters setting out to imitate the sun and break fascism for ever. It seemed that the only redemption left was to try fusing the enlightenment of his Institute back to the power of his atom-advisers. To play on them the music of the spheres. To Kitty that was too rarefied, and a losing of Robbie's grip on what was true between them.

Coming down from the Mesa, Robert Oppenheimer had felt as if he was over. Now the image of the face Robert shaved every morning was reproduced millions of times. It was mailed to kitchen tables throughout civilization on popular magazine covers. Meanwhile the official flesh and blood of Oppy travelled constantly, speaking at public science conventions and secret Washington

'Defence' committees. Along with Conant, Du Bridge, Fermi, Rabi, Rowe, Smith, Buckley and Seaborg, he was the clandestine Advisor of Advisors.

Everywhere, Oppy was heard to speak of the sin physicists had known, inviting mankind to join in it. Robert even composed on his face expressions of anxious melancholy so no one would forget. Forget that the Sandia factory at Sante Fe was now producing 1000 advanced Hiroshimas a year . . . that 12,000 would hopelessly contaminate the firmament . . . Robert knew that working on them was the price of retaining a certain influence. For if Teller's superbomb proved feasible, just ten of them might poison all life on earth. America had become a blindfolded boxer flailing about, doing everything it could to communicate its fear to Russia.

Even so, Robert sensed that most of his science allies only joined in guilt to claim some credit. Tragedy was a fashion. And to almost everyone outside the security veil, nuclear weapons were a magic act, an invisible vengeance. It was like asking mankind to share guilt with a ghost only its victims had seen. Each unresponsive stare provoked in Robert the guilty feeling that he was an ambitious man calling attention to himself. To prove to others, and to himself, this was not so, Robert began persecuting the remains of happiness in his private life. His suffering must be suitably unselfish. So Robert's fear of ignorant people became an intolerance he found it hard to control when the official Oppy was not exerting Power. That was part of his self-punishment now. He hated Power, but it drew him on.

The only person Doctor Oppenheimer did not need to influence was his wife. And because only Kitty was dependent on his life, it was his wife Robert influenced most.

Kitty had no authority to share in Robert's hope of saving mankind. She knew him only as a modestly virtuous, inconsistent human being. So Kitty felt far more immediately than Robert the horror her husband claimed guilt for. Like Jean, Haakon, Seth and everyone else on earth who could not identify with Oppy's exalted destiny, she was only a victim.

With Robert and Kitty's move back East, their fundamental argument about the meaning of their unrooted lives became a rift. That is, it was settled that nothing would be settled, that neither

222

through desire, romance, argument, intervention of friends or parenthood would either allow the other to impose a peaceful solution. The only rebellion left for Kitty was alcohol.

Seeing Robbie in his favourite chair under Olden Manor's mantel clock, or his white calves, the motions of his hands at the sink before bed, or in the scornful flash of his eyes at any intellectual weakness, Kitty felt in hyper-realism the crime this sober stranger had taken on himself. More than anyone else, Kitty needed to keep loving him, since she could never go back to Pittsburgh. But the cold veil of holiness Robbie had drawn around himself was growing insurmountable. Kitty felt herself freezing in the unnatural obsession Oppy was beaconing beyond her at mankind. Feeling how this woman's vulnerability gave him the upper hand, Robert began feeling for Kitty an old familiar contempt. How did you live with someone who thinks you are God?

But sometimes around the big house, her husband would seem to Kitty no more than a pompous spoiled child. It gave Kitty a curious sense of moral superiority.

Chapter 9

In the dangerous spring of 1949, anno nuclei 4, Kitty's impressions of her famous husband came together again. For a few weeks it seemed their life at Princeton might work.

On a warm cloudless weekend, they found themselves alone, face to face on canvas chairs by the tulip bed. The Institute Director had left off weeding the turned-up soil. Kitty paid no attention to the punch glass propped on the grass. Since hearing from Joe Volpe that their telephone and Robert's office were eavesdropped on, their free conversations tended to take place when they were alone in the garden. These days everyone who had ever been a utopian was making an appearance before a Subcommittee of Congress.

Next week Oppy himself was going into battle. For days he had been thinking out his tactics for carrying unpopular truths high into power without taking a fall.

But despite this Washington circus of official panic, nature had made a lovely hushed noon of it. Chalked high over the glinting gables were faint vapour trails smeared by some giant brush. Birds sailed over, purposefully as toys bobbed on a child's string. From the file of poplars, in exact line with the man and woman at the bottom of the lawn, came an astonishing buzz of honeybees, an obsessed droning concert, filled with the lawlessness of young things. From the tree house in the oak came the squeals of little Pete and Toni playing pirates with the neighbours.

Kitty folded the newspapers. The editorials were full of the grand-jury spy trial of Alger Hiss, the United Nations' first Secretary-General. The Communist Eugene Dennis was on trial too, and even Kitty's old Youngstown housemate Gus Hall. It made the woman safe in the garden feel a sick and lonely dread, and in need of Robbie. The long formal silence weighed down. Kitty had insisted he spend today with her.

'You're looking awfully pleased,' she broke in.

'I should have been a poet!' Robert held open his collected Yeats. He gave her a grim little smile.

'Maybe,' Kitty said. 'It's harder than you think.'

Kitty took off her dark glasses and shaded her eyes. Robert looked at her. He was going to accept it.

'Yes, maybe it is,' he laughed.

Then a little familiar thrill went between them. They were whispering. The spring afternoon was hushed, sacred as a library. In her hairband Kitty still looked like a college girl.

'I'm sure everything's harder,' Robert said. He twisted his thin neck in the tight collar.

'I wish I heard that more often!' she burst out happily.

'I'm always saying it!'

Kitty winced. 'Oh, not your contempt, Robbie! You only admit it in public,' she added.

'I'm sorry, darling,' he said politely. 'I've gotten bad on criticism.'

Robert struck a match and sucked the flame into his pipe. In the outdoor hush Kitty spread her paper across her girlish legs. They were talking!

'Robbie?' Kitty said suddenly. 'Why do you put us through it? They'll just turn on you in the end.'

'Think, Katie,' Robert reflected simply. 'What would it mean today if not even one Advisor at the top were capable of it? God isn't going to solve things.'

'Maybe if you hadn't gotten this far,' Kitty taunted nervously. 'It wouldn't be so much fun for you.'

'It's the other way, Katie,' he snapped. 'It's the leaders who suffer most.'

Robert had straightened up on the canvas chair. He frowned past the oleanders towards the children's voices. On the hot afternoon, this murmured debate seemed to Kitty strangely obscure, like some impertinent and senseless inventor's mistake that whirred confidently as the passions of nature grew over it.

Robbie sank back in the wood frame, closing his eyes; his delicate weight made sharp contours under the canvas. Kitty looked at his Adam's apple.

'The dissenters who are still healthy,' Robert added, 'are ordinary people.'

'Well, that's what I'd like us to be!' Kitty was vehement.

'No one listens to them!' he said, and they were silent.

'Robbie,' Kitty began again. 'Last night I had such a lovely dream.'

'You remembered it, Katie?'

Robert opened his eyes and looked at her. These days he only woke with vague unpleasant impressions.

This morning, for the first time in four years, Kitty had remembered her old feeling. Of the naked land, and simple folk close to life. It had sluiced up hot and bright in her cheeks like the easy passion of some young girl, and Kitty was set free from this pretence as the Director's wife, this egotism of manicured academic gardens. She shaded her eyes, not daring to look at her husband.

'I remembered it!' Kitty said almost angrily. 'And it was beautiful! Some was about Jed Holmes.' She flushed. 'I never told you about the old man in El Rito. The rest . . . Robbie do you remember the picnic we took with Steve Nelson before all this nightmare began?'

'I remember,' said the man apparently asleep in front of her, his voice pensive.

'Robbie, it was as if . . .' Kitty hurried on, '. . . as if we had left all this and were free again. Do you remember how you had just woken up from your privileged ways?'

'I was an aged fledgling.' Robert laughed sharply.

'We were pretty good together on that drive.'

'And Steve told you,' Robert said without opening his eyes. 'In Paris you'd been ready to lay your life on the line.'

Unshading her eyes, Kitty laughed happily. She stared up at the droning spring sky.

'And I was so jealous of her feeding her baby!' Kitty went on, a little desperate at the flat sound of her old self. 'You never did tell me what you and Steve talked about. You came back all brash and biblical.' Her voice trembled. 'Sometimes I do wish we could leave all this . . . of course it's not possible, but we could live for the things we used to. This life is killing us!'

Facing Kitty on the canvas chair by the tulip bed, the Director of the Institute of Advanced Studies stirred irritably. He did not open his eyes.

'We can't go back to that now, Katie,' he said. 'That was virtue on a small scale. In the position I'm in now, something really is on the line.'

'It's inhuman!' Kitty cried pitifully. 'It's like saying our lives are over!'

'This thing and I cannot be separated,' said Doctor Oppenheimer after a long summery silence. 'Neither can man be.'

Lying back, Kitty felt the wood frame under the canvas. The formal days of the Institute crushed down. The closer Robbie came to world influence, the less he seemed to feel his crime. Or was that fair? Maybe he needed public responsibility to find his goodness.

'I don't want a bureaucrat as a husband,' Kitty said sarcastically.

'I try to be a teller of truths, Katie,' Robert explained after a long silence, as if she were a student. 'I would go on telling the truth anywhere. Why not where it might bend history?'

'Telling the truth!' Kitty was half sitting up, holding back her anger. She knew he was listening. 'How can you tell the truth, out of contact with ordinary people and fun?'

'If we get into a Superbomb race,' her husband suddenly said, opening his eyes, 'there may not be many people left!'

'Damn it, Robbie!' Kitty fell back bitterly, looking away from the disturbing gaze. 'You've *always* been retreating from life. You fought it off for a while back before the war. But it has to go on for a lifetime. Since we left the desert, you've just been falling back and back.' She slipped her sunglasses on.

She heard the childishness of her words, here in this world Institute of sceptics. Catching herself doubting the best in herself, Kitty blushed angrily.

'Sure we've had to retreat Kitty,' Robert said quietly. 'But civilization isn't buried yet.'

'How can you look so happy about it?' Kitty asked with a sort of admiring horror. Did Robbie still dream of disarming the world . . . Atoms for Peace?

By the crisp new red tulips, Kitty had just played her last card. Once there had been so much life in her, and Robbie had needed to sheath himself in it. Now his sad face seemed only to turn away, to the final ascent of some strange Calvary.

'Things are not so hopeless yet, Katie,' Robert murmured. He sucked the lighter flame with his pipe bowl.

In the hot sun, his soft voice seemed to merge with the musical note of spring. The sharp excitement was back in his eyes. Robbie was playing his orchestra of souls.

'I ought to know, Kitty,' Robert went on with a sudden boyish smile. 'I'm keeping a close watch on it. Most of the Project – except Teller – seem ready to fall in with my line. Everyone here at the Institute seems to believe in it. I've worked out the Pentagon-business lobby pretty well. I have the top Advisory post at the Commission, and the ear of the smartest fellows around the President.'

'All except the Kremlin,' said Kitty, looking away behind her glasses. But the sophisticate beside her in the sun was hearing other voices.

'We already have enough bombs to cripple the Russians,' the bland voice beside Kitty said thoughtfully. 'And that's quite enough to keep us out of war. My ear's to the ground. The establishment seems pretty quiet and sane. I'd pick up right away the slightest stir of hysteria for supers, hoarding secrets, building armadas of missiles to beat down Communists. Or for the Army, Navy or Air Force to beat each other down.

'And you know Kitty?' Robert droned on excitedly. 'They really do seem pretty impressed – and willing to listen. It's time this country showed a little civilization. Time it controlled its absolute need to own everything!'

Kitty frowned behind her sunglasses. Sitting up, she lifted her rum punch off the grass beside the open book.

'All you have to do, darling,' she said grimly, 'is go on knowing more than everyone.' The ice in her glass had melted. The punch was weak.

'That's why I can't walk away from it, Kitty!' Robert smacked his fist in his hand, then poked the air with his pipe stem. 'No one else seems to keep his footing on this new ground.'

His wife's dark lenses regarded him across their knees. Why, he hasn't given up the frontiers of knowledge at all, she thought bitterly. He's just turned his moralism loose on the highest summits of power, a virus of inventing! Robbie did not love her, and never would again. Maybe he had never loved anything but his own conscience.

They both listened to the Olden Manor telephone ring for the third time. It was answered. Someone *else* wanting Doctor Oppenheimer's advice, no doubt. Robert's happy smile vanished. Kneeling by the tulips, he took the trowel in his thin hand and began turning the peat with little urgent stabs.

Seeing Katie in such a brave mood, he had had the wild hope that she was deciding to stand behind him. Seeing her drain the rum glass was a sharp disappointment.

'Robbie, do you care at *all*,' Kitty suddenly drawled, 'for the poor idiots who love you?'

Robert did not look up from his tulip patch.

'You don't have to remind me about Bohm and Lomanitz.'

'Not just your students.'

'They're bad enough.' When he saw her with a glass, he hated her. 'In New York at the Society, Wednesday,' he said abstractedly. 'A friend of Bernard Peters came up . . . he said I'd ruined Bernard's life. You might as well hear this. The wartime security men I tried to help, they've been leaking how I called Bernard "quite a red", and "dangerous". They must have taped every word!'

'You were too truthful,' Kitty said with formal irony. 'Teller of truths.'

'Thank you, Katie.' Robert paused. 'That's more charitable than the others. "Un-American Activities Committee" . . . it's ludicrous!'

'Might be less so, darling,' Kitty said thickly, 'if you weren't so big a cheese!'

His face hardened. 'When it's my turn, I'm not going to grovel and hide. There's nothing in any of our lives to be ashamed of. Why, the things we believed in back then, they're no different from Thoreau or the puritan brotherhood.'

'Mummy . . . mummy!' children's voices called.

Robert looked up from the weeding, shading his eyes. He had not heard Kitty's feet on the grass. Seeing her swinging walk already half way across the garden to the children's tree, he experienced an angry wave of grief. He was perspiring.

Well, this is no time to feel tragic! the Chief Advisor thought, digging gloomily between the bulbs. With the world hanging on a string. Probably the world had hung on a string before. But that string had never been Oppy. It was a funny feeling. At least his tulips were happy with him.

'Oh sorry, Doctor sir,' a man's voice said. 'It's you.' Two lean men were standing just across the tulip bed grinning down curiously. Robert was on all fours.

'Our monitor went dead,' one said.

'You cut our surveillance wire, Doctor.' The other man, bald, slightly older, squatted and felt in the tulip bed.

'Now you just wait!' Robert exploded. 'Whose home do you think this is?'

Standing to face these apparitions out of his past, he was suddenly helpless.

'An American house, Doctor.' The bald man was surprised.

'All right!' Robert began stuttering. 'I . . . I think you'd better leave right now!'

The bald man twisted some wires and pushed them into the mud.

'Okay Hank . . . thank you, Doctor.'

'I wouldn't say you needed any more tulips there, sir.'

After the two vanished among his oleanders, Robert stood in the hot sun panting with shock. Face to face with the Bureau men, he remembered to the last detail a foggy San Francisco night, on Telegraph Hill. A worried-looking halfbreed bodyguard dropping him off. Tasting the grief of that lost night and lost girl, it was like those stories of Yukon wolf packs, night after night closing more confidently around the traveller's shrinking campfire.

But the death these fools scented around Oppy was the mass death of humankind in some future Jornada of Superbombs. Robert's soul had become the mystery at Point Zero. He was the bomb.

Chapter 10

The argument with Kitty had spoiled the tulip gardener's absorption in Yeats and nuclear metaphysics. He felt acutely agitated. To regain his full concentration on next week's two hearings – one before the House, the other at the Senate – Robert shuffled down to the Princeton centre for a haircut and shave. It was exam time, and studiously quiet.

An hour later, Robert stepped back in the cool under the sycamores along Nassau street, head cropped short and fragrant with cologne. As the Director exchanged polite waves with Dr Einstein over the sunny street, he was taken aback to see his old student David Bohm approaching with another familiar face.

Einstein was on the track of solving Gravity. Regretfully overcoming his intense attraction, Robert waited for the two young men. The second was his old Berkeley student Joe Lomanitz. Revolutionary Lomanitz; during the war Robert had tried to keep Landsdale from drafting him into the Army. Strange, his having just mentioned them to Kitty! Now they recognised Oppy excitedly.

'Rossi!' Robert drew them out of the heat. 'What are *you* doing back East? And you David! This is grand!'

The shabbier young men emotionally shook their old teacher's hands under the rustling tree. They fell in along the brick sidewalk.

'We're getting summoned for our Un-American activities, that's what!' Lomanitz gave Robert a tough searching smile.

'Golly, don't worry about that!' Robert laughed. But he had to suffocate a wave of selfish suspicion. 'I'm seeing our pals too next week. So will Peters be, and a lot of others . . . thousands of us!'

'They sure have a bee in their bonnet about Berkeley radicals,' Lomanitz brooded.

'Treat you to an ice cream?'

'Thanks, Prof.' Bohm shrugged uncomfortably. 'Rossi will miss his train.' Didn't Oppy see how vulnerable they were?

'Anyway, here's some good advice.' Robert stopped presently to face his old disciples at the end of the sidewalk, under a thick elm bow. He gave their sombre faces a thoughtful glance.

'We have to fight this fear of the truth. It's the biggest threat to democracy. Tell them the whole works, proudly! Don't hide anyone, or anything they can inflate to a big secret. I learned that, the one time I tried to protect a friend. The truth is the only victory.'

He stared down with a gloomy frown at his polished Oxfords, beside the boys' worn loafers.

'You mean "we cannot tell a lie"?' Bohm offered affectionately. The three friends laughed in the studious Princeton twilight, and America was close around them.

But later that week as the Institute Director steered his car through drab Philadelphia under an overcast, on the highway to Washington, he was having his old trouble keeping to the speed limit. Yesterday, Robert had taken a look at a transcript of the Bohm-Lomanitz hearing. Both his students had pleaded the Fifth Amendment to avoid discussing their relation to Steve Nelson! It was a shock and made Robert feel unsure of them. Yes, even of Steve . . . and Bernard Peters! Didn't Bernard talk about doing violence to the American government? Was there a point at which you drew the line on trust?

In Washington the Chief Advisor spent a sleepless night above a steep brick Georgetown street. This was the house of his old Los Alamos secretary Anne Wilson, and her lawyer husband Herb Marks. Like Bohm and Lomanitz, the Markses were on the intricate chart of Doctor Oppenheimer's affections. The cloudy morning of the 7th, Robert parked behind the House of Representatives offices. He jumped nervously up the wide steps and was through the noisy lobby before the group of newspapermen saw him.

Everyone was over at the Grand Jury Trials. Precisely on time, Robert walked down the corridor of tall wood doors and was ushered into elegantly panelled Room 226.

He stepped into a crowded rustling silence. Oppy pulled back the witness chair beside Joe Volpe and a dozen men threw him tense indifferent looks. The Atom Advisor smiled charmingly up at the raised crescent table, along the dozen State Representatives and lawyers of the Un-American Activities Committee. He took in the baggy-suited law battlers and calloused campaigners who had for months been pounding and breaking men's careers over radical connections. They could break Oppy too and they all knew it. Against the facing wall sat Congressmen Velde, Nixon, Wood. There were three others. At a second table below, were two investigating lawyers, Taverner and Russell. Flashbulbs flickered, microphones hummed and scraped. Robert experienced the dread of powerful government.

Now the room's threatening rustle was silenced. With his hands clasped in front of him Robert began softly answering questions, talking with a sort of ready warmth. The last thing you did was show fear to growling dogs, he was thinking. And in minutes, strangely, the terrifying darkness of Communism, conspiracy and coverups cleared. The delicate flesh and blood Oppy gazed thoughtfully back at the inquisitors. The very magician of God's elements, who had given America dominion over the lesser nations and races of the globe!

'As General Groves has vouched for your loyalty Doctor,' Taverner was saying across the fifteen-foot gap, staring fixedly at Robert's loose tie knot, 'we have no interest in embarrassing you. We simply need your assistance on this matter of the Communist cell at Berkeley.'

Robert smiled over at them. Yes, he thought. I was loyal to Groves . . . but was Groves honest with me?

The rest of that morning, hour by hour, the formal charmless voices droned on. Robert could feel the luminous air he needed to breathe grow thick and weary (words dead as the flies under the closed Committee window). A passionate need rose in him to break the formal procedure. To insult this tedious legalism with human truths. But look at Szilard and the Federation zealots! No, he must wait.

Yes, Robert confided. At one time he belonged to every Communist front organization in California. No, he did not know of the activities of Lomanitz, Weinberg or the Englishman Eltonton.

The questions went on, but Doctor Oppenheimer's concentration was stronger than the politicians'. Now, feeling his old enthusiasm for Bernard Peters's passionate rebellion, wanting these ignorant bigots to feel it too, Robert admitted what a freedom-fighter, Communist and wild talker Bernard was. Wasn't that also true? Without showing guilt or nerves, Robert talked on proudly about his close friend Professor Chevalier. Haakon might be a parlour-pink, but he had been embarrassed by the talk he heard of passing the Kremlin nuclear knowledge.

The brilliant hearing-room lights and flashes lit Robert's head from all sides, as if to allow no shading of mystery. And so pleasant was it to the Congressmen to be set free from their cynical fears, no one even thought to ask Oppy why he had protected his friend Chevalier's name for eight months. When the witness begged them politely not to ask about his brother's Communism, to ask Frank himself, the politicians smiled and nodded generously.

Suddenly Committee chairs were scraping, papers rustled. But as the gaunt scholar rose to his feet he had still to endure the intimacy of his new converts. The satisfied politicians filed down. They crowded around to wring the right hand of the conjurer of the atom bomb, grateful to have found him good.

'I think we have been tremendously impressed with you,' said the vigorous young Californian, Nixon. 'We're mighty glad to have you in the position you're in!'

As the Chief Advisor drove back to Princeton in the soft summer dusk, thick green trees festooning the highway, he was experiencing a nervous exhilaration and anguish. He had saved moral truth to fight another round. But none of those tough congressional realists could know what it was costing Oppy to act out his innocence again and again.

What right do those fellows have, Robert thought, to possess the details of your deepest beliefs, simply because your soul and theirs are not from the same cookie mould? Still, he was learning to deal with them as he had with Groves. Did dealing low make you low?

Robert stared in a guilty trance over the steering wheel, at the darkening road. First you sold Groves your scholar's solitude, later you spoiled the Mesa. Coming to the Institute, you gave up your students. And just now you handed over your beliefs and friends to a congressional Committee. Robert felt exhausted, drained and bleached out. Well, at least he'd have a chance to expose a little moral truth next week before the Senate. But the beauty had fled from this evening, and Robert felt no urge to drive fast.

Just five nights later Director-Advisor Oppenheimer was again on Route 1, back to Washington. In an electrical storm that tore streams of green leaves from the heavy trees, a patrolman stopped him for breaking the limit outside Washington. All the last days, famous friends and thinkers had been pouring through Robert's pleasant Institute office.

But tonight as he drove alone into the Capitol, you could not see the Washington obelisk in the murk.

Chapter 11

Next morning, wrapped in his soaking English raincoat, rubbers and fedora hat, the Atom Advisor made a tiny figure on the lengths of the Senate steps. The grand foyer inside was bright and coolly dry. Murmuring groups stood here and there. The Joint Subcommittee on Atomic Energy was crowding into the huge columned auditorium of the Senate Caucus Room.

Passing in through the security check, Robert blinked in the near-white arc-lights. There was an excited hurrying of lawyers and aides among ranks of squared tables, lined with microphones. On their fatuous, confident faces, Robert detected no knowledge of the bleak terror out across the dying earth, weighing upon the sleep of little children . . . no dread of the crushing, flaming horror at Point Zero. He left Herb near the door, and made his way to Joe Volpe, waving from the forward witness table.

Doctor Oppenheimer took a hard leather chair, face to face with the long Committee table. Some of the summer-suited Senators and Congressmen had on sunglasses. Robert recognized Hickenlooper, McKeller, Knowland. Then he twisted to the row of chairs behind. He nodded thoughtfully to Atom-Commissioners Pike,

Dave Lilienthal and Bacher. Bob at least had been in the desert at Point Zero with him. Then Robert tried out a smile on Lewis Strauss.

Abruptly, the echoing rumble was dying back under the auditorium chandeliers. The silence tightened around Oppy in a radiance of expectant power. Flashbulbs flickered like distant artillery.

'Doctor Oppenheimer, Chay'man of the Gen'al Visory Ca-mittee . . .' Iowan Hickenlooper cut through the hush with satisfaction. And behind the glasses and three big mikes, the witness felt his hair bristle. The Senator sat at the centre of the long Committee table. And ten feet behind Oppy, facing the Conservative Senator over the closely cropped back of Robert's head with his arms tightly crossed, Lewis Strauss shared the mid-westerner's satisfaction.

For weeks now, a suspicion akin to a crisis of faith had torn banker Strauss's heart. A confusion over the giant head start his Renaissance protégé Oppenheimer had given America over Communist barbarism, a monopoly that Oppy, despite his benefactor's objections, now seemed dedicated to handing away in isotopes to foreign laboratories, to aliens perhaps not as unfriendly to dictators as Washington was. This saintly charity was a disloyalty Commissioner Strauss (who did not grasp the pity of a few iron isotopes when set beside the fleet of America's Hiroshima-laden bombers), was kept awake by. Turning over this mystery of Oppy, lying awake in his bed, it had taken on properties of the night.

But today, this blinding Caucus Room had a distinctly secure feeling. Commissioner Strauss no longer remembered the admiration he had once felt for the motionless figure now just ten feet in front of him, tentatively scratching the back of his greying head.

Waiting thoughtfully beside Joe at the polished witness table, Robert half sensed the bitterness somewhere behind his back in the cavernous silence. A paranoia of men who were disgracing humanity with their blindness to inevitable truths. Did Lewis really dream they could hold up the Russian Project everyone with Q-clearance knew about . . . by locking up iron isotopes? What could spur the Kremlin faster than to insult its tremendous victory with selfish ambitions for world supremacy?

'. . . this country,' Hickenlooper was saying, 'has been perty gen'rous with its radiais'topes . . .' From among the long panel of brooding faces above the profiled stenographers' heads, the Iowa Senator held the Chief Advisor's haughty depressed gaze without affection.

'Now it is called to this Committee's attenshin,' Hickenlooper went on grimly, 'that we have jus' shipped arn is'topes to Norway. In this Norwegian laboratory, Dr Oppenheimer, it seems there's what you might call a . . . Comminis. This is just tar'rible mis-mangmaint . . .'

There was a deep, expectant rustle, the packed assembly held its silence. At the table Robert heard himself clear his throat. He suppressed a wave of dread at having to repeat freshman inanities to rulers of the world. Outside the Senate walls, across the darkening continents, the trusting lamb was penned in ignorance.

'I think, Senator,' Robert heard a monstrous voice crackle down from the speakers. He leaned near the three mikes. 'The isotopes would be of no use to a weapons programme. To scientists they might be helpful for medical research . . . deepen understanding. But in an intensive reactor programme, the isotopes would be of little interest . . .'

There was a fresh stutter of flashbulbs along the columned walls. In the midst of crowded tables, the witness stared around him. He unhappily searched himself for the old inspired flash of prophecy. Was he completely used up?

'. . . still haven't convinced me, Doctor,' Hickenlooper was saying minutes later, 'is'topes could not be used for atomic en'gy!'

'Senator Hickenlooper, you can use a shovel for atomic energy.'

The witness had said it with a sudden rush of warm irony, freeing himself from the throttling weight of fear.

'. . . in fact you do!' Robert was warming up. 'But to get perspective, these materials played no significant part, and to my knowledge no part at all.'

A ripple of indulgent laughter stirred among the crowd of bemused faces. Hearing their sympathy, Commissioner Strauss's frightened heart lurched.

'Dr Oppenheimer,' Senator Knowland took up blandly. On the

next chair, Hickenlooper had taken off his glasses and was swabbing his brows. 'Would you mind assessing for us the military significance of these isotopes?'

The Senators' voices bounding from the column speakers, echoed back and forth off marble walls. And there was a blindness among the host, as strangers met in the shadow of the valley of death.

Far forward at the witness table, Doctor Oppenheimer was leaning near the microphone.

'Senator,' a voice Robert scarcely knew growled through the bleached-white Caucus Room light, 'no one can force me to say those isotopes cannot be used for atomic energy.' He tugged at his ear lobe. 'As for their military importance . . . less important than electronic devices. More important than, let us say, vitamins. Somewhere in between.'

Through the ranks of squared tables, all faces were turned towards the witness table. A quick responsive swell of laughter rolled through the auditorium and Robert felt again the glad healing flight of human mysteries. Up front, along the wide Joint Committee panel, there was a frustrated shifting, a tapping of pencils. Under the table, polished black and white toes were rearranged.

'Docta Oppinheimer!' Bourke Hickenlooper had replaced his spectacles, and looked down from among the impassive panel at the scholar's sad patient face. 'Since you have been so helpful, perhaps you would offah the Committee your views on the curnt campaign to give secu-ity parsonnel mar leeway.'

'Not very courageous!' the witness's voice crackled out, rolling down the great darkening canyons of the nuclear age. 'How little is understood already without this morbid fencing off of knowledge, and investigation! Sometimes, Senator, when we are afraid, it is not enough to speak of suppressing or destroying the object of our fears. Sometimes one must be brave. To quote the Russian poet Blok: "The trouble with our time is that we are too clever to believe in God, and too stupid to believe in ourselves."

'I think we must do everything gentlemen' – the witness's patient smile had been replaced by the old sharp glittering concentration – 'to believe openly in ourselves. As for security . . if you

237

want my opinion, the only security is in the grave!'

Half an hour later, by the Senate Caucus Room clock, there was an eager rumbling. As the witness rose unsteadily, the blind din of a Joint Hearing swept over his words. Gathering his papers with the disoriented frown of someone woken in a lovely dream, Robert glanced around the deep hall. But the crowd of confident officials were already grouping here and there through the tables and columns, heatedly gossiping. Discussing subjects other than the tragedy of man at his eleventh hour! And they were like tourists who have photographed an epic scene, only to hurry away. Robert met David Lilienthal's embarrassed grin, then searched on.

Still bent at the low table over by the auditorium door, Herb Marks sat soberly scribbling. Through his friend's flashes of wit, Herb had carefully kept watch on Commissioner Strauss's bleak profile. Now Robert was leaning on the table under the calling voices.

'Well, Herbert M.' Robert smiled uncertainly. 'How was I?'

Then his old friend too looked up in his face, as if at some enigma.

'Good . . . much too good.' Herb forced a smile. 'You always go the limit Oppy, always the limit.' The witness's face was sharply animated, as after a win at chess.

Robert did not wait for Herb. He was expected by Rabi and Bethe at the Cosmos Club in half an hour. But ten minutes later, when he clicked down the marble halls of government, out into the humid heat high on the Senate steps, Robert was feeling a vague guilty panic. A mournful Washington drizzle hissed through a sticky mist. Along the boulevard below, he saw no cabs. The few cars splashed through the puddles with their lights on. The sudden contrast of melancholy weather provoked an almost unbearable grief.

The Chief Advisor belted his wet raincoat, still cold from the air conditioning. He started down the long Senate steps into the rain. No, he had not found the words. Robert frowned. If they existed. He went before those mighty fellows with the word. Not even freedom-loving young America could *own* the violence on the Jornada, any more than it owned God. How could he worry about Lewis's feelings with a message like that?

238

And what if he *had* found the words? Robert had retreated from the downpour under a striped soda-fountain awning. Against the window stood a tramp wearing a veteran's pin. They exchanged indifferent glances. This was a strange scene for revelations. But Robert felt one growing on him.

What difference *could* it make? He concentrated on the traffic, glancing out in the roaring knee-deep spray. Who was he to shatter all these patriots who believed in freedom, greed and democracy which gave them dominion over their fellow men? Opposing armies still prayed to the same God to give them victory without heeding His words. At this rate, nations would end up praying to the same physicists for exclusive Power. So this is the government you sold the sun to, this splendidly naive team of lawmen and generals! What a piece of work was man, all right . . .

The weeping of the Capitol's sky that spring noon kept the world-famous Oppy trapped twenty minutes under the tramp's striped awning. Finally an empty cab pulled over. Robert was rescued from his thoughts.

Late that summer of 1949, anno nuclei 4, another mystery was upon the earth. And out of the secret continent of the east came a different weeping.

The west wind bore the second lamentation over wounded Japan, on towards the cypress cliffs of California. And sniffing it, obscure airborne physicists found it impure, for there was cerium in it, and they were not alone. There was another Doctor Oppenheimer on the earth, and another Los Alamos . . . another Jornada del Muerte, and another Trinity, and the free young democracy had no dominion over them. For they belonged to the tyrant Stalin, butcher of millions.

And in Washington, the President and Senators were afraid. Worshipping their exclusive knowledge, they were quite sure it was 'Security' which had allowed their divine powers to be stolen. Then among the physics priesthood (feeling his godhead rivalled), stirred the one uncontainable, primordial ambition.

So it was, as the Oppenheimer family arrived back at Princeton after their summer on San Francisco Bay and turned on the lights, that the telephone was ringing. Robert took the call in his leather armchair under the mantel. He sat bent, listening to the guttural European chatter.

'Yes, Edward.' Robert finally spoke. 'I'm afraid it is only too true.'

'You mean there is no question?' the tiny, faraway voice called, up the long well-shaft of the night. 'The Russians have it? Stalin has an atom-bomb?'

Kitty was watching him from the open cabinet with two martinis. She could faintly hear Teller's voice. She stared at her husband's drawn face.

'We aren't the world's only physicists. Does that surprise you, Edward?'

'What shall we do?' cried the little muffled voice. 'What shall we do?'

'Well, why not go back to Los Alamos . . . keep working.'

'For heaven's sake! Is that all?'

Across the six hundred miles of moonless Indian forest from Chicago, Teller's uncontrol leapt into the Director's heart. He fought it angrily.

'That's right, Ed.' He drawled. 'Simply keep your shirt on.'

'Keep my shirt on?' came the stricken voice. Was it not Teller, after all, whose passion it had always been to bring forth on to the Earth a new, far vaster power to burn human lives; a fusion-force that would be to Hiroshima as dynamite to a child's firecracker?

'That's right Edward,' Robert repeated. 'Try and keep calm.'

Then the conversation was over. Robert and Kitty sat a long time in the dusky living-room. Through Olden Manor and the sleeping Institute of Advanced Studies beyond, there was only the ticking clock. Robert waited, sucking his pipe-stem. Then, very strangely, feeling the doubled nuclear violence now a fact out in the innocent night, he was almost relieved. The young country's monopoly on atomic guilt was at an end. Any further, final, retreat would make the crime of Trinity almost insignificant. It was like another redemption long ago with Jean and Haakon, when a young narcissist from Riverside Drive, isolated by money, over-educated and morbidly sensitive, had discovered the other completeness. To be one with simple folk against the machine of greed.

Chapter 12

That summer at Eagle Hill, commanding the glittering lakes of San Francisco Bay, the Oppenheimers had come back again to Haakon Chevalier. Of the disintegrating circle of Robert's deepest friendships, only Haakon still forgave him everything.

He had seen at once his celebrated friend's loss of the old brilliant happiness. So he invited Robert and Kitty away from the big house, to share his little bungalow on Stinson's Beach while Barbara was in hospital. There on the Pacific surf, the writer set out to make his physics friend Oppy feel a romance in life, as Haakon himself had once run away to sea.

That afternoon by the open water where no agents could listen in, they stretched side by side on the sand under Haakon's parasol. Haakon and Kitty lay flopped on the sand, Robert between them, his nakedness wrapped in some armour of guilt. Their toes were towards the cracking waves, their closed eyes up under the shady parasol.

On Oppy's long, tanned body, limply bony as a Hindu sage, Haakon saw no traces of the strange children he had presented the world. There were no scars from the arena of Congressional hearings back east.

The day was getting on to dusk. But the sand out in the sun was still oven hot and hard. In the shade, the fine grains sifted coolly between their fingers. Here, shrunken in the hazy distances of sand dotted here and there with a coloured parasol, the three could speak. Utter thoughts that might sound obscene anywhere else, and never be understood.

Then sometimes the old friends would lie silent, all three listening to the muffled thump and hiss of the surf, the little buffets of the ocean breeze. Hearing again this canticle of the elements, feeling the heat and the caress of the breeze, Doctor Oppenheimer remembered the power of the sun. He felt the golden light behind his lids, saturating like Corsican wine the bleached whiteness of his soul.

'It's strange.' He broke their long expectant silence. 'It began as an expression of life.'

'I believe you,' Haakon's voice answered, stubbornly romantic.

'Robbie tends to sound like John on Patmos.' Kitty brushed the sandflies, not opening her eyes.

'It need not be extermination,' Robert reflected. 'If both sides accept equality.'

'If,' Kitty commented, 'they don't go mad first!'

'Yes,' Robert continued, after a thoughtful silence. 'It is the symbol of their delusions . . . the symbol.'

'Can we live without delusions, my friend?' murmured Haakon's voice.

A further silence, then Robert finally said: 'Love isn't a delusion.'

He propped himself up on his elbows, between the man and woman's closed faces. Robert looked out over gold-green ribbons of waves, into the dense haze. The thick bluish film suddenly was like smoke coming off the sea.

Neither was hate a delusion, or terror, he thought. Nor the shadings in between. It was a choice. Maybe you could only live without delusion if you had power. Maybe man was born powerless before nature, and delusions were men's only defence from it. Maybe Doctor Oppenheimer's grandiose guilt and responsibility was only the Power of a few, stolen from nature.

Gazing in the sun at the smoke pouring from the salt sea, a secret flush of fear weakened through him. He lay back between Kitty and Haakon under the drowsy striped umbrella.

Haakon's voice was saying, 'Humanity simply is not ready.'

'When has it ever been?' Kitty's laughter mingled with the waves.

'Probably,' Robert mused, 'we will never be ready to share the world with Communism . . . any more than with Indians or anyone else.'

'Neither can I . . . with the International,' Kitty said quickly in the sea breeze. 'They are not ready to share the world, even with their own people.'

'It is true, Uncle Joe ruined it,' Haakon grieved. 'At least set it back.'

Robert reflected: 'For the Russian people most of all.'

'Stalin was a mistake . . . a horrible one!' Haakon admitted.

'With ideology, Haakon,' Kitty said warmly, for she knew how good this free talk was for them all. 'With absolute rule, it's like with atom bombs. You can't afford mistakes.'

'The Russian people,' Robert's voice droned on after a pause. 'They are the most tragic of all time. To have had the Civil War. Stalin as their benefactor. Then Hitler as an enemy. Now to watch us build a nuclear armada? They have lost everything!'

'Yes,' Haakon said emotionally. 'It's no wonder innocent America fears Russian darkness.'

'Yes . . .'

There was a slap of flesh from Kitty's side of their drowsing trinity under the parasol. She did not open her eyes.

'. . . think how they must dream of American innocence!'

'Innocence, Katie?' Robert's voice lifted bitterly in the soft roar of the Pacific afternoon. At last they were saying the things that were so difficult to say.

'I want you both to hear,' Robert confessed with a sudden vehemence. 'Who would ever have thought that *any* leaders,' his hands clenched the sand in hard clumps, 'who were given that power, a power to wipe out whole cities of women and children, that even *that* would not cure them of selfishness and greed!'

'Is it so bad, my friend?' Haakon's voice spoke by Robert's right ear.

'Bad enough that our leaders hide it from us.'

The three bodies on the hot sand listened to the ocean. In the safety of affection they were risking uncut ideas, ideas that could bring down their last belief in human nature. This hour was free and belonged to everyone.

Not afford mistakes? Robert reflected. He dug his toes satisfyingly through the hot sand into the moist cool. What about all *my* mistakes? Suddenly he longed to crawl free and be close to life, part of the humble scheme of things. The nightmare in Washington seemed far away.

'And your brother Frank?' Haakon said.

On Robert's left, Kitty was throwing sand on her legs. The sandflies preferred her.

'I wouldn't worry about Frank!' she laughed pleasantly.

'Why? Have you protected him?'

243

'I can scarcely protect myself,' Robert smiled ironically.

'Our mutual friend Lawrence,' Kitty offered. 'He's fired Frank from the Radiation Lab. Congress leaked Frank's Party membership to the papers.'

'Uhuh, Haakon, Frank's not allowed in the laboratory.'

'Robbie, is this true?' Haakon sat up and looked at the placid dreaming face.

'Frank's buying a little sheep spread in Colorado. Pagosa Springs . . . isn't too far from Los Alamos. Rugged . . . quiet.'

Kitty forgot the sandflies. She opened her eyes and looked at Haakon.

'Frank, a shepherd?' Haakon shouted in disbelief.

'A shepherd.' Robert laughed. 'He's the only success in our whole bunch.'

Haakon was impressed. 'So you, Robbie, you'll be the last Utopian.'

'If I had any brains,' Robert said, 'I'd join Frank.'

Opening his eyes, he raised himself and stared out over the rippling line of combers, where the red sun lay almost on the sea. Haakon and Kitty followed his gaze.

'It's the oldest lesson of them all,' Robert was abruptly saying. 'You can only change the world from the bottom. Frank doesn't have to wait for Rome to mend its ways – he's making his rebellion, and I envy him. I dread going back. I know what I'll face.'

Kitty glanced around.

'Then why are we going?'

'You keep asking me that. I keep telling you.' Robert did not look at the scathing face on his left. Yet, confronting his enigmatic chains to the Mesa, inspiration failed him again.

'– I just do not know.'

'These sandflies are getting too much for me,' Kitty said, kicking on her sandals. 'You two stay, I'll have a shower.'

'Oh, don't go in, Kitty!' Haakon objected.

'No no, don't worry darling H. Robbie's happy on his own.'

Doctor Oppenheimer twisted to stare after his wife's bare legs, going slowly up into the beach grass. It worried him when she was alone.

Turning back to the sea, Robert took his pipe from the English tobacco pouch. He tugged loose some soft shredded leaves.

'Yes, Haakon!' he laughed. 'They are eating us . . . alive, alive-oh.'

The writer's parasol was the only one left on the long beach. The low red sun had little warmth. North along the slow curve of surf, the haze was a thick white mist across the littoral. The friends' long days by the open sea were almost over. After cooking them his cordon bleu dinner, Haakon must drive back over the Golden Gate. Soon Doctor Oppenheimer would fly east to the bitter conspiracies of the Capitol . . . to the 'Hill' called Congress, as long ago a certain Mesa had been called the 'Hill'.

At Haakon's elbow, Robert puffed his pipe. The most powerful man in the world lying by the least protected. They watched in deep emotion as the lively ranks of waves blackened. The red sun had slipped from its saturation, to a spent ripeness at the very edge of life. It was the tragic hour.

'Robbie, my friend?' Haakon began with embarrassed intensity, when they were alone. 'Robbie, I know why you go back . . .'

'Why, Haakon?' Hearing how his friend's great love for him had survived the security trauma, he felt a deep childlike safety. Their eyes followed the gliding drift of seagull silhouettes across the molten hemisphere of the sun. The sea breeze had died, but the waves came on.

'. . . tell me why I go back.'

'Because if you do not win,' Haakon said warmly, 'it will mean the entire evolution of human society was for evil motives.'

They both stared out in the sunset.

'Yes? Go on, Haakon.'

'If you do win,' Haakon went on, 'it will mean all the nightmares of history were failures on a road to human love.'

'And if we don't win . . .?'

Doctor Oppenheimer examined his friend's soft blond profile.

Haakon looked down, digging in the sand. 'If you do not win, my friend, then there will never have been such a thing as progress.'

Robert's coal glowed like an eye in the shadows.

'It will be proved,' Chevalier was intent, 'man's supreme passion was always for death. Robbie, my friend, you could never admit that.'

'Yes, I think that's it!' Robert let out his breath. 'That's it.'

'So, Robbie my friend?' Haakon scattered the sand. 'You go back.'

'Because I cannot admit my disbelief in man,' Robert completed it softly, nodding slowly in his amazement.

'Any more than I could admit a disbelief in you,' Haakon said, and a deep emotion passed between them.

'Thank you Haakon,' Robert said simply.

For a long time, the two men sat side by side on the chilly beach in a perfect silence. The twilight was closing around them. Way out, four Portuguese fishing smacks droned across the gold-scaled wake of the sun, their tiny running lights like stars.

'Well . . .' Haakon had gotten to one knee to collapse the parasol on its wood stem. 'Somewhere out there . . . *Russia!*'

'Think of that, old man!' Robert cried suddenly. 'Could there ever have been a time when we might all have shared everything?'

'If there ever was such a time we will never know now.'

'If we and they have fixed, equal destructiveness,' Robert rambled on, suddenly talking in a manner of the Capitol. 'It is still not too late for moderation. A lot of good people are fighting for that.'

'And if moderation fails?'

Abruptly, the friends sitting on the sand were very conscious of the security barrier. As if the fascist barbed wire – which 'Oppy' had imagined one cool night on the Mesa, with the condemned faces behind it he would soon set free – had somehow found its way through the bloodstream of history to this California beach.

'If moderation fails, Haakon? I can't even think about it.'

Robert roused himself, slipping stiffly to his knees. The sand-flies prickled along his legs. 'But if we go through the limits again,' Robert said softly in a rising tide of fresh anger, 'mark my words, Haakon, it will be worse. Much, much worse than the human mind can conceive!'

'In that case, you will not fail, my friend!' Haakon laughed enthusiastically, putting his arm over Robert's shoulder. 'I know you will not.' He stood up. 'Now come in the bungalow for some *nourriture*.'

'You have given me plenty of *nourriture* already, thank you Haakon,' Robert said.

246

Stinson's Beach was over. Haakon uprooted the parasol and smoothed the sand where they had talked. The first stars were out, the sun had sunk among feathery clouds. Low upon the distant horizon of the Pacific was a natural firestorm. And it was beautiful.

When Haakon had left Robert in the bungalow alone with Kitty – she had had too much sun, and drunk too much Napa wine – they sat at the low window and read. In the sweet forgiving Pacific night the Chief Advisor listened to the mournful fall of the waves.

Smoking his pipe without turning the page, Robert saw vividly in his imagination the weeks ahead. For the time was come of Teller's thermonuclear bomb. And he thought of all the faces who would accuse him for telling their truths, and for shouldering them with their guilts. No one wanting to give ground to Reason, all clinging to their freedom and attributing crimes committed by the system to him. Robert was too pessimistic now to keep up with people who disliked him. Power had done that. At least there was his little élite of physics colleagues. But all they believed in was their own minds . . . *les pensées indépassables*.

In the bamboo beach chair across from him, little Kitty dozed with an expression of childish disappointment. After another hour walking by the phosphorescent spume along the beach, Robert went to bed to search for sleep.

Chapter 13

From the fortress East the fear spread. From Washington, the panic of 'Joe I' raced out in hot flushes over the young land. And the great Senators and industrialists, and the Generals who had won untold conquests, and the President at their head who had known the battered Russian 'asiatics' would never have a bomb . . . all of them afraid of the unknown, unfaceable thing. All knowing the ancient thing was no more, that nothing that had been would ever be the same. In that American panic of the ninth and tenth months of the fourth year, far worse and more deranging to civilization than market crashes, camps, or all the invasions of Germans, Romans, Khans or Inquisitors or plagues, came a shock, like an earthquake among the moral foundations of the human soul. An earthquake of collective being to drive men wild, to jump from windows or burrow in the ground rather than live through another such. And this was the shock as the knowledge – called Los Alamos, Jornada, Point Zero – came home at last, maddening to the place of power.

A new bleached light was upon the earth, and this new light was a new world. A new light radiant from an unknown plateau in the red heartland desert, by the Rio Grande of the human spirit. And from the babbling and petulant reflected face of Washington rebounded waves of fear. Fear, panic, confusion, and further fear.

For visible, even to those half blinded in the new light, out of the fog of inequality and unrelation, was *another* fortress. Medieval butcher Stalin's fortress, containing the captive hundred races who for two years had borne in silence the possibility of having their cities and flesh crushed and poisoned by Jornadas from the Land of the Free. Suddenly oceans had rolled back, great plains and mountains had vanished. Now the virgin flesh of the free could equally be flattened by the war-battered tyrant, suddenly visible in his Marxist citadel. There was only trust to prevent it, and no wellbeing left in fortresses. War had come at last to American soil.

Panic raced out in hot flushes. Stumbling in the oxygen dreams of past mythologies, in the new abstract air, generals, statesmen and erratic physicists struck out to save their old wellbeing. Hysteria! Plans to transport their fortress, stone by stone, out of reach. Schemes to make it blastproof, move it underground (at least its throne room). To flatten and spatter the human flesh in the fortress over *there*, before it could multiply. Or to make it wither with threats and spells, or hollow mountains out for equipment. To eavesdrop, spy, even read monolithic minds. Weird hallucinations, of detecting and wiping out any country that dared to steal the New Light from its self-appointed master. Of rebuilding nirvana among the clouds, from which they could rule the world with superbombs. Where the unknown innocent women and men of the land would renounce their love of life and breed babies born with the nerves of commandos, skins of lead and lungs impervious to Plutonium. And all the time, from the first desert hours Doctor Oppenheimer had seen the light through the blockhouse door, one sane possibility left. To tear down obsolete fears . . . to embrace.

It was into this low pressure of 'Joe 1' on Capitol Hill that Robert returned that autumn. And with byzantine Stalin suddenly so close, the Chief Advisor's thoughtful unsurprise was a greater mystery than ever.

Chapter 14

The half-century was to end in a beautiful hot autumn.

Through America's places of ivied learning stirred the romance of epics in football stadiums, and another World-Series race. On the manicured New Jersey promontory of Princeton's Institute of Advanced Studies, there was an exciting new gathering of world intellects. Last year's poet T.S. Eliot had left behind him the cathedral incense of his murdered archbishop. Robert began over-hearing himself described by young colleagues, the ones who had not lived through the blasphemies of Trinity and the violence of Nagasaki, as a tragic saint.

Even here, in the devoted order and peace of his big office, among the new society of scholars, the world was not governed by reason. But that dread was nothing beside the constant tightness in Robert's sunken stomach since the Russian bomb, the premoni-tion of what was to come. And that if it was going to come it would be now. The ashes of civilization awaited a third coming, a bomb of bombs. Robert bent his ear to the network of personalities and power inside the veil of Secrets. Then in the first week of October it came, and all at once, and from several directions.

In the Capitol, model-Washingtonian Billy Borden of the missile trauma was able to get a top secret Subcommittee named. Together, the secret-statesmen flew out west to Los Alamos. Meanwhile in the catacombs of nuclear mysteries, Banker Strauss again exhorted the Atom Commissioners who had consistently voted him down. It was time American democracy had a techno-logy-fix. A thousand Hiroshimas were no longer enough. Russia must be left in the radioactive dust of a thermonuclear age. And in these same days, far out West on the Berkeley campus, Chevalier's 'Caliban' of the laboratory, Wendell Lattimer, hurried to Ernest Orlando Lawrence. Something had to be done! The two men were joined by ambitious young Alvarez, and the three flew south to Albuquerque, then on to Oppy's Mesa to collect their fourth

249

horseman. For Los Alamos had an airstrip now.

Above the changeless canyons of the Rio Grande, the Hungarian was waiting with Johnny von Neumann, Georgi Gamov of Göttingen days, and the Pole Stanislas Ulam. Were not all their homelands enslaved to Marxism? Gamov fanned their excitement with a parable of how once in Russia, Bukharin had offered him the whole Leningrad power supply for work on Stalin's atom-projects.

Still these seven were insignificant next to the man they had come for, like cardinals of darkness to elect a Pope, a passionate magician Robert had taken with him to his Utopia under the desert sky. Teller, who Robert had not been able to take back down with him from the brothel Mesa.

Now, thinking of Edward, behind his peaceful desk at Princeton, Robert felt something in him stir. That primordial genius, beloved of the elements, insatiable to stand alone at the hour of untouched ideas. Teller, who no matter how much responsibility Oppy assumed, no matter how many committees he punished himself with or prophecies he sung of doom, would never deny the cottonwood plateau where all of Robert longed still to be. An ego unfiltered, free, a creator irresponsible and childish . . . innocent, terrible and sublime.

To Oppy's glorious plateau the delegation went for Teller's counsel. Was there any other answer for the world and human happiness than to pursue the limitless fusion bomb? Each fusion bomb a Jornada of a thousand Hiroshimas. And Teller told them: 'There is no other answer than the Super.' Then like the ghosts of General Groves's ambition, and hidden within Groves's veil of security from the billions of innocent souls they would gamble – not to speak of the creatures of the earth, the fowl of the air, and fishes of the seas – the Horsemen flew to Washington.

As fall term got underway at Princeton, Robert was intimately aware, through his network of friends, of the top-secret delegation installed in an elegant suite in Washington. How Teller and Lawrence were evangelizing a paradise for frightened patriots, to be reached only by a new, more fabulous Gold Rush on the elements.

The urgent instinct came over a quiet Princeton scholar to speak out. And Robert discreetly prepared himself, knowing he must be understood.

He might not be a President or Secretary of State, Robert thought, turning nervously in his bed at Olden Manor the night he made the decision. But he had as much influence as he'd ever had. So he must fight Teller's fire. That would be a universal good, even though, to preach it, he had to enshrine an atom bomb.

What now of the humble brotherhood he had felt, working for the migrants of the orchards and artichoke fields? Now security was keeping them humble, ignorant as sheep going to slaughter. Robert would be practically alone in the struggle. It was quite a failure.

And within weeks of the Russian bomb, Oppy's top-secret Advisors were asked to meet and give judgment as to whether America could still hold its head up . . . having dominion only to crush and splatter the human multitudes of several dozen Moscows. Could the Pentagon not budget a more splendid celebration? A fireworks of a whole universe of poisoned paradises? As October 29 of Year 4 came near, agitated physicists arrived at Robert's Princeton office asking for reassurance and bearing extraordinary gossip . . . the old *hydrodynamics* problem from Teller's wartime fusion work might never be solved!

Recently another anxiety had begun for Robert. Was a time upon them when, no matter how beautiful and urgent the truth moralists spoke, no one would understand? When not even his advisors would be understood? *Maybe when you spoke in the voice of all men: few men understood you*! History was like a beach of decisions . . . 'yes' or 'no' grains of sand. Now the decision, yes or no to saving life on earth, would be made . . . and it was no more than a grain of sand. The truth was at the end of its tracks; morality might soon derail permanently.

Once Doctor Oppenheimer doubted the power of reason over absolute evil, he made a most unscientific mistake. In his need to hope, Robert began counting on Teller's technical failure. The Father of the Atomic Bomb had become a human being.

Chapter 15

Friday evening the Chief Advisor was steering yet again down through the innocent oblivious Maryland forest, Route 1 to the Capitol.

Robert had changed his baggy tweeds for neat grey flannels. In the briefcase on the seat was the 'undecided' letter mailed by the ninth Advisor, Glen Seaborg. Before Hiroshima, Glen had signed that Franck disarmament petition. He must have lost heart.

The gale had blown the last red leaves from the trees. The empty road through the windshield was a planing on soggy red. How secrecy veiled him from the simple lives in these little towns! Then Robert thought of his Russian doubles who knew him only through intelligence, or whatever the English spy Nunn had told them. Robert had warned Pash years ago. President Truman had so deceived himself he had even made Oppy sign an *oath* that the Russians were scientifically capable, before he believed it! Yes, he had known about Kurchatov and Peter Kapitza's work. And of Sakharov, Kikoin, Alekhanov and Golovin. Flerov even wrote pre-war warnings like Szilard's to the Soviet Defence Committee. But though Kurchatov started work before the war, no real programme got going. Not until Truman started raising the stake after Potsdam. Stalin even had a General Groves called Vannikov. Well there was no point getting idealistic about the Russians now. Political idiocy had spoiled that. If you had any doubts you had only to remember their chief was no pleasant Dave Lilienthal, but Lavrenti Beria, who had crushed and maimed millions of his own people like ants. Beria had only one double: Himmler. Well, if they had listened to him in '43 and again in '46, Robert thought bitterly, the Russian project might still be pottering along, and Beria not be involved.

Now it was 1949, and too late for appeasement. The price of saving humanity from fusion bombs was promoting atom bombs to keep Beria in line.

Is that a morality at all, Robert wondered, noticing the car's speedometer needle at 85 and lifting his foot. Or was he going mad, like the rest? Well, whether he was mad or not, or loved life or his family, they had better listen, or that would be that. Maybe he was only one grain on the beach of time, and Frank's way the only answer. But if he didn't handle this right, the whole human beach would end up as solid yellow glass. Surely they could not actually *want* that?

Outside Baltimore the lights were cozily on in the diners flanking the road. In the forest under the charcoal sky, outside the streaming windows, drifted the poison fog. It was permanent now. The lonely secret of the world's death bore down on the driver in the speeding car.

In the Capitol, Alger Hiss was in the fifth month of his treason trial. There was a demonstration daily outside the Grand Jury. Eugene Dennis had been convicted this week, and Gerhard Eisler fled the country on a Polish ship. Robert was feeling morbidly drowsy and had trouble not watching the wipers. Only fifty minutes now, he thought, enjoying that short freedom.

Saturday morning in Washington, the gale had passed. A cold steady rain fell on Constitution Avenue.

Robert easily found a parking place outside the ramshackle Atom Commission building. Inside there were already separate huddles of Air Force and Army personnel, whispering along the marble walls. Robert noticed Alvarez trying to look nonchalant and unexcluded. The meeting was so tip-top secret that no public interest existed. As if there was really no argument at all, no atom bomb, and no thermonuclear fusion, almost as if there was no public. The sun was just the sun, and everyone went to the grand jury trials. Military guards locked the doors behind Chief Advisor Oppenheimer and his sagging briefcase.

One flight up the wet stairs Robert caught sight of a different huddle. The seven advisers were waiting outside Room 213, the Kremlin-specialist Kennan too, and the Air Force's McCormack. No one was missing.

When these normally overbearing officials saw Oppy turn the corner in his raincoat and come towards them, their false geniality lightened (just as Robert's enemies found the sight of him sinister and subversive). The nine gentlemen made room around the mild scholar with the pipe and wet hat. A relieved light softened Robert's glance.

For ten seconds in the dim corridor, they made a shy grateful group. And in the Advisor's handshakes and subdued glances Robert suddenly was sure they knew very well why they were there, though Hartley Rowe ran the notorious United Fruit Company, Buckley designed guided missiles, and the rest had sold their souls to bomb makers. The Advisors were face to face with a 'crash programme', to build gargantuan sunstorms on the delicate earth.

'A large round table would be more suitable,' Robert said, walking ahead through the door into the fluorescent conference room.

There was a little explosion of nervous jollity. Overstuffed chairs were scraping back. One by one they were sitting, arranging documents down the polished table.

Then silence came. The world's fate crushed down. Over the Advisors' heads the cheerful conference-room air thickened and compressed, inhibiting eloquence, deforming reason, melting cold minds and freezing the warmest hearts. Urgency and concentration seized the seasoned negotiators. They must hurry, before their moral strength was dulled. Flanking faces turned away from Oppy to the chairs at the far end.

In the first hour the long table of Advisors heard testimony from Banker Strauss. Then from Lilienthal and his Commissioners. Following this the question was reviewed. Should the power stakes be raised from fission to fusion? Feeling Strauss's eyes shift his way, Robert barely spoke.

Then George Kennan moved forward to testify what 'Joe I' meant to the Russians. The Kremlin, he said, were more interested in bombs for their propaganda value, and in expansion on ideological fronts. One more hour passed, and Fermi had taken note of a large bluebottle fly making the rounds of the coffee cups. A vague stir of irritation was felt toward this impudent insect. Fermi got up with a shrug to open one of the streaming windows.

The conference door had just opened to admit General Omar Bradley in a neat olive uniform jacket. Kind honest eyes, and a thin wide mouth. Not long ago Robert had actually felt like a freedom fighter among such fellows.

'In conclusion, General Bradley,' he was soon saying, not resisting the instinct to hide his feelings in the boring jargon of the courtroom. 'Let us take the issue of the Super back to its cost as . . . as compared to the smaller atom bombs already in our arsenal, which, with boosting, already are capable of wiping out all the major cities of Russia. What military advantage is to be gained from such a huge expenditure on the Super?'

The Chairman of the Joint Chiefs was sitting with his back to the grey windows. He raised his handsome black eyebrows, his eyes twinkled with a foxy kindness.

'Well sir,' he said thoughtfully, 'only psychological I should say.'

When General Bradley saluted his way out of the conference room a few minutes later, Chairman Oppenheimer's face was still burning. The Air Force's McCormack was also abruptly leaving the Advisors to catch a flight to test site Eniwetok – the new Jornada in the Pacific – so Robert was spared looking at the others. (Their decision won't be handed down for weeks, McCormack was thinking as he pulled on his rain cape. The General found the eggheads horribly complicated.)

Soon Robert left the building for a low-voiced Saturday lunch with Alvarez and Joe Serber at a local spaghetti basement with checkered tablecloths. Then the Advisors locked themselves back in the conference room. Luis Alvarez was Teller's man. He had seemed quite taken aback that neither Oppy nor Joe seemed very excited by the new Gold Rush on the elements. What was being done to their glorious Superbomb?

'Well gentlemen, we seem to have a curious privilege,' Robert was musing later. Fermi had just described the uncertain state Teller's thermonuclear research was in. Then Hans Bethe had spoken to them, staring soberly over his friends' profiles at the glistening treetops outside.

The table head paused to suck his well-chewed pipe stem.

'This is a democratic country,' Robert went on. 'Yet we have no public opinion to contend with.'

'The boys know!' Fermi grinned. 'Not many would put up with it.'

'So it might be useful,' Robert went on, 'to imagine ourselves in a storm of controversy. Even with a lobby picketing us.'

'Quite right!' broke in Hartley Rowe. 'Throwing rotten tomatoes.'

255

'If you ask me,' Rabi shrugged, 'we should discuss this damn security once and for all.'

'One thing at a time, Isidor,' the Chief Advisor nodded. 'We're here to take a hard sane look at what our game with the Russians consists of. And what ground is to be won in raising the stakes by many hundred million lives.'

'To say the least . . .' Du Bridge muttered uncertainly. 'What makes some people want that so badly?'

For several seconds, the overtones of this question silenced the Advisors, as if someone had struck a giant gong. The Harvard President's spectacles eagerly followed the bluebottle's fruitless march among the empty cups. A light flickered over their heads.

'For the record, gentlemen,' Conant began with dignity, 'history has a precedent for removing the stakes altogether. In Japan, firearms were outlawed for a century on the grounds they were dishonourable.'

'Too late to cash in now, my man!' Cyril Smith replied in his jaunty sergeant-major style. 'If we veto the Super, we'll have to recommend stepping up atom bomb production and the booster in case Joe pushes on to the Super.'

'Correct,' commented the Chief Advisor. Along the wide table, both sides turned.

'All right,' Robert reflected, tugging his earlobe. 'Enrico's been into technical feasibility. Refrigeration for the Super might be so big that the Russians would have to build the thing for us on the target. Now, setting aside the moral issue, shall we consider the third point? The cost versus the military advantages.'

'But Robert! That is the same,' little Rabi interrupted. He looked up and down the table. 'The Joint Chiefs just told us the only advantage is psychological. But the cost of the weapon by present figures – well, it is the extermination of the human race on this planet!' Isidor's voice rose. 'How could we, as human beings, scientists, advisors whatever, approve a weapon to give us a psychological advantage . . . *at the cost of all human life*. I cannot listen to it!'

'The idea is repellent,' James Conant agreed primly. 'And I think . . . insane. That would not be too strong a word.'

Suddenly in this most secret Washington conference room, amid the labyrinth of Commission bureaucracy, everyone faced up the table wanted to talk at once. The fluorescent lights had taken on an unnatural brightness. Every rustle of fabric was clearly audible, the methodical 'snik-snik-snik' of the stenographer.

'Morally speaking gentlemen,' Hartley Rowe broke out, 'you would be using this bomb against civilization, not against armies. I don't like to see women and children killed wholesale, because the male element in the human race is so *stupid* – stupid, gentlemen! – they cannot get out of war and keep out of war!'

'Yes, yes, exactly!' Fermi leaned forward, fingertips pressed together, looking up under his brows at them with puckish ruthlessness. 'And you must not forget we are scientists. What I say is this: if *we* cannot resist, at least delay, the satisfactions of technical success, these dangerous developments, then how do we deny the Generals the satisfaction of using these portable extermination ovens which they call "devices"?'

'Absolutely, absolutely!' Rabi cut in, veins standing out on his temples. 'We cannot delude ourselves! This decision must be made knowing this country will use whatever weapons it has, no matter what are the consequences. No man, not even the President of the United States –'

'– least of all the President of a humanitarian country,' Conant interrupted vehemently.

'– must ever be given the power to annihilate the planet!'

Together several of the Advisors facing each other along the wide conference table glanced up at their Chairman. There was a quality of light over these heads, Robert was thinking, that he had never seen in life. The Chief Advisor had lowered his mournful eyes over his pipe and tobacco pouch.

For a beautiful excitement had stirred, deep under the weight of ice that six years of betrayals, abused happiness, guilt, despair and retreating from life had thickened on Robert's heart. Was it possible? He had scarcely put forward his own radical opinion. Yet for hours all these men had been getting more and more emotional over his strongest beliefs. Robert had hoped so many years for these ideas, and had so often been left alone at the moment of truth, that he scarcely knew how to react to hearing them agreed with. Knowing the deadly tide was rising out in the Capitol for drastic solutions to Communism, were all these men ready to risk swimming against it? He had felt nothing like it since Trinity! And suddenly Doctor Oppenheimer remembered his old dream, of a time when everyone would take responsibility for his fellow men. He could almost feel the madness subside across the world, even as far as the silent cottonwood Mesa he had betrayed.

An expectant silence fell. The hot, tight feeling in the Chief Advisor's throat had passed. He looked up pleasantly at the expectant faces.

'It seems, gentlemen, we are unanimous.' Robert lowered his eyes and shifted his pipe. 'To me that is such a surprising thing,' he added, so softly that everyone in the conference room held their breath to hear. Somehow such unanimity frightened him.

He looked up and smiled. 'So tomorrow we'll meet and solve the wording of the . . . the recommendation. To increase standard Plutonium production; and our three-point majority opinion on the crash-programme for the Super. And Enrico, Isidor, your addendum on the moral issue. Remember, no matter how clear we may be in our own minds, on paper we must be so simple, so clear any child could understand it.'

'Children?' Isidor Rabi grinned up and down the table. 'They will already understand. Words for adults will be trickier.'

And through the Atom Committee room, there spread a light warm laughter.

On the Advisors' Sunday, October 30th, the minutes went faster. Outside the four big windows, the weather was clearing and chilly. Locked inside the Committee room, as the eight Advisors at the summits of power and the mind composed their last declaration against nuclear psychosis, they experienced an inspiration rarely felt in Washington. That is, of men completely in the right.

Later that evening Robert sat, reading out their three reports. The simple typed sheets of white Commission stationery rustled in his fingers.

'If you will bear with me,' he said thoughtfully, 'I would feel proud to read out some significant paragraphs.

' "We believe," Robert read, "a super bomb should never be produced . . . our undertaking one will not prove a deterrent to the Russians. Should they use the weapon against us our large stock of atomic bombs would be comparably effective to the use of a Super. In determining not to proceed to develop the super bomb, we see a unique opportunity of providing by example some limitation on the totality of war, and thus of limiting fear and arousing the hopes of mankind." Enrico, will you read from your addendum?'

'With great pleasure.' The little man hunched forward delightedly. ' "Necessarily, such a weapon goes far beyond any military objective, and enters the range of very great natural catastrophes. It is clear the use of such a weapon cannot be justified by any ethical ground that gives the human being a certain individuality and dignity. The fact that no limit exists to the destructiveness of this weapon makes its practical effect almost one of genocide, and its existence and the knowledge of its construction a danger to humanity as a whole. It is necessarily an evil considered in any light. For these reasons we believe it important for the President of the United States to tell the American public, and all the world, that we think it wrong, on fundamental ethical principles, to initiate a programme of development of such a weapon." '

'I'm glad, gentlemen,' Robert said very softly when they had done. 'For if this had not been the majority, I would have resigned. I believe these conclusions are our most significant ever. That if we are . . . that if we are not listened to: the eventual outcome of the human adventure will have to be considered a very dark and uncertain thing.'

It took Doctor Oppenheimer's General Advisors one weekend to find the most fated words human ears had heard since the wilderness, words worthy of Trinity.

But as the football stadiums roared and America moved towards Thanksgiving, the five Atom-Commissioners were still not unanimous with their Advisors. For there was one vote now in favour of a duel with Communism unto the very extinction of life. And that was the vote of Commissioner Strauss. As the democratic process pressed them on, a great throng at their shoulders, the clique hungering for a further Gold Rush began spreading their suspicions of Oppy's Advisors outside the channels of decision. And again only one man felt more bitterly frustrated even than Teller and Lawrence to find himself put in the wrong.

One afternoon two weeks later, the sickness in Banker Strauss became too terrible to bear. Climbing with two aides into his limousine, he drove straight across Washington to the Defence Department building. He went straight up to the office of the Defence Secretary, American Legionnaire Louis Johnson, straight into the dapper patriot's office with its red, white and blue legionnaire's banner. He did not even have time to sit down.

'Mr Secretary!' Strauss came out with profound relief. 'Is it not an American tradition never to be less armed than our enemies?'

'Of course it is, Commissioner Strauss, that is the American way.'

'Well sir, Oppenheimer's Commission has just voted to reverse that American way.'

And for some reason, Lewis Strauss could not control a sly, thick-lipped grin of triumph.

Chapter 16

The season when hurricanes rake the coast from the Gulf to the Capital was behind. The first snows drifted over the busy Capitol buildings. But the invisible terror kept its grip inside the top secret leadership.

The magicians of Oppy's lonely desert Mesa had stolen the great mystery. Groves had brought it to Washington. Now it gathered like weather on the words of Oppy's Advisors. What did the words mean, that man's power had reached its final safe dominion over the firmament? That the only alternative was blind belief in Man, that one more step might jeopardize the creation of millions of years? Life was so sweet and bland in the villages of America. What *could* the Advisors mean?

And straining between the god of ultimate power, and the god of moral law, failed-haberdasher Truman convened in late January of '50 an even higher Committee to make his decision: AEC Chairman Lilienthal, Secretary of State Acheson, and the Secretary of Defence, Legionnaire Johnson. Now, smelling the wolfish reek of the power-state run by Stalin and Beria in the same nostrils as the new perfume of world humanism, Secretary Acheson too lost strength. At the bitter brink of his fall, Acheson interpreted the

Advisors' words to mean: that free men must accept second best to Genghis Khan. Forgetting the hundreds of Jornada del Muertes in his own arsenal, and the new booster principle – enough to wipe out several Russias – Secretary Acheson began babbling of his disbelief in a 'reliance on perpetual good will'. Now Oppy's faithful ally Dave Lilienthal stood his ground alone. The scaffolding of Reason was buckling.

Now it happened that in London at the end of January 1950 a certain sensitive fugitive from Hitler, gone to Los Alamos, was met at sooty Paddington station by Chief Inspector Skardon.

'Are you Dr Emil Klaus Fuchs?' Skardon asked politely.

Those three fabled New Mexico years, while Pash, Landsdale and de Silva encoded Oppy's dreaming steps on his desert Utopia, and wondered about his kitchen conversations, a dedicated Communist observer for Stalin, Beria and Kurchatov was living among them under the desert stars. Had even been with Oppy's circle at Trinity.

In New York later the same day, in the elegant Physical Society saloon, Robert sat with Hans Bethe in brass-studded leather chairs. The two gentlemen of Trinty were experiencing the emotion of a family which has had its heirlooms burgled by a son.

'How much did the man tell the Russians?' Robert looked grim and resigned. He was thinking of his and Fuchs' old teacher, Max Born in Edinburgh, who had refused all war work. If only the sharing had been done openly in the first place!

'I telephoned Los Alamos, Robert,' Bethe hung his head, not even bothering to push back his long grey hair. 'Fuchs knew everything,' the German said with simple sadness. 'He was even England's man at that conference to go over Teller's thermonuclear work.'

'Well, I suppose,' Robert nodded, 'whatever Kurchatov didn't know, he knows it now.'

Late that Manhattan evening, Bethe's and gentle Allison's voices – his the voice of the countdown at Trinity – were heard at an eleventh-hour press conference. Like captives, the scholars were signalling to the American people outside Groves's Security screen what was being planned for the fowl of the air, the beasts of the land – and for man. But Bethe's article in a magazine, comparing a

Washington armed with Superbombs to Genghis Khan, had already been confiscated by government agents. And tonight, the gentlemen of the news were not interested in monstrous scuffles in secret corridors. The coliseum's taste was for Spies, and for Big Bombs.

Just two days later, Edward Teller was in Washington testifying in secret to Congress on the Russian penetration of his, and America's, most secret organs of strength. And on January 31 Lilienthal was still standing alone, defending the Advisors' beautiful truths, when the final vote was taken on a 'Crash-Programme' to pursue the Thermonuclear Bomb.

The ultimate and infinitely more devastating Gold Rush on the elements was on. History had overpowered character.

Chapter 17

Only then, living quietly at the Institute, did Doctor Oppenheimer feel his moral chains to the Mesa weaken at last. Had he not done enough?

Robert still remembered how the cottonwood Mesa had been when men were born free, the long horseback rides and calling at Edith Warner's. Edith was gone now from the Mesa as his mother was gone from New York. The adventure he had shared beside Kitty was in the past.

But he could not help knowing of Teller's ambition set free at the new, lavish Los Alamos. Or that here at Princeton, Johnny Von Neumann would soon turn loose his giant new MANIAC computer on the thousands of thermonuclear formulae necessary to build a solar storm . . . Von Neumann, who long ago had taken over Neddermeyer's great American idea. Yet Oppy's old mystic influence to do good had not ended with the downfall of his Advisors. Just by declining to work with Teller, the Chief Advisor kept most of the important minds out of the desert. Only Bethe went back to the Mesa, 'to prove fusion impossible'. Robert's loyalty to Haakon was being repaid a hundredfold. He had become a leader. Hatred was clouding around Oppy, circling his quiet offices at the weather eye.

'Why do I go on with it?' Robert had sounded Kitty, one of the few Princeton evenings when they were not entertaining.

'The Kremlin!' he went on after a silence. 'They compromised our union work. Stalin turned his own saints, like Haakon, into informers. I try to help out Groves against Hitler. The army makes great sinners of us all. Now they've forgotten that. So I have to go around being their conscience!'

Curled in the armchair across the fireplace, Kitty looked at his strained expression and Robert's heart sank. The burning log snapped loudly. The children gazed up at their parents without understanding from their map of the Pony Express. They would be buying one of the new televisions soon.

'And our politicals!' Robert struggled alone for his hope. 'Why, I have counselled them and counselled them. One by one they've let us down. They can't sustain the simplest clarity. People will go mad! Then they suspect me for not being happy about it!'

'We are *not* playing martyrs tonight, darling,' Kitty drawled back. It was some cosy fireside conversation. Kitty depended on the powerful Oppy she knew. It scared her to see how human he could be. The children were old enough now to feel the security screen around their father's affections. And she could no longer distinguish her two impressions of Robbie. The Hindu sage or the vulture? Kitty almost preferred her children. Was she supposed to forgive him now?

She said: 'I don't see *you* sacrificing very much!'

After that conversation, Robert kept his new resignation to himself. Kitty was not going to let him off. He was a hero only for being with nuclear energy from the beginning like Kurchatov, and for keeping a moral log all the way. Right now, with Teller free to pursue his Super, one impression kept returning: his soul was overstretched to cover the whole canvas, good and evil were losing their strong lights and shadows. Oppy's labyrinthine guilt so few shouldered with him was neutering his life and the lives of others. Around the Commission, the Chief Advisor began to hear that Teller's thermonuclear research was going so badly that poor Edward was fighting with everyone at Los Alamos. It was as if Doctor Oppenheimer had brought down a curse on his civilized Mesa for the crimes of Generals. It was too much like playing God. Oppy did not want to be hated. He was happy to be human.

263

That Christmas at the Institute, he began openly trying to resign his position as Chief Advisor. A moral knot had relaxed. Doctor Oppenheimer was inching back toward humanity. But in the months of disintegration following Washington's espionage trauma, he was conscious of the top-secret frustration in the Crash-Programme. It began to appear that Teller would never win his nine-year struggle with the problem of too-slow heat radiation. Was the nightmare torturing humanists dispersing? Perhaps God would not leave man without the limits to protect him against himself! Then in May came 'Greenhouse', and Robert knew Teller's will had broken through.

In the early summer of 1951, anno nuclei 6, Teller convened at Oppy's plush Institute office, near the great electric-brain, a Q-cleared seminar of Commissioners and childlike physicists, to hear the New Idea he had cooked up for humanity with Stan Ulam. As Von Neumann, Fermi and Bradbury slipped in by taxi from the Princeton station, Robert's need to believe God had restored Nature her limits was so strong that he arranged for Teller himself to be left off the agenda. Had the time come to suppress knowledge? Oppy even took charge of the meeting. To them all it was like being back again at a hot desert morning in Theatre Two. And just as in the war days, Teller's suntanned face rose in front of the Director, demanding to be heard.

For the next two days, through hundreds of formulae never before seen on earth, Teller orated passionately at Oppy's blackboard. And gradually he worked up his marvellous idea: to dispense with the swimming-pool of tritium, using the fast X-rays at 300,000 degrees to beat pre-detonation. And finally, face to face with the loveliness of an absolute truth, needing to be at peace with it, Robert jumped up with his old excitement.

'That's it, Edward!' His eyes glittered over their faces. 'You've done it!'

When the secret meeting broke up, Fermi was waiting out in the summery vestibule for his American friend, looking miserable. He and Oppy were the only Atom Advisors there.

'Listen, Enrico,' Robert answered the little Roman gravely. 'When it is so technically sweet, you go ahead! And you worry what you will do with it when you have your technical success.'

Robert had come so far, he did not even argue with the disappointment in his friend's eyes. Was that now the law of knowledge their circle of scholars lived by? Did truth not always triumph? Yet from that hour, finally relaxing the chains to his Mesa, the one scholar-prince with the power to set limits loyal to human truth was himself out of control. It was like the second generation of the Revolution.

The chains to the mind-god were nearly thrown off. The world's leaders were squabbling pillagers in a run on the dwindling elements. Army Intelligence did not even inform Oppy or Teller that the Russians had already achieved Fusion. And still the confiscated Japanese film of bestiality and shame left by Robert's tiny bombs at Hiroshima and Nagasaki was not admitted on American screens.

The big screen was secrecy. God was Security.

Chapter 18

But it was not only Robert's apostles who refused to let him forget his chains.

That November 1st of Year 7, Civilization's sails were set at the edge of the moral canvas, like Columbus at the edge of the old flat planet. For, 1500 miles northwest of New Guinea in the Ralik chain of the Marshall Islands, at the site where Ahab's Pequod broke up in the vortex of the White Whale, on a flat sandspit named *Elugelab* among the Eniwetok atoll, Teller, Ulam, Von Neumann and the Atom Commissioners did a laboratory decree. Inside the great rectangular blockhouse was 'Mike', Point Zero of a hundred-mile circle of Navy cruisers, and the evil engine of Teller's and Johnny Von Neumann's genius. Not yet using the portable solid Lithium Deuteride, Mike was a 64-ton monolith of refrigeration equipment, and a fission bomb to ignite it at 300,000 degrees centigrade. On that morning a bland voice was heard, and in far-circling aeroplanes the boy flyers averted their eyes.

'. . . four . . . three . . . two . . . one . . . zero . . . plus one . . . plus two . . .'

Then again the bleached white light was upon the face of the firmament.

And circling the instantaneous mile-crater of vaporized sand and ocean, the boiling waters went white. And a mammoth spiriting genie raced out, a shock went down through the earth and a sound like a million thunderclaps roared. Then, in sepulchral silence, the horizon as far as the eye could see had lifted, rising very slowly . . . a white-purple, poisonous boiling-velvet Andes or Himalayas. And in its midst was an upsucking column of milk-white violence. Now as thousands of mindless boys' eyes came out to watch, from horizon to horizon, and to the very summits of the tropical sky where the island of Elugelab had been, were great black seething curtains of Hell. Then, ever higher, the four-mile pillow climbed steadily, mounting with magisterial solemnity in the astounded hush to escape even gravity . . . blasting the atmosphere with spite and hatred into the black nothingness of open space.

Alone at Berkeley, hiding by the seismograph at Haverland Hall, Edward Teller measured his baby with his mind: the thing they had done. And he knew his was a violence *one thousand times* the double Everest mushroom of Oppy's Hiroshima. Only now was Teller safe from dictators!

In Washington, Truman, Strauss and Borden also felt their presence announced upon the world. And in the Pentagon, no medalled breasts swelled more than that most excellent new breed of warrior, the godlike airmen Hoyt Vandenburg, Finletter and Roscoe 'Big-Bomb' Wilson, who had cleared the skies over Europe and the Pacific. Theirs was not the dominion of the sluggish temperamental ocean, nor of the humble land where crawling things went to die. To these simple clear-eyed men unversed in wax, the earth was no more than the place you crashed on, while the open skies were worthy of erecting lovely white mushroom clouds to veil the death-dance of millions below. And no longer did these big-bomb men need, two weeks later, to pay attention to the test of the mere boostered fission-bomb 'King', twenty-five times the size of Hiroshima and capable of wiping out Moscow in seconds, thus proving the words of Robert's Advisors. For, bomber-high, all that mattered was the grandeur of thermonuclear clouds.

The SAC air-heroes prepared their fine stable of flying machines to receive the mysterious new Trinity fire-storm, to deliver it to landlocked Muscovites. And they savoured their incomparable array of slim, gleaming birds. In the cold dry desert dawn at Edwards, clear-eyed Bridgemen and Yeager were rocketing against the sound barrier. The six-propeller, four-jet monster B36 was aloft with wings you could crawl through in flight. The all-jet B52 Stratofortress would soon be off the lines at Wichita. Already on the drawing-board in the city of Angels was the pretty mantis-like Hustler, to make the Journey of the Dead supersonic. And above and beyond all these was coming the exuberant new industry of superb wingless death-gods, the baby of the rocket-freak Von Braun. Soon, outside Detroit, Chrysler would give the Army *Jupiter*. Then the Douglas plant in Santa Monica would fabricate for the Air Force German *Thor*, and the Martin works in Maryland a 12,000 mile-per-hour *Titan*. Most glorious, at San Diego (with Los Alamos's own Critchfield presiding) would be born Convair's monstrous three-engine *Atlas*, capable of leaping the Pacific Ocean in a single bound. Then for the Navy, near Walt Disney's studios, Lockheed would a swift *Polaris* unsheath, to cruise, whale-like, the Russian shore aboard submarines.

Soon the Journey of the Dead – from Washington to Point Zero at Red Square, or from the Kremlin to Point Zero on the Mall – would take twenty minutes. Less time than Oppy's jeep ride, seven years ago, from the control bunker to the framework tower at Trinity. Moscow and Washington were being staged to join Hiroshima for the Dance of Death. (A later refinement might be to build Trinities right on target. But men cherish the illusion of individual honour. So it would be less fun – as duels take less courage than Russian roulette.) Wonderfully soon, the whole world would be Point Zero! But to Strauss, Lawrence and Borden and the big-bomb men – who did not frequent dances of death, only dreaming graceful Stratofortresses and the wonder of ever more majestic clouds – Teller's triumph at Eniwetok was a vindication. For had not the Chief Advisor called it 'unfeasible'? And 'undesirable'? Now, looking upon their glorious winged and wingless national armada, they knew it was feasible and desirable. Otherwise, why did they exist, and make the heart thrill? No one could be their equal in such power.

And feeling their last doubts about the strange new weapons relax in old-fashioned wellbeing, they experienced a need to be free too of the doubt about the powerful Doctor Oppenheimer. Suddenly Oppy's long, mournful opposition ceased to be a mystery.

Chapter 19

Two years before, Borden had been rewarded for his rocket trauma, repaid for his successful lobby in Congress for a crash programme to win the Super. Billy Borden became executive chairman of a Joint Congressional Committee on Atomic Energy.

So it was that one fine day Borden came to read a subtle, passionate narrative. The story of a poet, thinker and humanist, chronicled by those who were no more invited than Borden was. That is, those who hid in bushes and sniffed for spies. Security was no masterpiece. But Borden was not interested in fiction, he wanted facts. He had lived in Washington all his life, aside from dropping bombs on German civilians. But Billy Borden felt quite sure he had never met anyone trusted on Capitol Hill who married hard-core Communists, gave a fortune to unions, committed adultery or lied to security men! Borden was intensely relieved to find in private that Commissioner Strauss, who actually *knew* this strange being well, had much the same feeling about Oppy's file. And Lewis Strauss was relieved to find someone of the younger generation with views more disturbed than his own.

One sweltering August evening, after hours in Atom-Commissioner Strauss's office in that same temple to Nature's fires where Oppy's Advisors had made their prophecy, the two technocrats at last spoke openly. The Capitol was almost empty, and the silent Washington offices gave both men a sense of being the loyal sentinels of democracy.

'The man's name . . .' Borden's straight, weak mouth twitched. 'It's just all over the place. Nobody's advice is that good!'

'It's a riddle, Bill.'

Strauss leaned back in the twilight. His fingers knitted behind his balding head. The office air-conditioner was on full. Relaxed in his shirtsleeves, Strauss watched the missile-man's clean charmless face over his Commission desk, the desk from which each one of Strauss's own judgments had gone to defeat at Oppy's hands – until the Fuchs scandal. Yet power was still trickling from the nation's vaults.

'He's an *Expert*,' Borden muttered with masochistic awe. 'Advisor, Consultant or Chairman on almost every panel, Committee or Board in the country to do with nuclear weapons!'

'That could be conceit, I suppose.' Strauss raised his eyebrows innocently. Both men spoke in subtly lowered voices.

'OK.' The Commissioner's young visitor licked his lips. 'Just what, sir, what if our man was a masterspy?'

Borden sank back out of the desk light. Suddenly he was perspiring under his light blue jacket at the thing he had just said. Still he did feel a professional, that is an unnatural, safety with this illustrious older man.

'What if,' Borden went on hollow-eyed, 'he were a masterspy sir, with a directive to hold up this country's end of the thermonuclear race all he could?'

'He'd be doing an excellent job!' Strauss's smile gaped bitterly. 'But fortunately times are changing.'

'If it's not too late.' Borden swabbed his square brow and pushed his oiled blonde hair straight back. 'The story is that even the Defence Secretary said Oppy should be gotten out of the country.'

'Murray complains a lot about his Security Clearance.'

'His Clearance?' Borden gritted his teeth as if to keep his soul from being snatched between them. 'What about his Power? If he's a spy? And with *his* influence over all the physics gang!'

'There is not one single shred of direct evidence,' Strauss said. Listening to the deep silence, he shifted uncomfortably.

Borden was cunning. 'Now the Barber has tipped him off about surveillance: we're not likely to collect more.'

'Volpe, and our Advisor's friends: Lilienthal, Conant, Du Bridge.' The Commissioner's voice was soft and gruff. '. . . to say the least of every important physicist in this country,' Strauss went on with a sudden sly ferocity. 'Bethe, for instance! I offered the fellow money out of my own pocket to help Teller at Los Alamos. He agreed until our friend Oppy talked him out of it. I still remember that article of Conant's – a president of Harvard calling for more Radicals!'

'I heard Du Bridge at Berkeley!' Borden picked up with disgusted enthusiasm. 'He parroted a lot of squishy pacifism. Didn't make a shred of his own sense.'

'They think he's a saint, Bill.' He gazed up at the first street-lights playing on the ceiling. Night was falling over the unsuspect-ing beasts of the land, fowls of the air and fishes of the seas. In the Temple of the new God, Power, Commissioner Strauss carefully separated the reflected streetlamps from the coloured advertise-ments. 'But Oppy's a saint who goes everywhere. Everywhere he goes, his friends have a pinkish tinge.'

'Everyone ends up agreeing with him – it's just not democratic!' Billy Borden said. Strauss saw the blond young man turn pale.

For suddenly in his mind's eye, Chairman Borden was having a vision. In it he saw America's bland sweetness and virtue float out in the night, God's country. And Borden felt it pierced and gnawed by the worming loathsomeness of atheist Reds. Of vicious Marxist agents, working unmolested and laughing secretly at gullible Americans. At least men like Senator McCarthy – un-Washington as he was – were willing to hunt these people down.

'The real key . . .' Borden breathed in the shadows of the desk light, perspiring heavily despite the air-conditioner in the terror of his own vision, a vision as terrible in its way as Doctor Oppen-heimer's fear of Civilization given over to a thermonuclear race. '. . . the key is Fuchs!'

'Fuchs – and how he survived at Los Alamos. Strauss sighed deeply. It was a huge relief that the young fellow had said it first.

So that night, inside the 'Security' Groves had invented to divide and conquer, a bond sickened between Banker Strauss and Billy Borden. Neither man would now sleep easily until the elusive Oppy was not only tumbled from his authority but unmasked of his subtle saintliness. It must come soon. America's vaults would soon be empty.

Chapter 20

From the day Robert heard that his old friend Acheson had filed the deciding vote against his Advisors' report, he accepted it. No one man would stop frightened mankind clamouring and falling on their knees before Death.

What had Trinity ever been – and who had *he* been – to expect such courage from men who had not stood with him at Point Zero, or come to awareness with Hiroshima and Nagasaki in their dance of death? Well, they were deeper into the ethics of world responsibility than Robert could have imagined possible. It remained to be seen whether good or evil were stronger in a world that had banished God. (Or was it that God had been banished long before, and nuclear weapons a sort of cargo-cult to lure Him back?) Maybe there was an answer, but Robert knew he would ask not to be reinstated as Chief Advisor when 1952 expired. He had sold Washington dominion over the continents and the seas, but he made a lousy politician.

Only now did Robert at last come face to face with the other famous Oppy chained for ever on his cottonwood Mesa. For even back at his quiet ritual at the Princeton Institute, those who wanted salvation kept Oppy as their prophet. Those who wanted a submission to hatred felt the urgent need to track him down. Even Dr David Griggs came to see Robert in the cloister of his Princeton office.

Like all ambitious men who overcome a sense of mediocrity by enthusiasm, David Tressel Griggs felt a natural hostility to anyone who did not enthuse with him. However, as a Southern Cal physicist and the Air Force's Advisor, Griggs was the agent of the two groups on earth a person who had any feeling for the survival of living things could enthuse with least. That is, the Berkeley Thermonuclear-Horsemen and the SAC big-bomb men.

When Robert saw Griggs's dull hostile face come through the office door one showery May afternoon, an inexpressible disgust and grief rose in his throat. Instantly Robert felt this stranger's mistrust. Was he another one who thought the paper-Oppy was a spy? Why, Julius and Ethel Rosenberg were facing the electric chair just for *conspiring* to pass the Mesa's secrets! Maybe poor Haakon had been right then, to have had terrified moments at the US passport control when leaving for Paris? At the sight of Griggs Robert experienced a strange light-headed calm.

'Dr Griggs.' Robert grinned tensely. 'Come in, come in, you're right on time.'

'Thank you,' Griggs said heavily. 'How do you do, sir?'

The two men shook hands over the top of the desk, Robert shifting his pipe to his left hand. Griggs paused, eyeing Robert's long wall-cabinets of secret AEC files. Then he sat in the green armchair.

Griggs noticed his famous colleague watching him expressionlessly. He grinned. The AEC's twenty-four hour guard was out of hearing.

'What I am here for, Doctor,' Griggs broke the silence, 'is to read the minutes of the October '49 meeting of your Advisors.'

Robert smoothed the back of his head. 'Our conclusions at that meeting were overruled.'

'We at the Pentagon,' Griggs said, 'are looking for a pattern.'

'You must feel free, then. The next room will be quiet.'

One hour later, Griggs came back in Oppy's office. He resumed his armchair without smiling.

'To be frank, Doctor,' Griggs nervously sighed, 'we in the Air Force feel you and your colleagues are not being very enthusiastic, or very helpful, with the Super.'

'Dr Griggs, you've read the minutes.' Robert felt his face reddening. 'Our duty was strictly the advisability, technical and moral, of such a weapon.'

Griggs was abruptly alert. Waves of professional jealousy seethed across the desk. Kitty's photograph smiled at Robert with a glamorous irony.

'You confuse the issue, Doctor!' Griggs drew his nondescript head between his shoulders. 'Your attitudes, sir, are well known around Washington' Griggs spoke faster. 'The Russians are surely racing us to the Super. While you sit there talking about morality, good Americans are trying to keep the Kremlin from winning the race! And we're good and tired of this gossip! You know about Air Secretary Finletter saying . . .' Looking into the thoughtful face of the Father of the Atom Bomb, Griggs seemed to lose the thread. ". . . um, what did you say he said?'

'At a Pentagon briefing,' Robert offered very softly, 'Secretary Finletter said, "With a certain number of Hydrogen bombs, America could rule the world".'

Griggs sat forward. 'I was at that briefing. I heard no such remark!'

'I suggest, Dr Griggs,' Robert said coldly, 'you listen more carefully at important debates. My source is unquestionable. The comment is common knowledge.'

Griggs sat forward, one hand on Robert's desk. 'Just what are you suggesting, Doctor Oppenheimer?'

Looking across his familiar papers at Griggs's hard, suspicious eyes, Robert was horribly aware of his mortality. How alone he was before the clumsy machine of the law, with the electric chair at the end of it like an unfortunate accident. Disgust and mortification tightened around his mouth.

'Tell me, Dr Griggs.' Robert softened his voice still further. 'Have you been going around the Defence Department impugning my loyalty to my country?'

In the awful stillness the two men's reddened faces stared at each other. No one would save them from this silent office. Like grown men on a desert island, like Russia and America on the lonely globe.

'I don't have to!' Griggs snapped. 'A number of people up there have doubts about your loyalty, not only Finletter and General Vandenburg.'

Robert ground his teeth thoughtfully on the pipe stem. He smiled hotly. 'But you, Griggs.' His voice cracked. 'Do you think I am pro-Russian? Or am I merely a little confused?'

'I wish I knew!' Griggs shook his head threateningly. 'I wish I knew!'

'Well you, Doctor, are a paranoid.'

'More of your superior airs?' Griggs blurted back. 'Doctor, this is a dangerous game!'

'Compared to *your* game, Doctor Griggs,' Robert said, suddenly mild, 'my game is harmless indeed. In your game you are gambling the future of all life on earth.'

Strange to say, Griggs felt his disturbed emotions subside. His soul seemed to dilate. And for several seconds, it was as if David Tressel Griggs too were standing with Oppy in the new bleached whiteness of the Jornada del Muerte, about to join in the dance of death.

Be careful, Griggs thought quickly to himself, or he'll hypnotise you too. And immediately that mysterious apparition vanished from Griggs's imagination for ever.

It was not the last time Robert suffered the evil suspicions of David Griggs and his bosses. Worried that there might be a serious falling out between the Big-Bomb men and the eggheads who created the giant firestorms for their Stratofortress dreams of Power, they arranged a luncheon between Oppy and Secretary Finletter, in a private room of the Pentagon. Griggs took care to reveal to Finletter his side of their fight at the Princeton office. There would be two Deputies.

The flesh and blood Oppy walked in late. At the sight of these confident fellows, all Robert could think of was the ghastly toys they yearned for, the fragile membrane that separated their insane suspicions from the electric chair, and their insensitivity to the death-throes of the human heart. Did these same Brooks-Brothered cynics actually expect to woo him to their camp? Fear and contempt froze him, and Robert's soul joined his host's future victims in their dance of death. He could scarcely speak or smile. And when the terrible lunch ended, Robert unceremoniously fled Groves's Pentagon.

But the arrogant impression the Chief Advisor left behind would not matter much longer. Before Christmas 1953, five young AEC men drove up from the capital. After lengthily cataloguing the Chief Advisor's thirty feet of documents recording man's theft of universal fire, they carried them out of Oppy's office in locked cases. The last moral link binding the new American super-power to the enlightened dream on a desert Mesa was broken forever.

After that first Security barrier came down, barrier after barrier began falling. The hands and feet of the nuclear state quickly went to sleep. No further anaesthetics were needed for the leaders at the top, as the bomb and aircraft factories of America and Russia settled down to the serious business of crushing the spirit of future generations. *From now on, no human beings would be trusted on earth, save those willing to dance the dance of death.*

In January Truman, the Kansas City haberdasher who first sat face to face with the blood of Hiroshima, turned the Oval office over to General Eisenhower, who had a certain Senator Joe McCarthy among his backers. That March, patient Lewis Strauss at last inherited the Chairmanship of the Atomic Energy Commission. And a month later, only nine months after Teller's mammoth fireball vapourized Elugelab, Sakharov and Kurchatov fired a hundred times smaller, but portable, Lithium Deuteride Hydrogen Bomb. State banks had gone one neck ahead of the private sector; Chairman Strauss who knew who had much of this catastrophe to answer for, at once ordered up all the Commission files on isotope export. Then the Atom-Chairman ordered an ultra-secret 'preliminary study' of the ex-Advisor Chief's patriotism.

Robert and Kitty came home from a lecture tour of South Africa just weeks after the Rosenbergs were publicly burned alive in the Sing Sing electric chair for stealing worthless details of the mysterious new knowledge on the Mesa. The next day, Herb Marks drove up to Princeton.

The friends slipped out quickly for a milkshake, to avoid eavesdroppers. Someone in the Commission had called Herb with a message: better tell Oppy to sand his decks and strip for action. Barrier after security barrier, severing the flow of compassion. Maybe Robert was little more than a wealthy forty-nine-year-old New York physicist, with a pretty alcoholic wife and two children, who taught at Princeton. But hatred was sweeping up around the famous Oppy of Trinity.

The following month, for the first time in twenty years, Robert took Kitty back to Paris. He knew they would risk seeing Haakon and his new wife Carol in exile. Twenty-four years ago, young and homesick, Robert had taken Germany's New Physics and his tuberculosis to be cured in the pueblo country of the Rio Grande. Now, after all that had happened, he was falling back on Europe.

It did not matter. Anywhere you could go now, every face in the street was chained to the Utopia, and the sin of his cottonwood plateau. Robert Oppenheimer was going back.

Oppy being far from Washington lifted some of the shame model citizen Billy Borden felt over his trauma: the Father of the Atomic Bomb had been a Soviet masterspy all along. Borden's own dreams were coming true. Soon he would work at Westinghouse on giant atomic submarines, on which pure men without women would go to live for ever, like Captain Nemo under the sea, with Polaris missiles to protect them from the imperfect life on land. But before leaving for purer things, Billy composed a long letter. And on November 7th he mailed two copies, one to J. Edgar Hoover, one to the Congressional Joint Committee. J. Robert Oppenheimer (the letter said) had, since before the war, been a hardline Communist. Oppy had been undercover since 1942, but since then had pursued Soviet directives to hold back America's Hydrogen Bomb development. Perhaps he had been the 'spy at Los Alamos' Emil Klaus Fuchs said had passed the Russians the Uranium-diffusion method.

His conscience purified, Billy Borden set off for the Westinghouse boatworks.

Behind him, Borden left a political trauma in the highest, most secret crags of power, around President Eisenhower's office, the Republican leaders of Congress, the FBI, and in the offices of Chairman Strauss. Made public, the debate went, Oppy could be infinitely more embarrassing than the Rosenbergs, and much less easily disposed of. Why not simply throw Oppenheimer to McCarthy's witch-hunters, suggested Groves's old sidekick General Nichols? No, better a treason hearing, kept secret inside the security screen. Then Oppy must be pushed out of its protection to fare harmlessly for himself. Above all Oppy must not hear what was waiting for him at home, or he might flee Paris to Moscow.

Meanwhile out West, at the new Livermore Laboratory Ernest Orlando Lawrence had given to Teller to replace Oppy's prestige, that shameless soul was happily preparing 'Nectar' test, 'Yankee' test, 'Union', 'Romeo' and 'Koon' tests . . . and most splendid of all, 15 megaton 'Bravo'. Soon Communism would learn the meaning of Edward Teller.

And on December 3rd Eisenhower decreed that a blank wall be put between Doctor Oppenheimer and the knowledge he had sold Washington. From now on, the Great Mystery was exclusively for the likes of Strauss, Teller and the Big-Bomb men.

Chapter 21

A TWA Constellation carried Robert and Kitty Oppenheimer back to the city of Light. As Gander fell behind, Robert noticed the safe feeling.

The Oppenheimers slept through the night in their berths. At sunrise they were in London refuelling. Not long after, the riveted silver wing dipped. And below was Sacre Coeur, blinding white in the morning sun.

Kitty looked smart and pretty by the cabin window. They were both very moved.

'Do you think Haakon is down there right now?'

'He will be when he knows we're here.' Robert leaned close to Kitty.

'Think, Robbie. Last time I was here, so was Steve Nelson.'

'And Joe,' Robert said.

'Yes . . . Joe.' They looked at each other.

'Last time I was here,' Robert said, 'no one had heard about Hitler.'

'Or fission.' Kitty smiled.

'I'm certainly looking forward to seeing Haakon. All those people we know . . . I still only feel well with poets.'

'Well you'd better be particularly nice. He thinks you've left him for charmed circles.'

'That's a funny word.'

'You know what I mean!'

'It's not true,' Robert said. 'How can an engineer's daughter and a rag-trade Jew be charmed?'

'It's true if he thinks it is.' Kitty was winding on her safety belt. They were coming down. 'Anyway, I might have been a German princess.'

When they arrived by taxi at the George V, and the porter had brought their luggage to their sumptuous room, Robert telephoned for the number across town.

The address was in the quarter of poor painters, at the foot of Montmartre. Carol was there, but Haakon was away in Rome translating. He would surely come back before Robert and Kitty left Europe. After the call, he felt strangely complete and excited by the old feelings. He would have to keep an eye on Kitty though, what with all the wine. They were invited to lunch at the Embassy.

'Well,' he laughed, 'maybe I'm more than half European, after all.'

'Uhuh, seeing Haakon over here feels like growing up.'

For the next weeks, the Oppenheimers travelled as only Americans travel around Europe.

Robert's old hunger to consume knowledge and society was back. He tried out his languages and showed off his education, and they fought quite a bit. Many of the thinkers from the Mesa and the Institute had returned after the liberation. Robert had Atomic Energy business with NATO. Everywhere they went, prestigious persons fought to invite them. So they did not have to be alone, and Robert repeated himself a great deal. He took Kitty to see Göttingen, and Cambridge. And they visited Niels Bohr, Glen Seaborg and the rest. Over here, men like Teller and Von Braun seemed just bad memories of the war years. Despite American and Russian 'secrecy' everyone knew perfectly. And they shook their heads sadly at America's fumbling, headlong greed to pile up huger and huger destruction. He could see now how unready his young country had been for the German rot he helped plant in it.

Then on December 7th, twelve years from Pearl Harbour, the day the life struggle of millions had come to Doctor Oppenheimer, he and Kitty were back at the George V for their last night in Paris.

Tomorrow night they would fly back to New York. Robert was ready. In the last formal civilized weeks, he had proved he could be free and happy again. But personal happiness soon felt insipid, he had lost his taste for it. He was eager to go back and take up his moral chains. This time, when Robert sat on the huge hotel bed and gave the Montmartre number on the telephone, Haakon's voice answered.

The moment Robert heard Haakon's excited voice on the Hotel phone, coming from some poet's garret, he was set free. Tonight they were going back to have dinner in that simple time before the war, when they had been confident of universal good.

Robert and Kitty felt young and excited as their taxi turned down the long Roman vista of the Champs Elysées. Turning left at the Concorde of Robespierre's guillotine, they raced up the Rue de la Paix. Soon they were in dingy crowded backstreets.

'Mont-Cénis, Numero dix-neuf, Monsieur le Docteur,' said the man in the front seat. He had recognized the famous Oppy. The man refused to be paid, but solemnly shook their hands.

'They seem to like you over here,' Kitty said drily when they climbed down by the murky doorway.

There was a wintery night wind. Robert stood in his overcoat and scarf on the narrow pavement.

He was not prepared for the shock, finding his friend struck so low. Was it really *his* fault Haakon had been brought to this? But Frank and Haakon were the winners . . . and hadn't he come here tonight? They were back in the circle of Malraux and the great European Resistance – security be damned! He was undoing a betrayal.

There was just room for Kitty against Robert in the creaky elevator. Upstairs in the low-ceilinged garret, even the wood ice-box was piled high with books and papers. But there was enough room and electricity for the two tall men and their wives laughing and embracing, and one shy-looking dog. It was all the room in the world to have the happiest and freest evening of the trip.

Five minutes later, everyone was talking at once, and not knowing whether to stand or sit between the crannies of books.

'For heaven's sake, Robbie, let us hear of your famous dealings!'

'Futile and boring.' Robert poked his pipe stem. 'What's happening with you here? These are great days for France.'

'Not such great days maybe – even shameful days.' Haakon nodded thoughtfully, and popped a cork.

Then they were sitting on tattered couches. As the smoke, friendship and sharp smell of champagne spread through the dim low room, Robert felt his soul return to the softer world of moral culture. Now they spoke of the spirit of Europe and its condition, now of what was happening in America, and what had emerged from the war. And for Robert it was an almost physical relief, talking to someone who was romantically excited with life and ideas.

But towards the end of the excellent dinner, Chevalier spoke of the Algerian Camus's fine new book *The Rebel*, and Robert knew

279

his friend was thinking of that troublesome wartime evening ten years ago. And he felt depressed by Haakon's agitation when he asked if Robert could use his influence to prevent his citizenship difficulties ruining the Unesco job he and Carol lived by. The accusation in the request was depressing, but then so was Robert's delicate position, which was partly Haakon's fault. He was saddened by the spectacle of his own wealth and prestige, as well as by the elusive undercurrent of resentment, and the writer's willingnesss to lean on him.

Knowing Haakon's despair, Robert fought down these ugly rich-man's impulses. He suggested a Harvard friend to contact at the Embassy. Then he made them all laugh with a maliciously witty imitation of the powerful Washingtonian Robert most despised for casting the decisive vote for Teller's thermonuclear race, Dean Acheson.

The gesture seemed enough for Haakon, and the rest of the evening was a fine celebration. Still, the equality between them was tarnished, no meeting-ground left but dreams. The physicist, mind stuffed with defence 'secrets', had risked the security men to come here, outside the wire and barrages of power. But the writer had expected much more.

When the evening was almost over, Robert kept Haakon company walking the dog around the block.

Near the bright corner café, Haakon abruptly started talking to Robert very seriously about the trial and execution of Julius and Ethel Rosenberg. Of their miserable relative Greenglass at Los Alamos, who had perjured them to their deaths. Of the songs they sang each other in prison, and the kiss Ethel Rosenberg had given her prison matron, seconds before she climbed in the electric chair, watched by a gallery of reporters. Feeling vaguely alarmed, Robert changed the subject.

It was a cold windy Paris night. Clouds flew over the moon. Suddenly in place of the depression at his friend's martyrdom, Robert was feeling intensely the victory of the humble life upstairs, a foreboding of leaving romantic old Europe for the promontory of the Institute.

'Listen, Haakon . . .' Robert cut in. They stopped.

'Go ahead, Oppy my friend!' Haakon held both his friend's coatsleeves.

'I really do not feel at all good,' Robert said emotionally, '. . . not about going back.'

And strange to say, his friend understood instantly.

'Don't be afraid, little monk!' Haakon laughed as they started back. 'You are a great American. The Faust of Fisherman's Wharf! How could they harm you?'

'And you, Haakon?' Robert said softly in the dark.

'I am small fry,' Haakon laughed. 'But I have an idea. Listen. Tomorrow you do not leave Paris until night. I will take you out to meet Malraux. He would be immensely proud to meet Prometheus. And in a way, you fought in the same Resistance.'

'Only he won, without leaving bombs.'

'But you, Robbie . . .' The two men were back under the doorway of No. 19. Drunken shouts came from the café corner they had left. '. . . you were trying for very much more. In the end you must win.'

And that was the very first time, in the eight years since Hiroshima, anyone on earth had inspired Doctor Oppenheimer to wonder if his pacifism might really win through. Shuffling there in the murk of a cobbled Paris gutter, the winter moon sailing above, and Sacre Coeur bright-lit up through the gabled roofs, it sounded almost sane.

PART FOUR

Chapter 1

It was already cold night, two evenings later, when they came home from Europe to Princeton. Robert carried their bags into Olden Manor.

The cook came happily to meet them in the hall. There was nothing unusual in the thick stack of mail, and the children were well. Still for some reason Robert needed to pace among the silent colonial rooms upstairs. After the long weeks away, he felt more acutely than ever the fear he had admitted to no one . . . how the Rosenbergs had made their Jornada at Sing Sing, strapped to a machine of torture. Did he speak against the atom-spies to Haakon because he understood them? Robert thought of his friend Herb Marks's warning before they left. It was a very lonely feeling.

The next week of comfortable Christmas socializing, welcomed back by unsuspicious university faces, gave little substance to the news that Robert's Los Alamos neighbour Bill Parsons had suddenly died in Washington. Their kind old friend . . . but also the man who had ridden in the *Enola Gay*, and armed the bomb that vapourized Hiroshima. But had he really been a close friend? It was you who built the damn thing, a voice reminded Robert. Somehow the Old World had softened him, the material bomb returned to the unconscious. It shocked him now to think of the dangerous Yankee generals and politicians he had confidently faced down during the long campaign to cure the nuclear phobia. He could laugh off his regret at not being loved by them. But there was some relief in no longer being an Advisor. He would lose his last Defence Department post in a few months.

Over the weekend a call came from Lewis Strauss in Washington: top secret Commission business. Even that made Kitty nervous. But the statesman was Robert's patron, and wished the Oppenheimers well.

On Monday morning when Robert caught the New York–Washington Special, he was even feeling his old attraction to secret places of power. After lunch in Georgetown, Ann Marks drove Robert to the Atom-Power building.

A commission guard showed Doctor Oppenheimer in his heavy

overcoat up to Chairman Strauss in Room 236. The Washington street outside was bitterly cold. But this bright familiar office, having fiery dominion over all living things in a lonely universe, was pleasantly overheated. Waiting with Strauss, Robert found Groves's crass old side-kick General Nichols. Stiff West-Pointer Ken, whom Robert had annoyed with knowledgeable repartee during those heroic wartime train rides across America, when they were freedom fighters together. Nichols had been particularly fun to tease.

Robert shook hands with his old Army and government friends, and they sat down together. The generous desk-top was cleared. Nichols was in what, for the bald General, was a bouncy enervated mood.

'So tell us, Robert, how was your trip?' Chairman Strauss began, soberly arranging his legs somewhere under the desk. They grew still with power.

'Very good,' Robert smiled, and for some reason he felt something inside him shrivel. 'I dropped by NATO . . . saw the English and French as planned. But it's a shock to hear about Bill Parsons.'

Chairman Strauss and the General agreed that Parson's death was shocking, with the implication that it was more for Robert to be upset.

'By the by.' Chairman Strauss's enigmatic face came forward, hands folded under the desk. 'Your friend Herb Marks stopped by this morning.'

Sitting very straight by the window, General Nichols hugged his khaki arms. His pointed teeth appeared.

Robert innocently kept it going. 'Commission business?'

With a sudden shiver Strauss rocked his balding manicured head back. 'He wanted me to stop the Senate looking into your files.'

Across the glass-horse paperweights and huge unstained blotter, Robert stared back levelly at the two bleak faces. This is it, he thought. His face was stinging.

'Oh? Do I know something about that?'

'An inquiry, Oppy,' Nichols interrupted, familiarly grinning. 'Looking into your loyalty.'

'That again?' said Robert, and managed to sound contemptuous. 'Thought you settled it seven years ago, Lewis?'

Without answering Chairman Strauss rustled forward. He pushed a single sheaf of papers to Robert's edge of the desk.

'The Commission's letter of charges,' Nichols said. 'Until this is cleared up, the President has suspended clearance.'

Robert sat forward and rested his pipe on the desk. His favourite pipe, the one he had at Trinity. Thinking of the truths he had tried to tell, Robert forgot the pipe and lifted the papers. In the silence the prophet of the Mesa read through the twenty-four neatly typed accusations. Twenty-three were the usual: Communist relatives and students; Civil War donations up to his Los Alamos appointment, and recruiting radicals; some story about a closed Party meeting at Eagle Hill; the 'Chevalier incident'.

'What is item twenty-four?' Robert looked up haughtily at the two faces watching him, blank as a wall. It was General Nichols who answered, seeming scarcely in control of himself.

'In the autumn of '49 you opposed the Super on moral and technical grounds. You influenced others that way.'

'I certainly hope I did!' Robert cut in. 'What does that imply?'

Strauss's face went red and very hard. 'The delay allowed the Russians to gain eighteen months on us.'

'At the time, only you and the Air Force disagreed.' Robert concentrated so as not to lose the moral thread. 'It was your opinion against mine.'

'Be that as it may!' Chairman Strauss interrupted, curtly impatient. 'Of course, if you were to resign . . .'

'Is that what you would like?' Robert said. Did his last defence post not expire in a few months?

'We didn't say that,' Nichols snapped gruffly from the window.

'Well, I'll think about it,' Robert managed to say.

From the first mention of 'inquiry', Robert knew what his old friends were really talking about. Something vile, awesome and unmentionable suddenly stirred in the warm office air. Immense, well-oiled forces, advancing towards a single man. For a moment Robert clearly saw himself fallen from prestige and trust, himself and Kitty hounded by circumstantial evidence who *knew* how low! The UN Secretary-General Hiss had not been too high to send to Lewisburg Penitentiary, no evidence had been too circumstantial to be used against the Rosenbergs. The horror was in this office, the self-righteous gravity of these two familiar faces. Was *he*, then, to be the chosen one?

Minutes later when he left the room, Doctor Oppenheimer, who long ago on a desert Mesa had carried his pipe with a steady hand up the crowded aisle of Main Tech to announce the god-like destruction of a Japanese city, left the pipe lying on Lewis Strauss's desk blotter.

Chapter 2

Robert at once caught a cab to see his lawyer friends Joe Volpe and Herbert Marks. But despite the shocked rallying of his allies over the next day, and Kitty's instant outraged loyalty, a mysterious grief and pessimism was almost tenderly pressing down on Robert. The premonition of an ancient and fatal beauty.

The charges were so devilishly insidious that Oppy had at once written to Strauss that he would feel obliged to clear himself in a Hearing. What a fate, he thought bitterly. To be accused by the very same politicians he had lost so many good friends trying to compromise with. Yet through that first afternoon, and day after day throughout Princeton's festive Christmas recess, while in Washington the lawyers, Atom Commission and President's office went ahead with their complicated top-secret preparations for him, Robert asked himself: Why . . . why? And the inexplicable answer came, awesomely: his beliefs. When Robert looked back down the intricate channels of the life he had written himself, they seemed to stand out from his time, original and solitary. Yet now, instead of a consistent moral stream, they were broken in a mass of contradictions, vanity and inadequate ideology. And crowning the whole famous chaos of personalities and events with its vanity and its paradox, the Bomb. *Trinity*!

Ten days after the Charges, the Oppenheimers and the two lawyers met in Washington for the third time. They gathered in Herb Marks's pleasant Georgetown living-room – even Joe's law offices were tapped by the Bureau.

'I still can scarcely believe it . . .' Robert muttered with a melancholy smile, needing to hear them say something.

The two lawyers stared at the scholar crumpled in the corner chair by the curtains, like a timid lead-actor unwilling to go on, a man with a scarf wound on his thin neck who boyishly waved a new pipe. They all felt vaguely disturbed at his experience. It was New Year's Eve, the street outside was quiet.

'For Pete's sake, Robbie!' Kitty had never seen her husband with the fight gone from him. It was a fine time to get humble!

'They forgot how to trust you Robert,' Marks said brusquely.

'They want to make sure no one else trusts you,' Volpe added.

'What difference does it make?' Robert went on with a quizzical glance around their faces. 'I'll be out of office soon.'

'No you won't,' Herb said. 'All over this country you're a symbol of . . . of ethics.'

'Me, ethics?' Over his coffee cup Robert looked around their faces. But for an instant, he *did* feel again the way those who needed salvation worshipped him. Blinking in the sun, Robert nodded.

'It looks bad. Frankly, very bad,' Marks went on nervously. Joseph rested his spectacles on the stacked papers.

'Your hearing,' he said toughly, pausing between each sentence, 'will be in three or four months, probably hidden in one of the old Commission buildings. There will be a three-man board. The counsel who'll be cross-examining you may be a gent from Yale called Robb, Roger Robb. Apparently this fellow won a case for the head-communist Earl Browder. But mostly he argued on the other side.'

Marks relaxed back on his deep couch facing Oppy. This whole fratricidal business disturbed Herb more than any case had before.

'From what we could find out, he said, looking at his glass, 'this Robb is about the toughest, smartest trial lawyer in town. His speciality is prosecuting – and, I might add, convicting – murderers.'

Perhaps, thought Robert, lowering his eyes without affection to his new pipe and thinking of Trinity, perhaps that's appropriate.

'You're going to need the finest, most respected defence counsel the country's got,' Volpe went on brightly, ignoring Robert's bitter expression. 'Here's some good news. I've arranged for us to visit Lloyd Garrison in New York. He's on the board of your Institute. He'll help us find the man we need. Garrison is absolutely the finest and most respected liberal grand old man. You'll like him, Robert and he'll like you.'

'Yes, I remember him.' As Anne Marks joined them Robert looked up, grateful and perplexed.

'. . . though unfortunately Garrison won't be able to take you on himself,' Volpe said. The room sank back in its helpless gloom.

'My Lord!' Robert burst out in the long embarrassed silence. 'This is silly . . . how can anything so silly be happening?'

For several minutes no one could think of anything to say. Finally Volpe picked up his spectacles.

'Silly, Robert,' he said, 'but serious. It could be very serious.'

'At least,' Kitty said hotly, 'none of your colleagues can accuse you now of knuckling under!'

'Yes,' Robert nodded. 'I guess there's that.'

Chapter 3

Invisible within the new American Security machine, the news went out. In weeks every important scientist, from Eisenhower's Capitol, to the Plutonium works out west at Hanford, Washington, heard rumours that Oppy was facing a top-secret treason trial.

And through the great universities, which the Pentagon had turned into swamps of dark oaths and suspicion, through the weapons laboratories to which the protestors had crawled miserably to earn a living, even among those who felt let down by Oppy's Washington years, an emotion rose of sadness, mourning and fury. It was as if the modern power-state was setting out, in spite, to punish everything that was free and humane in civilization. To all but Teller's thermonuclear clique, Doctor Oppenheimer was become the nuclear age . . . all that Power had done to them all. And they waited, knowing that now Oppy would stand and fight.

But from the minute in Lewis Strauss's office that Robert saw the Nichols letter of official suspicions, the vigorous ranging hope died in his heart. He had spent his adult life questioning and accusing himself over a vast landscape of issues, far more disturbing and criminal than these twenty-four Charges. Now somehow, once the law had seized Robert's freedom, his innermost dreams shrank deep in him. He felt like some animal who has always roamed free and now stands listless in a narrow cage, with nothing to do but wait for the day when a trap door will open, leading to an unknown arena, an arena where Robert would only be a teller of truths – no longer for humanity but for himself.

Commuting from his famous Princeton Institute seminars, through January and February, while discussions continued in the spacious Manhattan offices of Volpe's grand old liberal, Lloyd Garrison, Robert noticed the change in his friends who knew. As often happens, seeing the wound in the powerful Doctor Oppenheimer's life, large numbers found the courage to rally at his side . . . the ones wanting salvation. It came as a surprise to find himself smothered with letters of affection and support in his defeat, as he had never been in the years of arrogant struggle and triumph. It only increased the humility Kitty had first seen in Herb's living-room that New Year's Eve. In this new modesty, Robert looked back on his old violent struggle with life. And it appeared mostly destruction and hate.

At each stage in your life, you thought you were so moral, he would think, standing frozen at his Princeton office blackboard. Maybe if you'd spent less time trying to be absolutely moral, you might have been virtuous. Well, maybe other people could still see some tragic Oppy tied to a New Mexico Mesa. But he was nothing but a man, and no example of anything but how not to abuse god-given gifts. He was the biggest sinner of them all. During those spring weeks, conscious of the Mesa's hideous bomb, and his own inner chaos, Doctor Oppenheimer caught himself feeling eager to stand before his judges, no matter what the verdict. This would be no trial of Socrates.

Yet Lloyd Garrison seemed not at all indifferent to the verdict of the newly named judges, the Gray Board. It was not proving easy to find an advocate with the courage to defend an accused Communist.

As April 12th came nearer, Robb flew to California in search of witnesses to Oppy's treason, and FBI agents passed to Chairman Strauss every word Robert and Kitty uttered. At his hushed New York desk, Garrison read deeper into Robert's background. And the tall, darkly distinguished gentleman of the bar, like so many before him, found himself enthralled by the story of the passionately cerebral, tubercular German-Jewish California scholar who overcame his privilege to take action beside the poor of the Depression, taking sides against the Falange of fascist ghouls when so many had remained passive. Who had accepted his country's request to mastermind the race with Hitler for an atom-bomb, and won it hands down. Who had suffered for his responsibility over Hiroshima, and not swerved from the thankless, harrowing task of pursuing the political power to defend moderation and human values against stupidity and hysteria. Who now was going on trial for his honour, before men who had done none of these uncomfortable things. The more the mild honest lawyer at the desk read, the more angry and moved he was, and proud to know such a man as Robert Oppenheimer. And all at once, Lloyd Garrison knew that it was he himself who must make the defence.

Then it was March. And in his scholar's life on the promontory of the Institute, Robert knew that the crash-programme for the ocean-leaping 'Atlas' rocket had gone through, to rain thermo-nuclear fire-mountains on the heads of Russians, and make them dance the dance. Because he had not enthused over these lovely crimes against mankind, Eisenhower had forbidden that Oppy should hear. But Robert knew. Then it was only a week to his hearing in the Capitol, and he could not help knowing too what young Teller was doing in the middle of the Pacific. Like hysterical spoiled boys needing to punish a rival gang of Russian street urchins for having shot off their little lithium deuteride bomb first, Strauss and Teller must now fire off a Chinese New Year of six secret big bangs in ten weeks. And this series of six thermonuclear Jornadas was called 'Castle', as if in mockery of paranoia. And the lovely cloud-yield of the six was 50 megatons, which, for those who dance below, means 2500 Hiroshimas. Who now would doubt the excellence and the virtue of Edward Teller?

Those cool early spring days in Year 9, among the famous scholars at Princeton (where resided the electric mind-god for which Johnny Von Neumann had left behind his Danube cafés for ever to play the damnation of the species on his MANIAC computer, like some Bach barren of music), Robert waited mutely for his secret hearing, proud and bitter, and ready to be judged. He was touched by Lloyd Garrison's enthusiastic idea of him. When he heard that such a man would stand for him, Robert even felt a faint hope. Meanwhile, interviewing witnesses in New York, Lloyd Garrison for the first time met Edward Teller.

And so shocked was Garrison by the Hungarian's passionate dislike of his old friend Oppy, the lawyer knew at once that Teller was someone he did not want to have on his side.

Chapter 4

In its floating barge at the Pacific testing range, Teller's third test, *Koon*, fizzled that Wednesday, April 7th. And a time would even come when a mammoth Trinity proposed by Teller's Livermore laboratories would be vetoed by Eisenhower because of its 'excessive power'.

In the capital, the following Monday of Oppy's secret Hearing, Herbert Marks drove Robert and Kitty past the innocent-looking White House, around the Washington obelisk. Parking off Constitution Avenue, the friends moved slowly, without speaking, along the budding trees. Kitty was still on crutches after her latest fall. Robert held his hat while a back door of the two-storey whitewood Atom Commission building T3 was unlocked for them. As he followed Herbert's stockinged ankles up a dingy metal staircase, he noticed his heart beating. You may be in this place all month, Robert thought. But at last he was caught up in the concrete procedures.

It seemed there were forty or more witnesses waiting out of his deepest past. Who could say anything about Robert's life he did not know better? How much could even *he* remember across fifteen years? What might there be in his FBI files? The strange argument over Garrison's clearance to the secret files meant that all this week Robert Robb was alone with Gray, Morgan and Evans . . . and his file! That spy-craze in the press had even infected him, Robert thought. He *knew* he was innocent. Still, it was wise to confide the charges to Reston at the *Times*. The secret powers were not going to use Security to get away with this unobserved.

With an electric shock of fear, the faces of his old Communist friends swept vividly up, far worse than anything in the pasts of Hiss or the Rosenbergs. Was he right to think them true, innocent and heroic? The trouble was, the more Robert thought of that angry, romantic time and his revolutionary friends, the more he became Haakon's old crusading radical Oppy. The only way was not to look back at those brief rebel years. To face his judges he needed his moral strength. To be strong he needed to be guiltless. To be guiltless, Robert could not afford to look closely at Steve Neslon, Eltonton, Folkoff, Lambert, Haakon and the others. That time of hope was spoiled and ugly now. Wasn't it punishment enough to carry the sin of Hiroshima? Anyway, the whole thing was buried. Who could dig up the details? So Robert tactfully glossed over the old anger to himself . . . even to Garrison. Instead he thought of the lost idealism of that time. So Robert had worked himself into a righteous indignation.

The friends were walking down a dark corridor of closed doors. They came to a sunny open room, Room 2022. Four men were talking outside. Robert's steps slowed. They were late. The men backed readily out of his way and Robert felt a vague excitement. Aztec virgins must have felt this way, going to have their hearts fed to them, he thought. He smiled thoughtfully at someone called Ecker, whose hand he was shaking.

Through the open door, Robert saw a wide polished floor. A long table ran down the middle, with a toughly grinning red-faced man facing Robert from the far side. Beyond were four tall, dismal venetian blind windows. Outside, over Constitution Avenue, huge lawns stretched out. He could hear voices, hidden behind the door to the right. On the long table's near side, he recognized Garrison's tall, immaculate back next to Silverman. As Herb showed him inside and to the left, the two facing men (must be Robb and Rolander, Robert thought) pointedly did not look up from their whispered conversation.

The room was about twenty-five feet along the window side. On the left past the lawyers' table was an empty chair. Further to the left an exhausted reddish-leather couch against the end wall, a dixie-cup dispenser. On his way to the couch, Robert absorbed it all in a glance.

'This'll be your place of honour, Robert!' Herbert had already mentioned a couch.

'Thanks, it's most fancy,' Robert said.

He sat at the centre of the couch. Then he slipped to the end, away from the window.

'Anything I can get you?' Herbert stood awkwardly, looking down at him.

'Well, perhaps an ashtray.'

Marks stepped to the counsels' table. He took a glass ashtray and brought it back.

For one instant then, Roger Robb's eye flickered past the couch. It was the biggest challenge of Robb's career, that glance said. How could this famous fellow be a spy? Then again, how could he not be?

The end of the couch was out of the warm sunshine. Robert balanced the ashtray on the worn arm. Then he lit his new pipe. Puffing it thoughtfully, he glanced ahead. Over the empty witness chair, between the profiled teams of lawyers, to the three Gray Board members, backs to the end wall.

The three officials stared back at him. In the middle, Gordon Gray was a clean dashing aristocrat of the golf-links about Robert's age, and, like the prosecutor Robb, from Yale. To his left by the window, bald, undistinguished Morgan blinked his wide disturbed eyes. Then the chemist Ward Evans, sitting to the right, gnomishly kind, with a long drooping nose. They did not look good company for a global humanist, Robert thought. A subtle and hostile awkwardness hung over these three, as of people caught gossiping. For, like Landsdale and then Billy Borden, Robb and the Gray Board had met Doctor Oppenheimer's file before they met Oppy himself. He crossed his knees, gazing back at them with quizzical dispassion. He watched Mitchell and two others step in, taking seats between the stenotypist and the door.

The Hearing door was being closed. Robert sucked his pipe with a series of vigorous little puffs. Curious, to think of human society lying out on this American spring morning, innocent of this room and what was being done to its first defender in the atomic age. Now Herb Marks was scraping back a chair facing the window. He sat between Garrison and Silverman. A blue haze from Robert's pipe smoke floated over the sunny floor by the windows. Sweetly perfumed as byzantine incense, it spread from the silent disturbing figure slumped lazily in the couch out over the crowded tables. It mingled suggestively with the clean classroom odours of ink, rubbers, chalk and mimeograph.

Behind the facing Board table, Gray rose irritably. He walked to the end window and pushed it wide. He returned and took his chair.

'Then is everyone heah?' Gray broke in softly. 'We call this hearin to ordah.'

At the other end of the tensely crowded room, Robert's world shrank to this exhausted leather couch, his pipe and tobacco pouch and balanced glass ashtray, and to the intimate mystery of Doctor Oppenheimer.

And during those two opening days in the hearing couch, Robert did begin to find his way back to things past, and what once he had been.

With his gracious drawl Gray read out General Nichol's Charges to the stenographer, followed by Robert's long dignified reply. The men present in the hearing-room listened in various poses of polite attention.

Then Robert carried his pack of cigarettes and glass tray to the witness chair. Garrison rose, pale and stately. He passed in front of Robert to the windows. And they began from the beginning . . . with Robert's German father marrying his artistic mother, and his birth in 1904. It was like a miracle! For despite the witness's embarrassment, with Garrison gently encouraging him, Robert suddenly felt himself going back.

Now once again he was in his heroic period, in that luminous time before Trinity, when all men were born free. Then, speaking without false modesty of Germany's new science and his return to California, of his political awakening, and the dream among the union movements and Lincoln brigade, of one day joining the Russian workers in a world fraternity, Robert remembered the old happiness. He felt again the mysterious light, the urge to do universal good. As the opening hours of his Hearing slipped densely by, Robert mused how the Atom-Project had seemed part of that struggle. But how gradually after their marriage and the Stalin–Hitler Pact, he and Kitty broke off from Party activities while keeping natural loyalties to friends like Professor Chevalier. Then Robert told of the scholars' quest on the Mesa to split the atom, the laboratory's success, and the later moral awakening among the scientists. About his long government service trying to defend a climate of trust dealing with the Soviets, without in any way jeopardizing his country's military integrity . . . all leading to his final cynicism about the Kremlin leaders. It was not a bad story. It was also beautifully true.

As Robert sat chain-smoking in the wooden armchair, quietly talking as the evening sun moved out of the hearing-room, he thought the hostile atmosphere seemed better too. As if his life story contained some magic power to restore health. Yet Oppy's old genius for keeping everyone around him feeling virtuous was faltering. Sometimes, when he looked towards the Gray Board past the counsel's long table, Robert was aware of Roger Robb on his left, alertly scanning, measuring, his expressions.

Hours before Garrison wound up their presentation, Herb Marks had made some comments to Gordon Gray. There was certain danger to Doctor Oppenheimer's reputation in any one-sided leak to the spy-rabid press. So a columnist, Reston, had been discreetly informed of mysterious proceedings inside the Security labyrinth.

'Excuse me, Mr Chairman!' Robert now heard Prosecutor Robb's sharp clear voice, nakedly threatening in this secret room. 'Am I to understand that Mr Marks is questioning this Board's discretion?!'

'Mr Marks, sir!' At the facing wall, Gray knitted his hands. 'It is of utmost importance to us all this case not be judged in the press.'

Garrison half-rose, inclined his head. 'As long as there is no likelihood, I will keep our message in its bottle.'

Two hours later, Garrison walked out to the dark corridor booth and telephoned Reston. The newspaperman had worrying news.

'Good God, man, are you quite sure you can't head it off?'

Garrison cupped his hand on the speaking horn. 'All right then . . . better let our side of the yarn rip.'

Out in the twinkling city of man that night, in his quiet guest room in Randolph Paul's house, Robert slept at last deep in the womb of the state. And downstairs on his breakfast plate next morning his own face stared at him from the front of the *Times*.

'Dr Oppenheimer's AEC clearance suspended,' it read. 'Loyalty hearing underway; Red ties alleged; Physicist denied access to secret files.'

Oppy was broken from the Security screen! Groves's crime, and the politicans', was in plain view of the man-woman-and-child flesh of future Point Zeros.

Chapter 5

An hour later, Herbert and Robert stepped warily through the open Hearing door. Immediately he felt the change . . . the respectful stuffiness was gone.

'I presume, Mr Garrison . . .' Chairman Gray was shutting the near window, to keep out the traffic sound. He leaned behind the table. '. . . we have all read the morning papers. Will you explain to me what you have done?'

'As I said yesterday, Mr Chairman . . .' Garrison was also standing. He did not look around as Robert resumed his couch. 'Better than half the story being leaked, or a third, or a quarter, that the case charges be out, for all to see.'

Gray felt for his chair between Morgan and Evans, then sat down heavily. 'You mean to tell me, sir, in our discussion yesterday, you gentlemen felt no inclination to tell me the documents themselves were in the hands of the press?'

'Indeed we did not,' Robert said from his couch with a kind of awe.

Garrison turned soberly among the dozen alert faces. 'May I point out that we did not disclose the names of this Board, where this hearing is being held, or anything else?'

'I see!' Chairman Gray muttered coldly. 'Doctor, will you take the stand please?'

'Certainly.'

'Naturally, you are still under oath.'

Carrying his cigarette and ashtray four steps across the rough wood floor, Robert sat in the wooden armchair.

'Doctor Oppenheimer,' Gray began, his soft voice settling with relief into the heavy impersonal rhetoric. 'From 1942 to 1945, you worked in the Manhattan District, as Director of the Atom Weapons laboratory at Los Alamos. Since then you have served in various capacities. Is that correct?'

'It is,' Robert said. How depressingly flat it sounded.

The silence drew taut over the tables. The six facing counsels in front of him sat back, Robb slightly sideways, pencils lying untouched. Straight ahead, the three board members faced Robert over their black top-secret files. With these opening moves a threatening atmosphere stirred. Now their performance would be world famous. That put the stakes way up!

The sunshine of another day retreated, hour by hour, across the musty floor. Finally inching up to the window sills, it left the room.

It was past mid-afternoon. Robert's ashtray was rank with cigarette butts. The consistent rudeness of suspicion bore down on Robert's doubting conscience like a dentist's probe. It was beginning to wear him down. Even Ed Teller did not have the confidence to face him down like this! Where was their certain tone coming from?

'Doctor, in your testimony yesterday,' Gray was saying, 'you made the distinction between Communist party members, and what you called "fellow travellers" . . . those in sympathy, but who never actually commit themselves.'

'That distinction, in terms of discipline,' Robert repeated, 'is quite significant.'

'You said further, sir,' Gray looked at him, 'that in recruiting staff for Los Alamos, your policy was to overlook radical backgrounds. Except in the case of Party membership?'

'As I pointed out to Colonel Landsdale . . .' Was there no way of sharpening these tedious questions? '. . . party discipline is severe enough to interfere with our objective at Los Alamos. However, we needed the best minds to do the best kind of work. So we could not become sidetracked on the issue of political alignments. Besides, in 1942, I knew many patriotic Americans who were in sympathy with the Russians.'

'Would you include yourself?' Chairman Gray said instantly.

'No, I'd say that after the Nazi–Soviet Pact,' Robert said quietly after a pause, 'and for a number of reasons, by 1942 my sympathy for the Soviet system had declined sharply.'

Gray had just nodded to Roger Robb. Suddenly Robert was conscious of a vigorous impatient bustle to his left. He felt a wave of almost physical alarm.

'That was the year, in fact . . .' Robb took up with a sort of robust dogged satisfaction. He paced to the window on Robert's extreme left, and gazed up toward the White House. Then he turned back. Robert was watched on two fronts. How aggressive the fellow was! '. . . the year the Army assigned you the direction of the Atomic Weapons project?'

'I see no relation between the two events.' Relaxed on his chair, Robert focused his concentration. 'And on the preceding point, let me add that we had very few "fellow travellers" at Los Alamos . . . less than at Berkeley.'

'Let us speak bluntly, Doctor.' Prosecutor Robb paced slowly along the windows. 'By 1943, you knew the Party was an instrument of espionage?'

'I was not clear about it.'

'Surely you suspected it?' Robb turned with an incredulous look.

'No,' Robert said limply, shocked to hear the word at last spoken out loud. Was solidarity espionage?

'That was your reason . . . Party membership seemed to you inconsistent with work on a secret war project. Was it not?'

For the first time Robert wondered why no one was rescuing his responsibility from this offensive fellow. 'I think I have stated the reason about right.'

'I am asking you now if fear of espionage was not *one* reason?'

'Well, perhaps.' Robert shrugged.

'Your answer is that it was?' Robb's voice hardened.

'Yes.' Robert tried to find Herbert's eyes among the swimming tables. Could the fellow get away with such insinuations?

'You gave considerable support to relief for the Spanish Civil War?'

'Uhuh, yes.' Robert met Robb's eyes contemptuously, then looked away.

'Donations contributed,' Robb insisted, 'through California Communist organizations?'

'Particularly after my father's death in 1937. I became far better off than the rest of my friends. I guess I gave quite a lot.'

'Those donations were cut off in 1942?'

'Well now,' Robert fought back gently, 'let us be careful . . .'

Robb advanced, leaning on the corner of the counsel's table five feet away. The stenographer's 'snik-snik' paused.

'I want you to be, Doctor!'

'I gave increasingly less.' Robert held his coal to a fresh cigarette.

'Less, as America became involved on the continent. I remember no cut-off date.'

'How often did you see Rudy Lambert in those days?'

"Oh, half a dozen times,' Robert smiled. 'I think the party saw me as a soft touch for funds.'

'Could you describe Lambert?' Robb said vaguely.

Robert managed a thumbnail description.

'It is unfortunate you are unfamiliar with the Bureau files,' Robb said drily. 'You might remember back in 1943 telling Colonel Landsdale you could not describe Lambert.'

During that instant, propped in the witness chair, Oppy thought he might faint. Had the government men taped every conversation he had with Security?! He felt his own remembered being, torn by facts.

Though Robert was saved five minutes later by an adjournment, it was almost immediately Thursday. And like a nightmare of accusing evil and destruction, Robb was once again standing over Oppy before the eyes of his helpless friends and merciless inquisitors.

'Now, Doctor . . .' Robb recommenced with the breezy charm of a man who is only warming up. 'We have touched on your liaison with Jean Tatlock.'

'Yes, Jean and I were engaged twice,' Robert said, remotely, as always when he spoke of the sensitive moral things in his life.

'But – and remember you are under oath –' Robb turned at the window, to the left of the witness chair. '– did not your liaison continue after your engagement? After, in fact, your marriage to your present wife?'

'No particular contact,' Robert said icily. 'What are you getting at?'

Robb moved ahead down the windows to get an angle. 'Doctor Oppenheimer, was Jean Tatlock a Communist?'

'In a way she was.'

'You mean she was not a Communist?' Robb was impatient.

'I did not say that,' Robert said politely. And facing him at the far window corner, prosecutor Robb thought: So this is the superb brain of Doctor Oppenheimer.

'Then she *was* a Communist, Doctor,' he said. 'As were your wife, your brother Frank, and his wife.'

'You have made all three points before,' Robert said.

'By current security standards,' Robb pressed harder, stopping by the Board table, 'would not your wife's politics alone invalidate you for clearance in security matters?'

'Mr Chairman!'

Robert heard Herb's voice, like an angel. Garrison was on his feet facing the young prosecutor.

'I withdraw the question,' Robb muttered.

'Mr Chairman!' Garrison turned with polite indignation. 'By current security standards, Mrs Oppenheimer's past politics would indeed render the Doctor liable for invalidation. But the final judgment must be one of common sense.'

'That is a very fine hair to split, Mr Garrison.' Gray looked away. 'Mr Robb?'

'Doctor Oppenheimer, did you in June 1943 . . .' Robb circled the bare wood floor between the witness chair and centre table, '. . . more than two years after your marriage to Katherine Dallet, the widow of a Communist, spend the night with another Communist, Jean Tatlock?'

Disgust, fear and shame rose in the throat of the scholar slumped in the witness chair. In the silence Robert felt the accusing eyes of the Board, Garrison – and beyond, of Kitty and Lewis Strauss somewhere out in Washington. Of the whole sinful nuclear-state before which he now stood stripped of honour.

'Yes, that's true,' he said quietly. 'I felt I had to.'

'Why did you feel you had to?' Robb moved behind Robert's back.

'I received notes from her,' Robert said. 'She was under psychiatric treatment. She was extremely unhappy.'

'Did you find out why she had to see you?' Robb stood back watching him, polished toes pointed out.

'We had a drink at the Top of the Mark, overlooking San Francisco Bay,' Robert said in a trance. *Where did he exist . . . but in the other secrecy of his soul*? 'Then we went to her home.'

'Where was that?' Robb's voice lowered too now.

'On Telegraph Hill.'

Robert tried to catch Robb's eyes. But the prosecutor stared at his forehead.

'When did you next see her?'

'She took me to the airport.' Robert gazed out of the second window. There was a late afternoon light. 'I never saw her again.'

'So you spent the night with her, did you not?'

Robb cut off Robert's view.

'Yes.' His own voice was almost inaudible.

'That is when you were working on a secret war project?'

'Yes.' In the secret hearing room, their voices were so soft as to be alone.

'Did you think that consistent with good security?' Robb said pityingly.

'It was, as a matter of fact,' Robert stammered, choking on futility and revulsion. 'Not a word . . . it was not good politics.'

Robb broke the embarrassed silence. 'Now I will ask you again, Doctor. Did you not, in July of 1941, play host at your Berkeley home to a closed meeting of the Communist Party?'

The man in the witness chair straightened with a sort of stoic anger. On his right, Garrison was rising among the seated figures.

'I would very much like,' Robert snapped, 'to have your witness – Crouch? – here in this room under oath! I have never heard of the man.'

'Mr Chairman!' Garrison stood, handsomely profiled to Robb, his left hand extended. 'As President Eisenhower has recently observed, this is a country where a man may stand face to face with the man who accuses him.'

'I am sorry, Mr Garrison.' Chairman Gray folded his hands on the open secret file. 'For reasons of security the witness Crouch will not be available for questioning. But you have my assurance his testimony has been double-checked.'

That night over Washington, there was an electric storm. Spring showers thrashed windows of the bedrooms (all within two miles of each other) where the Board members, Garrison, Robb and Doctor Oppenheimer were all lying awake after midnight, listening to the storm and wondering what had happened to them. For something had definitely happened today in Room 2022, something terrible and mysterious and beyond all their understandings. Something to do with man's cosmic solitude in the nuclear age, and his savagery toward himself. And as often happens, all six men felt deeply fascinated with each other.

Roger Robb, expert at breaking down the hard shells of criminals who lived by betrayal and lies, wondered at the helplessness of America's top nuclear magician. Either the man is a supreme manipulator living a life of deception, or a dreaming imbecile, Robb thought. Wondering if he had not overdone it, Robb vowed to show he could be a gentleman too. He would try to understand what the enigmatic doctor really did believe in. As for Robert, carrying in his soul the morbid beauty of Western cultivation, and the weight of his country's crime, he felt tonight the ruin and horror of a young and fanciful girl who has been violently raped. Had he not always been adored and respected? How was it this Robb's uncouth and brilliant honesty could befoul him with such ugliness? In his heart, though, Robert could not help the strange feeling that the attorney's ruthless factualism was correct. Tomorrow, Robert vowed, he would meet his destroyer will to will.

That same hour Garrison too lay awake, grim with remorse at the crucial moves on security and tactics he had misplayed at the opening of the game. But why must Oppy be so extreme in his vow not to defend himself?

As for Morgan and Gray, they lay awake in bitter apprehension of the world press, sharpening its teeth to devour all of them back in Room 2022. And as for eccentric little Ward Evans, he was thinking, What a sensitive, confused, great man the fellow is . . . I'd proudly trust him with the kids. And Evans turned over, and he went straight to sleep.

Chapter 6

'Doctor Oppenheimer,' Robb opened with a genial grin on that overcast Friday morning in Room 2022. 'This Board would genuinely like to understand your position as a moral leader among scientists.'

'If I am one.' Robert was haughtily wary. 'Go ahead.'

Roger Robb retreated slowly along the windows, comfortably in the witnesses' view. He turned and waited for a moment, hands clasped. Today he was in a dark blue double-breasted suit.

'Doctor, were you morally opposed to the dropping of the bomb on Hiroshima?'

'We set forth –' Robert began willingly.

'I am asking about *it*, not *we*!' Robb interrupted. It was the exact tone Oppy had used on lesser intellects!

'. . . I set forth my anxieties, arguments on the other side.'

'You mean you argued against dropping the bomb?'

'Yes,' Robert said sadly. 'But I did not endorse them.'

'Having worked three years, "rather excellently" as you put it . . .' Robb lowered his voice incredulously. '. . . you then argued it should never be used?'

Robert blinked pensively. Had not most of the scientists thought that . . . even Szilard, who started the whole damn business? Couldn't this fellow even grasp the issue between duties to science, country and mankind?'

'No,' Robert replied. 'I was asked for the views of scientists, for and against.'

'But you supported the dropping . . . you helped pick the target!'

'Los Alamos, then, was not a platform for policy. I did,' Robert muttered, 'what I was told to.'

'Even worked to produce the thermonuclear bomb?'

'It was unfeasible . . .'

'I didn't ask you that!' Robb interrupted. 'If you could have discovered it, you'd have done so?'

'Oh yes,' Robert mused truthfully. Wondering, as he lit his second cigarette, at the naive fool he had once been.

Still listening near the window in the dull grey light, Robb's hands involuntarily fell to his sides. Stepping to the desk, the prosecutor briskly picked up his notes. He walked to the corner behind Robert, by the dixie cup dispenser. To calm his disgust that a man with so little hold on mortal issues could use such a condescending tone with him, Robb emptied a paper cup. *Unless, of course, the man's motives were hidden.* No one could be that naive!

'Doctor Oppenheimer,' Robb said. 'Did you ever actually tell General Groves about your brother Frank's Communist membership?'

'I can't remember . . . I can't be certain,' Robert said, with a spasm of the dread he felt at any mention of radicalism. 'However, I don't really think I should have told Groves such a thing about my own brother.'

'If then you told General Groves,' Robb had resumed his hammering rhythm, 'that you did not know if Frank was, or wasn't, Doctor, would that not be a lie?'

'It would,' Robert said, thinking of the people he had betrayed trying to be honest with Groves. 'Had I made that statement.'

'Would you now,' Robb said, inching back into the witness's field of vision, 'deny you made such a statement to General Groves?'

'Oh?' Robert looked over his shoulder. 'I couldn't.'

'Mr Chairman!'

Garrison was half standing. The overhead lights flickered, went on. He looked very tall under the low ceiling, in this cramped office.

'Mr Garrison sir?' Chairman Gray stared at the pale manicured hand.

'May I take exception,' Garrison said, 'to Mr Robb's technique? Testing a witness's veracity against detailed twelve-year-old documents!'

'You may, Mr Garrison.' Chairman Gray was gracious. 'But as you know this is not a trial, it is a hearing. I am sure you are familiar with hearing procedures? Proceed, Mr Robb.'

'Doctor Oppenheimer,' Robb spoke up somewhere behind the witness chair. 'Do you deny you told General Groves you did not know your brother was a Communist?'

'I couldn't for certain,' Robert muttered.

'In other words, you *might* have told General Groves something untrue?'

'Well, I hope I didn't!'

'But *might* have, Doctor! Might you not?' Robb snapped. He was standing at the witness's right shoulder.

'Obviously I might have,' Robert said with a morbid pessimism.

'Mr Chairman . . .' Garrison was speaking in his noblest Lincoln-esque manner. '. . . may I call General Leslie Groves to the witness chair?'

306

In the dingy little upstairs office 2022 of Atomic Commission building T-3, stifling with the intimate emotions of combat and debate, and with the father of the nuclear age seated with a sort of prophetic melancholy at their centre, it was Monday of the second week in his treason trial. Over that weekend, the first distinguished statesmen, generals and scholars had begun converging on Washington from all over the country, as once they had flocked to Los Alamos, and later to the Institute of Advanced Study.

A pouring rain blotted out the pewter sky, and the south lawns outside. In the hearing-room, there was a clammy chill. Robert sat puffing his third pipe. He could just see around Groves's wide khaki bulk, caged in the witness chair. Poor fat patriotic Groves, to whom Robert had sold the forces of nature, his friends and his integrity! Groves who had used him to make 150,000 Japanese dance the dance, and then to terrorize the tragic Russians! He puffed his already well-chewed pipe stem thoughtfully.

'. . . so, General, when the pressure from your security men was too much,' Robb was saying, standing at some distance from the swollen presence decked with medals, '. . . you ordered the Director of Los Alamos to reveal the name of the intermediary he had withheld eight months. And the name he gave you was Chevalier?'

'That's right . . . the name of his close friend,' the General's familiar unctuous voice said, and his fat trembled vigorously. At long last it was Groves who felt guilty.

'As far as Doctor Oppenheimer's work for his country is concerned,' Groves hurried on, 'few men I know are as loyal, discreet or patriotic as he is. No other man could have done the job he did. I was there, I saw it!'

'I'm sure that's very reassuring to hear, General,' said Robb, and eleven faces turned his way. 'But by security standards today, General – a security risk being someone who, among other things, has a Communist in their family – would you still consider yourself free to extend Doctor Oppenheimer's Clearance?'

There was a long contorted silence. The windows rattled.

'No . . .' Groves retreated disappointedly. 'I guess I wouldn't.'

After Groves left the room, passing out of marvellous Oppy's life for ever, the scholar on the couch sat alone, stuffing his pipe bowl.

When Robert lifted his eyes, John Landsdale was watching him fixedly. He turned and quickly sat.

'. . . of course Doctor Oppenheimer isn't a security risk!' Landsdale was saying with quiet disdain an hour later. Landsdale the gentleman hunter still lay bitterly awake nights, imagining himself tracking down the century's greatest quarry, the master spy Fuchs.

'The questions put by this young man,' Landsdale nodded toward Robb, 'make me doubt whether it is the truth which is to be discovered here. This is all a manifestation of the hysteria of the times, and disturbs me in the extreme.'

'This enquiry is a manifestation of hysteria?' Robb's voice rose a register. He unbuttoned his jacket.

'I think –' Landsdale went on.

'Yes or no!' Robb moved in from the left. But it was like a hammer which clicks on a wet cartridge.

'If you let me continue!' Landsdale's cold blue eyes glittered. 'I will be glad to answer you, sir.'

Roger Robb lowered his papers. 'Very well.'

'I think the current hysteria over Communism threatens our way of life.' Landsdale crossed his legs. 'To regard Communist associations of the '30s in the same light as those of today seems to me hysterical.'

Behind the Board table, Ward Evans made a sign.

'On a secret war project, Mr Landsdale,' Evans said, 'can there be one hundred per cent security?'

Landsdale answered at once. 'Not unless we are prepared to abandon all the freedom we want to defend.'

'Thank you, Mr Landsdale.' Gray grinned over the Board table.

On the couch, watching the leathery back of the southerner's neck as he rose, Robert puffed vigorously and faintly smiled.

'Mr Garrison?' Robb was saying, as Landsdale went out the door. 'Would you be so kind as to furnish us with a list of your witnesses?'

'I have already prepared one for you.' Garrison reached over the low table beyond the empty chair. 'A list of yours would not be unhelpful.'

'I'll see what I can do, Mr Garrison,' Robb grinned quickly.

The rain had passed later on when Robert carried his ashtray back to the witness chair.

'All right, Doctor,' Roger Robb began. 'Let us leave aside Peters, Nelson, Folkoff, Lambert, Eltonton. Let us finally go back to the interview we have all heard played on the speakers. I mean your interview with Colonel Pash, and to the cock and bull story you told him about the so-called "kitchen conversation". You were not, we have all heard, telling the truth?'

'No,' Robert said with dignity.

'You lied to him?'

'Yes,' he said, watching the gloating red face with pity.

'You claimed Chevalier had approached three people,' Robb pressed, like someone who scarcely believes his luck.

'Probably.'

'That's wasn't true?' Robb said it greedily, almost intimately.

'That is right. The whole thing was a fabrication except the name of George Eltonton.'

Robb drew nearer with a sad, cautious compassion. 'Isn't it fair to say, Doctor, that according to your testimony you told not one lie to Colonel Pash, but a whole fabrication and tissue of lies?'

'Right,' Robert said bitterly, and he was thinking of a country he had tried to serve, a friend he had tried to protect, a humanity he had hoped to save.

'Why did you do that, Doctor?' Robb bent curiously.

'Because I was an idiot.'

Chapter 7

In the Chairman's comfortable office over in the Atomic Energy building, where once he had sat with Billy Borden discussing whether Doctor Oppenheimer was a Soviet masterspy, banker Strauss had still not recovered from the shock of publicity through the Capitols of the West.

Now, seeing from Garrison's witness list that a wave of distinguished outrage was sweeping to the rescue of the limitless arrogance seated on the couch in Room 2022, Chairman Strauss's sick alarm intensified.

309

Hearing finally that his star witness, Ernest Orlando Lawrence, was pleading bad health and taking Luis Alvarez with him, thus leaving only Teller and a few Air Force and security men to face the ranks of America's top scientists and statesmen, Strauss could almost hear Doctor Oppenheimer's sly laughter. Waiting until after dark, Strauss telephoned three thousand miles to Berkeley.

'Lawrence asked me not to testify,' Alvarez's slow heavy voice answered. 'Frankly, I'm happy to be let off.'

'Of course you can testify, Luis,' Strauss begged in a low voice. 'It is your duty, as an American.'

'That may or may not be, Lewis. But I'm afraid I just can't help you out.'

Then, to the shock of the sick lonely man in the Chairman's office, the phone went dead. Yet somehow the next morning there came a reluctant cable of assent from Teller's thermonuclear ally.

Across the planet, that April night, as in its floating barge in the Pacific Ocean Teller, Ulam and Bradbury prepared Von Neumann's fission-fusion-fission bomb, capable of a 300-square-mile wasteland, the fourth thermonuclear Trinity of that spring, all powerless men, women and children, the innocent beasts of the earth and fowls of the air, were smothered in a blanket of deliberate terror controlled by weak, cowardly Russian and American politicians and generals. And it was the reign of cynics.

Doctor Oppenheimer sat thoughtfully on his couch listening to great men speak for him, as he no longer spoke for himself. Without hope none of this seemed to possess meaning. Robb had uglied even that. It was too late, the bonds of human responsibility tying Oppy to the Mesa had been torn out.

'Really gifted and able people,' the Kremlinologist Kennan had testified that morning, 'should be considered in a special category.'

'That's absurd,' James Conant was saying now, the man who had argued face to face with the mad cynicism of Molotov, Gromyko, the big-bomb men, Strauss and Teller. The urbane world traveller sat erect on the sunny witness chair five feet in front of Robert. 'If Oppenheimer is a security risk for opposing the Super, so am I! I opposed it just as strongly.'

Robb paced the wood floor, slowly circling Conant.

'Of course you don't know what the record before the Board

discloses. Nor what the testimony before us has been.'

'I only know,' Conant replied, 'the Nichols Letter of Charges.'

Counsel Marks leaned forward, pencil raised.

'Mr Chairman,' he said, 'the majority of your evidence is beyond the reach of witnesses. Why question any witnesses at all?'

'Mr Marks,' Robb said, 'I seek perspective on the witness's judgment.'

'I hope you remember that,' Marks snapped, 'when we question your witnesses!'

'I shall, Mr Marks, I shall.'

At the left end of his couch, Robert was feeling at home with his new pipe. Now, in the enactment of Oppy's past, Fermi's elbows were on the arms of the witness chair.

'In my opinion, Teller's super was not feasible!' Fermi's voice, full of generous humour. 'And we had no need. It is nice to dream of bombs into infinity, but this one would have no other usefulness than the suicide of the species.'

'Is there no contradiction . . .' Robb acted out his incredulity. '. . . between the Doctor's indifference to the A-bomb being used and later opposing the Super?'

'To compare the two bombs,' Fermi shrugged, 'is to compare an eagle with a cricket because they both fly. Also Robert's viewpoint developed as he discovered politicians are not rational in their attitudes to this thing.'

'It is all very well, Doctor Fermi, to go about feeling guilty . . .'

'Many from Los Alamos,' Fermi interrupted, sitting with his knees spread and his big dapper shoes together, 'admitted guilt to claim credit. Robert's guilt was a way of life. Not many people can face such unpleasantness indefinitely. But for his country and humanity Oppenheimer has done it.'

The Washington sun had retreated from Robert's end of the crumpled couch. In Fermi's words he had almost smelled the presence of the old scholar's circle somewhere beyond.

After the Italian left office 2022, Robert listened to Bob Bacher of Point Zero. He was trying to overcome the Board's suspicion that Oppy had recruited his gentle student Serber *because* of his radical background. Then David Lilienthal took the witness chair. Lilienthal, who had bravely held out to the very last against the

Super. Robb turned to the Board table. 'Mr Chairman, I have classified material to discuss with this witness.'

'Say, what's going on here?' Lilienthal cut in. He sat forward on the witness chair, watching Garrison, Marks and Silverman file out the door. 'Is Doctor Oppenheimer being tried without counsel?'

'The point is,' observed Chairman Gray, 'that this is not a trial, but a hearing.'

Five minutes later, Robert's counsels were back ranked in their chairs at the centre table.

'And so you are quite certain . . .' Robb was pressing Lilienthal. (Chairman Strauss's predecessor had visited General Nichols at the Commission building. Now he was discovering he had not been shown all the files.) '. . . that you are intimate with all the AEC files on the issue of Doctor Oppenheimer's security clearance?'

'I am beginning to wonder!' Lilienthal admitted grimly.

'You *insist* you did not suggest a review-board such as this one gathered here?' Robb turned at the window. 'I have here a memorandum in your writing that you spoke to Mr Clifford –'

Garrison was on his feet, his cheeks flushed.

'I object in the strongest terms! A lapse of memory is not a lie.'

'Mr Garrison!' Robb left the bright windows. The room inside was murky. 'Do you question my methods? It is an axiom that the greatest invention known to man for the discovery of truth is cross-examination! This witness's memory has just been proved unreliable.'

'I am the first to admit it,' Lilienthal said evenly. 'But this technique confuses me. This Board wants facts, the facts are on file. I ask for the files and some of them are denied me!'

Against the rear walls, Robert felt the blows rain on him. The series of men in this scarred witness chair, were shades of himself. Their words about him seemed to carry away the pigment of his being, as dust off a butterfly's wings. The closest friends disturbed him most.

Now Isidor Rabi sat in front of Robert without being able to meet his stricken friend's eyes.

'What I have to say is,' Rabi said in a quick gruff monotone, 'Los Alamos was a miracle of a laboratory. After all Oppenheimer has done, this whole security mess is most unfortunate.'

At the Board table, Ward Evans leaned forward.

'In other words . . .' Rabi looked right and left, at each expectant face in this dusty depressing room. 'There he was! He was a consultant! If you don't want to consult the guy, you don't consult him . . . period! Why must you then suspend security clearance and go through this sort of thing? He's only there when he's called, that's all there is to it. It does not call for such a procedure when someone has accomplished what Doctor Oppenheimer has. There is a positive record – we have an A-bomb, and a whole series of developments and more bombs, God help us. What more do you want, mermaids? This a tremendous achievement!'

'It is four thirty, Mr Chairman,' Robb suddenly announced, with a thin smile at Rabi. 'Perhaps we might adjourn.'

Week two of Doctor Oppenheimer's treason trial was almost over. As Chairman Gray sat listening to the last of Robert's Advisors – Rowe, then Du Bridge – saying it did not disturb them Oppenheimer had lied to security men to protect his friend Haakon and brother Frank, Gray felt more and more disturbed: just as Robert's friends would one day accuse him for not screening Haakon more effectively. Knowledge was indivisible.

'Before I call my last witness,' Garrison was murmuring politely, 'might Mr Robb provide me with that list of his witnesses?'

'Unless ordered to,' Robb finessed elegantly, 'we will not disclose our witnesses in advance.'

'This Board,' Chairman Gray took the point up, 'wishes no further leaks, Mr Garrison, such as might embarrass and inhibit witnesses from the science community. Now, please show in Dr Vannevar Bush.'

'I had at the time of the Los Alamos appointment,' Bush spoke with quaint vehemence, twisting his bow-tie, 'complete confidence in the loyalty, judgment and integrity of Doctor Oppenheimer. I've had no reason to change my opinion. I do think neither this, or any other Board should sit on the question of whether a man should serve his country because he has expressed strong opinions. If you want to try this case, try me! I have expressed strong opinions many times, and I intend to do so again. Sometimes they have been unpopular. When a man is pilloried for that, this country is in a sorry state.'

313

And humanity too, reflected the man who had built the death of the world, like someone on his own judgment day.

Chapter 8

That next Capitol morning, as far out on the Pacific the secret cruisers of the Eniwetok test-site steamed in on the poisonous evidence of Teller and Lewis Strauss's 7-megaton *Union* firestorm, Robert felt the new atmosphere the instant he came in. He sat at the shady end of the couch. It was almost as if he could feel the build-up of strontium contamination secretly being detected from India to Australia, in Europe, and even here in Washington.

Roger Robb was waiting over by the sunny windows. His and Doctor Oppenheimer's eyes met. Robb gave him a quick charming smile.

Leaning in a row on the far table Gray, Morgan and Evans bantered good naturedly about golf-courses. It was time for Robb's witnesses, all of them either Teller's thermonuclear horsemen or men intimate with Oppy only as a file. There were even some men who had seen neither Robert nor a thermonuclear firestorm. Nobody in office 2022 would have to believe now in Oppy's tragic prophecy.

'Mr Chairman.' Robb faced the door. 'May I call Dr Wendell Lattimer to the stand?'

As Robert lit his pipe, Haakon's Caliban of the Berkeley labs came into the hearing-room. He turned his large head from side to side, trailing cigar smoke. Chairman Gray leaned forward with a welcoming smile. The room concentrated as a single mind.

'And so between 1945 and 1949,' Lattimer was saying in a quavery, grating voice, 'we did not develop anywhere in our programmes, largely due to Oppenheimer's influence. This influence he has is a prodigious thing really. I make studies of character – not bad at it either. I can tell you, this power to persuade people is in Doctor Oppenheimer a very powerful thing indeed.'

Roger Robb's first witnesses were not going very well. But the faces of Chairman Gray and Morgan expressed no disapproval at the poor performances.

'First I would like to say,' testified a witness called Kenneth

Pitzer, whose office had once been in this room, 'that I have no wish to be testifying here. I am testifying at the specific and urgent request of General Manager Nichols.'

'Mr Chairman,' Robb said confidently hours later, after Roscoe 'Big-Bomb' Wilson had made a sales-pitch for the great skies as the only approaches for making landlocked Russians dance the dance. 'I call David Griggs to the stand.'

'Mr Griggs,' the laconic Silverman persisted during the cross-examination, 'again and again you refer to Doctor Oppenheimer's supposed antagonism to the Air Force, in terms of your one heated meeting at his Princeton office, which however you cannot remember.'

'Do you expect me,' Griggs snapped aggressively, 'to remember what Doctor Oppenheimer said word for word?'

'From what knowledge, then, did your doubts about Doctor Oppenheimer's loyalty extend?'

'Since 1946, the witness said, twisting into a curious posture before Robert's desolate stare, 'I have been aware he was considered a security risk. Also it is fair to say that it has been my experience that when you are in a hot controversy (and the Air Force one over the Super was like Civil War) it is awfully hard not to question the motives of people who oppose you.'

'In other words,' Silverman enquired with some relief, in the embarrassed silence, 'in the heat of battle, your judgment might have clouded?'

'Something along those lines,' Griggs apologized.

Finally the towering, slow, blond figure of Luis Alvarez did appear, straight from California. He sat on the witness chair, twisted awkwardly as if in deference to the silent figure on the couch behind him. Alvarez of the Pacific testing ranges, Alvarez who at Tinian had written the message to the Japanese scientists, to flutter like cherry blossoms from the firestorm on the Inland Sea. Lloyd Garrison took over cross-examination.

'To summarize your testimony: while between 1945 and 1949 you, Lawrence and Teller were promoting the Superbomb throughout the country, you became aware that Doctor Oppenheimer was opposing you, and having a widespread influence impeding your success.'

'Yes, that's correct.' The witness's voice was muffled.

'Doctor Alvarez,' Ward Evans broke in. Evans had begun engaging each famous colleague in a short droll exchange. 'Does any of this have any bearing on security matters? What do you think it means?'

'By itself,' said Alvarez with almost physical relief, 'it means nothing. Absolutely nothing!'

'Does it mean Doctor Oppenheimer is disloyal?' Evans persisted.

'Absolutely not, sir, absolutely not.' Alvarez coughed indignantly.

'Mr Chairman?' Robb said quickly. 'May I call William Liscum Borden to testify?'

But, face to face with clean, blandly neat Billy Borden, boy champion of superbombs, even Robb could not hide his embarrassment.

'We are all in this room, Mr Borden . . .'' Robb gazed out of the windows at the gathering stormclouds. '. . . because of your letter to the FBI. Have you realized that the charges it contains, which we have just been discussing – for instance, that Doctor Oppenheimer is an "agent of the Soviet Union", has "more than one Communist mistress" – that a number of your charges go beyond those in the Nichols letter of charges?'

'I don't see that the implication,' Borden said stiffly, 'is much different.' His blue eyes darted righteously.

'I see. I think I understand.' Robb looked coldly at the even colder face seated among them. 'Now let me see if you feel any hesitation about answering questions I might put to you because of the presence of Doctor Oppenheimer and his counsel?'

'Not at all,' Borden said.

'The answer is no?' Robb tilted his head to one side. And not until this moment was Robert sure that he was in no danger of a formal spy trial.

'The answer is no!' Borden repeated.

'I think,' said Robb softly, 'that is all I care to ask.'

Chapter 9

As the hearing in the ramshackle commission building went into its third week, the feverish excitement of spring spread across the young land.

In classrooms across the land, children who knew that the glory of just living was theirs for ever felt summer vacation very near. They writhed at their desks, with wise impatience at the stupidity of learning. In Washington Chairman Gray writhed too, even fruitlessly asking Robb if the Hearing could be called off. And when Joe Volpe heard how Oppy was being treated he burst out: 'Shove it! Leave it! Because I don't think you are going to win!'

But here they all were, gathered again among the chairs and tables of top-secret office 2022, the scientists of the magical atom which had rent the adult world, and the statesmen and university professors. The Jews and the Gentiles. Men of the Old World and those of the New. Men rooted among files and bureaucracy, men drugged with Stratofortress dreams of flight, and men living in the misfit underworld of espionage. Men who knew love and desire and the great soaring force of the human spirit. And men who had denied their personal passions to serve an ideal of the patria. Here they all were this morning, taking up the strange argument: whether or not this gentle vain sentimentalist, who had just spent his fiftieth birthday puffing his pipe on the fallen leather couch while the sensitive mystery of his life was torn from him, was a danger to humanity because he had dreamed of world utopias, and lobbied for some limit on the mad destructiveness of the human species. And, strangest of all, it was only Doctor Oppenheimer who knew the full extent of his crime.

This morning, Robert was feeling a sad peace at his own persecution.

'Mr Chairman,' Roger Robb's voice rose above the whispering rustle. 'I would like to call Colonel Boris Pash to the witness chair.'

Robert watched a heavy, barely familiar head approach without seeming to notice him. Then Pash became another pair of shoulders in the witness chair. Robert vaguely remembered: this fellow had been among the first into liberated Paris, on the campaign to snare captive European scientists.

317

'Yes sir,' Pash was soon saying. 'In May 1943, I was investigating a reported case of espionage at Berkeley. We knew that a man called Steve Nelson had attempted to secure information on the Radiation Laboratory through a man we knew as "Joe". At first we thought it was Giovanni Lomanitz, so we recommended his draft deferment not be renewed.'

'What happened then?' Robb said with quiet anticipation.

'When Lomanitz heard . . .' Pash's pink hand appeared over his shoulder, felt nervously at the back of his neck. '. . . I believe he called Doctor Oppenheimer. At the time it seemed to us strange that whoever we investigated ran to our subject. When we gave them problems, it resulted in the subject intervening. We also discussed the subject's large contributions to causes through the Communist Party, broken off the late winter of that year.'

'At the time,' Robb said softly, 'he took up his Los Alamos position?'

'Yes.' Pash nodded twice, adjusting his thick glasses.

'What did you recommend?'

'That the subject had probably been a Communist agent,' Pash said simply.

Robert sat sucking his pipe in the sun. Pash's solid shoulders squirmed slightly against the chair back.

'. . . that the subject had direct connections with Steve Nelson, who may have been promoted in the Party because of his contact with Mrs Oppenheimer. We recommended heavy surveillance with two bodyguards.'

'Were the bodyguards assigned?' Robb said.

'I regret to say they were not . . . at that time.'

'Thank you, Colonel.' Robb took his chair. 'Mr Garrison, you may cross-examine the witness.'

'Colonel Pash,' said Garrison softly. 'Do you consider yourself an expert on the character and political thought of Doctor Oppenheimer?'

'That is my job,' said the ex-physical education instructor. 'And I'm not bad at it, if I may say so.'

'Colonel Pash . . .' Garrison paced slowly, hands behind back. 'How often have you met Doctor Oppenheimer?'

'Once for that interview,' Pash said uncomfortably, though it

318

was unclear what made him so. 'But from evaluating our files I am intensely familiar with him.'

'That interview was in August 1943. Have his opinions changed since?'

'I don't think I can speak for Doctor Oppenheimer.'

Garrison's gleaming shoes stopped beside Robert's couch, a little behind the faceless agent in the witness chair. 'How long has Doctor Oppenheimer been under FBI surveillance?'

'Since 1942,' Pash reflected. 'That is, fourteen years.'

'On the information of 1943 you consider him a security risk?'

'Yes I do.'

'You know he is?' Garrison turned.

'Yes I think I do. I do, yes.'

'Have you ever had clear proof of his disloyalty?'

'No proof,' Pash said coldly. 'But I thought it was his duty to disclose Chevalier's name. And it was irresponsible for a scientist with his classified knowledge to risk visiting Chevalier five months ago, when he could have been taken at gunpoint to Russia.'

'You mean he was more loyal to a friend than his country's security requirements?'

'I would say so.'

'Did Chevalier prove to be innocent?' Garrison raised his thick eyebrows.

'It was not possible,' Pash said with a nervous yawn, 'to prove he was guilty.'

'And can one, Colonel Pash, know a man better from his file, or from actual conversation with him?'

'In our work,' Colonel Pash replied with professional pride, 'I would give preference to files. They are the sum total of all the impressions of a man which a single person can't get, just by himself.'

'Thank you, Colonel.' Garrison straightened. 'That is all I wish to ask.'

Just behind on the couch, Robert felt the strangest emotion watching his constant shadow in the underworld stand and walk out of his life for ever.

Only then did Robert hear Robb speak a name so strange his pipe slipped to his lap. Robert glanced at the stocky, beetling figure with the deep Pacific tan who stood in the open doorway.

Robb turned ceremoniously. 'Mr Chairman, I call my last witness . . . Dr Edward Teller.'

A nervous excitement stirred among the cramped hearing tables. Yet one person present had already seen Teller today at lunch.

Despite himself, the Hungarian had drifted to Washington even without Garrison's invitation, drawn by the inexorable force of all he owed, and would continue to owe, to Chairman Strauss, General Nichols and the 'Big-Bomb' men. They at least had wanted Teller's genius, and supported what he tried to do against all odds, to defend free men from the total eclipse of Communist tyranny.

Just hours ago, out in the Capitol, as *they* had asked him to, Edward had sat down with Robb in his club. And though in New York Garrison had described Robert to Teller as a saint, Robb now spoke of him as the devil incarnate. Then Edward Teller saw for the first time in his life the secret files on the man he had known most of his career. There they lay, spread on a cocktail table.

Teller had turned the pages one after another. Was it possible? Had soulful, gifted Oppy been all along intimate and in the thick with high-up agents and sympathizers of the very dictators, thugs and ghouls who had enslaved his beloved Budapest? The agents of darkness who were plotting the violent overthrow of American democracy?

It had been too great a shock; there had been too little time to digest any of it. The Hungarian had walked through the sunny unsuspecting streets seething with strong emotions. He was in a daze now, standing by the empty witness chair.

Teller looked down, with a sort of accusing misery, at the delicate, familiar face on the couch. Robert gazed back wonderingly.

'Hello Robert,' he said thickly. 'How or-r-r you?'

'Good afternoon, Edward,' said Robert uncertainly.

Teller sat in the witness chair. He took the oath.

At the right end of the darkened couch, Robert had exchanged his pipe for cigarettes. For a while he could not understand what was said. The two overhead lights flickered on.

'. . . and so after work on the atom bomb was successfully completed in 1945,' Robb said with a slow and formal precision, pacing slowly along the windows, past the Father of the Hydrogen Bomb to the Father of the Atom Bomb and then back again, 'it was your assumption that the laboratory would continue research into the Super or "fusion" bomb?'

'This line of research was by no means free of obstacles, you understand,' Teller said with an abrupt explosion of his usual physics excitedness. 'But if we had begun building the bomb at that point, we probably could have had it by 1949.'

Behind the Board table, Ward Evans raised his hand with a puckish grin, chewing his cigar to the other side.

'Do you not speak from a historically privileged viewpoint, Doctor Teller? Were not the majority of your colleagues, not minor scientists but men like Fermi, Bethe and Oppenheimer here, all convinced of the immediate unfeasibility of the Super?'

'Scientific knowledge,' Teller said, with the growing excitement (not unlike alarm) the sound of his voice always caused him, 'has always expanded when the human mind has been willing to take on what appear impossible problems.'

'So you believe in pushing knowledge as far as it will go?' Evans reflected in a fatherly tone. 'Reasonably though, Doctor Teller, could not the Superbomb as easily have taken 103 years to develop, as the three it took you?'

'It would have taken less time,' Teller said brightly, 'to prove it impossible.'

Standing at the furthest window, Robb cut in impatiently.

'So you feel,' he went on, 'your colleagues should have demonstrated appropriate moral support?'

'Militarily as well as scientifically!' Teller looked hopefully from the one man to the others. 'By 1949, we knew the Russian project was underway.'

'Is it your view,' Robb moved slowly forward, 'Doctor Oppenheimer was a source of disenchantment?'

'That is my opinion,' said the bulky figure in front of Robert. 'I even remember Conant saying that not over his dead body would the Super be approved!'

'Do you feel, Doctor Teller,' Evans cut in again, 'you fully understand Doctor Oppenheimer's reasoning at the time of the 1949 Advisor's report?'

'Back in 1945 I approached Doctor Oppenheimer, as did Szilard. We had petitions against the drop on Japan. He told me matters were being dealt with on a higher level. In 1949 the man himself was dealing on a higher level and was opposing bomb development. I cannot say I fully understand Doctor Oppenheimer's thinking.'

For several seconds Robb did not say anything. Evans went on.

'Doctor Teller,' Evans said pleasantly. 'I would like to understand *your* thinking. In 1945 you opposed use of the bomb, in 1949 you were working to build a much larger bomb.'

'Building bombs and using them?' Teller exploded. 'That is not the same thing!'

At the far table Evans leaned back, thumbs in braces. 'They were the same in 1945, Doctor Teller. You and Doctor Oppenheimer could agree at least on that today?'

Robb hurried from the window. He paused in front of Teller.

'Do you feel, then,' he said quickly, 'that Doctor Oppenheimer's confused attitudes were a threat to this country's military security?'

'I do.'

'Doctor Teller?' Robb's voice rose. 'Have you ever suspected Doctor Oppenheimer of disloyalty?'

'No, I never have.' Teller shook his head shaggily.

Robb took in the room of concentrating faces. Cocking his papers on his hip, he leaned forward.

'Do you or do you not, Doctor Teller, consider Doctor Oppenheimer a security risk?'

As he chain-lit another cigarette Robert suddenly was hearing again the childishly coy guttural voice from Main Tech. It spoke as if to vapourize all opposition with its speed and length of delivery.

'In a great number of cases,' Teller's voice went on in its exotic Danubian accent, 'I have seen Doctor Oppenheimer act in a way that is for me exceedingly hard to understand. I thoroughly disagreed with him on numerous issues and his actions frankly appear to me confused and complicated.' Teller heaved a breath. 'To this extent, I feel I would like to see the vital interests of this country in hands I understand better and therefore trust more. In this very limited sense, I would like to express a feeling that I would personally feel more secure if public matters would rest in other hands. If it is a question of wisdom and judgment, as demonstrated by actions since 1945, then I would say it would be wiser not to grant clearance.'

Through the dull evening glow in office 2022, there was a stunned silence. And there was not one person there who did not feel like a cricket in the presence of an eagle. But Edward, Robert thought, you have just described the way everyone feels about you!

Robb broke the silence, his cheeks pink and his eyes bright. 'Thank you for your testimony, Doctor Teller. I have no further questions.'

Feeling a sense of great creative release, Teller sighed deeply and got to his feet. Just behind him Oppy was still there, crumpled on the couch like some knight of the mournful countenance. Will you disgrace everything I represent because *you* cannot understand it? said Robert's quizzical frown.

'I am sorry, Robert,' said Teller, squeezing his friend's thin fingers.

'After what you have just said, Edward,' said the man against the wall softly, 'I don't know what you mean.'

On the overcast morning of May 6th, 1954, Lloyd Garrison stood. Beginning his two hour summation, he was speaking to a dozen men who had just listened through the parable of their age.

Only one man under the yellow lights of office 2022 heard Garrison's closing words without emotion. Robert knew now that the truth could not be spoken aloud even though his life had been monitored by circles of men, agents and instruments, though he was in plain view of the galleries of nations, of armies and governments – of *History*, and the future dancers of the dance. Robert was listening, but he could not hear it. Oppy had stolen the absolute power of Gods. This was a last judgment. But it was not his.

'As Mr Robb himself has pointed out in his conclusion, we have reviewed the entire life of the man supremely entrusted with the secrets of America's great nuclear strength. We have relived wartime episodes by tape and witness: just as if they were here in this room with us in the year 1954. And nowhere during the last weeks,' dark, stately Garrison said with feeling, slowly pacing the dreary windows, sometimes pausing near Robert's couch to gaze up toward the overcast White House, 'have we found Doctor Oppenheimer wanting in patriotism, or any actual evidence of disloyalty.'

For a time, sitting on his tattered couch, Robert's hopes lifted. He felt the barbed wire around enlightenment loosen.

'But there is more than Doctor Oppenheimer on trial in this room.' Garrison faced the Gray Board an hour later. 'The Government of the United States and our whole security process is on trial here. You have in Doctor Oppenheimer an extraordinarily gifted person, a man complicated beyond what nature can ordinarily do no more than once in a very great while. Like all gifted men unique, not conventional, not quite like anybody else that ever was or ever will be.' On his couch Robert sat back gloomily. The vast human lesson of his life was sinking in the obscurity of historical crime. 'When we ask such a man if he considers Chevalier a dangerous subversive, or whether the Hydrogen bomb would be advantageous to national security, and after careful deliberation he informs us "no" and "no", and those conclusions do not agree with our own, then we do not, as Americans, question this man's loyalty because we do not agree with him.

'There is an anxiety that in a Cold War climate this country's security procedures will be applied artificially, rigidly, like some monolithic test of patriotism that may destroy men with great gifts. Mr Chairman, members of this Board, *America must not devour her children*! Some men are awfully simple and their minds are simple. That does not mean standards should be different for them! This man, who is subtle and gifted, bears the *same* close examination of what he really is, and what he stands for, and what he means to this country! I believe by recommending this man be trusted with our secret knowledge you will most deeply serve the interests of the United States of America, which all of us love and want to protect and further.'

Leaning back, knees crossed at the centre of the couch in office 2022, puffing his new pipe, a great mystery was listening. But nowhere could Robert hear the force of the truth. Not with the vivid clarity he had once heard it, long ago, on a brilliant noon of the soul, fishing by a river among the live oaks of the Santa Cruz mountains. Nothing was left of it. The great positive had become the great negative, and you could not think about it.

324

Chapter 10

Inside Olden Manor at Princeton, the telephone was ringing. It was a hot late June, two days before the last of Oppy's thirty-four Advisory posts expired. Robert sat outside in a patio chair, his eyes shut, a book on his lap. The morning sun darkened in and out of high, lazy Atlantic clouds. He did not stir.

It was a month now since Chairman Gray and Morgan had overruled Ward Evans's favourable vote and handed down their decision. 'The American government had proved it could examine Doctor Oppenheimer's soul, find it discreet and loyal, though unworthy of security clearance.' One month since Robert, Herb Marks and Garrison had sat in a state of shock in the Manhattan offices, trying to keep hope alive with an appeal, and since a five man 'Review-Commission' had been set up – under Lewis Strauss, of all people! Since then, the Reviewers had been racing to settle Oppy's clearance before they had nothing to return to him, or to take away.

And what was Robert supposed to do either way? Forget the universal laws of nature he grasped and they could not? It was death's carnival of the absurd, an empire of fire and destruction. A hell no longer in the darkness of the human soul, but a Himalayas of poison and incineration. Speechless, Robert was trying to find the words . . . words were all he had left. There was scarcely even a weed patch on his life which had not been trampled through. The great mystery on the Mesa, at Point Zero, was amputated from him behind fences of security guards.

This morning Robert lay listening to the ocean sound of the breeze in the forest. He heard Kitty's quick firm step.

'It's for you . . . Mr Reston.'

Robert's heart jumped despite himself. He got up and went into the dark living-room. Kitty stood, listening to her husband's questioning mutter. There were long pauses, then a silence. And then in the open door Kitty saw his face.

Robert's sharp glance did not meet hers. 'Well, you would think Lewis might have told me himself.'

Kitty's voice went liquid with fury. 'What have they done? How could they do such a thing? It's incredible!'

'Katie . . .?' Robert turned away in the hot sun, head bent. 'There is something I'm going to tell you, right now.

'I don't know how to say this,' Robert smoothed his greying head. 'But I have been wrong. You were always right. We should have come down in the beginning. Now I will have no more voice officially. You have lived your life . . . like this. Probably it's a waste.'

Kitty came close on the patio tiles without touching her husband. Suddenly, terrified tears were in her eyes. Was he surrendering? Kitty had never heard this proud man speak without romantic hope, or admit fundamental wrongness. Instantly she felt their great role go dim.

'No . . . you are *wrong*!' Little Kitty raised her pointed chin desperately, scarcely understanding what she said. 'It's a triumph . . . it's *our* triumph! No one can say now that you didn't fight longest and hardest! No one can say you didn't hurt those fascists! They have crowned you with thorns – I've never been so proud of anything in my life!'

In the suburban hush, Kitty clutched her husband's hand defiantly. She broke off with an expression of pain.

'Thank you . . . let's not overdo things,' Robert said vaguely. 'Now I think it would be better if I were alone for a while . . . could you forgive me . . . yes? I won't be too long.'

Robert went out of Olden Manor through the kitchen door. Forgetting the dead pipe at the corner of his mouth, he pushed his hands in his trouser pockets. He shuffled vaguely down toward Princeton village, passing the quiet summery houses where children were playing on flexy-racers under the heavy oak branches. Someone's son polished the spokes of an English sports car. All of this, everywhere, was damnation.

A half hour later, Robert was turning the corner into Nassau Street when he caught sight of a familiar head of woolly white hair coming his way. With a sudden shame, he started the other way. But there was a 'chink-chink' of keys. Robert's colleague appeared at his left arm. This man's vigour and fluffy hair made him feel more shaven-headed and pitiful than ever. They strolled together.

'Doctor Oppenheimer! The very man I want to see.'

'Thank you.' Robert frowned apologetically. 'Sometimes that is easier for others.'

'Aha!' His companion wisely nodded his long wrinkled head.

The two professors walked along some way in silence. They passed in and out of the shade. Gradually Robert began feeling glad of the old man's company, of being gently seen through and warmed by fatherly understanding. It was a lovely day.

'So! They are saying unpleasant things about you, my young friend?' The old man smiled ironically. 'Do not be upset. Of all of us who opposed – Rabinovitch, Szilard, the rest – you lasted longest. So it is flattery.'

'My wife says that . . .' Robert sighed heavily.

'Women understand such things.' Einstein delicately held Robert's arm. 'Look, let us sit on this bench! We will be like two gentlemen sitting in the Tanzgarten by the Limmatquai. Ah . . . there is nothing like the Swiss lakes!'

Robert sat down gratefully by the old man. The bench was set in a grass bank. It faced across the street to the candy and sports shops.

'How I have missed pure work . . .' Robert gently broke the long patient silence. 'It is time I grew my hair long again.'

The scholar beside him on the wood bench answered the confession with a little blowing sound. He waggled his head humorously.

'You do not need such ornaments.'

Robert had turned sideways on the bench. He drew one knee up.

'I would be interested to hear . . . how is gravity coming along?'

'Ah-ha! The Grand Unifying Theory!' the German whispered. 'But you know, I have been thinking. Please light that pipe. I have thought. Ach! What a weapon gravity would make.'

'Yes,' Robert agreed, feeling the laughter come. 'We could reverse it to get rid of the evil ones.'

'And lighten it for the good!' Einstein burst out.

'But what speed,' Robert knit his brows, 'would the evil chaps reach as they left the atmosphere?'

'Never mind.' The old physicist was laughing, all but his kind sagging pelican's eyes. 'Unquestionably the evil would make off with it!'

'Then we would have to get gravity back too!' Robert said.

On the shady bench between the chestnut trunks, the two rumpled professors could not stop their tragic laughter for a half minute. Then they sat still in a deep understanding.

'You never did do any real war work?' Robert finally said.

'Oh yes,' Einstein nodded pensively. 'A neat little guidance system for torpedos . . . I could not resist.'

'But listen . . .' The old scientist hesitated. He leaned closer. 'My dear boy, if I could have imagined it would ever lead to *ziss*. I would happily have remained a clock-maker! A clock-maker who listens to Bach Passions in the chapels of the Oberland.'

There was an emotion between the colleagues; a special moment, the kind of moment which must not be interrupted by intrusions from the sidewalk.

'Come, let me buy you a milk shake, Oppenheimer!' The old man was bustling to his feet. 'Ziss American invention is so cooling to inflamed tonsils, like mine last month. I will never lose my gratitude for milkshakes.'

Robert smiled. 'Do you think they will work on consciences?'

'Oh no, never!' Einstein stopped him with a polite anxiety. 'Our consciences must *remain* inflamed!'

Doctor Oppenheimer would not have much time after his fiftieth year to think over Einstein's words that afternoon. As often happens, not long after – as if even his voice rebelled at the burden of prophecy – Robert's throat developed a growth, the kind of growth for which cool drinks would not be enough. But he had done his important dying so long before.

During the twelve years left to him, the exact span of time from his rise as General Groves's Chief-Alchemist of Elements to his fall at Chairman Strauss's hand, the public Oppy's voice was heard all over the planet, even in Japan. It spoke with disgust and melancholy of the disgraceful spectacle the leaders of the intelligent species were making of paradise and of themselves. As once medals had gathered on General Groves's chest for the flesh-splattering violence of Hiroshima, honours and degrees now collected in Oppy's cabinets like tokens of absolution. President Johnson even presented Robert with a 'Fermi Award' in the White House, days after the hero of a first Nuclear Crisis in Cuba was assassinated in Texas. For in anno nuclei 18 missiles and Jornadas were already worldwide. At Berkeley and in Paris, thousands stood emotionally to cheer. Not because the Doctor was good or evil, but because he was the captain with them on their raft, carrying the logbook of the disaster, in which were written the coordinates back to a golden time when men were free. And it is said that in Italy, when Oppy mentioned before a packed audience an invention made at Los Alamos, he wept. But now the ties of hope that bound him to his Mesa, like reins with which to deflect the runaway terror of statesmen with the power of gods, were severed, and hung limp in Robert's hands. Even his son Peter failed to enter Princeton, and fled west to his uncle Frank.

The world looked very different. Today when Robert walked the streets of man, the oblivious faces seemed already engaged in their dance. Men were become cannon fodder for cynical politicians. And everywhere Robert looked he saw Point Zero. Architecture tumbled and vapourized, great cities seemed already bound on their Journey of the Dead. He had turned to ice.

Doctor Oppenheimer died without a sign of weakness at sixty-three, and his final thoughts were of mankind. And Edward Teller's oldest friends would not hold his hand in theirs.

Chapter 11

In New Mexico on a Mesa overlooking the Valley of the Rio Grande, like some vast, silent printing block of souls under a vacant blue desert sky, the memory of Doctor Oppenheimer is still bound to its rock. There is even a tiny street named after him.

Back east in Princeton Kitty tried for some time after he died to live on at the Institute being Oppy's widow. For a while Robert's old student, gaunt gentle Joe Serber, came out, and they tried it together. But without their teacher it was not the same. And watching the newspapers, the Atomic Age seemed a cursed and unendurable waiting without her husband's hopeful words. It was not long before Kitty grew unclear who Robbie had been. For the first time, alone with staggering memories of what they had gone through, Kitty wondered: who was she, who was left alone in these scholar's rooms, with her two children Kitty knew could not love their name? Alone, with Robbie's cabinets of honours and diplomas and scrapbooks of clippings, kept with all his fascination for anything to do with himself. And somehow, feeling moved by these signs of pitiful childishness, Kitty missed Robert as a child. As only a woman knows to miss a man – even one like Robert.

But who was she, then, this Katarina Puening? German in her early childhood under the Kaiser. Then a Pittsburgh engineer's daughter, biologist of fungi and romantic revolutionary . . . the wife of an atom-bomb physicist of German immigrant background. Now Robbie had left her marooned on this sterile American promontory. You are a woman without a home, she told herself. It was necessary to drink a great deal.

But gradually, even at Princeton among the stilted minds of the Institute, Kitty became aware of ordinary people doing ordinary things. A passionate conviction began in her that she must be free, get away from the frozen crushing weight of the sacrilege Doctor Oppenheimer had committed. Kitty thought then of her old promise outside the adobe farm at El Rito never to forget Jed Holmes. So Kitty struggled with her past.

Then abruptly their daughter Toni killed herself. This was the future. Selling all she needed to sell at Princeton, Kitty bought a large sailing boat for charter, like ones she and Robbie had vacationed on together. Leaving the nuclear age to deal with itself, Kitty went to sea. She was beginning again.

And the sea was there. At first it was only the desert cays of the Gulf Stream, with its warm-rolling, shallow-blue waves that glazed the woodwork in salt. Then out into the slow deep-blue Atlantic swell, and up the lovely Georgia banks and Carolina forests to galey Cape Hatteras. Then there would come the secret rotting jungle of Brazil and Panama. And there would be another sea and another sea after that! And in her mind, the handsome sun-blackened woman with the greying black hair saw all the seas of the world she would sail again. There would be the tepid and temperamental Indian Ocean of typhoons, and the cold majestic North Pacific rolling against the cliffs of Oregon, the German Baltic, China Sea and Mediterranean of the Greeks . . . and the sick cities of the mind would roll back before them . . .

And so for Kitty too there came a day as they were crowding sail on the greatest sea, on a course due west, that her life gave out at last.